TRAITORS' GATE

In this challenging novel of World War II, a
bestseller in its hardcover edition, Catherine
Gavin creates two Frenchmen, Mike Marchand
and Jacques Brunel, who are faced with the
terrible division of loyalties imposed upon them by
the fall of France. Mike's passion for Dina da
Costa, a Brazilian girl of mixed race who is a
pilot like himself, has to take second place to his
determination to fight with the RAF. Jacques,
who has fought in the Norwegian campaign, falls
in love with Alison Grant, the girl he meets when
the French wounded of Namsos are taken to
hospital in Scotland. Their love is not fated to be
fulfilled, and Jacques must work out his own
salvation inside defeated France. The scene shifts
from Glasgow to Rio de Janeiro and on to
Sierra Leone, but the principal background for
this penetrating and controversial novel is London
in its finest hour.

Traitors' Gate enhances even further the
author's already formidable reputation as a
novelist. In this challenging book, written from a
deeply felt personal experience and with profound
conviction, Catherine Gavin shows us the dark
side of the bomber's moon.

261 Our nan!

Traitors' Gate

Catherine Gavin

CORONET BOOKS
Hodder and Stoughton

First published in Great Britain 1976
by Hodder and Stoughton Limited

Coronet Edition 1977

Printed and bound in Great Britain for
Hodder and Stoughton Paperbacks, a
division of Hodder and Stoughton Ltd.,
Mill Road, Dunton Green, Sevenoaks,
Kent (Editorial Office: 47 Bedford
Square, London, WC1 3DP)
by Richard Clay (The Chaucer Press), Ltd,
Bungay, Suffolk

ISBN 0 340 21997 1

TO MICHAEL ATTENBOROUGH

I

THERE WAS A HUSH in the broad Glasgow street on the day the French soldiers hauled down their flag. They marched from their base in a quickstep, after the early rush of workers was over, with two policemen to give their little column an element of dignity, and two stray dogs, running alongside, to lend it an element of farce. When they halted, only the husky words of command and the slap of hands on rifle butts broke the stillness of the summer day.

The troops, Marchand saw, were in terrible shape. Most of them had been in Scotland for several weeks, but beneath the shabby berets their strained faces still bore the marks of the disastrous campaign in Norway. Their boots were scarred by the Namsos rocks, their uniforms frayed and barely clean, so that Marchand, bitterly aware of his own civilian clothing, was glad there were so few spectators. Where some of the Victorian tenements had been turned into offices he could see elderly men watching from the open windows, and on the opposite side of the street a straggle of women, some with infants in pushcarts, had halted on their way to the neighbourhood shops. Among them was a girl in a red dress, who had been watching Marchand before the pathetic ceremony began. If it had been five years earlier, when pictures of Mike Marchand were appearing in every illustrated paper in Europe, he would have said she recognised him.

Now she was watching the Tricolore hauled down, and so was he. The improvised flagpole shook ominously; the blue, white and red came down in uneven jerks. No one, least of all the officer in command, seemed to have any idea of the drill; but then, it was seventy years since France had last surrendered to an enemy, when Napoleon III drove beaten from the battlefield of Sedan.

"Thank God there isn't a band," Marchand said beneath his breath. "At least we'll be spared the *Marseillaise*."

The elderly gentleman by his side, wearing funereal black and

7

the rosette of the Légion d'Honneur, looked at him reproach-fully but said nothing. Only two months before, Monsieur Dupetit had been a respected servant of the Third Republic, calmly anticipating an early retirement to his charming little property in the Ile de France. Now it was June 1940; the Germans in their lightning war had overrun the little property along with so much else, and forced a defeated country to sign a humiliating armistice. The French government was at Bordeaux, not Paris; Monsieur Dupetit was in Glasgow, and to him the monstrous fact was that his pension, the reward for years of faithful service, might well be in jeopardy. He did not intend to say a word which would commit him to one French viewpoint or another. He was not impressed by the young man they had sent up from London. Tall, hatless, with his fair hair ruffled, and his casual grey flannel suit rumpled after a night in the corner of a first class railway carriage, he was not Monsieur Dupetit's idea of a diplomat, nor, admittedly, did Marchand claim to be a career diplomat at all. But such as he was the young man represented the French Embassy, the one remaining bastion in Monsieur Dupetit's crumbling world: he had made up his mind to agree with everything that Marchand said. He waited in a pained silence until the parade ended and the company was marched away.

"It's over now, monsieur," he said nervously. "Will you come back with me to the *Quartier-Général*?"

"The *Quartier*—oh, you mean to the St. Andrew's Halls. No, there's nothing more I can do there. The commandant has been given his movement orders, and we heard him telephone the British RTO at the Central Station. All he has to do now is clear the post and entrain his men."

"And you're quite satisfied about the money?" Monsieur Dupetit persisted. "I've had so many complaints about the arrears of pay."

"The commandant has the money for a month's back pay, and you've got a signed carbon copy of the receipt he gave me. I only hope he's smart enough not to put his pay clerks to work until the pubs close this afternoon!"

Monsieur Dupetit visualised disgruntled Frenchmen, suddenly affluent, drowning their sorrows in the Glasgow bars, and nodded agreement.

"Then we'll meet again at luncheon, Monsieur Marchand? I

know the officers are counting on your company at a farewell luncheon in the mess. And I assure you that one eats there—in spite of everything—very well indeed!"

"I told the commandant I'd be there if I can find my cousin and get back to town in time. Otherwise I'll grab a sandwich at the railway buffet."

Monsieur Dupetit shuddered. "The buffet will be overrun with servicemen—*and* women," he said. "I do hope the Committee can provide a car for you. Shall I come along with you and see what I can do? The ladies all speak French, but still . . . Of course, your English must be very fluent . . ."

"We'll understand each other." There were five minutes more of inane exchanges to be endured before Marchand was able to set off down Berkeley Street alone, and walk off his ill-temper at what he thought of as a pitiful charade, a public exhibition of the bleeding wounds of France. He had detested the parade as much as he detested the emotionalism of the officers who called a municipal auditorium and its side-rooms their *"Quartier-Général"*, and had bombarded him with questions about their repatriation to France. He had had enough emotionalism in the past six weeks to last a lifetime! And his pace unconsciously slackened as he remembered his morning walks across Hyde Park, where the trenches begun at the time of Munich were being extended, and supplemented by anti-aircraft gun emplacements, to the French Embassy at Albert Gate. He had grown to dread the emotion he would find there, and the tears as the teleprinter in the vestibule stuttered out its endless message of defeat. The Wehrmacht had rolled up the map of France behind it, until the day came when Hitler sat in the very railway carriage where the Kaiser's envoys signed their surrender, gloating as the French, defeated, accepted the harsh terms of an armistice.

That armistice was less than forty-eight hours old, and to Marchand, through the long painful Sunday and his sleepless night in the train, they had been so many hours on the rack. It was almost soothing to be out of London and in Glasgow, and the further he got from the St. Andrew's Halls the more it struck him how little impact the war seemed to have made on this old-fashioned, shabby street. He saw a milk cart go by and then a baker's van, both horse-drawn; he saw a cat on a doorstep, licking its ginger fur, and purple pansies growing in a window box. It was all peaceful, ordinary: only a barrage balloon, glinting

9

silver high above the street, was a reminder that in the very near future Glasgow might be as vulnerable as Paris was, before the day that Paris fell.

The commandant had given him a name and an address on a piece of paper, but as Marchand came to the far end of the street he saw a fat French soldier, lounging against an iron gate which had so far escaped the drive for scrap metal, and guessed that he was at his destination. The soldier, who was bare-headed, and wore a grimy Red Cross brassard on one rolled-up sleeve, moved aside amiably enough to let Marchand read the notice on the gate.

A sheet of white paper, pasted on a larger sheet of cardboard attached to the bars with string, bore five rubber-stamped lines in purple ink:

AVEC NOS MEILLEURS
VOEUX: LE COMITÉ DU
CONFORT POUR LES
BLESSÉS FRANÇAIS EN
ÉCOSSE

Underneath was added, in a firm handwriting, "All gifts gratefully received between twelve noon and six p.m."

Twelve noon, and his watch told him it was barely ten! Marchand addressed the bored soldier. "I've come from your commandant," he said, showing his paper. "Aren't the offices open? Is Madame Gavin here?"

"She just came in, monsieur, and two of the other ladies are here too. Go in if you like, the office is upstairs." And he pushed open the iron gate to let Marchand pass under an archway and into what might once have been a stable yard.

There were no stalls for horses now, but there were barns, two of them fastened with brand new padlocks, and one with its door ajar, showing a table and several chairs. There was an ancient smell of corn and oats, mixed with tallow and rotting wood. The yard was roofed in, and the June sunlight struggled through a large skylight, thick with dust. Opposite the archway he saw a ramshackle staircase, built against the wall but little more than a ladder, with open spaces between the risers, and a single wooden rail on the left hand side. The landing above was almost in darkness.

The office is upstairs, the soldier at the gate had said. Marchand, with a questing look round the empty yard, began to climb.

"Can I help you?"

It was a woman's voice, coming from below, and he turned on one step to answer. At once, his head swam, his vision blurred: all he could see was a shaft of light striking through the skylight and turning the dun cobbles of the yard to the colours of the desert. He heard a familiar roaring in his ears. With a groan, Marchand collapsed on the stair, which shook beneath his weight, and clung with all his strength to the handrail, fighting the terrible pull which drew him downwards to the ground.

"Hold on!"

Through the kaleidoscope of colours revolving before his eyes he saw the flash of a red dress, a lock of brown hair falling across a startled face, and a girl's hand held out to his. Then Marchand's senses cleared. If she tried to pull him up his height and weight might bring them both crashing through the handrail, and with a huge effort he unlocked his muscles and used his own strength to drag himself to his feet.

"Terribly sorry to be so clumsy!"

He meant to be very English, very casual, but the words came out in French, and in French the girl in the red dress said it was all her fault, she had startled him, and the stair was really a disgrace, they all said so! Would he please come into the little office, and sit down?

She piloted him into a very small room with a window wide open on the street, and Marchand leaned against the window sill, fighting the nausea which always followed his attacks of vertigo, swallowing the bitter water in his mouth. He felt he had made a fool of himself in front of a woman: to be sick would be the final humiliation.

"I didn't hear you come in," she was saying apologetically. "I went down to what we call our waiting room, to make sure it was tidy for the afternoon, and I sat down at the back to check out a list of stores . . . Roger should have told me you were here. Would you excuse me for five minutes, please?"

Marchand was thankful to be left alone. He wiped the cold sweat from his face and hands with his handkerchief and did his best to brush the dust of the staircase from his suit. The slight breeze from the open window was clearing his head, and his surroundings began to come into sharper focus.

Most of the space in the little office was taken up by a wooden kitchen table, holding a Remington portable typewriter, a pile of penny notebooks in red or brown covers, and a china marmalade jar containing pencils and a fountain pen. A rubber stamp, obviously the stamp which read "With our best wishes: the Comforts Committee for the French Wounded in Scotland", was lying on top of a closed ink pad. There were two stools, but no chairs, and a shelf along the back wall held cardboard box files. An antique telephone was fixed to the wall beside the door. In spite of its deficiencies, the makeshift office was as neat and functional as a flight deck.

The girl in the red dress kicked the door wide open and came in carrying two mugs of steaming tea on a round japanned tray.

"There!" she said, "I was pretty sure they'd have a kettle going on the gas ring. Have some tea, monsieur, it'll do you good."

He knew the touching British faith in tea as a restorative, but the drink, to which sugar and milk had been added all too generously, was comforting in its way. Marchand sat down on the stool she indicated, and drank it gratefully.

"Have a piece of buttered oatcake, you won't find that too sweet."

"Thank you very much."

"Did you have anything to eat this morning?"

"Railway tea from a trolley at Carlisle. And then the train was late, there wasn't time for breakfast at the hotel."

"You must be hungry."

"You're very kind, madame, to someone silly enough to trip on your staircase. You *are* Madame Gavin, aren't you?"

"Yes, I'm Catherine Gavin." Her smile widened. "And I don't need to ask your name! When Monsieur Dupetit telephoned me at home last night to say the air attaché was coming up from London, I didn't realise he was talking about Mike Marchand."

"I wondered, out there in the street, if it was possible you recognised me."

"Why not? It's not so very long since we were all cheering you like mad in the Place de la Concorde. Almost exactly five years ago."

"It seems like longer than that to me."

"It seems like longer to all of us." Now that there was only

12

the table between them, Marchand saw that his hostess was hardly the girl he had taken her at first sight to be. He was talking to a woman of about his own age, which was twenty-nine.

"Were you really in the Place de la Concorde that Fourteenth of July?" he asked. "What were you doing in Paris? Were you on holiday?"

"Bastille Day's always a holiday," she said easily. "I was there all right. I was jammed up against one of the statues when you came out on the balcony of the Hotel Crillon, yelling 'Mich-el Mar-chand, Mich-el Mar-chand' with the best of them."

"Oh, don't remind me," he said (but he liked to be reminded of the cheering and the shouts), "I've always hated my first name. Michel Marchand—it sounds like a hairdresser's apprentice!"

"Who started calling you Mike?"

"Some of the Yankee flyers, when I was a test pilot with Trans-Andean."

"That was before your record-breaking flight?"

"Quite a while before. And as for the record, it wasn't really one of the great ones, you know. Montreal–Bucharest non-stop— it was more like an exercise in showing the flag. From French Canada to a country of the Petite Entente, that was the way my sponsors saw it. I thought it was just good promotion for Air France."

"You're too modest," she told him. "Remember, I was there. I saw you take Paris by storm that Bastille Day. After the Stavisky scandals the year before, and the February riots, people were delighted to have somebody—something—they could really cheer! I'm sure you were the most famous man in France that night—"

"But it didn't last long. About nine months, to be exact."

"You had wretched luck. Everybody was backing you to break the round-Africa record."

"What I wanted most was to beat Tommy Rose's record from London to Cape Town. And in the end Amy Johnson beat us both."

She turned round to put the tea-tray on the shelf which held the cardboard files. It was painful to look into a face so like the faces of the French soldiers when the flag came down, so etched with bitterness. And the bad luck which overtook Mike Marchand when his plane crashed in Senegal was nothing to the disaster which had overwhelmed France.

With an attempt at a lighter tone, she said, "So now you're an air attaché. Have you been at the London embassy long?"

"Only since last September, they took me on when I was turned down for the Air Force at the beginning of the war. And I'm not the attaché, madame. I'm graded Temporary, and Acting, and everything else that means I'm just a dogsbody to the whole establishment. But I did fix it so I could take the air attaché's place today."

"Why?"

"Because I want to find out about a cousin of mine, who's reported to be in one of your Scottish hospitals. But first of all I want to say"—he made her a little formal bow—"I know His Excellency would wish me to say, how grateful we are for all you and your friends have done for our wounded. Monsieur Dupetit has been singing your praises to me, and so have the senior officers at the St. Andrew's Halls. I only wish His Excellency and all of us had known earlier what you were doing."

"Well," she said drily, "we sometimes wondered what *you* were doing, when we saw your men wandering up and down the streets, completely lost, without a word of the language, or a penny in their pockets!"

"You think they were neglected, madame?"

"I know they were! They weren't quartered in Glasgow, they were stranded in Glasgow! I don't care what was happening in France, the French Military Mission should have made some provision for the men who fought in Norway!"

"But they *were* provided for, after the first confusion. Every man received his pay before the main contingent was shipped back to France—"

"Just in time to be taken prisoners by the Germans. They were in the fighting at Brest, I know."

"I'm afraid they were. But I still don't know how long your Committee's been in existence—"

"Not long by the calendar. The retreat from Norway began on the third of May, didn't it? It was the thirteenth, I'll always remember because it was my birthday, when I first got a chance to do something for the French."

"The day of the German breakthrough at Sedan," he said, and saw her shiver.

"That name!" she said. "Another Sedan—after seventy years! I would have done anything—I was so grateful when they telephoned and asked me . . . Monsieur Marchand, I'm telling this badly. It really all began because of the mules."

"The *mules*?"

"Yes, the Chasseurs Alpins brought their mules from France. And when they got here on the way back from Namsos the mule lines were laid out in a park near the church I belong to, and the minister started a canteen for the mule drivers in the church hall. It was packed every evening. They got tea and sandwiches and cakes, all free of course, and people sent cigarettes, and the church ladies played the piano and did their best to talk French. The men were so good—so grateful—and it was so terrible for them, not understanding English, and being without home letters or any news from France."

"And your pastor asked you to help in this canteen?"

"He asked me to go there in the evening and translate the news bulletins for them."

"From the BBC or the newspapers?"

"The BBC news at nine. Somebody lent us a wireless set, so we could listen to the news together, and then I translated it into French."

Marchand thought of what that news had been: the destruction of Rotterdam and the surrender of the Dutch army, the uselessness of the Maginot Line, the German *Blitzkrieg* raging across France, the Belgian king giving up the struggle, the British Expeditionary Force chased off the continent, leaving its arms and armour at Dunkirk. "That must have been tough," he said.

"It was hell." For the first time he saw emotion in the calm face before him, and half expected a burst of tears. But with only a catch in her voice she went on: "It was at the canteen that we heard about the wounded men, and how lonely they were, scattered among all the different hospitals. So then some of us decided to start the Comforts Committee, but there was an awful lot of red tape to cut through first. Even the letter I wrote to the *Glasgow Herald*, asking for help, was held up for days before they got permission to publish it. Some pompous ass even came and lectured me about *infiltrating* the hospitals with civilians who might be spies—what sort of spying he thought they could do on helpless men, he didn't explain."

"Yes, well, we've all learned what a Fifth Column is, and how loyal soldiers can be subverted—"

"But the Lord Provost was on our side, and he gave us £25

out of the Central War Fund to start buying things. And after the letter did appear, there were so many gifts, so many boxes and bundles, that we had to move out of our first room in the St. Andrew's Halls and come down here. This place was requisitioned for us, and Roger was detailed to help with the heavy things. It's an old grain and feed store, with plenty of storage room even for the biggest packages, and a place for people to sit and talk when they bring their gifts. We don't ask them to walk up that horrible stair," she finished with a smile.

"Do they still come?" the man asked. "Even now?"

"Now? Oh, you mean because of the surrender? That hasn't made any difference. The French wounded are still in hospital, and as long as they're there, we'll carry on." She opened one of the penny notebooks. "Would you like to see what they got first? Toilet articles—they hadn't any. We got three hundred and fifteen bags from the Red Cross to put them in."

Marchand read from the page she indicated. "Ten French cigarettes. A comb. A mirror. A packet of razor blades. A toothbrush. Shaving cream. Soap. A packet of writing paper and envelopes. A pencil. *Avec nos meilleurs voeux.*"

She was watching his face anxiously. "You don't think it's very much, do you?"

"On the contrary," said Mike Marchand, "I think it's a very great deal."

"Oh, I'm so glad!" She picked up a brown notebook, which he saw was only a school exercise book with warnings about road safety on the back. "Danger Don'ts!" Marchand read silently. "Don't play at being 'Last Across' on any road or street!" She flipped the pages over and handed the book to him. "People have been very generous," she said. "Look, those are their names and addresses, and the contributions. We never get less than a shilling, and usually it's half a crown or five bob. Look! Once or twice we got a guinea."

He thought of the war which was costing millions every day, and was so much moved that he hardly heard what she was saying next, until he became aware that she had repeated his name.

"Monsieur Marchand! We all know that careless talk costs lives, and I wouldn't dream of asking you about troop movements. But the fact that you're here at all, here in Glasgow I mean, shows that something is going on, and probably the men at the

St. Andrew's Halls will be leaving soon. But what about the wounded? What's going to become of them?"

He was going to say that the British were setting up concentration camps for them, but caught the wretched words back in time. The wounded would continue to receive care, he explained, in the Midlands or in London, where over one hundred thousand Frenchmen, sailors, refugee merchantmen, survivors of Norway and Dunkirk, were being assembled while arrangements were made for their repatriation.

"Some of them may want to join General de Gaulle," she said.

"Any of them tell you so?"

"I've heard some of the officers discussing it."

"Did you listen to his first broadcast, by any chance?"

"On the eighteenth of June? I did indeed."

"Then you're the first British person I've met who did. Most of my London friends could talk of nothing but Churchill's great speech in the House that afternoon."

" 'This was their finest hour.' Do you wonder at it? And then de Gaulle was speaking in French at six o'clock. I only heard him myself by accident. Some of the French officers billeted at the Beresford Hotel heard that an important announcement would be made on the BBC, and asked if I could arrange for them to hear it. I borrowed a wireless set from the manager and we listened to the speech together."

"What was their reaction?"

"Two mornings later some of them tried to enlist in the British Army."

"*Two* mornings later? Not the next morning?"

"No, they waited too long. De Gaulle had broadcast for the second time, claiming that he spoke in the name of France. So when they went to the Scottish Command headquarters here, taking me along as the interpreter, to find out about enlisting, we never got past the duty officer. He told them if they wanted to go on fighting they had to join up with General de Gaulle. And we were politely shown out to the street."

"That's very interesting," said Mike Marchand slowly. "That was a very fast reaction to the general's claim . . . Did you hear the second broadcast yourself, madame?"

"I've heard them all. 'The flame of French resistance must not go out'—I heard that at the Beresford; then the claim to speak for France, at home, and then the announcement of a French National Committee with jurisdiction over all French citizens in Britain. De Gaulle's done a lot, hasn't he, in just six days? Even God took seven to make the world."

"I gather you're not impressed by the gentleman."

"Oh! I think de Gaulle has a great future—in radio."

"Is that quite fair to a man who wants to carry on the fight against Germany?"

"From inside Britain," she said sharply. "That's the whole point! That's what I thought of the very first time, the time in the Beresford. No doubt he wants to fight, but he wants to fight on the winning side so that he can go back to France in triumph. Only he'll never be able to go back alone! And there'll always be Frenchmen to say he went back 'in the baggage wagons of the Allies', like the Bourbons at the Restoration—"

"The Bourbons, madame! Isn't that a bit far-fetched for 1940?"

"Sorry, that's the way my mind works, I'm afraid."

"'The baggage wagons of the Allies'. That takes me back to my schooldays . . . What Allies have you in mind, if I may ask?"

"Ourselves and the Americans, when the time comes."

He might have reminded her that since the 'miracle' of Dunkirk, the euphoric name given to a shattering defeat, Gibraltar was the only foothold left to the British in Western Europe. Instead—"You're an optimist," he said. "Don't you know that just before the end in France, when Paul Reynaud was still prime minister, he sent a desperate appeal to Roosevelt for American intervention, which was refused?"

"The Americans will come in later on," she said confidently. "Now they'll see we mean to fight on till we win."

"Now that you've got rid of the Ally who let you down, you mean."

"I think you only hurt yourself, when you say that."

It was true, and Marchand despised himself for having said it. In his heart he knew—and he was one of the few Frenchmen in London who did know—that the British would never give in, never surrender; that the Empire, along with the beleaguered island, would turn defeat to victory; it was his sense of personal humiliation which had driven him to the self-inflicted wound. But the Scotswoman gave him no time to fumble for an apology. She looked at her watch, and said, "Our delivery truck will be here any minute, the driver's very punctual. Didn't you want to ask me something about a cousin of yours, in hospital?"

"Yes," he said gratefully, "His name's Brunel. He was reported wounded in the retreat from Namsos, and that's the last his parents heard of him, except that he was hospitalised somewhere in Scotland. They got a letter out to me in the last diplomatic bag from Bordeaux, asking me to find out which hospital, and how he is; but there wasn't much they knew about it at the St. Andrew's Halls—"

"We'll have him on file." She turned confidently to the row of cardboard boxes, which he saw had once contained shoes. Two of them still carried scraps of the manufacturers' labels, all were carefully marked with the letters of the alphabet.

"Brunel, you said?"

"Jacques Brunel, Chasseurs Alpins. He was a captain in the reserve."

The lid of the shoebox marked A–D was removed, the typed five-by-three filing cards quickly sorted out.

"Here he is. 'Brunel, Jacques André, captain, 53rd Chasseurs Alpins, home address Villa Mon Bijou, Menton, Alpes Maritimes. Next of kin, father, Maître Théophile César Brunel, attorney-at-law. Admitted May 7, 1940, to Dykefaulds Hospital, Lanarkshire.' Well, now we know where he is, at least!"

"But not how he is?"

"We don't keep the medical records, I'm afraid. You'd have to ask about that at the hospital."

"Which isn't in the city?"

"No, but it's not very far away. Hardly any of the French wounded were brought right into the city; many of them were taken as far as Gleneagles, a good two hours' drive."

Her brown eyes met his troubled blue gaze in a look of shared understanding. It was a matter of policy to keep the city hospitals as empty as possible: every bed would be needed in the event of a massive air raid or invasion by German paratroops.

"You want to see him, of course, and that's easy to arrange," she said, rising. "Our truck's going to Dykefaulds this very morning. How much time have you got?"

"I'd like to be back in the city by one o'clock, if I can."

"We'll fix it. Oh heavens!" she broke off. "There's the truck now. Roger'll be hunting after me to get at the stores."

In the street below a 15-cwt Army lorry had pulled up to the kerb, and the driver, wearing a lance-corporal's stripe, was making vigorous signs to the French sentry called Roger.

"You've got Army transport too, madame?"

"For a few hours every day. Now come and meet one of our committee, Alison Grant, who knows Captain Brunel far better than I do, and the whole Dykefaulds set-up. She's working in the big room with Mrs. Tait."

He followed her into the room next door, which was not only bigger but very much brighter than the cubbyhole they had left, with a skylight as well as two high windows, and long trestle tables on which piles of garments were laid out. Two women were checking the piles: one dozen undershirts, one dozen pairs of underpants, one dozen pairs of knitted socks, and so on. They stopped when 'Monsieur Marchand' was introduced, and smiled as he made his formal bow, and repeated his little speech of thanks, on behalf of the French Ambassador, for their "devotion to our brave men". He saw that Mrs. Tait, a large woman of forty wearing a cashmere twin-set, a tweed skirt and a cairngorm brooch, was only waiting for him to stop talking to ask him if he was feeling all right now, after what could have been a nasty accident on that terrible stair. He made the usual excuses for his own clumsiness, and was glad when a decided voice cut in with a question to Miss Grant.

"Alison, will you be a darling and take the things to Dykefaulds instead of me? And take Monsieur Marchand with you? He's come to see his cousin, Captain Brunel."

"I'd love to!" said Alison Grant. "Captain Brunel's cousin—I think it's wonderful you've come all this way to see him. But Catherine, don't you think Dr. Skinner may be sticky?"

"Captain Fletcher too. That's why I'd like you to go, Alison. You're a favourite with the staff at Dykefaulds."

"Your cousin's the favourite," said Alison, turning to Marchand. "He's a great hero to the nurses, because his English is so good. They call him 'Captain Jack'."

"Jacques always was the clever one when we were boys at school," said Marchand. "He had a tutoring job in England one summer, just before he began to study law. He's Maître Brunel in civilian life, like his father—he was called to the Bar at Nice two years ago."

"Captain Fletcher will be most impressed to hear that."

"Is he the army doctor at this hospital?"

"Captain Fletcher is a lady," said Alison with a giggle. "What we call a QA nurse. She keeps them all in order in the French wards. The boys are terrified of her—they call her *la seesterre*."

"Catherine, don't you think you ought to telephone to Dykefaulds before they start, and sort of explain things?" said Mrs. Tait.

"That's a good idea. Come on, Alison, let's do it together. I'd like you to get back by half past twelve, and then I can take the lorry on with the clothing to Greenock."

"What seems to be the trouble?" Marchand asked, when the two younger women had left the room. "Don't they allow morning visitors at this Dykefaulds? Perhaps I could hire a taxi and go out later—"

"Oh, they all have their own ideas about visiting hours," said Mrs. Tait. "And Dr. Skinner's a real martinet. He even fusses about the things we send out to the men. Wine especially. And there's nothing they appreciate more."

"I'm sure of that. Are you sending wine today?"

Mrs. Tait read from a list pinned to a cork bulletin board: "Twelve cartons of Gauloises, two baskets of fruit, twenty packs of cards, a draught board and draughts, a dart board and darts, and—yes, here we are—two dozen bottles of red wine and so on."

"I gather they're all convalescent," said Marchand.

"Nearly all, I think. But remember, they only get one glass of wine and one cigarette at a time. And the Glasgow tobacconists are running out of Gauloises. I hope we can send some down to the Sailors' Home at Greenock, as well as the underwear."

Marchand looked at the piles of underclothing on the tables. "Are these for your own sailors?" he enquired.

"Of course not; everything here is for the French. We had an emergency appeal for twelve of your boys, survivors of a freighter bound from Martinique for the Clyde, and torpedoed when she was almost in sight of port. They've been kitted out at Greenock, but we want them to have a change of underwear, and luckily there was enough in store."

"You're doing a wonderful job," he said. "And if I may say so, you all speak wonderful French."

Mrs. Tait smiled. "Mine's a bit rusty. I was a governess in a French family for five years before I married, but that's quite a while ago."

"In what part of France, madame?"

"Paris."

He was going to ask her, where in Paris, but Mrs. Tait went on quickly, "Now little Alison, bless her heart, she's really fluent. She was at a finishing school in Paris for a year before she came home to take a secretarial training. We're going to lose her soon; she's off to a fine job in London."

"London might be a good place to keep away from now."

"Because of air raids, do you mean? I don't think it matters where you are, any longer."

He thought savagely that the shield of France was gone, and the enemy stood on the Channel coast. But before he could reply Alison Grant was in the room again, breathless and excited, and Mike Marchand for the first time realised all her attraction. She was a very pretty girl with red-gold hair and dancing blue eyes, but at first sight he had been aware of nothing but her clumsy clothes. The French finishing school must have specialised in cookery, not *couture*, he thought, summing up the grey flannel suit with the boxy jacket and pleated skirt which made her shape unnecessarily square, the lisle stockings and brown brogues with big flat heels. On her head Alison wore a blue crochet turban, the style suggestive of a munitions worker which had become fashionable among British girls waiting for the call-up, and escaping from the turban her bright hair had been tortured into half a dozen lacquered curls—'plastic curls', they had been called a few years earlier—which to Marchand looked uncomfortably like horns.

"It's all right!" she announced gaily. "They're expecting you. Captain Fletcher's going to tell your cousin that you're here, and that you've heard from his parents, and so it won't be a shock to him—"

"Is he so very ill, mademoiselle?"

"Not Captain Jack, no; he's getting on well now, but they have to think of the other men in the ward . . . the doctors don't want any of them to be excited by a stranger's visit . . ." She looked enquiringly at Mrs. Tait, who nodded encouragement, and then went on:

"I think I ought to tell you this, monsieur, before we go. It's not that they want to be—obstructive, or make difficulties. But they really do have to take special care. Because Dykefaulds is a hospital for the mentally disturbed."

2

DYKEFAULDS HOSPITAL STOOD where the moorland country began beyond the Glasgow city boundary, and even on a bright June day it was a gloomy and forbidding place. It had been built in the mock baronial style by a Glasgow textile manufacturer who made his fortune by selling bandages to both sides in the Franco-Prussian War, and he, about the year 1875, had tried to soften the outlines of his home by extensive planting of scrub pines and larches, which had never thriven. His son sold the place in 1915. Then it became a hospital for the shell-shocked soldiers of World War I, and between the wars the addition of pebble-and-dash bungalow wards ended any outward distinction which Dykefaulds had ever possessed.

Sitting behind the broad back of the lance-corporal driver, Alison Grant spent the first few miles of the journey across Glasgow in some distress, assuring Marchand that, whatever the nature of the hospital, his kinsman's mental health was excellent. Yes, there were shell-shocked men among the survivors of Namsos, but Captain Jack was not one of them; he was always cheerful and kept everybody's spirits up. But many of the Frenchmen were excitable, she had to admit; they had been greatly upset, and had upset others in the psychiatric wards by their grief and anger, when the news of the surrender came. That brief reference was as far as she, or either of the women he had met in Glasgow, seemed prepared to go in alluding to the fall of France.

"I only wish I'd known about all this sooner," said Marchand wretchedly. "Jacques and I have never been great correspondents. I haven't heard from him since the New Year, and then he was at Chamonix, training the Scots Guards to ski before the expedition to Finland."

"Which was given up when the poor Finns surrendered to Russia."

And there they were again, back at the word surrender. In the jolting lorry, with the crates and boxes inefficiently arranged by the French soldier bumping up against their legs, Marchand tried to draw the girl out on her finishing school in Paris. Had she been taken to the Opéra, the Comédie Française, the Louvre? But Alison preferred to talk about the secretarial job waiting for her in the Ministry of Economic Warfare. Her brother had arranged it for her; he was a Member of Parliament, and had something to do with the Ministry, in what way she did not disclose. Alison was going to live with her brother and his wife at their home near Kingsmead-on-Thames, at least for the time being. A new baby was expected in the family, and she would be able to help out until Lucy was up and about again.

It was all pleasant and open, and Mike Marchand, listening with half his mind, had time to think how strange it was that all three devoted women at the Comforts Committee had shied away from any discussion of their time in Paris. The former governess and the schoolgirl had nothing to say about it, nor had Catherine Gavin told him why she was in the Place de la Concorde on that Bastille Day of 1935. It was exactly contrary to Mike's experience in London. There, everyone remotely connected with official France, whether through the embassy, the French Institute, the Alliance Française or any other group —anyone who had even been on a day trip to Boulogne—had brimmed over with tears, had written or telephoned useless expressions of sympathy when France was overrun and Paris fell. He remembered one lachrymose lady novelist who seemed to think that the whole of European culture lay in the valley of the Dordogne, and at the last embassy reception he had longed to offer her the sewers of Paris for her enthusiasm instead. It struck him suddenly that why the three Scotswomen had refused to speak of Paris was because the pain of losing Paris went too deep.

His first sight of Dykefaulds was intimidating, although the pretentious double doorway and the mullioned windows of the hall were softened by Virginia creeper and cotoneaster. Behind the façade there was what he detested, the hospital smell which always reminded him of the three stifling months he had spent in the French hospital at Dakar after the plane crash which ended his flying career. The sub-smell of disinfectant and anaesthetics seemed to pursue him as he walked behind Alison into the office where the medical superintendent of Dykefaulds rose to receive them with a wintry smile.

Dr. Skinner was a small man with thick horn-rimmed glasses,

clad from neck to knee in an immaculate white coat. He was flanked by Captain Fletcher who, Mike had been warned, could be as sticky as her boss. She was resplendent in grey and scarlet, and her expression was not so much sticky as glued with disapproval. She gave the visitor a thorough but silent inspection.

"Mr. Marchand, you've come a long way," said the doctor without shaking hands. "I can't refuse to let you see Captain Brunel. I'll make this one exception to the rule I made less than a week ago: no visitors for the French wounded until further notice."

Mike heard Alison gasp. "Why was that, sir?" he asked.

"On the day after the—h'm—the surrender," said Dr. Skinner with an ineffable curl of the lip. "A priest from the Glasgow base came out to visit them. Monsieur l'Aumônier, I was asked to call him. Unfortunately his visit was the reverse of comforting. The men were agitated to the last degree, crying and shouting, struggling out of their beds and clamouring to be taken home to their families. The only way to calm them was by sedation. Wasn't it, Captain Fletcher?"

"It was indeed, sir."

"So you can see Captain Brunel for twenty minutes in my private sitting room. When he leaves the ward the other men will be told that he's gone out for treatment—"

"I don't even know the nature of his wounds," said Mike.

"He had a severe case of frostbite, like so many of the Namsos men, but we were able to save his fingers, and they won't be badly deformed. He was wounded on the last day of the evacuation and buried in débris near the harbour. After they got him on board his wounds were neglected, and infection set in; we've been treating him for severe kidney damage. Understand, there's no question of his leaving here for the next few weeks, I won't allow it. None of the patients at Dykefaulds are to be railroaded back to France, or anywhere else, and you can tell your ambassador I said so."

"Won't I be allowed to visit the wards today?" asked Alison, and Dr. Skinner's expression softened.

"Not today, Miss Grant. But Captain Brunel will be disappointed to miss you. We'll allow you five minutes with him after he's seen Mr. Marchand. Goodbye, monsieur. Captain Fletcher, come with me."

"I thought you said they didn't mean to be obstructive," said

Mike ruefully, when he and Alison were alone. "I don't think they exactly smoothed our path, do you?"

"Monsieur Marchand"—Alison's pretty face was pale—"I hate to be the one to tell you disagreeable things, but there *is* a reason for Dr. Skinner's attitude. It's got nothing to do with Monsieur l'Aumônier's visit. It's because his own son is a prisoner of war in Germany."

"I'm sorry," said Marchand, "Was he captured at Dunkirk?"

"No, at St. Valéry, just two weeks ago. When nearly the whole of the 51st Highland Division was cut off, and had to surrender."

"They had very bad luck, I know."

"They had a very good chance of escaping, if the French High Command hadn't kept them at Dieppe too long, and they couldn't reach Le Havre in time to be rescued. So young Dr. Skinner was taken, and Captain Fletcher's brother, and—eight thousand other men of the Fifty-first."

"The French Ninth Corps surrendered at St. Valéry too," said Marchand. "And may I remind you, mademoiselle, that a million and a half French soldiers are now prisoners of war in Germany?"

"I know they are, it's dreadful; but Scotland's such a little country, everybody seems to have someone, or know someone, in the Highland Division. It's a very special part of our history, almost like the French Foreign Legion, don't you see?"

"The Legion had better luck at Narvik." And just then Captain Fletcher came back, to take Marchand into custody and march him off down a slippery corridor which added floor polish to the hospital smells and into a small room with a glass door standing open on a patch of garden.

"You're to wait here for Captain Brunel. Twenty minutes, mind, not more!"

"*Oui, mon capitaine.*"

She gave him another searching look. "I can't see any resemblance between the two of you. Except maybe for the height. Are you first cousins?"

"Our mothers were first cousins."

She said "Aye!" on a long negative breath, and left Marchand with an impression that she thought he was there under false pretences. He shrugged, and looked about him. It seemed as if the father of young Dr. Skinner, prisoner of war, might be a widower, because there was no trace of any feminine influence in the little room with the sad-coloured wallpaper and carpet, the tweed-covered fireside chairs and the pictures of Glasgow University football teams hanging above the black malachite presentation clock on the mantel. But the garden was a riot of colour, of delphiniums, lupins and Canterbury bells massed round a beautifully tended lawn behind a protective screen of Douglas firs, and Mike stood staring at it, beginning to realise what it was to be, through his country's fall, an object of contempt and aversion.

It was along the tiled paving which separated the garden door from the lawn that Jacques Brunel was brought to him, not on a nursing orderly's arm as he had half expected, but in a wheel chair with a man pushing it and his own hands lying lightly bandaged in his lap. Mike gasped at the sight of him—so thin, so pale, and above all so pathetic in a totally unexpected way, being dressed in the old hospital uniform of the British Tommies, with a bright red tie knotted above a bright blue suit. Jacques was as dark as Mike was fair, and when they were boys at the Ecole des Roches he had been considered not only the clever one but the good-looking one, his finely-cut features and large dark eyes being what French girls thought handsome. The good looks had been ravaged by combat and by pain, and whatever comforts had been provided for the French wounded at Dykefaulds the services of a barber were not amongst them, for Captain Brunel's black hair lay over his ears and forehead, and hung on the blue collar of his hospital suit.

They had one other point of resemblance as well as their height. They were not demonstrative, and their meeting, the first for nearly a year and in such tragic circumstances, was not emotional. Mike's gasp was all; then he held out his right hand impulsively, saw the bandaged hands unmoving on the light blanket laid across his cousin's knees, and changed the greeting to a gentle pat on the shoulder of the wounded man.

"Jacques, it's great to see you!"

"You too, Michel. Where the devil did you spring from?"

"Came up with money to the Glasgow base." Then the Scots orderly, who had understood not one word, pushed the wheel-chair inside the sitting room and turned it outwards to face the garden, while Mike pulled up one of the stiff fireside chairs and sat down beside the open door.

"Too much fresh air for you?"

"Not a bit. Most of us sit outdoors when the sun shines. We're all on the mend, you see."

"How are you really, old boy?"

"Fine, really fine. All this" (indicating the blanket and the high wheels of the chair) "is only window-dressing to impress the visitors." Jacques laughed. He was twenty-eight, one year younger than Marchand, and until he laughed he looked like forty. As soon as the orderly had left the room he leaned forward eagerly and asked to see his mother's letter.

Mike held it up for him to read—the inert hands never moved—and Jacques' eyes scanned the few lines it contained.

"Thank God for that," he said, "they're still at Oradour. When the 'phone message was passed on to me about a letter in the bag from Bordeaux, I panicked. I thought they must have gone to Bordeaux themselves, along those awful roads, but this was sent on from Limoges by a friend."

"You should have trusted your father. With his kind of contacts he could have had that letter delivered by special messenger to Buckingham Palace. And obviously they mean to stay on at Oradour until things settle down."

"There's not much point in going home, is there? Not with those Italian bastards lolling all over the Villa Mon Bijou. Michel! Wasn't it the mercy of providence that they left Menton at the beginning of June, to see Marcelle and the baby, and attend the christening?"

"I can't think of a safer place for any two people in France to be than the doctor's house at Oradour," Marchand assured him. "But they must be going crazy without news of you."

"I wrote them twice, at least I dictated letters twice," said Jacques with a glance at his hands. "I suppose they got lost between here and Menton, and I got nothing through my APO number. Michel, you'll send them a telegram, won't you, and tell them I'm well, and send my love?"

"The moment I get back to Glasgow," Marchand promised. Though how long a wire would take to transmit from Glasgow to the peaceful little town of Oradour-sur-Glâne, fourteen miles from Limoges in the department of the Haute Vienne, he was not prepared to say.

"Good, that's one load off my mind," said the patient. "Now the next thing. What are the terms of the Italian armistice?"

"They haven't been announced yet. Our delegation only flew on to Italy yesterday."

"Some delegation! Cadging for peace all the way from Compiègne to Rome! The Boches have grabbed two thirds of France; what do you bet the Italians will claim all the Mediterranean shore as far as Nice, and maybe further?"

"They tried to fight their way through Menton to Nice last week, but our troops held them at the strong point on Cap Martin."

"I wish I'd been there, fighting on my home ground, and not at the Arctic Circle."

"The Norwegian campaign was pretty rough going."

"It wasn't a campaign, it was a massacre."

"Do you want to tell me about it, or have you had enough?"

"We've all talked ourselves silly about it, and I don't suppose I can tell you anything you don't know."

"I'm not so sure. I learned today that seven months after German tanks mowed down the Polish cavalry, the French took mules along on the expedition to Norway."

"The mules? Oh, sure, we had mules; we left most of them dead in the snow, poor brutes. At least the mules were shipped from France, what they forgot to ship was the skis. Or if the skis were there to be unloaded, they'd been shipped without the bindings. I don't know what the situation was at Narvik, but at Namsos we were completely immobilised, wading through snow a metre deep, just sitting ducks for the Luftwaffe."

"General Béthouart took Narvik, just before the end of May."

"Yes, and destroyed the port, and had to pull out in less than a week because his men were needed back in France. Not that it mattered a damn, because the Gulf of Bothnia was free of ice by that time, and the Boches could take the ore out by sea." He shook his head angrily. "Why the hell didn't we concentrate on Narvik, us and the British too? It looked so good on paper—to enter Norway as soon as Hitler invaded, and cut the route of the Swedish iron ore supply to Germany. But then some master strategist dreamed up the idea of keeping a southern port open by seizing Trondheim in a pincers movement from Andalsnes and Namsos. Operation Hammer, they called that. We got the hammering."

"How was your air support?"

"Terrible. Operation Hammer was a dress rehearsal for the

Blitzkrieg. We were sold so long on the Maginot Line defence that we'd forgotten how to attack, and the British had listened to their pacifists so long they hadn't got the arms or the *matériel*. The Boches soon had us both on the run, and the last I saw of Namsos, on the last day, there wasn't any town—it was obliterated.''

His voice had risen, and his colour was rising too, so that Mike began to be alarmed. But Jacques controlled himself, and went on quietly, ''When you've been here for weeks, in a decent, clean place like this, you begin to think Namsos didn't happen. You can't realise any of it happened.'' Mike knew that 'any of it' meant France, not Norway, and he understood. Here in Dr. Skinner's pleasant garden the two of them were insulated from the tragedy.

''The doctor has only one hobby, and that's gardening,'' said Jacques, as if he followed Marchand's thought. ''Isn't that lawn a sight to see? When the boys were first allowed out in the grounds, they were amazed to see such green grass: it never grows so green at home in Provence. And we'd all had a touch of snow-blindness, because the dark glasses had been forgotten too. That green grass looked good to us after the snow.''

''Thank God you're out of it all right,'' Mike muttered. ''Better here than a POW in Germany.''

''Yes, well, that's the end of Chapter One,'' said Jacques. ''Operation Hammer. What about Chapter Two, Michel? You didn't come all the way from London just to see me.''

''I came as soon as I got the letter from Cousin Marguerite,'' Mike protested. ''I fixed it so I was given the job of carrying the men's back pay to Glasgow.'' He decided to say nothing about the movement orders.''Monsieur l'Aumônier means to distribute all the hospital pay tomorrow.''

''Oh! Dykefaulds hasn't recovered from his last visit yet.''

''This time will be different. And speaking of money'' —Mike took his wallet from an inside pocket—''I'm on a little money mission of my own. You remember my Uncle Pedro in Brazil?''

''Of course I do.''

''He wrote to me, air-mail, after the Germans invaded France. Said in time of war there was nothing like having a little cash in hand in case of accidents, and enclosed a cheque for £500, to split fifty-fifty between you and me. Here's your cut. Why don't you give it to Dr. Skinner to keep for you?''

Jacques stared at the folded paper. "What the hell!" he said. "Why should Monsieur Ferreira send all that to me? What does he think I'm going to do with it?"

"Spend it on some decent clothes, to start with," Mike said flippantly. "You're going to need a new outfit when you're demobilised. Go on, take it, Jacques. Why shouldn't he send you some ready money, he's as rich as Croesus, and he liked you a lot, that winter he spent at Monte Carlo. He thinks of you as family, man! Okay, my mother was his wife's sister, but your mother was his wife's cousin, right? Here, I'm going to put it in your pocket." He saw that the bandaged hands would fumble with the paper slip.

"Open it out and let me see it first."

The cheque was for £250, and signed M. D. A. Marchand.

"It's your signature, and your bank! I'm not going to take charity from you!"

"Of course it's my cheque, you fool, don't be so touchy! What did you think I would do—cut old Pedro's cheque in half like the judgment of Solomon? I banked the lot and wrote a new cheque for you. Here's his letter, if you don't believe me."

"You know I can't read Portuguese. But—all right, Michel, he's very generous. Please let him know I'm really grateful." Jacques allowed Mike to put the cheque into his jacket pocket, and watched while the letter from Brazil, with the air-mail stamps on the envelope, was folded up.

"I suppose he wants you to go back to Rio now."

Mike's pleasant face, blunt-featured under the fair hair, hardened slightly. "I've got other plans," he said. ". . . Cigarette? I've got Churchmans, not Gauloises."

"Just a drag."

Mike lit two cigarettes and held one to his cousin's lips. Then as Jacques looked at him expectantly, he went on: "I don't mean to chuck the embassy as long as there's any sort of job needing to be done. But that bunch at Bordeaux may decide to recall the lot of us and put in their own men, in which case I'm going to do my damnedest to enlist in the RAF. I only hope to God I haven't left it too late."

"Thanks." Jacques took a final drag at the cigarette and allowed Mike to stub it out. "Do you think you've any chance, Michel? You were turned down for our own Air Force at the time of Munich, and again at the beginning of last September; wouldn't that be on your record?"

"The situation's changed since last September, and the RAF's short of experienced pilots. I happen to know that Dowding's quota of fighter pilots isn't nearly filled. And the casualty rate is bound to go up like a rocket before too long."

"They won't enlist an experienced pilot who's known to have been grounded for medical reasons. And yours got a lot of publicity after the Dakar crash."

"Then I'll join up as a fitter mechanic," said Marchand. "I was a perfectly competent ground engineer when I was with Trans-Andean."

"Michel, have you seen this man de Gaulle? He's asking for engineers."

"I saw him once at the Hyde Park Hotel. He came to London twice after Reynaud made him Under-Secretary for National Defence in his last cabinet. De Gaulle was promoting that crackpot scheme for an indissoluble Franco-British Union that Jean Monnet and Vansittart dreamed up, and the government turned down at Bordeaux."

"Yes, well, I don't know anything about that. But when General de Gaulle came back to London last week, it was to save the honour of France."

"He came to London because he was out of a job," said Marchand with a grin. "When Reynaud resigned, and Marshal Pétain became prime minister, there was no more Under-Secretaryship for Temporary Brigadier de Gaulle. And considering that he'd made a violent scene in the Port Admiral's office at Brest, accusing Pétain and Weygand of treason, he may have been right in thinking Weygand would have him arrested, once the surrender was a fact."

"Did he think that?"

"He must have been pretty well sure of it when he latched on to the British General Spears, who was in Bordeaux representing Churchill. He went out to the airfield with Spears on the morning of the eighteenth, and when Spears was about to take off in his own plane he hauled de Gaulle aboard at the last minute, just like a sack of old potatoes. In a few hours, our hero was broadcasting his first appeal. Did you hear it?"

"We haven't had wireless privileges for the past week. But look here, when I asked you if you'd seen de Gaulle, I really meant had you been to see him. Got in touch with him. The newspapers say he's asking all Frenchmen who want to stay in the fight to get in touch with him—"

"I haven't done that yet," said Marchand.

"Do you know *how* to reach him? He's not at the embassy, I suppose?"

"Hardly. We only get the telegrams from the new War Minister at the embassy, ordering de Gaulle to go back to France and be court-martialled—for desertion, I suppose. He's already been struck off the army list."

"Michel, that's not the point," said Jacques patiently. "You can't call a man a deserter who fights on when everybody else gives in! And he's a fine soldier. The papers say he was the only general who won a victory in the Battle of France."

"Since when did you and I believe all we read in the newspapers? De Gaulle fought two local engagements in the month of May. First he tried to attack at Montcornet with the Fourth Armoured, without infantry support and under heavy attack by the Luftwaffe; General Georges ordered the engagement broken off. Next, on the twenty-ninth I think it was, he tried and failed to reduce the German bridgehead at Abbeville: the 4th Camerons and the 4th Seaforths of the Highland Division had to get him out of that mess. Then his men were pulled back to rest, and he went off to start his game of politics."

"You know far more about it than I do," said the invalid wistfully, "and I suppose it's all true enough. But you can hardly blame him if the bridge at Abbeville wasn't another Lodi. He mayn't be a Bonaparte, but you seem to be condemning him unheard, Michel—"

"Hardly unheard," said Mike. "De Gaulle's been very eloquent on the radio. It's just—there's something in his broadcasts that makes my hackles rise. '*Moi de Gaulle—moi de Gaulle*', he keeps repeating it: always that *me*, as if he was on some personal adventure, and perhaps he is. And I can't help feeling that a man who was only in action for five days in this campaign, and a junior Minister for eleven, has what our English friends would call *a bloody good cheek* when he announces that he's speaking in the name of France."

"You've never taken so much interest in politics before."

"No, I haven't, have I? I had my bellyful of all the politicians in France when they betrayed *La Ligne* and everything the pioneer flyers did in South America. I've never joined any political party; you were the one who planned to become Deputy and mayor of Menton some day. What do you think of your chances now?"

"Not very much, but after this Pétain lot have had their day, and we restore the Republic—"

"What kind of a Republic will it be? One of those women in Glasgow was talking about Stavisky, neither you nor I can have forgotten him. A con man who nearly brought down the Republic, only six years ago. What if de Gaulle turns out to be a super con man who sees himself as some kind of phoney emperor?"

"Oh come now, you're going too far," said Jacques. "It's not the same thing at all. General de Gaulle seems to be the only one with the guts to speak up for France in England. I want to know more about him—more than his broadcasts and the newspapers can tell us. And *you* haven't told me if you even know where he can be reached."

"Someone lent him a service flat just off Park Lane. I don't know the exact address, but it's not ten minutes' walk from where I live. You weren't thinking of writing to him, were you?"

"There's not much point in that; I wouldn't be any use to him at present. But couldn't you go and see him, Michel? Find out what he means to do, and what the British mean to do for him? And then write and tell me all about it?"

Marchand was silent.

"What have you got to lose?" insisted Jacques.

"Nothing, of course." It was true. Mike Marchand had no parents, no wife, no home in France, no relatives nearer than the kind-hearted old uncle in Rio de Janeiro. He was the perfect recruit for a soldier of misfortune like de Gaulle.

"I'll think about it," he said reluctantly. "And you think about getting well, *mon vieux*. When Dr. Skinner lets you go, you'd better come to me in London and make up your own mind about de Gaulle. The flat's paid for up to the end of September; it's not very big, but there's room enough for two. And it may be months before the repatriation is completed."

"I'm not going to ask to be repatriated."

"No?"

"Good God, Michel, how can I earn a living in France under the Germans? How long will it be before they move into the Unoccupied Zone? What sort of justice will we be allowed to

34

administer in the courts at Nice? And even if justice prevails, do you think I mean to spend my days pleading cases of eviction for non-payment of rent, or defending musical buffs who play their gramophones too loud after ten o'clock at night? That's the sort of neighbourhood litigation I've been involved in since I was called to the bar, and even if those Italian jackals are kept out of Nice, I'm not going on with it."

Jacques Brunel's pale face was alarmingly flushed, and Mike in distress looked round for a glass of water, a bell to ring for assistance—anything to quiet the agitated man. Finding nothing, he produced his cigarettes again, and said helplessly, "Here, have another drag."

Jacques shook his head. "I'm not going back to France," he said again. "My parents are all right at Oradour, and even if they go home to Menton I pity any Italian who gets into an argument with my father. If de Gaulle can't find a place for me I'll go to Casablanca—my God, when you think of the Army of Africa, that hasn't fired a shot in anger—"

"Take it easy, man, for pity's sake," Mike begged him. "Dr. Skinner will flay me alive if he sees you in a state like this. I'm only supposed to be with you for twenty minutes—"

"But you'll come back tomorrow?"

"I've got to be in London tomorrow morning, Jacques. But now I know you're being well looked after, we'll keep in touch. I'll get the phone number before I leave, and ask Dr. Skinner to let you speak to me on this extension." He indicated the black handset on a table beside the empty grate.

"I'm sure he won't be very keen on that."

"Then I'll call the Comforts Committee in Glasgow and get your friend Alison Grant to fix it. Those girls are the champion fixers of all time."

"Did Alison come here with you today?" said Jacques.

"She didn't come here with me, she brought me—in an army lorry. She's coming to say hello to you"—Mike looked at his watch—"any minute now. I'm sure punctuality's one of her Committee's higher virtues."

"Don't be sarcastic," said Jacques, "they're doing a wonderful job."

"Who's being sarcastic? Even if I did have to listen to a lecture on the deficiencies of the French Military Mission from one lady, and a bit of sermonising from another, I thought our friends in Glasgow were remarkable. They've got a requisitioned building, they've got army transportation and a driver, they've got funds and stores and willing helpers, probably what I really felt for that Committee was plain jealousy. They've made something out of nothing; France has made nothing out of everything."

"But didn't you like them as people?" Jacques persisted.

"They're very pleasant women, from what little I saw of them."

"But not quite your style, eh? Not chic enough for you?"

"I haven't encountered the Scottish style before."

Jacques turned his head towards the door. "Here comes Alison now," he said. Mike had not heard the light footfall, but although he hated to admit it he knew himself to be more than a little deaf. It was one of the consequences of the air crash which had changed his life.

Alison came in smiling, and Mike observed his cousin's answering smile with interest. If I weren't here I believe she'd kiss him, he thought, watching how tenderly the girl laid her fingers on the bandaged hands, and bent over Jacques to ask how he was feeling now, and if he had been sleeping well, and if he wasn't glad to see Monsieur Marchand.

"Very glad, if seeing him hadn't meant seeing less of you," said Jacques. "Have you been in the wards at all?"

"Not today," said Alison cheerfully, "but Dr. Skinner says I may come back again on Wednesday, so I'll see everybody then."

"We'll look forward to that," said Jacques, and added to Mike, "Did you know Miss Grant was going off to work in London next Monday?"

"I didn't know it was as soon as that. . . . You'll have to buck up and join me in Mount Street as soon as you can." He was amazed to see that both the girl and the Frenchman looked self-conscious. Could it be possible that Jacques Brunel, that serious young barrister and patriotic soldier, had taken a fancy to this little Scots redhead with the plastic curls? Mike knew about hospital romances: in tropical Dakar the wards had positively throbbed with the emotions of the patients and the nurses, white and coloured, but Miss Grant was not a probationer, nor even a VAD, only an occasional visitor from the Comforts Committee. They've got something going, he thought, I ought to clear out and leave them to it. Pity to waste the privacy of Skinner's dismal den.

36

"Meantime we'd better get you back to your ward, *mon vieux,*" he said. "I'll go and hunt up that orderly." He was stepping out into the pretty garden when a word from the wounded man recalled him.

"You won't forget all the things you're going to do for me?"

"I won't forget, First, a telegram to Oradour-sur-Glâne. And second, a message to Uncle Pedro when I write. Okay?"

"But above all"—and Jacques' drawn face was very serious—"you're going to see that man we were discussing. Remember?"

"I'll go and see him," promised Mike Marchand, "but I've some unfinished business to attend to first."

3

THERE WAS NO such thing, Mike Marchand soon discovered, as unfinished business in the summer of 1940. Once the shock of the French surrender was over, life went on. In France the Italians occupied Menton, the only town which had really suffered from their invasion, and the German troops in the south withdrew beyond the demarcation line into the Occupied Zone. The government, which had hoped to return to Paris, soon found itself on the road again, like any other travelling circus, and wended its way to Clermont-Ferrand in the high country of the Auvergne, where Julius Caesar had been defeated by the Gauls.

In London the French colony was shaken by the news that the ambassador had resigned. *En poste* for seven years, he had proved himself a true friend to England, and was resigning in protest at his own government's abandonment of its Ally. When the Minister took charge of the embassy, some of the younger diplomats went unostentatiously to call on General de Gaulle. They brought back widely differing accounts of the man and his personality, but they were all agreed on one thing, that 'French National Committee' was a figure of speech. None of the leading Frenchmen in London were members, and no general or Minister had left France to join de Gaulle. He was, for the time being, a one man band.

Mike Marchand was not among the general's visitors, although he read in *The Times* of the Thursday after his return from Glasgow that General de Gaulle was forming a legion of French volunteers 'with full British backing, financial and otherwise', and also 'a French centre for armament and scientific research which will form a rallying point for all French technical experts and scientists'. Before he committed himself, Mike spent nearly four days in using all his contacts at the Air Ministry and the Royal Aircraft Establishment in a vain attempt to enlist in the RAF. The form of words of his rejection hardly varied from "Jolly bad luck, old boy!" to "Why don't you have a go at this de Gaulle chappie?" although one chair-borne Air Commodore was original enough to remind him that flying was a young man's game, what? and aircraft had developed since the old days of the Aéropostale.

"I never flew for *La Ligne*, I wish I had," said Mike. He might have added that it was only five years since Michel Marchand had been important enough to be invited to watch the first flight of the Fury monoplane at Brooklands aerodrome, and the tests of the prototype Spitfire. Looking on, he admitted, didn't mean that a man nearly thirty could fly a Spitfire or a Hurricane, as the Fury was now called, as well as the kids on whom all depended in a conflict with the Luftwaffe. He went home with his confidence badly shaken. He had no belief that General de Gaulle's volunteer legion would at once include an air squadron. The British had lost nearly five hundred aircraft in support of the British Expeditionary Force on the Continent; they were unlikely to release a single Blenheim to the man who claimed to speak for France.

When Friday came, the most personal part of his unfinished business was with him in his rented flat, supine in a corner of the sofa with Mike's arms around her, and her beautifully manicured hands pressed lightly against his chest.

"Michel, you really must be good!"

He felt as if they were back at the beginning of their affair again. Except that it was summer, with the sound of a lawn mower coming through the open window instead of a February afternoon with the curtains drawn, the setting was identical, and so were the words she could scarcely expect him to take seriously. Mike smiled as he kissed her. He remembered how intently he had watched Denise in the early part of the winter, when they met from time to time at dinners and cocktail parties in the days of the 'phoney war'. She was very pretty, a Parisienne to her finger tips, and bored to tears, he guessed, with her fat pink slug of a husband, a banker on loan to the French Purchasing Commission. Adrien Lambert was said to have peculiar tastes, and to neglect his wife; Mike Marchand had waited until the reception when she told him carelessly that she meant to go and see an exhibition of French Impressionists in Cork Street at four next afternoon—there was a good deal of that kind of thing in the blackout winter, cultural values being supposed to be among the assets which would bring the Allies victory. He had been in the salon shortly after four, and from there it was only a taxi ride to his flat in Mount Street, and a seduction scene for which any writer of novelettes could have written the script. Mike had learned that Denise's repertoire was limited: even so, he was surprised to hear her whisper again:

"Michel, no, you must be good."

"Are you punishing me because I had to be away last Monday? I really had to go to Scotland on a job."

"Yes, I know, it isn't that. Michel, let me sit up. I can't talk, I can't even think, when you're kissing me."

"Who wants to think?" He poured her another glass of champagne and one for himself. Denise liked champagne in moderation, it was part of the ritual of a *cinq à sept* for her: the bottle in the ice-bucket and the plate of *petits fours* from Fortnum and Mason on the cocktail table beside the vase of sweet peas or roses. Her own scent was Guerlain's *'Pois de Senteur'*, and she was fastidious about keeping it beneath her ears and on her wrists and away from her beautifully cut black dress. Her tiny hat with its wreathed prune-coloured veil, her long black suède gloves and her handbag from the Faubourg St. Honoré were lying as usual on the sideboard where more fresh flowers stood.

"Darling, I've been thinking so much about you and me," Denise began, and her lips were trembling. "I'm afraid what I'm going to say will make you dreadfully unhappy."

"What is it, darling?"

"It's—it's simply that I feel, I do feel, now that this awful thing has happened to France, we oughtn't to go on seeing one another."

It was the last thing Mike had expected her to say. How far she was sincere, he didn't know; he had come to believe that every word she spoke, every line of dialogue, was taken straight from the serials in *Marie Claire*, and certainly 'we oughtn't to go on seeing one another' was a euphemism to please magazine readers. But the fall of France was too grave a theme for Denise to handle, or to connect with a rendezvous in a bachelor's apartment: the tears she had shed at the time of the surrender were conventional tears, falling because all her friends were crying too.

"My dear," he said solemnly, "we mustn't let it ruin our lives." And was totally amazed at her reply.

"What if we've ruined our lives already? You know what Marshal Pétain said when he called for a day of national mourning, that our defeat sprang from our laxity. That we have all taken more than we have given. As he said, the spirit of enjoyment destroys what the—the—"

"'What the spirit of sacrifice has built up'," said Mike gravely, and wondered at himself for remembering what the old hypocrite had said. He was as much surprised to hear Denise Lambert quoting from any political speech as if one of the Mayfair pigeons cooing in the trees outside the open windows had started to whistle the *Marseillaise*.

"Yes, the time has come when we must all make sacrifices," she said solemnly. "And mine must be—to give up seeing you."

"Don't be a little fool." He caught her roughly to him, hardly realising, in his burst of injured pride, that she was giving him the chance to get out he had been hoping for, not so much giving it as handing it to him on a plate. She whimpered at once that he was hurting her, creasing her dress, and that, he knew, was the ultimate crime in the eyes of Denise Lambert. I should have taken her to bed the minute she came in and not wasted time on the champagne and *petits fours* routine, he thought; and then he remembered that even in the small excitements of her passion Denise never forgot what love could do to mascara and an expensive hair-do. She always kept her pretty satin slip on when they went to bed.

So Mike released her, and when she rose from the sofa got to his feet at once, taking her in his arms again, but lightly, and smiling down at her as she laid her head appealingly against his arm. Denise was a little woman, insinuating as a pet cat; wearing her four-inch-heeled, black suède pumps she hardly reached his shoulder. He was going to say, "What the hell has old Pétain got to do with you and me?" when she forestalled him, and said,

"Michel, Adrien and I had a long talk last night."

"About us?"

"Good heavens, no!" Denise backed away from him at once. "Adrien has no idea—I mean, it would be absolutely fatal if he ever found out—"

"He won't." Reassurance on this point was one of the moves in the game, and Denise had often arrived delightfully breathless, certain that she had been followed to Mount Street by somebody spying for her husband.

"We talked about going back to France, Michel."

"Ah! Monsieur Lambert doesn't want to stay in England, then?"

Her light brown eyes, never her best feature, narrowed in calculation. "He thinks it isn't safe to stay. The invasion may begin any day, and General Weygand himself said that when it did, England would have its neck wrung like a chicken in three weeks."

"He hopes," said Mike.

"Surely Weygand ought to know! Michel, you don't mean to stay in London, do you?"

"Maybe."

"And join de Gaulle?"

"Don't know yet."

"Monsieur Monnet thinks de Gaulle's making a great mistake in starting a new movement under British protection. He won't have anything to do with it, and Adrien won't either. Especially since he's been offered this wonderful new job in Africa."

"In North Africa?"

"No, at Dakar, for the Banque de France. It's to do with the gold—" She caught her breath. "I'm not supposed to tell!"

"With the gold reserves; I know all about that," said Mike Marchand. "Is he going to take it?"

"He says he would be foolish to refuse. And you know he was really very sweet to me last night, poor Adrien. He said he didn't deserve me, and he asked me to give him another chance to show he loves me in spite—in spite of everything. He reminded me of all the Marshal's been saying about sacrifice and the rebirth of France. He begged me to go with him to Dakar."

Denise looked at her lover imploringly. She wanted him to understand, and let her go; at the same time she wanted to keep him for ever, the tall, blond, unruly young man who was the first and only one to bring her body to its full awareness of pleasure, and who had told her tales of a legendary and liquidated airline, La Ligne, the Aéropostale, with more emotion than he ever showed to her.

"You'll be the sacrifice if you go to Dakar, my child. Let Lambert go alone, and you go to your mother's villa at Mougins for a bit. You couldn't stand the climate at Dakar for more than a few weeks."

"Other French women have, so why not me?" Denise said defiantly. "I can't let Adrien go off to that horrible place alone!"

It was wifely solicitude, it was touching, it was also essentially false. Mike remembered that Adrien Lambert, as well as being a valued officer of the Banque de France, was also an extremely rich man in his own right. Any sacrifice Denise might make was certain to be gold-plated.

He took her hand and kissed it. "My dear," he said, "may you be happier in the future than I have ever been able to make you. I have no right to ask you to remain with me."

She was back in his arms then, tearfully, whispering that he had made her happy, so happy, happier than she had ever been; and in the same breath telling him that Adrien had arranged their passage on a Swedish boat to Casablanca. She picked up her hat and gloves. Even then Denise had to prolong the scene, looking wistfully round the living room, into which the late sunshine was streaming through two long windows, inhaling the scent of the sweet peas and even taking a last sip of champagne. As usual he insisted on getting a taxi for her, and as usual she protested that they ought not to be seen in Mount Street together. He didn't think it mattered now if they were seen lunching at the Ritz, so he took her downstairs firmly, and was unexpectedly touched when in the hall she flung herself into his arms and kissed him with real passion, before giving a sly glance into the hall mirror to see that the prune-coloured tulle veil was properly adjusted. He whistled to a passing cab and kissed her hand as he helped her in, standing on the pavement until the taxi reached the corner and the affair was over.

Mike turned back to his apartment building, put up in the Dutch style of warm red bricks and corbels when Victoria was queen, and pushed open the main door. There was no need to take out his key ring, for he had never yet found that door latched, although an ancient couple who lived in the basement and kept the stairs and landings tidy were supposed to lock up at midnight—by which time, he supposed, they were asleep and snoring. Mike Marchand had thought himself lucky to rent his furnished flat, for the building was very quiet, and he seldom saw or heard the elderly lady who lived alone with her Pekinese dog in the other apartment on his landing. A well-proportioned staircase with wrought iron banisters led up to the landing where his own front door stood open, and between that door and his neighbour's there was an alcove with a girandole of electric candles, big enough to hold a console table and a big vase of fresh rhododendrons, rose and white.

Mike went into the living room which smelled of Guerlain

scent, and lit a cigarette. The ice in the bucket had melted and the glaze on the *petits fours* had begun to crack. He intended to leave the whole mess to be picked up, and the cakes eaten, by the cleaning lady who arrived every weekday morning at eight o'clock, coming from some vague address in Paddington to make his coffee and tidy up the flat.

From a window seat he looked down through tree branches into a pretty little park below. The lawn-mowing was finished, and the gardener, sweeping up the cut grass, was the only person to be seen. Nobody was enjoying the sunshine on the benches or the paths, or looking at the flower beds, and Mike, in his disturbed state, felt there was something ominous in the silence. The bells of Grosvenor Chapel on the corner had ceased to ring, and would only be rung if and when the invasion started; the children of the elementary school opposite, whose laughing and shouting marked their play breaks as clearly as the bells, seemed to have gone on holiday earlier than usual. Mike sat alone at his window, in frustration of body and vexation of heart.

Admit it—he was glad the affair was over. He had been tired of it within two months of its beginning, and he should be glad that she had been the one to end it. And yet his male pride resented being so gently set aside, like the amusement of an idle spring, in favour of the husband over whose misdeeds she had so often and so boringly wept. He remembered other affairs when he had been the one to say goodbye, and the fireworks and raging which had accompanied the farewells. Especially the end of one spirited affair in Santiago de Chile, which the discarded lady had tried to settle with a Toledo blade.

But this time there was the gold at Dakar. Just the sort of secret a silly woman would let slip, and although Mike had heard one or two guarded references at the embassy to the loading of a vessel called the *Primaguet* and its sailing from Le Verdon for West Africa, he had understood that the gold of the Bank of France was to be taken far inland, either to Fort Bamako or Fort Keyes in the French Sudan. Now if Adrien Lambert had accepted a highly responsible post in Dakar itself, that could only mean the French gold was being taken to Fort Croisé, at no great distance from the city. He wondered how many people knew about the change of plan.

Meantime there was the evening to be got through, and it was barely seven o'clock. Remembering the clean linen on his bed,

44

and the sheets turned down invitingly, he thought with tense nerves that he would go to Soho, dine at Kettners, and visit one of the French girls with whom he had had transactions in the days before Denise. But that meant tears and politics again—*ces dames* were devoted to the father-figure of *le maréchal*—and Marchand had had enough of that. He mixed and drank a stiff whisky and soda before walking through the empty byways of Mayfair to dine at a little Italian restaurant on Curzon Street. From there he went to a club where he sat down to three profitable rubbers of bridge with three taciturn Englishmen, any of whom would have thought it the height of bad form to mention French affairs to him.

He therefore missed the communiqué in which the British government officially recognised General de Gaulle as 'the Leader of All Free Frenchmen, wherever they may be', and the broadcast in which the Leader, now sure of his status, shifted from the 'we' of his Committee's statement and declared that he, *Moi de Gaulle*, took under his authority all French citizens living on British territory, and all who might come there.

* * *

It was impossible to know how many French citizens living on French territory heard the general's claim. Most listeners in Britain switched off their wireless sets when his broadcasts began, and few noticed that the harsh, badly paced voice was already smoother than it had been ten days before. So many refugees, exiles, victims of persecution and lost human beings were crowded inside the tiny island fortress, separated by less than twenty-five miles of water from the enemy, that the French had no better claim to sympathy than any of the others. The King of Norway was in London, with his government. The Queen of the Netherlands was there too, with her government, and the Belgian government was there, conspicuously without its king. There were Czechs and Poles whose representatives were called governments-in-exile, and as they crowded the pavements of Piccadilly on a beautiful Saturday evening, the last in June, nobody cared that the Leader of All Free Frenchmen had won yet another concession from his British hosts, and was now going personally among the French camps calling for recruits.

Mike Marchand, driving down Park Lane and along Knights-bridge, saw crowds of strollers moving between the parks and into

Kensington, where he was bound. But the side streets of Kensington were as deserted as the byways of Mayfair, and when he pulled up his borrowed car at the foot of Young Street and dutifully took out the rotor arm, he saw only two more cars parked in the whole expanse of Kensington Square. He looked up at the windows of Castlewood Close, saw a small boy waving eagerly, waved back, and went into the building with a smile.

He was going to dinner with two good friends, Edmond and Betty Leblanc, and however grim the days might be he was sure of enjoyment in their home. Betty had made it pleasant, although Castlewood Close was a seedy place where the lift was always out of order and the corridors littered with unwashed milk bottles and children's scooters, and certainly not worth the rent her husband paid for a three-bedroom flat of which two of the bedrooms were mere cubbyholes. She was always bright and glowing when their friends were expected, so that Mike was disconcerted when she opened the door wearing her kitchen apron, with a tag of brown hair uncoiling on her neck.

"Oh Mike, darling, I'm so sorry, dinner isn't nearly ready, it's been a hellish day!" she flung at him, while Edmond, coming quickly from the living room which was also the dining room, tried to give the guest a heartier welcome. He was a lean, grizzled Frenchman with a quizzical smile and a cigarette perpetually adhering to his lower lip. The children were hugging Mike's knees, and he saw that they were already in their dressing-gowns and slippers, while Babette, who was seven, had her long hair plaited for the night. Timmy, a fat four-year-old, dragged at Mike's hand and demanded a story, the same story as last time, and lots more of it.

"Gently, *mon petit vieux*," said Mike, "let me give your mother some fruit first. Much better for you than chocolate!" He handed over a large basket of cherries and one of early strawberries, and the over-excited children shrieked with delight.

"You've been in the country," said their father. "You didn't buy fruit like that in London!"

"Uncle Mike came in a car tonight," said Timmy. "Babs and me saw him."

"I thought you sold your car when petrol rationing began," his mother said to Mike. She was dragging the apron over her head, making her hair wilder in the process.

"I did. I borrowed one of the embassy cars for the day," he

46

said, and turning to follow Edmond into the front room, almost fell over a large suitcase, with its lid open, lying in the dark little vestibule.

"We're going to the country too!" shrilled Babette. "We're packing, because we're going down to stay with granny and granpa tomorrow, ever and ever so long!"

"I'm going to pack you both off to bed," said Betty Leblanc. "Mike, I'm sorry this is such a madhouse. But Edmund scrounged some petrol today, don't ask him where, and he's driving us to Bath tomorrow. I won't keep the kids in London another day longer. Timmy, do shut up!" she finished almost hysterically. For Timmy had wriggled his plump form into Mike's lap, and was begging him to go on with the story about the fifty-three take-offs of Jean Mermoz.

"I have to get the ice cubes," said Babette importantly, and she ran off to the kitchen to fetch the six little mounds of ice, like miniature sand castles, which as Mike well knew were turned out by six metal containers kept on a tiny shelf at the top of the Leblancs' erratic fridge. A bottle of Cinzano, with three glasses, had already been placed on a low table.

"I think you're smart to go," said Mike to Betty, while the little girl was out of the room. "Even if it's a rush, it's a good idea to go down on Sunday, when Edmond has a bit of free time. *Bon voyage!*" he said, raising the glass his host had filled.

"Edmond has all the time in the world," said Betty, and two spots of colour came up in her tired face. "He's lost his job."

Edmond Leblanc tried to smile. He was forty-five, much older than his wife, and had been a flyer in what the French called the Other War. In the 1920s he had been the aviation columnist of a Paris newspaper, and could entertain Mike by the hour with stories of the Aéropostale at Montaudon in the great days of *Courrier Sud*. Ten years back, Leblanc had become the London correspondent of a Paris magazine, to which he sometimes contributed articles on the new planes and the men who flew them. He had known Marchand since the summer when the young French flyer took part in a series of air displays in Britain.

"Yes, *Paris-Lendemain* has folded, Mike," he said to fill the awkward silence. "Paris-Tomorrow is now Paris-Yesterday. Not that there was anything else to do. The paper came out strong against everything from the German occupation of the Rhineland to Pétain's request for an armistice, and Monsieur Edelmann knew his name was on the Nazi Black List. He cabled me on Thursday from Lisbon, telling me he'd got out all right, and was waiting for a place on the Clipper to New York. It was that or be marched off to a German concentration camp."

"And the paper has actually ceased publication?"

"That's right. And it's not the only one, as you probably know."

"Tough luck, Edmond, but you've so many good contacts in Fleet Street you'll land another job before the end of next week."

"You make it sound as if that little rat Edelmann did him a good turn by running away," snapped Betty. "What makes you think there'll be any jobs for a Frenchman in the Street? The French let us down; why should we rush to pat them on the back and say everything's fine, you were terrific, now here's a nice job for you, we'd rather employ you than any old Englishman, just try not to let us down again—oh, I'm sorry, Edmond, I'm sorry, Mike, I don't mean *you*—"

Marchand saw that she hardly knew what she was saying, and made a soothing gesture, but Betty had not finished yet. "But we won't starve!" she went on defiantly. "I'll get a job if I have to! And not any of your voluntary war jobs either! I'll find something in Bath and mummy can look after the kids, she promised me that at Christmas, if the worst comes to the worst—"

"It's not the worst yet, Betty," said her husband, and she began to cry. Timmy struggled down from Mike's knee and went to pat her face with his fat hands, and Babette took fast hold of her mother's dress. Betty put her arms round them both.

"I'm a fool," she managed to say weakly, "I didn't mean to say all that. Come on and help me, you two, or poor Uncle Mike's dinner'll be burned to a cinder!"

"She did mean it, though," said Edmond quietly, when the two men were alone.

"She's terribly upset," said Mike. "You told me she'd taken the whole thing so well."

"She doesn't really want to go to Bath, you know. And leaving the kids with mummy won't work out, at least not for long. It was the damned newsreel she saw yesterday when Babs and Timmy were at a birthday party—she saw the refugees on the French roads before the surrender, sleeping in the fields, hunting for lost kids, and the German bombers coming over . . . On top of the

48

job folding, it was just too much. She's been running round in circles ever since."

"You should have called me up and told me not to come."

"We both wanted to see you."

"How would it be if the whole lot of you got in the car, and I take you down to some place like the 'Compleat Angler' at Marlow for dinner? It would take her mind off—"

"It's too late for the small fry, and besides, it might hurt her feelings. She's got something special in the oven, something for what she calls our farewell dinner—"

"Oh hell," said Mike, stubbing out his cigarette, "I can't stand this. Come on out and talk to her."

In the kitchen Betty was stirring the contents of a saucepan, with a tear-smudged face and a smear of flour down the front of her dress, while the children, very subdued, looked on. Mike, picking up a lettuce from the draining board, sniffed appreciatively. "Nothing burned here," he said. "It smells delicious. Need any help?"

"Can you cook, Uncle Mike?" squealed Babette.

"I can mix a salad. I can hull the strawberries. I can take the stems off the cherries. Edmond can open the wine and set the table."

"What a pair of clowns you are," said Betty, laughing at last. "I'm not going to turn you loose in my kitchen, Mike! No, this is what we'll do. I need half an hour to get these two into bed and make myself presentable. You go on over to the local and have a drink there, and everything'll be nice when you come back. Please, Edmond?"—with an undertone of appeal. Her husband stooped, and kissed her.

Dusk, even the late dusk of an English June, was falling as the two men walked the very short distance to the Leblancs' local, which was called the 'Greyhound', where the management had already done the blackout for the night. Heavy cloth curtains on the windows and the screening of the door seemed to keep the faintest current of air from the saloon bar, which like the public bar was as crowded as if the streets of Kensington had spilled human beings into this one hostelry, which had known a long history of troubled times. Edmond Leblanc heard his native language, and the languages of at least three other foreign countries, as he edged his way forward to the counter. From another room came the click of billiard balls as a few resolute

Englishmen stuck to the Saturday night pastime of a world at peace.

"Two half pints of bitter, miss."

"Thanks, Edmond." Mike seized the glass tankard his friend handed back to him over a soldier's khaki-clad arm, clasping the shoulders of a girl in a summer dress, and rescued an open mustard pot on the verge of falling off the metal counter. They stood in the middle of the scrum for a few minutes, taking a long pull at the beer, and then Mike proposed that they take their drinks out to the street. With so much noise going on around him, he was finding it impossible to hear. Edmond Leblanc mopped his face as they sidled towards the door.

"Stuffy in there."

"My God, yes!"

Other men had taken their drinks and their girls into the half-darkness of Young Street, and were leaning against the stonework which still held the heat of the long summer day. The 'Greyhound' did not encourage music indoors, but up the street someone was playing a harmonica, a trickle of sound making a statement about hanging out the washing on the Siegfried Line, which at that moment of British history was equivalent to whistling in the dark.

The two Frenchmen strolled along to the corner of Kensington Square. Mike knew nothing of its more than two hundred years of history, not even that many of his countrymen, including the great Talleyrand in the days of the Revolution, had found a refuge there in times of distress, but the square had always appealed to him as resembling a backwater in some quiet French provincial town. The little Catholic church, the flat white stucco façades of the eighteenth century houses, the well-tended central garden all breathed a sedate bourgeois peace. There was a scent of tea roses, and trails of wistaria and clematis in varying shades of mauve and purple were wreathed above some of the closed front doors. But as Mike's eyes grew accustomed to the light he saw that the railings which had guarded the Square garden had been taken for scrap iron, and as an air raid precaution a huge tank of static water had been installed at one side of the already neglected lawn.

He swirled the beer in his glass reflectively, too perturbed by that ugly little scene between the French husband and his English wife to know how to begin a conversation. He left it to the older man to say, "So what's new at the embassy? How did they react to the British recognition of de Gaulle?"

"Predictably. The official line is that nobody, least of all a rebel general, can impose his authority on French citizens while the embassy and the consuls are still there to represent them. And to represent the President of the Republic, who is with the government; that government being, wherever it may be, the legal government of France. Sorry to sound so pompous," he concluded, "but that's the substance of the *démarche* they want to make to Lord Halifax."

He had no intention of telling any newspaperman, even one temporarily out of work, that the real business of the morning had been transacted in the Old Building of the Admiralty, where the French Naval Mission had its offices. Mike had gone there from Albert Gate with the Service attachés and listened to their discussion of the biggest problem since the armistice: the disposition of the French fleet. The British had offered to release the French from their solemn vow never to sue for a separate armistice only on condition that their great fleet should be sailed to British ports. French naval pride, still seared by the memory of Trafalgar, could not bend to this condition, and now the armistice terms demanded the demobilisation and disarming of the whole war fleet under German and Italian control.

As early as June 27, Britain had refused to allow the French ships already in British harbours to sail back to France. There were at least fourteen capital ships at Plymouth and Portsmouth, with other naval auxiliaries, and they were manned by twelve hundred crewmen, all now complaining vocally of British harassment. Every aspect of a delicate situation was discussed by the anxious group in the Old Building without any practical conclusion having been reached.

"I'm sorry, Edmond?"

"I asked you, what was your *own* reaction to the recognition of de Gaulle?"

"I got a car and a fair allowance of petrol, drove down to White Waltham, and tried to enlist in the Air Transport Auxiliary."

"What happened?"

"The usual—another turn-down." He stepped nearer the privet hedge, no longer protected by the railings, to let a boy and girl in uniform go by. "Lord knows I've given up all hope of combat duty, but I did think I could ferry aircraft between the factories and the RAF bases."

"Have you ever flown a twin-engine bomber, Mike?"

"Like an Oxford? They send you on a Heavy Conversion Course for that. At the Central Flying School."

"But they're not sending you."

"No. Many thanks for my personal visit, delighted to offer me a drink in the mess, but No. And yet they've taken on Jim Mollison, and God knows I'm a more reliable pilot than poor old Jim. Or I used to be. But now I'm Mike Marchand, who piled up his plane outside Dakar, broke every bone in his body and killed his navigator. And was grounded permanently because he suffers from vertigo."

Edmond's mutter was intended to be sympathetic. "I can't picture you ferrying aircraft from one British village to another," he said. "I thought you meant to try for a ground job, or something in admin.?"

"Even for that, after last night's declaration, I'd have to join de Gaulle. So I might as well keep my promise to my cousin, and go and see what the general has to offer."

"I may end up with the general too, before very long."

In the shadows, Mike could just see the quizzical face, and the dark hair brindled with grey. "You, Edmond? You're well over military age—"

"Ah, but the general means to fight with the pen as well as with the sword. No, he doesn't need a speechwriter! I'll give him this credit: the broadcasts are his own unaided work, as the pavement artists say. But now he's got financial backing from the British, it should be possible to start a Free French newspaper, telling all about the Leader, and the movement, and the heroic followers; one or two men I know, who were at the Ministry of Information in Paris, are working on the idea this weekend."

"The idea being just straight propaganda for de Gaulle?"

"More or less."

"And you'd want to work for a rag like that?"

"It's a case of any port in a storm, Mike. We haven't all got rich uncles in Brazil! And if I don't take the job, there are plenty of bigger guns than me who may turn up any day from Paris, and jump at the chance. Henri de Kerillis and Elie Bois are in London already."

"What kind of readership do you expect for a thing like that?"

"French groups. French teachers, students of French—and of course all the French communities in the country, who are shaking in their shoes already for fear of being interned if they don't rally to the Leader of All Free Frenchmen."

"There you are!" said Mike. "That's what needs explaining, and not in French either. That word *Leader*—they hate it here. There's a *Führer* and a *Duce* in Europe already: why did *we* have to get stuck with a Leader?"

"*Chef des Forces Françaises Libres*—you know it's an exact translation from the French."

"Yes, *I* know, but someone ought to explain it to the British."

"Don't worry," said Leblanc, with a little jarring laugh, "the British are going to hear a lot more about de Gaulle in the very near future. General Spears realised that his boy would take a bit of selling, so he's persuaded Mr. Churchill to pay a press agent's fee to put the general over to the British public. They're saying in the Street that Spears asked for £1000 but Winston would only go as far as £500, at least to start with. They've hired a good man, though—Richmond Temple."

Mike Marchand upended his tankard and let the last drops fall on the dusty pavement, as if the bitter had become too bitter for his taste. "What simpletons they are," he said. "As if de Gaulle needed any PR man, with Churchill as his patron, and the BBC at his disposal any night of the week."

"And you must admit he's done a lot with it. My God, it's not a fortnight since he turned up in England penniless, with nothing but the uniform he stood up in and one spare shirt. Now he's the acknowledged Leader, backed by Britain—"

"You sound pretty well sold on him yourself."

"Not really. If I get the job I really want you won't hear of Leblanc in *mon général's* entourage."

"You mean you *have* a job in view?"

"You know I often do a Saturday turn in Fleet Street, subbing for the *Sunday Journal*? I've got to know a lot of chaps in the company, and there's an even chance Mac might take me on at the *Daily Journal*, in the newsroom. But remember, Betty mustn't have an inkling. I don't want to raise her hopes."

"I understand." Mike looked away and across the dark garden. The boy and girl who had passed them on the pavement were sitting now under a hawthorn tree. They were locked in each other's arms, unmoving, moulded into one body, and Mike felt a sharp envy of that boy in khaki. He was sick of inaction, sick of his own past which tripped him at every step, he wanted—like those kids beneath the flowering thorn—to snatch at the life which might end for all of them tomorrow. He said,

"I'll go to the Free French headquarters on Monday. Do you want the other half?"

"Thanks, but we ought to be getting home to Betty, she must be ready for us now."

"Right, let's take the glasses back. I'll do it! No sense in two of us struggling through that mob." He struggled alone, and when he rejoined Edmond outside the 'Greyhound' Mike was laughing.

"Something funny?"

"I was just thinking of a girl I met in Glasgow who said when the Allies won the war and took de Gaulle back with them to Paris—I know, I know, that's what she said—he'd be like the Bourbons at the Restoration."

" 'Having learned nothing and forgotten nothing'? She may very well be right."

"At the embassy they prefer to compare him to General Boulanger."

"Not very flattering. After all, Boulanger's effort at a *coup d'état* fizzled out in the Café Weber on the Rue Royale."

"You think this fellow means to go further than the Rue Royale?"

"I think he's planning to go right on up the Faubourg St. Honoré. Maybe as far as the Elysée."

4

GENERAL CHARLES DE GAULLE was rising slowly in the world. He had never been as destitute as the publicity stories about his arrival in England in the clothes he stood up in and one clean shirt had implied, for before he left France Paul Reynaud, while still prime minister, had given him about £600 from the secret funds. It was enough to tide him over until support from the British taxpayer was forthcoming, and the general had moved from his borrowed apartment in Mayfair to a modest hotel in the Buckingham Palace Road. More important, he had moved himself and his French National Committee, such as it then was, into a suite of offices.

This he owed to the British general, Edward Spears, who, having scooped de Gaulle up from the airfield at Bordeaux, had dumped him down in the very heart of London's power and splendour. The zealous general, who was also a Member of Parliament, arranged office space for the Leader of All Free Frenchmen in St. Stephen's House, just across the road from the House of Commons and across the Thames from the ornate headquarters of the London County Council. Whitehall opened to the north, and Westminster Abbey was visible beyond a parterre of flowers and trees, while if de Gaulle cared to look out of his office windows he could see a statue of Boadicea, Queen of the Iceni, driving her chariot furiously against the Roman invader.

The German invader was now expected hourly. The tipsters were giving July 8 as the date for his arrival, but on Monday, July 1, it was felt that invasion week had opened, and when Mike Marchand walked across the parks to St. Stephen's House he saw trenches being dug and more artillery hauled into place. A thin trickle of arms purchased in the United States had just begun to arrive.

Now that he had committed himself to approaching de Gaulle, Mike turned down the Embankment, if not eagerly, at least without reluctance. Two more days of witnessing the exchanges between the French Embassy and the Foreign Office in London with Admiral Darlan and Marshal Pétain in France, always on the burning question of the French fleet in Axis hands, had left him with an overriding sense of futility. They were doing everything and getting nowhere, running on the spot; de Gaulle to give him his due was getting somewhere. As soon as the British allowed him to recruit in person he was off to Staffordshire to address the survivors of the Narvik division: he had been there, at Trentham Park, while Mike was driving down to White Waltham on Saturday afternoon. Since then he had addressed the members of the French colony in London, dolefully assembled in the YMCA building in the Tottenham Court Road. Not even his PR man could claim that those meetings were successful, the general having as yet no idea of how to appeal to a mass audience, but at least he had been seen and heard, and had impressed by his great height. The newspaper stories written from the PR handouts stressed that the general had been known since his cadet days as *le Grand Charles*, the inference being that quality could be measured in centimetres. There was little else that could so far be said. His failure to carry the bridgehead at Abbeville was revised, and made to sound like another Austerlitz: General de Gaulle, British readers were assured, had to all intents and purposes invented the tank.

It was impolitic to add that his arrogance and vanity had antagonised all his superior officers throughout his military career, and that Marshal Pétain, whom he had used prime time on the BBC to revile, had twice intervened in the highest quarters to save a younger de Gaulle from the consequences of his own folly.

There was no queue of eager recruits to the Free French Forces outside the grimy doorway of St. Stephen's House, but two British Army cars were drawn up under the plane trees which edged the pavement, poignantly reminiscent of the plane trees fringing the banks of the Seine. Some English girls in the uniform of the MTC were sitting on a bench in the lobby, and on one of the tiled walls which made the interior of St. Stephen's House look like a public lavatory Mike saw an arrow pointing to a door marked '*Service de Presse*'. The Cockney liftman, deceived by Mike's dark blue civilian suit, shook his head when he asked for the offices of General de Gaulle, but finally said, "Oh, the French gent!" and took him slowly upward to the third floor.

After the bright sunshine out of doors, the premises of the

French gent seemed dark and gloomy, but the sound of voices came from both sides of the right-angled corridor, and a middle-aged officer came forward at once to introduce himself as *"le commandant du Quartier-Général"*.

"Michel Marchand."

"Ah yes, from the embassy. Very glad to see you here, monsieur."

"Not officially from the embassy."

"No, of course not. But very welcome in your own right! I have a son in the Air Force, he used to follow your exploits. Just take a seat in the waiting room, I'll send Lieutenant Larron to you at once."

There was no one in the small waiting room but another middle-aged man, a civilian, who jumped up eagerly when Mike and the commandant went in. He was obviously bursting to offer his services, in what capacity could only be guessed, for he had just time to tell Mike that he had lived in London for twenty years before a little bustling officer with the Chasseur insignia came in to say, "The general will see you now!"

"Lieutenant Larron, this is Monsieur Marchand, from the embassy," said the commandant.

"*Enchanté, monsieur*," said the little officer, "Just give me a minute to take this gentleman to General de Gaulle, and I'll be right with you. I'll send one of the girls in to take down your particulars . . . Now, sir, this way if you please!"

Mike was left alone to study his surroundings. Bare, well-polished linoleum on the floor, faded curtains, a table holding a battered typewriter and stationery—the empty room was no more impressive than the improvised office of the Comforts Committee in Glasgow. But there was a good deal of coming and going in the corridor beyond the open door, where men in uniform were moving purposefully about with cardboard folders in their hands, and he could hear women's voices in the room next door. Then a tall French girl with the face of a startled hare came in and smiled at him as she sat down and fitted three sheets of paper and two carbons into the typewriter and asked him for his full name.

"Marchand, Michel Dieudonné Antoine. Born at 239, rue St. Honoré, Paris 1, November 15, 1910. Unmarried. Present address care of the French Embassy, Albert Gate House, London, SW." Mike had given these particulars so many times before, knowing them to be a preliminary to any official business in

France, that he spoke mechanically and hardly listened to the click of the typewriter keys.

His father's Christian names? Jules Hubert. Killed at Douaumont in 1916. By a coincidence, in the same action of the Battle of Verdun in which Captain de Gaulle had been taken prisoner of war. He saw the hare's face, more startled than ever, raised reprovingly above the typewriter.

His mother's name? Rose Amélie Verbier, died in Paris, 1928. His national service? With the Air Force, 1929–1930. His home address in France? None. His near relatives in France and their addresses? None.

"Then, monsieur, you will have no objection to enlisting under your own name?"

"How else?"

"The Statute permits enlistment under a *nom de guerre*, if the recruit has reason to fear reprisals against his family in France."

"That doesn't apply in my case."

"Then I'll have your declaration processed at once."

"Thank you, mademoiselle . . Is somebody in trouble?"

There was a rush of feet on the landing, the commandant's voice saying something inaudible, and then another voice, loud with despair: "He said he didn't want me! He said, 'What use is a one-armed man to me?' I told him I was some use to him at Abbeville before the Highlanders came up—" Mike saw a little scuffle, heard the bell for the lift ringing sharply, and then the girl moved between him and the door.

"Poor man, he ought not to have insisted," she said unhappily. "Thank you, Monsieur Marchand—and good luck."

There was something unnerving in the waiting alone, smoking and listening. The next sounds were more reassuring, for the middle-aged civilian was out on the landing, obviously delighted with his reception.

"So gracious, such a noble figure . . . understands our problems here so well. I told him my car was at his personal service —with my chauffeur. A Delahaye, bought in France last year. He says more typewriters would be welcome; I can supply three. Will tomorrow morning suit for the delivery, *mon commandant*?" Tomorrow morning would suit very well.

"Now then, Monsieur from-the-embassy, *à nous deux*! The commandant has been telling me about your record in Brazil." Lieutenant Larron was back in the waiting room, more important than ever, with one of the cardboard files, which everybody seemed to carry, in his hand. "I've brought a copy of the enlistment oath for you to sign, and then we'll arrange for your medical at the Service de Santé.'

"Just a minute," said Mike. The little officer had pulled a chair up beside him, the smell of garlic was overpowering. "I don't want to sign anything until I've had a word with General de Gaulle."

"He's very busy this afternoon."

"He's been appealing for people to get in touch with him personally, and that's what I mean to do, *mon lieutenant*."

"Yes, that sounds great, but you ought to have come sooner. It's two weeks since he made his first call for recruits."

"It doesn't look as if he's exactly packing them in."

"All the better for the ones who got here first," said Lieutenant Larron with a wink. "The best jobs are nearly all spoken for. Look at Captain Dewavrin—he showed up two days after he heard the general speak at Trentham Park. Now he's head of the Second and Third Bureaus, working with Hettier and Tissier, very close to the general—"

"Set up a *Deuxième Bureau* already, has he? Espionage and counter-espionage?"

"We've got to take precautions against the British, haven't we? They're no fools; they want to feather their nests out of the situation—if we let them! But that's another story; let's get on with *you*. Read the oath and sign it, and then I'll try to work you in for three minutes with the Leader."

Mike took the printed form, and saw that it was already complete but for his own signature.

Forces Françaises Libres [he read]
Acte d'Engagement

Before [here followed the illegible signature, 'Larron'] representing General de Gaulle, Commander-in-Chief of the Free French Forces,
Mr. *Marchand, Michel Dieudonné Antoine* [in typescript] declares that he has made himself acquainted with the Statute of the Personnel of the Free French Forces, that he enlists and will serve with Honour, Faith and Discipline in the Free French Forces for the duration of the war now in progress plus three months.

There followed provisos about a medical examination and the approval of General de Gaulle's personal staff, and then a space for the signature of the recruit and two witnesses. There was also an omission, which made Mike knit his brows, but all he said to the lieutenant was, "I haven't seen whatever this may be—the Statute of the Personnel."

"It's only in draft form at present."

"Surely you've a copy somewhere? You don't want a perjured signature, do you?"

"What we want are recruits, not barrack-room lawyers. Oh, very well, if you insist!" Lieutenant Larron took a few sheets of thin paper, typed in single spacing, from his folder, and handed them sulkily to Mike Marchand.

Who was aware, as he ran his eyes over the four codifications of the Statute, of the repetition of one name—de Gaulle.

Conditions of admission to the armed forces will be regulated by General de Gaulle.

Conditions of employment in the auxiliary forces—ditto.

All promotions to the rank of officer will be made by General de Gaulle.

All reductions to the ranks will be made by General de Gaulle. His decision will not be affected by the findings of a council of enquiry.

The right of pardon for penal offences is in the hands of General de Gaulle.

And so on.

"Satisfied?" asked the lieutenant as Mike came to the end of the last page.

"Satisfied that I've seen it, yes."

"And you understand it?"

"Perfectly."

"Will you sign the oath, then?"

"Not till I've seen *him*."

"Oh hell!" said Lieutenant Larron, "I'll take you to his aide-de-camp . . . *Je m'excuse, mon capitaine!*" For as he bustled out the little man had collided with a tall, blond officer, and dropped his folder in the act.

"Another civilian recruit, Larron?" The newcomer was coldly handsome, with regular features; he looked down with amusement at the man scrambling to pick up his scattered papers.

"Captain Dewavrin," said the lieutenant, pulling himself together, "this is Monsieur Marchand—from the embassy."

"*Mon capitaine*," said Mike automatically, and stopped short. Whatever interest he might have had in meeting the man who, after the briefest of encounters, had become the head of de Gaulle's Intelligence Service, was eclipsed by the sight of the man at Dewavrin's back—another handsome young officer in the familiar uniform of the Chasseurs Alpins.

"Good Lord, Schnaebel!" he said, "what in the world are you doing here?"

"I beg your pardon?"

"Schnaebel, don't you remember me? Michel Marchand?"

"You're mistaking me for somebody else," said the Chasseur pleasantly. "I've only just arrived from France."

"This is Lieutenant Carreau, monsieur," said the head of the *Deuxième Bureau*. "He reported today, after a remarkable escape by fishing boat from Brest . . . Larron, I want him to see the general without delay. Can you arrange it?"

"But I met you twice in Brazil," persisted Mike. "Once in Rio and once at—at Recife, I think it was. You were flying for Condor, between Recife and Natal—"

"I've never been in Brazil in my life, monsieur," said the lieutenant. "Sorry! Mistaken identity, I'm afraid!"

"Just give us five minutes, *mon capitaine*," said Larron. "This won't take long."

But more than five minutes passed before Mike Marchand was admitted to the presence of General de Gaulle. His conducting officer was summoned by a cavalry lieutenant with an aquiline nose, and conferred with him behind closed doors, while Mike was left in the corridor, looking in at a big room where four attractive girls were typing under the supervision of the nervous young lady who had taken down his own particulars. He had time to wonder if the Leader, who had no use for a one-armed man, would have any use for one whom two military doctors had declared to be suffering from vertigo and unfit to fly a plane, and who now appeared to be suffering from delusions as well. He had almost convinced himself that his memory, at least five years old, of Arthur Schnaebel, chief pilot of Condor Air, had tricked him in the matter of a chance resemblance. Then the cavalry lieutenant, who was the general's ADC, ushered him through an anteroom where telephones were ringing, into the sparsely furnished office overlooking the Thames where Charles de Gaulle sat, beside a large map of France, alone.

Mike snapped to attention and waited to be addressed.

Without inviting him to be seated, de Gaulle got up and moved away from the desk on which a large ashtray was overflowing with the stubs of half-smoked cigarettes, as if to indicate that the interview would be a short one. His great height, which had earned him the nickname of *le Grand Charles*, did not automatically give him a commanding presence, for years of the parade ground had not corrected his sway-backed posture, and in proportion his head was too small for his big womanish hips. It was the general's face which interested Mike Marchand. He had only caught a glimpse of de Gaulle on one of his visits to London before the French surrender, but he remembered the haughty, confident expression very well. Having listened to all the broadcasts but one since the eighteenth of June, he had half expected to see the broadcaster emotionally ravaged by his own passion. Instead, it was as if the general had drawn a mask of icy indifference over his features, to conceal whatever hell of patriotism and devouring ambition raged beneath.

"Your name?" said General de Gaulle.

"Michel Marchand, *mon général*."

"Where have you been employed since the outbreak of war?"

"At the French Embassy in London."

"In what capacity?"

"Temporary attaché."

The pouting lips under the little Hitler moustache twitched for a moment in disdain. "So you speak English, I presume. Where did you perform your military service, and with what rank?"

"In the Air Force, *mon général*. Finally, with the rank of Sergeant Pilot."

"What are your further qualifications? What foreign languages do you speak, other than English?"

"Spanish and Portuguese."

The cold grey eyes appraised him. "Have you lived in Portugal?"

"Sir, I lived and worked for some years in Brazil."

Mike Marchand was aware that their dialogue was as false as the patter of the music halls; that the general had been briefed on his record in Brazil as well as on his record in the air, and that this briefing was the result of the conclave between the two young officers in the anteroom. He decided it was time to take the lead in the conversation.

"*Mon général*, I understand that a group of our own airmen have enlisted in the Free French forces, and are billetted, or are in camp, at St. Athan. I want to join them. I want to fight, in whatever capacity, as one of the Free French Air Force."

"The men at St. Athan are survivors of the Battle of France, as you are no doubt aware. The British were not generous in sending us planes during that battle. When do you think they will be liberal enough to supply me with Blenheims, Spitfires, Hurricanes, to continue the struggle?"

"When their own losses are made good at the factories, or by purchase from the United States."

"I've no time to waste on fantasies, monsieur. You will be far more useful to me in Brazil than among the pilots of St. Athan. No doubt they will be, one day, the nucleus of my Air Force, but your qualifications can be used to better purpose now. You have relatives living in Rio de Janeiro?"

"Relatives by marriage, *mon général*. My uncle lives there, yes; my cousins in the state of Minas Gerais."

"Very well. You will be attached, in the first place, to my Press Service, to make a thorough study of my aims. Then, as soon as possible, you will return to Rio de Janeiro: perhaps as one of a mission, perhaps alone, as my personal representative in Brazil. You will have the honour of being one of the first, if not the first, to make my aims known in South America—"

"*Sir!*"

The pale eyes glittered in the sallow face. "How dare you interrupt me, monsieur?"

"*Mon général*, with respect, I must interrupt you. I should be useless at the kind of work you mean. Propaganda. Politics. I answered your appeals because I want to fight for France, in the air if I can, on the ground if I must. You asked for engineers and technicians; I'm a qualified engineer. I could service your vehicles if I can't service your aircraft as yet. But I can't go back to Rio and play politics—"

"You will go wherever de Gaulle sends you, Marchand. And he is not interested in those who attempt to pose conditions."

"It's not a question of conditions, sir. It's a question of fighting the Germans, that's all *I'm* interested in. And the Germans stand on the Channel today—not in Brazil."

Now the mask of indifference cracked and the suppressed rage flared out. "I don't need any lessons from a whipper-snapper like

63

you," barked Charles de Gaulle. "You will obey me as you would obey the voice of France." He sat down abruptly and pulled some papers towards him, to indicate that Mike Marchand's audience was over. "Report immediately to my ADC."

If he expected to hear the respectful *"A vos ordres, mon général!"* it never came. Mike turned on his heel and left the room quietly, closing the door very gently as he entered the anteroom where the cavalry officer was sitting with a telephone in one hand and another tucked between his shoulder and his ear. He ignored the signal which the ADC made to him with the handset, and went out to the corridor where Lieutenant Larron was waiting.

"Allez, Marchand, you're one of us now!" the little man began breezily, when Mike cut in, "Like hell I am!"

"You mean you didn't—"

"I mean I'm not joining a private army," said Marchand. "I want to serve my country, not one man." His only desire was to get out of the place, where he was too well aware that he had a considerable audience: the man who said he wasn't Schnaebel, and another man by his side, shorter, squarer, but also vaguely familiar; the hare-faced girl and one of her typists, and the cavalry lieutenant who had come to the door of the anteroom and was listening horrified. "Here's your enlistment oath," he said, taking the crumpled paper from his pocket. "It's the same kind of personal oath as the German Army had to take to Hitler, as far back as 1934—"

"Don't be a damned fool, Marchand!"

"And there's something your boy missed out," he said, with a last look at the printed form. "Just three words. Oh, he's got three in all right! 'Serve with Honour, Faith and Discipline'—to the Leader, of course, that's great. But what happened to Liberty, Equality, Fraternity? Remember them?"

5

TWO WEEKS HAD passed since General de Gaulle made his first broadcast, on the same day as Winston Churchill made one of his greatest orations in the House of Commons. The Battle of Britain was about to begin, Churchill warned his fellow-countrymen, and bade them 'so bear themselves that if the British Empire and its Commonwealth last for a thousand years, men will say "This was their finest hour".'

These two speeches were made on the eighteenth of June, the anniversary of the battle of Waterloo. It was the irony of fate that when the great guns of Britain roared for the first time since the retreat from Dunkirk, they were turned—for the first time since Waterloo—upon the French.

It was on the day of Mike Marchand's abortive visit to St. Stephen's House that Mr. Churchill ordered Operation Catapult to be embarked upon. De Gaulle was not told about Operation Catapult, nor was anybody at the French Embassy, where most of next day was spent discussing the new developments in France. Over the weekend the French government, with the President of the Republic in tow, had ended its three weeks' odyssey at a watering-place called Vichy, some forty miles north of Clermont-Ferrand. Far from the splendid palaces where they had deliberated in Paris, the Deputies and Senators assembled in the casinos of Vichy, and entered upon the creation of a new French State, dedicated—in the words of Pierre Laval, the Deputy Prime Minister—to 'a policy of honest collaboration with Germany and Italy'.

Mike Marchand was too junior, and too little versed in the juridical niceties of the Vichy situation, to take much part in the discussions among his colleagues. He did remark that, since the Pétain cabinet had chosen 'Work, Family and Motherland' as its watchword, and de Gaulle had chosen 'Honour, Faith and Discipline,' *Liberté Egalité Fraternité* seemed to have been dropped from the language of France. There was some exasperated comment from his seniors, and then he was called to the telephone. His caller was Edmond Leblanc, in high good humour, telling him that the even chance had come up at the *Daily Journal*.

"That's great, *mon vieux*! When d'you start?"

"I started last night, right after the interview."

"Does Betty know?"

"Sure, I called her as soon as I'd a minute. She's delighted, of course, wants to leave the kids in Bath and come home to look after me."

"Wiser not."

"That's what I told her. And now what about yourself? Did you see . . . You-Know-Who?"

"For about five minutes."

"And?"

"Nothing doing, I'm afraid."

"You mean he didn't offer—"

"I mean I wouldn't play," said Mike. "Look, I can't talk about it on this line, you know that. Let's have lunch together one day soon. I'll buy you a celebration drink at the 'Cheshire Cheese' and tell you the whole story."

"Fine, but if you call me at the DJ remember to ask for Eddie White. That's my new byline; the boss doesn't care for foreign names in his publications. The readers might think it unpatriotic—"

"I'd understand that if your name was Hitler," Mike retorted. "Never mind, Ed, I was only kidding. Best of luck, and I'll call you soon."

He laid down the handset with a grimace. We're turning into a bunch of cloak-and-dagger boys, he thought, saying You-Know-Who when we mean de Gaulle, and worried about who may be listening on the extension. He drew a sheet of writing paper towards him. He didn't mean to play cloak-and-dagger with Jacques Brunel, waiting patiently for news in his hospital ward, even if—remembering those bandaged hands—whatever he wrote might have to be read aloud to his cousin. Let them know at Dykefaulds that the psychos were not confined to Lanarkshire.

You'll have to make up your own mind about the general when you come to London [he ended his letter]. For my money, he's not a military leader but a political adventurer who's been given the chance of a lifetime and means to use it for all he's worth. The British are fighting for survival, and they're too busy to notice—even if the censorship allowed them to find out—what he's up to with his personal representatives and his committees. He doesn't seem to have the faintest idea that the enemy is Germany, not Vichy; Adolf Hitler, not Philippe Pétain; but he does mean to create a political network across the world for the glorification of Charles de Gaulle.

He addressed the envelope without reading the letter over, stamped it, and was sufficiently impressed by the climate of unease to post it in a red pillar box, not in the embassy mail box, on his way home that evening. Afterwards, Mike Marchand was glad that his letter was on its way to Glasgow, and himself absolved of all further comment, when Operation Catapult was unleashed at daybreak the next morning.

Catapult was the result of as painful a decision as ever a British cabinet had had to make. From the Bordeaux days onward, the French had been adamant in refusing to allow the fleet to sail to British ports, other than the vessels which were there already. They had accepted the armistice terms of demobilisation and disarming under Axis control, and had also swallowed the German declaration that the French war fleet would not be used for German purposes. Admiral Darlan, the French Minister of Marine, had further declared that sooner than allow his warships to be used by the Germans, he would order his captains to scuttle their commands.

The British, in their hour of mortal danger, could accept neither the German pledge nor Admiral Darlan's. Already the enemy was in occupation of the Channel and Atlantic shores of France, using all the ports as bases of attack on British convoys. A German order could at any moment halt the disarming of the French fleet and send any or all of the squadrons to sea, with German crews, against the island fortress and its lifelines with the world. Therefore the French fleet had to be rendered harmless —and by the British.

So ran the logic behind the British descent, in armed strength, on all the French vessels in British harbours at about four o'clock in the morning of the third of July. Taken completely by surprise, the French crews surrendered and were marched off to internment with very few casualties. One Frenchman killed, one British

leading seaman killed, a few men wounded, a few broken heads
—such was the casualty list for the first part of the exercise; but
as the French diplomats gathered at the embassy, pale with shock
and anger, they knew that there was more to come. When Roger
Cambon, the Minister, left for the Foreign Office to present a
formal protest against the seizure of French ships in British
waters, the end of an era had been reached.

Monsieur Cambon bore one of the great names in French
diplomacy. His uncle Paul, then ambassador to London, had been
one of the architects of the Entente Cordiale which had united
France and Britain for nearly forty years, through the long ordeal
of the first World War. Now, as he drove back to Albert Gate,
messages were beginning to come in from Vichy, from North
Africa and from Egypt, which showed that the morning's work
at Portsmouth and Plymouth had only been a dress rehearsal for
humiliation.

At Alexandria, from the British point of view, Operation
Catapult was a success. There the French Force X, in harbour,
was covered by Admiral Cunningham's squadron, and in spite of
direct orders from Darlan to weigh anchor and leave Alexandria,
using force if necessary, Admiral Godefroy was finally persuaded
to immobilise his own ships. All fuel oil was discharged, all guns
disarmed, and two-thirds of the crews taken ashore for eventual
repatriation, while the British vessels lay like a boom across the
harbour.

But before all this could be completed—before the great
battleship *Richelieu*, lying at far-off Dakar, could be attacked by
HMS *Hermes* and seriously damaged by an air torpedo—the full
fury of Operation Catapult had broken in the western Mediterranean. There, in the afternoon of July 3, it came to open warfare
between the British and the French. At Mers-el-Kebir, the military port three miles west of the city of Oran, the very best of the
French Atlantic Fleet lay under the command of Admiral
Gensoul, who upon the arrival of a British force from Gibraltar,
flatly refused to accept any of the alternatives offered to him. He
would neither turn his ships over to the British, nor allow them
to be disarmed by the British, nor scuttle them. He defied the
British ultimatum which followed, and at 5.54 the Royal Navy
opened fire on the French ships and the shore batteries of Mers-el-
Kebir.

It was a short engagement. It was a British victory. It completed the elimination of the French Navy from the war. It cost the lives of over twelve hundred French officers and men.

*   *   *

At the French Embassy the day of Catapult dragged by, much as the days had dragged in the middle of June when defeat drew nearer hour by hour. The teleprinter chattered in the vestibule, the messengers roared up on their motorcycles from the Old Building at the Admiralty, and if any man thought, like Mike Marchand, that the British, fighting for their very existence as a nation, were right in what they had done, he knew better than to say it then.

"*Perfide Albion!*" said one grey-haired man. "Less than three weeks ago they wanted us to join them in an indissoluble, ever-lasting, to-all-eternity Franco-British Union: today, they're blowing our ships out of the water."

"They say they can't trust Hitler's word. Say he's broken every promise he ever made—"

"They've got something there."

"They had Darlan's word, *our* word, that the Fleet would never pass into German hands . . ."

Silence.

"Monsieur Cambon means to resign tomorrow," somebody said inconsequently. There was no particular consequence in anything that was said as the July sun began to set over Hyde Park and the sounds of traffic in Knightsbridge slowly grew less.

"What else can he do? Tell me, gentlemen, what can any of us do? Wait for orders from Vichy? I think we all know what these orders will be, do we not?"

"I wonder how *le Grand Charles* is taking it. I wonder what he thinks of his British paymasters now."

"I hear he's taking it very badly. Considering if he ought to retire to private life in Canada."

"Retire!" said Mike. "Not he. Think! He's a man nearly fifty, quite unknown outside France, and he's just been handed the chance of a lifetime by Winston Churchill and the BBC. His whole future is at stake now; he'll put up with a lot more than what the papers call 'the Battle of the Brothers'."

"Don't make me sick."

"What will really make me sick is if de Gaulle broadcasts tonight."

69

But the familiar *'Moi de Gaulle'* was not heard on the BBC that evening. It was Mr. Churchill who had to face a silent and sombre, finally a cheering, House of Commons next day and justify the mounting of Operation Catapult. It was not until July 8 that the Leader of All Free Frenchmen went to the microphone and admitted that the French ships were 'better destroyed'. In the meantime Churchill had attacked the 'callous and malevolent' conduct of the French government, and the French had dropped a few bombs on Gibraltar by way of a token reprisal. Darlan, it was known, was ready for war with Britain, but Pierre Laval, the Deputy Prime Minister at Vichy, announced that the cabinet was against it. Nothing must interfere with the task of revising the Constitution to bring France into line with the totalitarian states. All that was necessary was to break off diplomatic relations with Great Britain.

This was done; and on July 8 the Foreign Office was officially informed that the French Embassy was to be withdrawn from London. The two distinguished men who had already resigned were going to live in England, to which they said they were bound by so many ties, and all the others would be repatriated to France in about ten days' time.

The undiplomatic activity which followed was very great. Seats on the train, berths aboard the *Orduna*, giving up of leases, auction of furniture, above all packing up of clothes, books and household goods, gave the entire embassy staff more wholesome occupation than it had known for three weeks. It was an activity which made Mike Marchand miserably aware of his own isolated position. He was one of the very few who would acknowledge neither Vichy nor de Gaulle; who wanted to remain in England and fight with the RAF, and who stood a good chance of following the French sailors into one of the internment camps at Huyton or Aintree.

On the night of July 11, after the Deputies and Senators in session at Vichy had put an end to the Third Republic and the Presidency of Albert Lebrun, and installed Marshal Pétain as Chief of the French State by the sweeping majority of 569 votes to 80, Mike was so sick of his own company that he decided, in a real spirit of bravado, to accept the last invitation sent him as an attaché of the French Embassy.

He had always lived in the present, and the present had been so shattering that he had forgotten all about the occasion until he noticed the solitary square of pasteboard sticking in the gilt frame of the mirror above his mantel. At Christmas, in the middle of the 'phoney war', the mirror had been stuck two deep with invitations to luncheons, dinners, *vernissages*, and parties of all sorts. This one was from the Brazilian Embassy. Not one of the very grand ones, for it came from the commercial attaché, not from the ambassador himself, but then the nephew of Senhor Pedro Ferreira was on the list for every entertainment, whether he still had diplomatic rank or not. Guiltily, Mike couldn't remember if he had accepted, for the thing was dated two weeks back and a world away, but he took a perverse pleasure in turning up to see their faces on this night when France was down and out. He wondered if there would be an emissary from de Gaulle among the guests, getting into training for being the Leader's personal representative at Rio de Janeiro.

The Brazilian Embassy in Upper Brook Street was only a short walk away, through streets bathed in the endless sunlight of 1940. Rather to Mike's surprise the ambassador himself was there, ready to greet him warmly and enquire after Senhor Ferreira's health.

"You know most of these people, don't you?" he said. "If there's anybody you specially want to meet, tell José-Carlos to introduce you."

"I will, Excellency: thank you very much. It's very pleasant to be here again." And Marchand thought, as he bowed and moved towards José-Carlos, the commercial attaché, who greeted him with the warm embrace of South America, that it was indeed relaxing to be in this neutral embassy, where the salons glowed with rare woods and fabrics which were not English, and where a guitarist ensconced in a huge tapestried chair was softly playing a prelude by Villa-Lobos.

The guests were pretty much the crowd he had expected, people from the United States and South American embassies, more brightly dressed than their English counterparts, of whom only one or two were present. The women were beautifully groomed and hung with jewels. There was no clothes rationing in Britain yet, but most of the young women were in uniform, and a threat of imminent shabbiness hung over the capital. With a glass of champagne in his hand Mike chatted with some vivid creatures from Buenos Aires and Santiago de Chile, moved on to another group and looked around. There were no French guests, as far as he could see. This was the sort of party the French Purchasing Commission had attended in force; Denise Lambert, he remembered, had affected to despise Latin American ideas of chic. He wondered how chic Denise was now, in fever-ridden Senegal, and if the Lamberts had been in Dakar when HMS *Hermes* attacked the *Richelieu*.

"Good evening, Mr. Marchand!"

A pretty girl was smiling at him, and Mike had so completely failed to recognise her in a dress of sea-green taffeta, with the plastic curls gone and her red hair brushed into a shining wave on her forehead, that he had to try to hide his embarrassment as he bowed to Miss Alison Grant—last seen waving from the back of an army lorry, when she dropped him off at a Glasgow post office to send a telegram to France for Jacques Brunel.

"Miss Grant, this is a very nice surprise—"

"I think it's nice to see you, too. Neil!" She pulled the sleeve of a stocky red-haired man who had been seized upon by somebody else. "Come and meet Mr. Marchand. I told you about our trip out to Dykefaulds, didn't I?"

"Mr. Grant and I have met before," said Mike. For he recognised the brother in Parliament, one of the youngest MPs in the House of Commons, who had got this pretty kid a job in London and who might even have taught her how to do her hair. "At a reception last February, in Berkeley Square."

"At the Ministry, of course I remember," said the professional. "Before your time, Alison, my child. No cocktail parties in Berkeley Square nowadays!"

"Are you enjoying your new job?" Mike asked Alison.

"It's a lot tougher than I thought it would be, but it's fun." And as her brother, with a word of apology, turned back to the man waiting to go on with his monologue, she added quickly, "I saw Captain Jack again, just before I left Glasgow."

"Oh, you did manage to get back to Dykefaulds?"

"Yes, and found him very much better. Your visit did him a lot of good, everybody said so—even Dr. Skinner."

"I've written to Jacques twice, but I suppose he isn't able to write letters yet."

"He soon will be. The bandages on his hands were due to come off this week, and they say his fingers won't be very much distorted."

"I'm very glad to hear that," said Mike soberly. And with an

72

attempt at a smile, he added, "How about the Comforts Committee? Is it still flourishing?"

"They've had the staircase repaired, you'll be glad to hear. But things began to slacken off, even before I left. Most of the men at Gleneagles were passed fit to travel south, with about ten of Captain Jack's own company from Dykefaulds."

"So what happens to all your marvellous supplies?"

"Whatever is left over when they close down will be sent to the Refugee Committee here. Do you know it? Not far from Marble Arch."

"I've been there. It's an Anglo-French concern, very well run." I may be a refugee myself before very long, thought Mike with fury, grateful for a free meal and a parcel of cast-off clothing.

"I'm sorry," said Neil Grant, rejoining them and taking a glass of champagne from the tray a footman offered. "That fellow would talk the hind leg off a donkey . . . Alison, don't you see any sign of the guest of honour? I do want to have a word with him before we go."

"I wouldn't know him if I saw him," his sister retorted, "but His Excellency seems to be holding the fort alone."

"I didn't know there was a guest of honour," said Mike. "The invitation didn't say 'To Meet'."

"I believe he was a last minute inspiration, hence the presence of the ambassador," said Neil Grant with a smile. "Senhor Antonio da Costa. He and his sister are on a short visit to London. A very able fellow, and very generous. He's given £1000 to the Lord Mayor's Fund, to buy two X-ray mobile units for the use of the Red Cross."

"Neil gave a luncheon for him at the House today," said Alison. "Mr. da Costa was nearly forty minutes late!"

"He's just as unpunctual tonight."

"He wouldn't be a Brazilian if he weren't," said Mike. "Antonio da Costa. That's hardly an unusual name in Rio de Janeiro. Is he from Rio, by the way? What brings him to Britain at a time like this?"

"He's from São Paulo, I believe."

"Oh, *that* da Costa? Tony da Costa, Capricorn Airways? I've heard of him, of course; who hasn't?"

"But you don't know him?"

"He's a new young comer since my time in Brazil."

"He can't be much older than you are."

"But he came up faster. What's his sister like?"

"Here they are now," said Neil Grant quietly. "Judge for yourself."

There was a ripple of interest in the room, as heads were turned towards the ambassador, greeting a cheerful-looking man in his early thirties, and a tall girl in a white dress, with black hair falling to her shoulders. Soon they were all hidden by a forward movement of the Brazilians present, brushing their foreign guests aside in their eagerness to welcome the president of Capricorn Airways.

"They're making a big fuss of him," said the MP. "He's known to be very close to President Getulio Vargas, and that counts."

"Don't you think his sister counts?" said Alison. "*I* think she's sensational! But you know, I thought she'd be dripping with jewels, like most of the other women; imagine, she's got no ornament but that little gold kid belt."

"Well, come and meet them both, Alison," said her brother. "And then we really must push off . . . I'm sorry we haven't had much chance to talk, Mr. Marchand. Er—I don't know what your plans are, but if I can help in any way, don't hesitate to give me a ring. I'm at the Ministry every morning, and at the House in the afternoon."

"That's very kind of you," said Mike. "Goodbye." It was the first time he had spoken since the da Costas entered the room. He took the hand Alison was holding out. "Goodbye," the friendly Scots voice repeated. "I'm sorry we have to dash, but my baby niece is only four days old, and we're both rather anxious to get home to her and her mamma."

"Of course you are! I'm awfully glad to have seen you again—"

"Give my love to Captain Jack!" It was a hurried whisper, for Alison's brother was already forging through the crowd towards the too fashionably dressed young man from São Paulo with the sharply polished black shoes and the lacquered black hair, who had the ear of President Getulio Vargas and apparently of the Ministry of Economic Warfare as well. Mike made no attempt to follow in the wake of the Grants. He talked to a man from Montevideo, who thought Mike Marchand was the name of a former gentleman jockey, and to a flirtatious lady from Asunción, and then he sought out José-Carlos, who was to introduce him to anybody he especially wanted to meet.

The girl he wanted to meet had moved away from her brother's side, and she stood a head taller and a good deal slimmer than the vivacious little ladies around her. And now that Mike was close to her, he could see that what made her looks sensational, as little Alison had said, was not only the hair like black silk and the skin like clover honey, but the hint of more than one southern race in her features, contradicted by eyes which, fringed by long black lashes, were a clear northern grey.

"Senhorina da Costa, may I have the honour to present Monsieur Marchand?" said José-Carlos.

"But I know him already," she said, and smiled at Mike. "I asked you for your autograph at Santos Dumont airfield, the day you won the race from Buenos Aires. And you gave it me. You wrote 'With love to Dina'."

* * *

"Maria da Gloria Divininha da Costa," she said. "That really and truly is my full name. You were the first person ever to tell me it was too long."

"You mean you wanted me to write the whole thing in your autograph album?"

"You'd done it for all the other girls. Maybe you were tired by the time you got around to me."

"I don't see how I could have been."

Dina da Costa laughed. "It was eight years ago," she said, "I was sixteen, with puppy fat, and all I could do was blurt out 'Can I have your autograph, Captain Marchand, please?' I must have been quite forgettable. Admit you'd forgotten all about it."

Mike shook his head apologetically. There had always been a giggle of schoolgirls in unbecoming blue uniforms hanging round Santos Dumont on race days, and the race from Buenos Aires had only been one of many. But that a plump schoolgirl had turned into the exotic creature beside him was as incredible as his own luck in getting her away from the party at the Brazilian Embassy and having her all to himself, sitting knee to knee in the crowded little bar of the Ecu de France.

The gilt chairs were packed so close together, the cocktail tables so precarious, that Dina held a little wisp of blond fur in her lap, with the gold kid purse which matched her belt. Mike steadied their glasses every time a new wave of young men in uniform pushed through the swing doors and the blackout curtains. He could see the texture of her skin, and smell the scent she was wearing—based he thought on lilies, but more evocative than the Paris perfumes he knew so well. They were speaking Portuguese, not the most beautiful language in the world, and Mike's was a little rusty, but the faintly nasal, faintly guttural sounds seemed to suit the vocal chords of the girl by his side, as the Villa-Lobos preludes had suited the guitarist's strings.

"I had a terrific crush on you when I was sixteen," she said. "But so I had on Chico Sanchez, and Roberto Chaves, and Gismondi. Going out to the airfield to watch them fly was about the only thing that made boarding-school in Rio bearable."

"Your schoolmistress must have been a liberal-minded lady."

"She was," said Dina seriously. "She knew that flying meant more to me than having a schoolgirl crush on pilots. Amy Johnson was my great heroine always—far more important than any of you glamour boys!"

"I was talking to Amy Johnson just the other day."

"You were? Is she in England now?"

"Very much so. She's a ferry pilot with the Air Transport Auxiliary."

"A ferry pilot, with her record?"

"Sure. She says she's very happy to be in the Service. Dina—" it seemed so natural to call her Dina—"would you like to meet Amy Johnson? She's at Hatfield with the women's section of the ATA, it's not far away. I could call up and find out her flight times, and drive you down there in one of the embassy cars." He stopped, wondering if the French Embassy cars were still available.

"You're very sweet to think of it, and I only wish I could. But Tony and I must catch the Irish boat tomorrow. We're flying from Foynes to Lisbon on Saturday, to get the Sunday Clipper to New York. Tony's in a hurry to get home."

"That's a tight schedule, even for VIPs like you. D'you mind telling me how it's done?"

"The only problem was the flight from Foynes. Do you remember Jerry O'Hanlon, who used to fly for Panair do Brasil? He's station manager at Foynes now. He got us top priorities to Lisbon."

"I know Jerry, and I'm sure you'll be all right ex Foynes, but

Lisbon might be a tough connection. I think you'll find there's a huge backlog of French passengers piling up at Estoril. You're not planning to stop over for a day or two?"

"We spent some time in Lisbon on the eastbound trip, with some ancient relatives we have out at Cascaís. I felt they didn't approve at all of a girl who was helping to run an airline."

"I could hardly believe my ears when José-Carlos told me you had your 'A' licence, and flew your own Puss Moth."

"I fly Tony in the Beechcraft when we're going to São Paulo at weekends, and he has papers to work at in the cabin. What José-Carlos—is that the commercial attaché?—didn't tell you was that I worked for Panair do Brasil as a stewardess for six months, and I often fly stewardess for Capricorn. I want to learn every bit of the airline business—"

"Including the paperwork?"

"I rather like the paperwork. But what I want now is my 'B' licence, so I can pilot our commercial flights on the short leg between São Paulo and Santos."

"Flying what?"

"Our four-seater Beechcrafts, to begin with."

The noise of the cocktail bar grew louder, and Mike had to strain to catch everything that Dina said. It was the talk he had missed since he took up his uneasy post at the embassy, talk, not of the war potential of military aircraft, but of the development of civil aviation in the country he knew so well. And the piquancy of the talk was that the younger pilot was a girl, so striking, so attractive that many appraising glances came her way, but who was completely lost in the story of her brother's enterprise and her pride in helping him to realise his dream of opening up Brazil by a system of air bridges between the vast inland territories and the coast. He knew what she meant by her 'crush' on himself and the other pilots of his day. It was pure hero-worship, devoid of sex; it was exactly what he himself had felt for his own seniors, Antoine de St. Exupéry and Jean Mermoz. He remembered how, as a schoolboy of eighteen, brought to Brazil after his mother's death, he had haunted that block of the Avenida Rio Branco where the Aéropostale had its offices, in the hope of seeing one of the heroes of *La Ligne* coming in to confer with the chairman after bringing the night mail to Rio de Janeiro from Punta Arenas. That passion had made an airman of him, as it had made an airwoman of Dina da Costa, and he took one of her thin muscled hands into his own in a gesture of sympathy which he thought had nothing to do with the flesh.

She stopped at once and smiled apologetically. "I've been talking too much," she said.

"It's a wonderful story, I'm very envious." He emptied his glass as she raised hers, and said, "They're keeping us waiting the devil of a time for a table. Where's that waiter?"

"It's very crowded," said Dina. "I'd no idea London was so lively! This would be like some of the little places we go to at Copacabana, if only they had a band."

Mike stood up, trying to catch the barman's eye at least, and sat down again quickly. Leaning against the far end of the bar, engrossed in their own conversation, were four men in uniform, three of whom he had confronted at General de Gaulle's headquarters, and with them a fourth, shorter, squarer, ruddy-faced, seen there only for a moment but somehow familiar then and still.

He took out his cigarette case to gain time, to think what to do next. "Dina, I forgot to ask you if you smoke?"

"I don't, thank you. But don't let that stop you."

He lit his own cigarette and said casually, "Do you see those men standing between the bar and the restaurant?"

"Two of them very tall and blond? Yes, are they friends of yours?"

"Not exactly, but I know their names. The little fat guy's name is Larron—Lieutenant Larron last week, Captain Larron now—and the tall fair one who just turned round, he's got his back to us now, is called Dewavrin . . . Take a good look at the other two. Did you ever see them in Brazil?"

"Where in Brazil?"—with a startled look.

"At Natal, for instance."

"Capricorn doesn't go in to Natal."

"Well then, at Rio. Anywhere."

Dina moved her chair slightly, took out her powder compact, and studied the two men in Chasseur uniform over the top of the mirror. "I'm not sure," she said. "Perhaps . . . isn't the other fair one Arthur Schnaebel, who used to fly for Condor?"

"He calls himself Carreau."

"Oh, then, I must be wrong. But no, wait, I do know the red-faced man. I met him stunt-flying once, at an air pageant in Recife. I think his name's Lachmann, Anders or Andy Lachmann, and he *did* fly for Condor; he was flying one of their Junkers in the show."

"You're certain?"

"Positive."

"And Condor Air's Nazi-controlled."

"Brazilian licensed, Mike."

"I know it was called after the Condor Legion, that the Nazis sent to the Spanish Civil War."

"But these men don't have to be Nazis, even if they did fly in Brazil! You're a Frenchman, and yet you flew for Trans-Andean, before you joined Air France! Those are French uniforms they're wearing, aren't they?"

"Of course they are," said Mike soothingly. "They're loyal followers of General de Gaulle. They made a heroic escape from Brest, nearly as heroic as his own from Bordeaux." Taking out his note case, he thought of the heavy fighting round Brest before France surrendered, and how easy it would have been to take Chasseur uniforms from the bodies of the dead.

"I've had an idea," he said, "How would you like to go to a restaurant where there *is* a band, and dance? We could go to the Hungaria, it's only just across the street."

"But you said the food was so good here!"

"So it is, but we can't seem to get at it. I think you'll like the Hungaria just as well."

"All right then, let's go . . . It really would be nice to dance."

Thank God, she was standing up, turning towards the door, and Mike laid the scrap of summer fur round her shoulders and a ten-shilling note on the table, almost in the same movement. His one wish now was to get Dina da Costa outside and into the street before any of those self-absorbed men could turn round and identify a Brazilian girl of such conspicuous good looks. The last thing he wanted was to involve her in a Gaullist quarrel. Luckily the men were busy ordering another round of drinks. They seemed to have money enough to buy whatever they wanted.

Mike and Dina were at the corner of Jermyn Street when the Alert sounded, with a whine of sirens which echoed across the darkened streets.

"What on earth's that awful noise?" said Dina.

"It's an air raid warning. Don't be scared, it doesn't mean the Boches are anywhere near London."

"I'm not scared!" Dina was looking up fascinated at the

blue-black sky, where the silver beams of London's searchlights were criss-crossed in Cubist patterns. Nobody in crowded Piccadilly appeared to be scared either, although a few people ran past Mike and Dina into the nearest entrance to the Tube.

Mike slipped his hand through the girl's arm. "Would you like to go back to the Carlton?" he said. "We could have dinner downstairs in the Grill. But the Hungaria's below street level too, it's nearly as safe as the Underground."

"Let's dance!" she said, and they hurried across Lower Regent Street into a haven of soft lights and flowers, and of music loud enough to drown the sound of a barrage which Mike was straining his ears to hear. It was a long time since the Alert had been heard in the capital.

The Hungaria, on that July night in 1940, was like every place of its kind in London—crowded with the young, the strong, the hopeful, snatching at every hour of enjoyment which might come their way. In its own way, it was like the 'Greyhound' public house and the shadowed garden of Kensington Square, where the Service boys and girls embraced in the darkness, for the lights on the dancing floor were shaded and the girls in their thin summer dresses laid their cheeks to the flushed cheeks of their partners, and tightened their fingers on the khaki or blue cloth of the uniforms. Mike held Dina closely in his arms. They were dancing to a Paris waltz, which he knew quite well, for Denise Lambert had liked to hear it on his record-player, as part of the build-up with the flowers, the sweet cakes and champagne.

Je me sens dans tes bras si petite,
Si petite auprès de toi—

Dancing with Dina da Costa he could hardly remember the words. And anyhow she was not *petite*, he only had to bend his head a little to look into those grey eyes, lowered beneath the preposterously long lashes. He could smell the scent of lilies, and beneath them the green leaves and the lily pool.

"That was wonderful," he said as the music stopped.

"Do you suppose the band could play a samba?"

"I don't think it would go down very well here. The English aren't geared to samba rhythm."

"Are you?" said Dina as they settled themselves on their banquette and the waiters hurried up with food and wine.

"I used to be, when I lived in Rio."

"Tell me how that came about."

He told her, between dances, between bites of food and sips of the excellent Bordeaux he had chosen, about his first stay in Brazil after his mother's death, his return to France for Air Force service, and then the wonderful years with Trans-Andean, flying the length and breadth of South America. Dina watched him intently, saying very little except to show that she knew the people, the places, the planes, which had once made Marchand's world. She knew that as he talked the tragedies of the past weeks were being obliterated, overlaid by memory pictures of that world—that in fancy he was again coming in to land over Guanabara Bay, with the Sugar Loaf to starboard and the statue of Christ the Redeemer on his port wing, and the whole panorama of the *cidade maravilhosa* spread below.

"I wish you and Tony could have a long talk," she said as the dessert plates were being cleared away. "I wish we didn't have to catch the boat train so terribly early tomorrow morning!"

"You don't wish it any more than I do," said Mike. "Let's dance again. Come on, they're playing *J'attendrai*."

A girl singer was standing behind the tall microphone now, on the platform which raised the orchestra above the dancers. As she sang the song which had swept Paris in the winter, when French girls were waiting for men far away in the suspect safety of the Maginot Line, the spotlights swept in circles of pink and pale green on her long white evening dress. Over the darkened dance floor the circles moved, lighting the relaxed mouths and languid faces, touching Dina's honey skin to rose. The song ended, the beat changed, and Dina whispered, "I don't know this one, it must be very new."

"It's very English."

> We'll meet again, don't know where,
> Don't know when,
> But I know we'll meet again some sunny day.
> Keep smiling through, just like you always do,
> Till the blue skies drive the dark clouds far away

It was the perfect song for the mood of that night, for the youth of a country at war, completely alone, without foreign Allies, in an island besieged, but sure of itself and its survival.

The singing and the music died to a thread of sound; the bodies of the dancers, closely embraced, moved under the spotlights in a ritual harmony of sex and war.

"Do you believe in love at first sight, Dina? Our first sight?"

"Tonight? Or eight years ago, out at Santos Dumont?"

"Tonight's when we began."

She was silent, pressing closer to him, and shaking her head.

"Dina?"

"I don't—don't know about beginning. But I do believe we'll meet again—"

"Some sunny day."

Mike kept her hand in his as they walked back to their table, where an officious waiter was ready to suggest coffee and liqueurs.

"Coffee, Dina? I warn you, it won't be as good as a São Paulo *cafézinho*."

"Please, I'd like some coffee."

She was thankful that the arrival of the coffee, with a brandy for Mike, kept them at their table in the shadows at the side of the room when the next song began. It was as new to her as 'We'll Meet Again', but at the first verse Mike Marchand's face hardened, and he ground out his cigarette viciously in the ashtray.

> The last time I saw Paris
> Her streets were decked with spring,
> And lovers walked beneath those trees,
> And birds had songs to sing

He said nothing at all until the song ended, with a melting promise to remember lost Paris 'that way', and then he only said, "It didn't take Tin Pan Alley long to cash in on that one, did it?"

"You'll see Paris again," was all Dina could find to say.

"Yes, but how? When?"

"Have you still a home in Paris? Family?"

"Nothing and nobody."

"Then—Mike—why don't you come back to Brazil?"

She was sorry she had spoken when she saw Mike's twisted smile. "You're the second person who suggested that this week," he said.

"Who was the first one?"

"General de Gaulle."

"Oh! That man!"—with a little dismissing flick of her fingers. "But it makes sense for you, Mike! You could be like my French grandfather, and have a great future in Brazil—"

"You had a French grandfather?" That probably accounted for the clear grey eyes, so unexpected above the high cheekbones handed down by the Indian element in her Brazilian heritage.

"He emigrated to Brazil alone when he was only eighteen, two years after the Franco-Prussian War. His family lived in an Occupied province, like people in the Occupied Zone now—"

"Alsace?"

"Lorraine. He left a town called Metz, where his home was, because he couldn't bear to see the Prussians strutting about the streets, and he went to Rio because he'd heard about the Minas Gerais, and thought the beach would be covered with emeralds and rubies just for the picking up. Well, he soon found it wasn't so. But he turned his hand to anything, and then he went up to São Paulo and started a cannery—"

"What was his name, Dina?"

"Bernard Bresson. Have you heard of him?"

"I've heard my uncle Ferreira speak of him. Of course I didn't associate him with the name da Costa."

"He was my mother's father," she said, not quite sure how to take the little smile which twitched Mike's mouth. "I only mentioned him, just to show you—"

"To show me what I could do if I tried. And it isn't that I don't want to try! But you've got to remember the difference between your grandfather and me: he went to Brazil when the Franco-Prussian war was over. This war with Germany is still going on."

Dina said no more. The mood between them, the awareness of something beginning, was ruined; she knew it, and so did Mike. When he asked her to dance again she shook her head, and made a show of consulting the little diamond watch hidden by the sleeve of her dress. It was after one o'clock, she said, and time to go. Mike's protest that the Carlton Hotel was just across the street was a formality. He wanted to get out of the overheated restaurant and be alone in the starlit street with her.

But Lower Regent Street, like Piccadilly, was still full of strolling and apparently carefree people, and when Mike asked the attendant who offered to get them a taxi what had happened to the air raid, he was answered by a reassuring laugh.

"Bless your 'eart, sir, Jerry didn't get anywhere near London tonight. The All Clear went hours ago. Glad you was enjoying yourselves, and didn't 'ear it."

"Just another false alarm," said Mike, "Good night."

6

CAPTAIN JACQUES BRUNEL sat at Dr. Skinner's desk in
Dr. Skinner's private office and waited for the Dykefaulds
switchboard operator to put in a call to London.

In the three weeks since Mike Marchand's visit his looks, like
his health, had improved considerably. His thin face had lost its
cadaverous look, and afternoons spent in a deck chair in the sun
had given him a tan which could hardly have been bettered on the
beach at Menton. Even his hands, bandaged for so long, had
begun to take on a healthy brown, and while he waited for the
'phone to ring he flexed them as he had been taught to do, noting
that they were more obedient every day. He was quite capable of
getting out his cigarettes and matches from the breast pocket of his
hospital uniform and lighting up by striking a match on his thumb.

He was smoking, all the more confidently because the ashtray
before him contained the foul dottle of Dr. Skinner's last pipe,
when the operator rang once and said, "Here's London for ye,
Captain Jack," and he was through to Mike.

"*Allô, allô! Michel? Ici Jacques.*"

The line spluttered and buzzed, and then he heard Mike's
delighted greeting.

"Did I wake you up?"

"At half past eight? I'm just finishing breakfast. Jacques, how
are you?"

"Much better. Didn't you get my letter? Could you read it?"

"Of course I could."

"Good. It looked to me more like hen's tracks than handwriting when I read it through, but I didn't want to dictate it to a
nurse. We can talk it over when I get to London."

"And when's that going to be?"

"Dr. Skinner still won't give a definite date, but I hope before
the first of August."

"This is only the twelfth of July. However."

"The British are being difficult about our uniforms."

"What uniforms?"

"Well, I still have mine, but the men's were filthy and in rags when we got here, so they were destroyed. They have to travel south in British battle-dress to the demobilisation point. And the uniforms haven't arrived yet."

"They've got to kit out the whole Home Guard first," said Mike.

"The what?"

"The Home Guard. I'm thinking of joining them. No oaths of allegiance to de Gaulle needed there."

"Michel, don't play the fool. Here's what I'm calling about. If the embassy is closed, then the French Military Mission is disbanded too, no?"

"Correct."

"Who does the demobilising?"

"The consulate-general, I suppose. I'll check on that and let you know."

"Oh, the consulate's still open? I have to be sure, *vieux*: I don't want to be interned like our sailors at Aintree."

"That's a special case, Jacques—"

"And a damn bad one, if you ask me."

"Thrr-rree minutes, please," cut in the voice of authority.

"*Mademoiselle, mademoiselle, une petite seconde, s'il vous plaît!*" cried Jacques, losing his head. "Michel! Can you hear me?"

"Listen, *mon brave*, your movement orders will tell you where to proceed for demobilisation. Just keep calm, and you'll soon be out of there."

"There's another thing," said Jacques, relaxing slightly. "I had a letter last night from one of the men in my company, he was here until ten days ago. Now he's in London, interned at the White City—"

"Nobody's interned at the White City, any more than they are at Olympia. They're not under guard, and they're free to go anywhere in London they want to go—"

"Yes, yes, but Dupont says de Gaulle's recruiting officers are harassing them, and the British authorities are doing nothing to stop it. De Gaulle himself went down, and there was nearly a free fight afterwards, when his men went over from Olympia—"

Mike groaned. "Those two camps—I knew it wouldn't work. Jacques, what do you want me to do?"

"I want you to go to the White City and find out what's really going on. And then make representations in the proper quarter

86

to get privacy and better conditions for the men awaiting repatriation."

"You don't want much, do you?" said Mike sarcastically. "Just remember I've got no status now. I'm only an unemployed Frenchman, with some money in the bank that may be frozen any day, and what used to be called on a man's military record, *esprit politique suspect*. But I'll go and see your chap; what did you say his name was, Durand?"

"Jean Dupont, *caporal-chef*."

"You're joking! Look for a Jean Dupont in a place the size of the White City? . . . All right, all right, I'll do my best."

"Thanks, Michel." The three pips went again, and Mike said hastily, "You'd better get the Comforts Committee to fix up the battle-dress uniforms."

"They're working on it. Madame Gavin has been in touch with Scottish Command—"

"*Avec nos meilleurs voeux*," said Mike. "Wait!" as a faint "*à bientôt!*" came down the wire from Lanarkshire. "I saw your friend Alison last night. She sent her love. Jacques—" The line went dead. And Mike, going back to the folding table on which the cleaning lady set out his coffee with rolls from the United Dairies a few doors away, poured himself a final tepid cup and stood drinking it, feeling that the message from Alison might have been more tactfully conveyed. "I saw your friend Alison last night"—he probably thought I asked her for a date.

With that, the thoughts of last night came flooding back, so that when the woman had taken his cup away, washed up the breakfast things with the maximum of clatter, and had accepted her money for the week with a jaunty "Ta, Mr. Merchant, see you Monday if old 'Itler don't turn up first," he indulged himself in dreaming about Dina da Costa. Love at first sight—she was probably right in saying she didn't believe in it, although he had given her the lead; and that was part of Dina's overwhelming charm for Mike. With that exotic appearance, which singled her out from every other woman in the crowded rooms where he had seen her, Maria da Gloria Divininha had a good hard streak of bourgeois common sense. Mike grinned (going into his bedroom and hunting for a tie) at her production of *grandpère* Bresson as the model for an expatriate Frenchman in Brazil. Young Bresson had started in Rio as a butcher's boy down by the docks, had taken rotting meat from the butcher's dustbins (if they had dustbins in 1872) and sold it to the fishermen for bait. With the money he had bought meat not quite rotten from his employer and sold it round the shacks for food; then he rendered down the butcher's fat, and sold it in scrubbed-out kerosene tins for cooking, and so on, and on, until as his granddaughter said (skipping over the gory details) he had opened his cannery in São Paulo, the first of the great Bresson chain. Mike had seen why the dynamic Tony da Costa was being wooed by the Ministry of Economic Warfare, representing a Britain which more stringent rationing would make only too eager to import canned foods in neutral ships.

He wondered if Dina seriously meant that he himself should start on the way to a great future by peddling offal round the hotels of the Avenida Atlántica.

He intended to telephone the MEW at the earliest moment, which he took to be half past nine, and certainly not on his own behalf as Neil Grant had suggested. When he called the Ministry he realised that the young MP was not in the higher echelons of power, for he was actually in his office already, and his secretary, with no more than mild petulance at not engaging in a duel of precedence with somebody else's secretary, put Mike through with only five minutes' delay. He had been rehearsing a few English idioms to help him say what he wanted to say in a guarded manner, but the Scotsman took the initiative at once.

"I was talking about you at seven o'clock this morning, before I was out of bed."

"About me, Mr. Grant?"

"Yes. That gentleman who was the principal guest at last night's reception called me at my home before he left London."

"Ah!" said Mike, seeing the light.

"Apparently he had a long talk with his sister in the small hours of the morning—"

"About a matter of positive identification, I suppose."

"Exactly. And a very serious matter too, which I would like to discuss with you. Could you make it convenient to call here on Monday morning, say ten o'clock?"

"Certainly. But Mr. Grant, those two identifications, as you call them, may be only two of many. The place where the men came from is an open door to infiltrators from the enemy camp. Would it not be wise to set up some sort of screening process of the—er—volunteers, without delay?"

"It's a very delicate situation," said Neil Grant. "I'll be

grateful for any information you can give me on Monday. Thank you for calling—"

The British weekend is Hitler's best friend. Mike knew the saying well enough, and here it was being fully illustrated on a Friday morning. Between ten a.m. on Friday and ten a.m. on Monday, how many more new arrivals (by fishing-boat, stolen aircraft or swimming the Channel) might not have presented themselves at St. Stephen's House, to be welcomed with open arms and offered 'personal representation' in Guatemala, Kenya or Iceland? And go on to relay information from the heart of Britain back to Berlin or Rome—even to Vichy?

Mike Marchand went out slamming his own front door with a violence which made him apologise at once to his next-door neighbour, Mrs. Lindsay, who had just emerged from her own flat. She was, as on all the rare occasions when they met, entangled with the leash of her little Pekinese dog, So Long, the strings of a shopping net, a parasol, and this morning with books falling out of a wicker basket. Mike picked them up and gave them back to her.

"Oh, thank you, Mr. Marchand, I'm just going round to the library. So Long doesn't like that, does oo, booty-boy. They make me tie him up to the hat-stand in the lobby."

"Poor So Long," said Mike, stepping back hastily from the animal, which was snapping at his ankles. "Are you keeping well, Mrs. Lindsay?"

"Very well, thank you, but really, Mr. Marchand, don't you think we should protest about the way this building is being *kept*? I know you and I are the only tenants here at present, but the hall and the landings are *not* being properly swept, and I don't know when they last put fresh flowers in the vases!"

"I hadn't noticed," Mike said truthfully. He saw that the console table in the alcove between the flats was empty of the usual bouquet. He knew nothing about what went on in the basement, but suspected that the old girl down there was taking advantage of the national emergency to cut corners on her job. He escorted the other old girl, his neighbour, to the street, and raised his hat as she went trotting off round the corner to the public library—not a bad example, in her feeble way, of the song the milkmen whistled about 'There'll Always be an England'. He went off to the Underground and the White City.

The British talent for improvisation had been strained to

breaking point to provide centres for the French troops still in Britain. In Staffordshire the Légionnaires and others who had been in Norway were under canvas, which in summer weather was no great hardship to the professionals of the Foreign Legion. At Liverpool the great Aintree racecourse, or rather the office buildings and rooms under the stands, housed the Frenchmen who had been interned when their ships were seized, and who not unnaturally were violently anti-British and anti-de Gaulle. Furious at the 'massacre', as they called it, of Mers-el-Kebir, they had hissed and booed the general, Britain's lackey, when he made a personal appearance to drum up recruits, and there had been brawls and clashes between Frenchmen and English in the streets of Liverpool. It was no wonder that Hitler delayed his invasion when the former Allies were doing such a fine job of destroying one another.

The trouble in London came a little later, for it was not long since the sheep had been separated from the goats in the capital. There, as at Liverpool, sports arenas were being used to house the Frenchmen, although the London arenas were entirely under cover. The White City, used before the war for dog racing, was occupied by those who had chosen repatriation to France. The few hundreds who had opted for de Gaulle were in the stadium or exhibition hall called Olympia. There may have been some humorous intention in this, for just as the White City was associated in the public mind with the coursing of electric hares, so the name of Olympia had become synonymous with Fascism since the pre-war demonstrations of the British Union of Fascists under their Leader Oswald Mosley. Humour or not, Olympia and the White City were too close to each other for peace between the sheep and the goats.

In only a few days, the future repatriates had given the White City a somewhat derelict appearance. This was not quite their own fault, as sleeping bags on top of straw, mixed with such bedding-rolls as had been salvaged from Norway, were all they had as sleeping facilities, and the few washrooms provided for the patrons of dog racing were not equipped with showers or bathtubs. But the same breakdown of discipline as Marchand had seen after the defeat, in Glasgow, had turned conditions at the White City into what the men themselves liked to call *la grande pagaille*, complete disorder. Nobody appeared to be responsible for restoring order. The two bored policemen at the main door hardly let their eyes rest on the soldiers, some in shabby French uniforms and some in British battle-dress with odds and ends of insignia pinned to their shoulders or lapels, who slouched out and in as the spirit moved them. Inside the huge arena what appeared to be outposts of British charitable organisations had been set up. Marchand talked to a group of distracted ladies who told him they were planning a *Cantine du Soldat* outside the gates, where the poor fellows could play dominoes and look at the British picture papers. Further along, he talked to Salvation Army workers who were efficiently pouring coffee for a thirsty queue. Nowhere could he find an office like the one set up by the Comforts Committee in Glasgow, where the shoe-box files would immediately have disgorged the name, home address and next of kin of Dupont, Jean, *caporal-chef* in the 53rd Chasseurs Alpins.

And yet, among the hundreds of men perched where the patrons of dog racing had watched the hare and the hounds on the flood-lighted track, by the quenched light of the July day, Mike Marchand did find his cousin's corporal. He did it by patiently quartering the stadium, asking questions here and there, but most of all looking for men with the metal badge of the 53rd: the head of a girl wearing a cross on her necklace, set inside a bandsman's horn. Dupont wore his in his big shabby beret; even in a badly-fitting British battle-dress he was tidier than most of the men slouching beside him on the lower tiers of one of the stands opposite the main entrance to the White City. They moved over when Mike came up, but stayed near Dupont, and looked suspicious when the Chasseur identified himself.

"The lads seem to be a bit on edge," said Mike, and Dupont nodded. He was a typical Provençal, short and stocky; he looked reliable enough. "They're not too keen on toffs in civvy suits," he said, and raising his voice, told his friends that this was his officer's cousin, with a message from Dykefaulds. The watching men nodded but stood their ground.

"Captain Brunel says you're having trouble here, Dupont. What exactly are the complaints?"

"Well, sir, you can see for yourself the White City's not a palace, but that can't be helped. The lads complain of the food, and it's true they don't serve us ortolans, but there's nothing wrong with what we get. There's been a lot of bitching about the control checks by the English, and the curfew—the lads don't like to feel they can be pushed about—"

"But they're free to come and go within the permitted hours, aren't they?"

"Oh yes, sir."

"Then I'm afraid you'll all have to put up with the curfew until you get your movement orders for repatriation."

"When will that be, sir?"

"I wish I knew. As soon as ships can come from France—"

"If the English have left any to come—"

"Or until *they* can spare ships to send you. Are you eligible for passage in a hospital ship, Dupont?"

"Don't know, sir, it was frozen feet I had, couldn't walk for weeks. I tell you, it's a big change, the White City after Dykefaulds, they looked after us like newborn babies there."

"You didn't think of staying on in England—in the army?"

The suntanned face grew grim. "With General de Gaulle, d'you mean? Were you sent here to ask us that?"

"I? On the contrary, I refused to join de Gaulle myself last week. It was a foolish question, forget I asked it."

"I only want to get home to the wife and kids, sir . . . You know, when de Gaulle came here, and stood up in front of us like a camel with a pile of dirt beneath his nose, and told us we were traitors if we didn't rally to him, one of the lads sang out, 'It's all very fine for you, *mon général*! You've got your wife and family here snug beside you; my old girl's over there in the Occupied Zone!' General! We've all had our bellyful of generals, they went and sold us, that's what they did!"

"But Captain Brunel says the general's recruiting officers have been here too."

"Yes, sir, they have, threatening us with all sorts of pains and penalties if we don't go over to Olympia and sign the enlistment oath. The worst is, they come here out of uniform, because they're in the SR—the Information Service—and want our lads, if they do go home to France, to send back any news that might be useful to the Gaullists."

"About the German occupation, do you mean?"

"Not so much that, as who among their family and friends support de Gaulle and who don't. They're to make a list of the names and keep it till some courier can pick it up . . . I call it a pack of rubbish, sir, and so do most of us."

"What do you mean to do if they come back?"

"You'll soon find out," said Corporal Dupont. "They're here now."

Mike looked sharply round. Four men in civilian clothes, with perhaps twenty in French uniforms at their heels, were walking unconcernedly through the main door of the White City. It was obvious that the twenty had not been hospitalised, for they were powerful, tough young men who shouldered their way in much as Mosley's flying squad of Blackshirts had cleared the gangways of Olympia when their Leader was holding a Nuremberg-style rally. Two of them commandeered a table and stood back while a short, square officer seated himself behind it.

"Now, lads!" he said—and Marchand knew him to be the man Dina da Costa had 'positively identified' as Anders Lachmann—"You've had time to think over your position. We're going to give you another chance to sign on with the Free French Forces, and follow the general to the deliverance of France. *Allez vite!* We have your names, you know, the lot of you—"

Marchand was before him in three long strides. "Lachmann," he said, "why don't you and your bully-boys get the hell out of here and leave these men alone?"

The other man looked up at him with a smile. He had a ruddy complexion and small brown eyes which twinkled with derision.

"Well!" he said, "if it isn't Michel Marchand, throwing his weight about again! You don't scare me, you Vichy swine; you won't kill me as you killed your navigator outside Dakar."

Mike leaned across the table and hit him in the face with the flat of his hand. Lachmann kicked the table over; it went down in a flutter of printed papers, and Mike went down too, with one of the men from Olympia at his throat. He fought back, the boy was ten years younger and very strong, but Marchand had the height and the weight and the fury, he dragged his opponent to his knees and knocked him backwards into a scrum of Frenchmen hitting each other indiscriminately, while the organisers of the *Cantine du Soldat* ran outside shrieking "Police!" and the Salvation Army men automatically got out their first-aid kits. The squad from Olympia was outnumbered but better organised; they went through the mob in a wedge formation, kicking and gouging, while glass and crockery from the canteens were splintered and one of the stands came down in a thunder of wooden benches. Then, to the sound of police whistles, a squad of British redcaps stormed in, and it was all over.

"You see what we've been up against, sir?" panted Corporal Dupont, at Mike's elbow. He said he got the general idea. His hat had been trampled and was unwearable, and one jacket sleeve was ripped at the armpit, but apart from bruised knuckles he didn't think he was marked. Certainly the Metropolitan Police sergeant, who had arrived on the scene with six men, approached Mike very civilly when he asked for his identification.

"Just a moment, sergeant." Mike took a £5 note from his wallet and pressed it into Dupont's hand. "Buy a drink for yourself and the boys when the pubs open," he said. "I'll tell Captain Brunel. Good luck to you!"

He took out the little folder which contained his driving licence and his Aliens' Registration Card, and flipped it over to show the policeman his diplomatic accreditation. "You can find me at the French Embassy if you need me, sergeant," he said —the man saluted. He walked out through the smashed furniture and knots of arguing men without turning back to look for Lachmann. But as he went he saw the man he knew as Schnaebel in earnest conversation with the policeman.

*   *   *

Olympia o—White City o

Our former Allies the French, so eager for peace last month, showed willing to continue the fight—amongst themselves— in a punch-up which our overworked police force had to settle yesterday forenoon. The venue was the White City, better known for dog racing and cat shows than for boxing . . .

That was the *Daily Mirror* in its best sarcastic vein, but as Mike Marchand finished his study of the newspapers in the embassy's press section—they were still being delivered, and would be until the end of the following week—he was glad to see that the *Mirror* was the only paper which carried a reference to the row at the White City. Even then no names were mentioned. 'The match ended in a draw', was the punch-line, the reporter or the rewrite man having mixed his sporting metaphors, and apart from the standard jeer at the French surrender, no harm was done. It confirmed Mike's belief that Edmond Leblanc, renamed by the *Daily Journal* Eddie White, had been exaggerating wildly when he telephoned on Friday night.

"Mike, have you gone crazy? What possessed you to go out to the White City and start a brawl with the recruiting officers?"

"The recruiting officers, as you call them, hadn't the vestige of a right to be there—"

"They were representing de Gaulle, and the British have given him the right to recruit anywhere! You're alleged to have called them Fascist thugs and bully-boys, and they accuse you of being a Vichy saboteur—"

"A *what*? What the hell are you talking about?"

"The report the censors killed this evening, and lucky for you they did."

"Look, Edmond, there *was* a bit of a dust-up this morning, but I don't believe there were any reporters on the scene—not that it would have made any difference to me if there had been—so where did your story come from?"

"The *Service de Presse* at St. Stephen's House."

"I thought so," said Mike contemptuously, "Well, I know you've got pals there, Georges Boris, and Comert, and all the rest of the refugees: tell them next time you see them that I'm no more a saboteur than I am a Vichyist; I'm sure they know already that I'm not a Gaullist—"

"You have to be one or the other, Mike."

"Oh hell!"

Eventually they agreed to have dinner together on Saturday evening. Edmond was still doing a Saturday turn on the *Journal*'s Sunday paper, but he could take an hour off for dinner at nine o'clock and proposed a meeting at the Wellington—"if you don't mind coming as far as the Street," he said. "That old rascal Emile can always produce a first-rate *steak pommes frites*."

"Nine it is." It would mean an argument, of course, but it would take up the slack of Saturday evening, and Saturday afternoon dragged by somehow in the denuded flat of one of the younger Secretaries, whose wife, with all her packing done, was sticking to the protocol of a goodbye tea. Mike remembered later that the chief topic had been the problem of getting a safe conduct across the line of demarcation, for those who had to pass, once they reached France, from the Unoccupied to the Occupied Zone.

It was only seven o'clock when he got back to Mount Street, and rather than face his own empty flat he turned in to the saloon bar of a public house on the South Audley Street corner and asked for a Scotch and soda. It was normally a quiet place, frequented before the war by gentlemen's gentlemen from the great houses of Grosvenor Square. It was some months since Mike had dropped in, and he supposed it was a sign of the changing times that there was a rougher element in the saloon bar than he had ever seen in the 'Audley Arms' before. He carried his drink to a corner table, apologised to a stout lady taking up more than her fair share of room, and took out his cigarettes.

"Could you oblige me with a light, sir?" said a watery-eyed little man reading the *Star*, with a packet of Weights in his hand.

"Certainly," said Mike. He pushed a book of matches across the table. "Keep it. I've got plenty more at home."

"That's very kind of you." The little man withdrew behind his paper, the fat woman seemed to swell to superhuman proportions, and Mike mused on the man Lachmann's gibe, "You won't kill me as you killed your navigator outside Dakar!"

It had never left his mind since the scene at the White City. He had gone over all the details of that crash four years ago, in which Francolin had died and Mike's own injuries had ended his flying career for ever. For the hundredth time, he had tried to think what he could have done to save them both in those last moments above the desert. He had tried in vain to land at Yoff airfield, but there had been witnesses to the crash at Fort Croisé: it was a military ambulance from the fort which had brought Marchand in alive. The enquiry had attached no blame to the pilot. It was a clear case of engine failure, and the responsibility was laid in the lap of the manufacturers of the Goëland '36. But the man who felt himself responsible was Mike Marchand.

He walked slowly back to his apartment. The street door was off the latch, as usual, but the lobby seemed unusually dark as he went in. The three-lamp chandelier was lighted, but the electric candles set in girandoles round the walls and in the empty first-floor alcove had been switched off, no doubt as a war economy measure. It was time to draw all the blackout curtains in the silent flat.

Mike changed into a sports jacket and slacks for an evening which, if he knew Fleet Street, might well progress from a steak at the Wellington into a pub crawl covering the whole area from Ludgate Circus to Temple Bar. He had been out with Edmond in the intervals of a Saturday turn before.

Before leaving he checked the contents of his wallet, on the writing desk, making sure that he had plenty of money and his identification. It was due to be endorsed within the next few days at the nearest Aliens' Registration Office. The lamp on the desk top was particularly bright, and the well of the stairs, when he came out on the landing, was dark by contrast. There seemed to be a darker shadow in the alcove where the big vase of flowers had been.

"Marchand! Marchand!"

He looked down into the lobby, where the light from the chandelier lay in a pool on the sand-coloured carpet. Someone had spoken from the shadows beyond, and Mike felt his head beginning to swim in the onset of vertigo. He clung to the banister, trembling from head to foot. There was no rickety stair here, no excuse, it had happened to him again, he would never be cured, and he lost balance as the roaring in his ears began and the coloured kaleidoscope whirled with the metal spokes of the banister around his head. Then there was a crushing pain, and darkness.

7

WHEN HE WAS able to focus his eyes again Mike was first aware of a light where no light should be, as if his bedroom window had changed position in the night, and then of a vast expanse of white: white ceiling, white curtains, white bed-linen inside which he had been trussed like a chicken skewered for roasting. He moved slightly, and felt a painful constriction. He turned his head, which ached and stung, and instead of the usual clutter of his bedside table—wristwatch, travelling alarm clock, cigarettes, paperback—a square of bare white wood came into his line of vision. Beyond the square he saw more white, a high iron bed and a humped form beneath the counterpane. He realised, with his first real flicker of intelligence, that he was in a hospital.

The instant revulsion blew the flicker out at once, and Mike relapsed into a stupor, half coma and half sleep, from which he was roused by the sound of trolleys moving on rubber wheels along polished linoleum, and the awareness that something annoying, something that involved touching and more light, was happening to his eyes. He had a feeling that this interference, or inspection, had happened more than once before.

"How are you feeling now?" The voice came out of another blur in his consciousness, which might have lasted five minutes or an hour, and from a point above his head. His vision was clearer now, and Mike saw a rather pretty girl, whose question he wanted to answer politely: unfortunately the answer came in French. The girl shook her head and went off down the ward with a swish of starched skirts, and Mike was left to practise what he wanted to say next in English, while the long ward full of male patients was rousing to the beginning of a new day.

Mike investigated the cause of his constriction. His hands, which were flexible and not painful, told him that he was bandaged under the hospital shirt. He was nerving himself to touch the back of his head, when the young nurse appeared by his side again, escorting a presence in a different uniform, who announced uncompromisingly, "I'm Sister Laidlaw and *je parle français.*"

"It's all right." Mike tried to smile. "Please, Sister, will you tell me where I am?"

"You're in St. George's Hospital. You were brought up here from Casualty at a quarter to eleven last night. Now will you tell us if you feel more comfortable this morning?"

"If I knew what happened—"

"You had a very nasty fall." Sister Laidlaw's look was as stern as her accent was Scottish: if she had been a real battle-axe like Captain Fletcher at Dykefaulds it would have seemed quite natural, but as the Ward Sister was younger than Mike, very young indeed for her position, her grave look of reproach was merely droll. There was a smile in Mike's voice as he told her it was very kind of them to have looked after him, and now he would like to leave as soon as possible.

"I dare say!" said Sister Laidlaw, scandalised. "You'll leave when the doctors say so, and not before. Now just bide at peace for a wee while, and you'll see the house-surgeon when he makes his rounds."

After that there were various humiliations to be undergone, and an argument with the little nurse about sitting up to drink tea instead of taking it through a feeding cup, but there was no return of the stupefied feeling or the drowsiness. Breakfasts were served, and the ward grew talkative, although the humped shape on Mike's left was only moved for ablutions, and the little boy on his right, who had a broken leg, was too small and scared for more than a solemn "Hallo!" Mike lay in silence, assembling his thoughts, until a bustle in the ward indicated the arrival of the house-surgeon.

In about ten minutes he reached Mike's bedside, and bade the patient a cheerful "Good morning!" He unhooked the temperature chart, gave it a quick look, and with his fingers on Mike's pulse said something to Sister Laidlaw, standing at attention by his side, which resulted in a movement in the ward and the placing of screens round Mike Marchand's bed.

"Don't be alarmed, you're not on the danger list," he said breezily. ". . . Thank you, nurse," as a chair was brought, "that's fine . . . If we'd taken you seriously last night," he returned to Mike, "you'd have a bobby sitting here with his notebook and pencil, waiting to take your deposition. But this morning, Sister tells me, you didn't even know you'd had a nasty fall."

"That's what *she* told *me*, doctor."

"All right then, let's begin at the beginning. What's your name?"

He listened approvingly as Mike recited all the particulars already given on the card found in his wallet.

"What's the last thing you remember before the accident took place?"

"Standing at the desk in the living room of my flat and making sure I'd enough money for the evening."

"You were alone?"

"Quite alone. I was going to dine with a man at the Wellington Restaurant in Fleet Street."

"You don't remember leaving the flat?"

"The next thing I knew I was here, in hospital."

"Had you been drinking?"

"Good God, no! I had one Scotch and soda at the 'Audley Arms'."

"This was when?"

"I didn't check the time. I was due at the Wellington at nine, so I suppose I left the pub about eight o'clock."

"Your neighbour found you at the foot of the stairs, passed out cold, with your head bashed against the banister when she came back from a bridge party at ten. She called the police and they brought you here to Casualty. We had to give one of the coppers first aid too, the lady's little dog bit his hand nearly to the bone."

"So Long!" said Mike.

"Come on, you're not leaving us yet—"

"I didn't mean 'so long, goodbye', I mean that's the dog's name."

"Do you know the lady's name too?"

"Mrs. Lindsay. She was complaining about the flowers on the landing—" And with that the first thread of memory wove itself through the amnesia which had overtaken Mike Marchand.

"That's clear enough, anyway," said the doctor. "Now, if you weren't drinking, and hadn't company, what do *you* think happened? You tripped on the stair, maybe? To the tune of a bruised rib and a cut on your scalp we had to put three stitches in?"

"I've had occasional attacks of vertigo since I was in an air crash four years ago."

"Humph!" said the doctor, "The X-ray did show you'd knocked yourself about a bit. You lead an active life, Mr. Marchand."

"Not as active as I'd like," said Mike. "When can I get out of here and go home?"

"Tonight, if you behave yourself."

"I've got to get home *now*."

"Something on your mind?"

"No, why?"

"Look, Mr. Marchand. You talked your head off in the ambulance about a fight, and a chap who slugged you from behind, and you named a lot of French names I don't suppose the cops could spell correctly, and you went through the same rigmarole in Casualty until you were put under sedation. That's what I meant when I said there might have been a policeman waiting with his notebook now. That's why I'm trying to find out what you remember this morning instead of consoling little Ronnie Smith for his broken leg—"

"Don't waste another minute on me," said Mike. "I'm grateful for all you've done, and now I want to go. I hate hospitals. You can put the bed to better use for someone else."

"Something in that," said the doctor, rising. "We'll see what the consultant says." He patted Mike's shoulder gently. "You French have had a bad time lately. Sorry and all that."

"You thought I'd been drowning my sorrows, didn't you?" The doctor gave him an enigmatic smile as the screens round his bed were taken away.

It was ten o'clock before the consultant began his stately progress round the ward, with the house-surgeon and Sister Laidlaw in attendance, and all the hierarchical rules of St. George's obeyed to the letter. He did not deign to enter into a discussion with Mike Marchand, whose presence indeed he almost ignored, but after a few questions said icily, "You understand that you have been suffering from a severe concussion, and should remain in bed for twenty-four hours? You do, and you still insist on leaving hospital? Are you prepared to take your own discharge and sign a form releasing St. George's from all responsibility? . . . Very well then," with a comprehensive glance at his entourage, "this man may go."

Mike went back to Mount Street in a taxi. The street was lapped in Sunday calm, the door of his apartment building stood unlatched as usual, and there was no sign, indoors, of the commotion which must have taken place before Mrs. Lindsay sent for the police and the ambulance to cope with his prone body. He would have to go to the nearest florist on Monday and send roses or carnations to the poor old girl.

He examined the foot of the stair. There were stains on the rugs, probably from the back of his own head, but no smears on the iron banisters or the risers of the staircase. The pain at the base of his skull and his aching ribs were the only evidence that he had fallen downstairs.

He opened the door of the flat cautiously. He remembered quite well that the blackout was in place, and switched on all the lights in the living room before he took a step inside. Nothing was disturbed, as far as he could see. No one had taken his keys from his pocket as he lay insensible in the hall to ransack the flat. Everything was just as he had left it.

It was as much of an effort to undress as it had been to put his clothes on in hospital, and he didn't feel equal to getting into a tub he might find difficulty in getting out of. But a sponge dipped in cold water refreshed him, and at last Mike was able to pull on old slacks and a clean shirt and lie down on top of the bed. There the drowsiness overcame him again and he slept for an hour.

When he woke up he was disgusted to see bloodstains on the pillow, and getting some sterile cotton from the bathroom, swabbed the place where they had cut away his hair to put in the stitches. All the mirrors in the flat were fixtures, and he couldn't see if the shorn hair and the surgical sewing were obvious.

Now he began to feel the first pangs of hunger. There was some food in the house; he ate a slice of bread and butter and drank a glass of milk from the fridge. The kitchen mirror showed a villainous reflection, for he had not the energy to shave, but the natural sleep and the nourishment had refreshed him to the point where he was able to lift the telephone and dial the number of the embassy.

Not to call the embassy doctor—oh no! The hospital had said he should, but Mike knew better: the fewer people who knew about last night's incident the fewer there would be to draw the wrong conclusions. Mike Marchand was learning, after nearly thirty years, to be cunning and mistrustful; London, since the fall of France, had become his personal jungle of suspicion.

He wanted to find out about Edmond Leblanc.

There was still a switchboard girl on duty at the embassy, coping with the last minute appeals for help in getting diplomatic visas, exit permits, anything that might get the distraught and terrified out of Britain and into the safety of Canada or the United States. That morning—but it was after one now, his watch told him—the girl on duty was Jacqueline, herself as distraught as any of the callers, and Mike made his voice as casual and cheerful as he could when he asked if there were any messages for him.

"Nothing this morning, monsieur, but there's a note saying Monsieur Leblanc called you at ten o'clock last night."

"Is that all? No message?"

"Just that he'd been calling your apartment and got no reply."

"All right, Jacqueline, many thanks."

Mike sat back and closed his eyes. None of it made sense: that ugly crowd of strangers in the pub, the lights extinguished in the lobby, the damage done to his body which might have been inflicted by kicking and a cosh all looked like a frame-up, but one which would have failed in its purpose if Mike Marchand had spent the evening behind the stout oak doors of his apartment. Only one man knew for certain that he intended to go out again, and that man was Edmond Leblanc.

Who had Gaullist contacts, and who could in all innocence have mentioned to one of them that he was dining with Marchand at nine o'clock.

Because if he *had* been attacked, and the amnesia came from a blow instead of a fall, then his attacker could only be one of the young thugs he had confronted at the White City. Perhaps even Anders Lachmann himself . . .

His watch said three-fifteen, which meant he had been asleep again, sprawled uncomfortably in an easy chair, and he was chilled, in the hot summer afternoon, with the effects of delayed shock. He thought he must have been dreaming, acting a scene from the movies, to suppose he could have been attacked in his own quiet building, on a Saturday evening in London . . . It was the vertigo he dreaded, not any human agency, which had sent him headlong to the foot of the stair. It had nearly happened in Glasgow three weeks ago.

There was a table which held the telephone and a malachite ashtray beside his chair, and his still unfocused eyes were caught by an engagement calendar which stood there too; one of the French ring-leaf variety, showing two days at a time. He saw his own notation of dinner at the Wellington—that was last night, and this, he realised, was Sunday the fourteenth of July.

Bastille Day. Just five years since Mike Marchand stood on that balcony above the Place de la Concorde, while the crowd roared: that famous Bastille Day when the Fascists demonstrated at the Etoile, the Communists in the Place de la Bastille, and Mike Marchand had stood between the two like a symbol of courage and youth. This fourteenth, in London, was to be dedicated to General de Gaulle.

He had no idea that he had torn the page from the calendar and was rolling it between his clenched hands until he heard the ringing of the front door bell.

It was so unexpected, on that strange Sunday afternoon, that the bell rang twice, and a third time, before Mike made up his mind to open the door. Even then, he did what he had never done before: he put up the safety chain before he eased the door back a mere three inches, and said "Yes?"

"Monsieur Marchand?"

"Yes?"

A man's hand held an identification close to the reluctant opening, and a voice said, "Major Dempster. Special Branch. The street door was open, sir; that isn't very wise."

* * *

Major Dempster was a thick-set man of about fifty, wearing a heavy dark suit and a tie easily mistaken for an Old Etonian tie, with the light blue stripe only fractionally too wide to be authentic. He was smoking when he came in, and before taking a chair at Mike's invitation he stubbed out his cigarette in a small ornamental bowl of Lalique glass.

"You had quite a nasty accident last night, I hear, sir," he began. "I was surprised to find you'd been discharged from hospital."

Mike shrugged. "There wasn't much the matter with me. I was back here before noon."

"But you missed the Fourteenth of July parade of the Free French Forces?"

"I never meant to attend it. I don't much care for that sort of charade."

"Pity. It was a very striking ceremony—or two ceremonies, rather. The Londoners turned out in thousands to cheer General de Gaulle when he marched his men down Whitehall and laid a wreath at the base of the Cenotaph."

"Which, strictly speaking, has nothing to do with the storming of the Bastille."

"Perhaps not," the major conceded. "Perhaps that was why the parade continued to Grosvenor Gardens, where the general laid another wreath beside the statue of Foch."

"Really?" said Mike. "I'm sure Marshal Foch would have felt honoured. Was that in the original plan?"

"The original plan was improved upon, by a special directive from the Prime Minister. Mr. Churchill wanted as many people as possible to see and applaud General de Gaulle."

"And you say they were there by the thousand. How many hundreds did the general muster?"

Major Dempster smiled. "Two battalions," he said.

"Was that all?"

"Plus about a dozen airmen. And a coachload of French wounded, who got the biggest cheer of the day."

"Too bad he couldn't parade some of the sailors from Mers-el-Kebir."

It was out before he could stop himself—the bitter gibe; and as the Englishman's dark brows drew together Mike realised his mistake. He studied the burly figure, the polished black boots and bowler hat, the starched white collar and the pseudo-Old Etonian tie, and knew he was confronted by an enemy.

"Did you disapprove of the action at Mers-el-Kebir, sir?"

"Not in principle, but I wish it could have been carried out without loss of life."

"Naturally." Major Dempster lit another cigarette and looked round the room, taking his time. "Nice place you've got here," he said. "Rented furnished, I believe?"

"Yes."

"By the year or by the quarter?"

"By the quarter, payable in advance . . . Major Dempster, what is all this about? You didn't come here to interrogate me about the terms of my lease—the house agents could have given you the details tomorrow morning."

"They gave us the details on Friday afternoon, after your visit to the White City and nearly twenty-four hours before you—fell downstairs." The major took out a black notebook. "The police officers called to an accident here late on Saturday night had an interesting report to make when they returned to the West Central station. They stated that when you were lifted into the ambulance you revived sufficiently to insist that you had been attacked, struck down from behind, apparently by one or more persons, whom you successively identified as Franklin, Stables, and Gauld. There are four witnesses to attest that you repeated these charges at St. George's when you were admitted to Casualty."

"Charges!" said Mike. "A drunk doesn't always know what he's talking about—"

"Now you're saying you were intoxicated last night? You only had one drink at the 'Audley Arms', where you stayed just long enough to pass a small object to an unidentified party—"

"Am I crazy or are you?" said Mike. "It was a book of matches, and I never saw the old fellow in my life before . . . Do you mean to tell me I was being watched in the public house?"

"You've been under surveillance since Friday afternoon, Mr. Marchand. And now I want to ask you one or two questions. Who were the men you accused of attacking you? Franklin, Stables and Gauld?"

Mike actually laughed. "Franklin is Francolin," he said. "A French airman who died four years ago. Stables is Schnaebel" —he spelled out the name, for Major Dempster was busily writing in his notebook—"the real name of one of de Gaulle's officer recruits, who now calls himself Carreau. I believe he crossed the Channel walking on the water."

With a "tchk!" of disapproval, Major Dempster asked the identity of Gauld.

"You'll have to work that one out for yourself, major."

"You're not very co-operative, Mr. Marchand."

"Give me a good reason why I should be."

"I'll give you several reasons," said Major Dempster, and his fat face was suffused with blood. "Just answer one more question first: why haven't you applied for an exit permit to leave England next Friday in the *Orduna*?"

"Because I'm not sailing in the *Orduna*, major. I'm still hoping to join one of the Services in England. If not, there must be some kind of war work I can do."

"Having first applied for a residence permit—an alien's permit, without diplomatic status?"

"Yes, of course," said Mike, taken aback. "I hadn't thought about the need for a residence permit."

"I doubt if it would be granted."

"My ambassador and Monsieur Cambon intend to remain in England—"

"They're in a rather different position from yourself. And the ambassador is definitely leaving England. He's sailing from Southampton in the RMS *Highland Brigade*—"

"Not to France?"

"To Rio de Janeiro, on the twenty-second of July."

Mike sat dumbfounded. It was the last thing he had expected to hear about the former ambassador, Britain's devoted friend. To cover his shock, he said, "What makes you say I wouldn't be granted a residence permit?"

"Because of your persistent and public criticism of General de Gaulle."

"I've exercised the right of free speech in a free country—"

"There's no such thing as free speech in total war."

"Or else it's all on one side," said Mike. "I know about the press release circulated in Fleet Street, calling me a Vichy saboteur—"

"Of course that never passed the censorship. No one believes you're a saboteur, Mr. Marchand, not as we understand the term; but aren't you a supporter of Vichy?"

"I think the Vichy set-up stinks," said Mike. "It's the people going home on the *Orduna* who've come out for Vichy."

"But you must come out for one or the other, can't you see? Decide for Vichy and go back to France with the soldiers or the diplomats; but if you want to stay in Britain you must join de Gaulle."

"Nothing doing," said Mike.

"Why?"

"I'm not compelled to tell you why."

"One more scene like that row at the White City, and you may be compelled to tell it in a court of justice—and *in camera.*"

"Under what law?"

"Under the Defence Regulations, 1939. Specifically under Regulation 18B, which allows the arrest of a suspect for treason 'without charge or trial, contrary to the liberties granted by the Great Charter and the Bill of Rights','' recited the man from Special Branch.

"And if the suspect is found guilty?"

"Then he or she will have to make a long stay in the Isle of Man."

"Have you a warrant for my arrest, Major Dempster? Because if so I'm going to call the embassy—"

"There isn't even a duty officer at the French Embassy today," said Dempster calmly, "and I doubt if you'd find the switchboard girl much use . . . No, I've no warrant, sir. You mustn't think of this as a visit of intimidation—"

"What do you call it then?"

"Just a warning."

"All right," said Mike, rising, "I'll think it over. I'll make up my mind in a day or two if it's to be the *Orduna* or the Isle of Man. One thing I can tell you, it won't be your half-price Hitler at St. Stephen's House. No, wait, major!"—over a protest—"you've asked all the questions; let me do the talking now . . . De Gaulle has Churchill and the BBC on his side, and it's very easy for his PR men to present him as the hero and poor old dotty Pétain as the villain . . . while anyone like me, who says to hell with both of them, is supposed to be working for the enemy and sabotaging the war effort . . . No, I haven't finished, I want to tell you something. I came to London first on a Whitsuntide holiday trip, with a group of other boys from the Ecole des Roches. We saw Buckingham Palace, Madame Tussaud's, the Houses of Parliament . . . and of course the Tower of London. We were all fascinated by the Crown Jewels. But what I liked best was what our guide called Traitors' Gate: those steps by the Thames where State prisoners entered the Tower on their way to execution, after they'd been tried and found guilty in Westminster Hall. You've got another Traitors' Gate wide open in St. Stephen's House right now, because that man de Gaulle, in his ambition and his vanity, will welcome anybody, *anybody* who will give his movement strength and numbers and carry him to power. That's all, major; don't bother to put it in your notebook. I intend to say all that all over again at the Ministry of Economic Warfare tomorrow morning."

While Mike was talking, he was unconscious of his overwrought and protesting body. The aches and pains, side, head, all over, came back again as he moved forward politely to open his front door for the man from Special Branch.

"Your Mr. Churchill's a romantic fellow," he said. "Let's hope his romance with *le Grand Charlatan* won't turn into Operation Boomerang."

With a pleasant consciousness of having had the last word he shut the door and sat down at the writing desk. As far as Marchand, Michel Dieudonné Antoine, was concerned, it *was* the last word: he'd had enough. It was not his accident, not even the undercurrent of awareness that it might have been no accident, which made him suddenly decide to cut his losses and leave London. Keep his appointment with Neil Grant—that, certainly; but after that, what was there to keep himself in England? The feeling of rejection, begun when France surrendered, intensified in Scotland when he learned of the feeling roused by the capture of the Highland Division at St. Valéry, had been fostered by the tragedy of Mers-el-Kebir, but these were troubles on the national scale. Now his personal freedom was threatened, first by a surveillance which made him feel soiled, then by the positive prospect of an internment camp—no, it was too much! He had wanted to fight with Britain and for Britain, and now Britain was ready to treat him as an enemy because he had refused to genuflect to a man who carried within himself like a time bomb a latent hostility to the land of his benefactors. So be it! Mike pulled paper and pen towards him, intending to write to Jacques Brunel, and then, changing his mind, he went to the telephone and asked the operator for a personal call to Captain Gerald O'Hanlon, at Foynes airport in Ireland.

8

To Alison Grant, trying to control her restlessness in the lounge of the Euston Hotel, the high whine of the sirens came as a personal affront. Since six o'clock she had been moving between the hotel lobby and the main platform of Euston station, hoping for some magic increase in the speed of the Glasgow train, already posted one and a half hours late. Now it was after seven, and there was an air raid warning.

The lounge was so crowded that she didn't dare leave her table again. The Up trains to London were disgorging all round the clock their cargoes of Service men, some moving to the defence of 'invasion corner'—uninvaded still—many more to the ports of embarkation for the long journey round the Cape of Good Hope to the Middle East. Every canteen, snack bar, and public bar in the station was as crowded, on this last Monday of July, as the hotel lounge and restaurants. Alison, doing her best to reserve the empty chair beside her, was relieved to see her brother making his determined way through the throng.

"Neil, thank goodness!" she exclaimed, as he dropped into the place beside her and laid his black briefcase on the table. "I was so afraid you'd be held up when I heard the Alert!"

"Yes, well, we got a flash when they went from Yellow to Red," said Neill. "I had the car out of Berkeley Square just as the sirens sounded, and took the back streets to Euston. The car's in the yard now . . . Two dry sherries, please," he said to the waiter, and then to Alison, "How long have we got?"

"Ten minutes, if the train's on time."

"Right. Well, after you called me, I rang home, and told Lucy we'd have something to eat in town. It seems more friendly to give Captain Brunel some dinner, now that we're running late, instead of just gulping a drink, don't you think?"

"I'm sure he'll be delighted," said Alison. "Let's gulp this, and then you wait here—will you?" She sipped quickly at her sherry.

"I'll organise a table in the grill. Look, Alison, just one thing!

Don't mention Mike Marchand until I do. I want to see how his cousin reacts to his—escapade."

"I won't say a word more than I have to," she assured him, and with a quick nod slipped out of her chair and ran to reassure herself, by a searching look in the mirror of the ladies' room, that above the black office dress her white Peter Pan collar was as spotless as the white gloves she had been carrying in her handbag, her red hair brushed into a long smooth wing. She went into the main station and waited in the lee of the bookstall, while the tide of khaki, Air Force blue and Navy blue swept past as if the whole of Britain was on the march. She heard the sound of taxi horns and wheels: vehicles were no longer being stopped because there was an Alert on. Since Hitler's impudent peace bid had failed, ten days ago, there had been many more Alerts in London, and since Saturday, when the Luftwaffe attacked in strength at Dover and along the Suffolk coast, RAF Fighter Command had been in combat for most of the daylight hours.

The minute hand of the station clock jerked round to half past seven, and the Glasgow train arrived in a cloud of steam and smoke. The carriage doors banged, the passengers poured out, most of them burdened with rifles and packs, and as the tide of their friends broke upon them from behind the ticket-collectors' barrier, Alison saw the tall form of Captain Jacques Brunel.

He was walking along quickly and easily—and it struck Alison that she had never seen him walk before—wearing his Chasseur uniform, which had been carefully mended and pressed, and carrying a light valise. When he saw her coming he set the valise down on the dusty platform, and almost lifted her off her feet in a spontaneous embrace: not kissing her, not saying her name, but simply enfolding her in a grasp so strong that when she had breath to speak Alison stammered, "Hey! You're better—"

"Quite better, quite well again!" he assured her. "And you—how wonderful you came to meet me, Alison!"

"But of course I came," she said, not much more coherently. "And Neil—my brother—he came too. He's waiting in the hotel—he wants us to have dinner together—"

"That's very kind of him." A porter came up, and Jacques asked him to look after the valise; Alison had almost forgotten that he was not quite a stranger to London and the routine of the railway termini. The crowd was thinning out round the Glasgow train, and they were able to walk quickly to the exit. "I can't get over how well you look!" said Alison.

"I can't get over how pretty you look. Black suits you—and you've done something to your hair."

"I'm growing it into a pageboy bob." She was proud of his admiration, and proud of her French officer, as confident as if the French had just won the Battle of the Marne, when he shook hands with her brother at the door of the hotel lounge.

"Very glad to meet you, Captain Brunel," said Neil Grant. "Let's take Alison to our table, shall we? And then I expect you'd like a wash."

"If you care for sherry, we're one ahead of you," Neil continued cheerfully when they returned to the grill room. Jacques asked if he might have a Scotch and soda.

"Splendid! I didn't know you drank it, 'fraid I don't know much about French tastes."

"I developed a taste for Scotch last winter, when the Scots Guards were training with us at Chamonix," said Jacques. "Besides, this is a special occasion. Can you imagine what it feels like to be out of Dykefaulds, and back in the land of the living?"

"I can," said Alison, and Jacques gave her a grateful look. But it was to Neil that he said something graceful about the wonderful care and hospitality given in Scotland to the men from Namsos, and Alison saw, as they opened their menus, that the Member for Carrick was very pleased indeed. They agreed on a mixed grill, a salad, with biscuits and cheese to follow, and Neil ordered a bottle of Beaujolais.

"Another Scotch, while we're waiting for the grill?"

"No thanks, I'm out of training for two Scotches, I'm afraid."

"Did you have anything to eat on the train?"

"Tea and a sandwich off a Salvation Army trolley, at a station where we stopped for a long time. I don't know where it was, because of course all the signs are down." And Jacques began to tell them about the sailors in the carriage next to his, who had sung popular songs untiringly for most of the long journey, including a parody of 'There'll Always be an England', which he repeated:

> There'll always be an England
> As long as Scotland stands,
> It's jist on puir auld Scotland
> That England's wealth depends

Neil Grant laughed, and attacked his food with gusto, while Alison thought for the first time that Jacques Brunel was clever. She had thought of him in his hospital ward as brave, intense, mercurial, but not clever in the sense that he knew how to interest and draw out a character so reticent as her brother. Now Jacques was asking for Mrs. Grant and the baby, and here was Neil, so taciturn where his own family was concerned, actually boasting about his two boys and their delighted surprise at the appearance of a little sister.

"Have you any news of your parents, Jacques?" asked Alison.

Yes, he said. He had had a letter from his mother, sent with three weeks' delay, telling him that they were back in their own house at Menton. It was in fair condition, not too much vandalised by the Italian troops compared with others in the town; Maître Brunel's office was working overtime to record all the claims for looting and damage, and between that and organising shelter for some of the refugees—six millions, it was estimated—who had poured into the Unoccupied Zone, Jacques' father was in his element.

"My father's a politician *manqué*," he explained to Neil Grant with a smile. "He once had great dreams of being elected to the Chambre des Députés. Perhaps now he should be glad they were frustrated."

"What party does he belong to?"

"Radical. He's a great supporter of Edouard Herriot, who is —who was—the President of the Chamber. The Speaker, you would say." And, changing the subject slightly, and away from any allusion to the Casino at Vichy, Jacques went on, "Have you come from the House of Commons now, Mr. Grant?"

"No, the House wasn't in session today. Which meant I had more time to give to my work at the Ministry."

"Economic Warfare, isn't it?" said Jacques with a glance at Alison. "What does that mean exactly? Organisation of the blockades?"

"Amongst other things. For instance, tomorrow in the House the Minister will have questions to answer on American exports of oil to Spain. We have to oppose re-export to Germany, now that—"

"Now that the Germans stand on the Spanish border at the Pyrenees," concluded Jacques. "It's all right, Mr. Grant. You don't have to, how do you say, pull any punches with me. I've had plenty of time to get used to the idea that France has lost the war, and you British are landed with a lot of problems because of that. But the war's not over yet, and I think we'll come into it again before it's finished."

"Of course you will," said Alison loyally. But Neil's only comment was, "Your cousin seemed to think so too, in his own way. Too bad he couldn't have stayed in London until you got out of hospital." She noted with an inward smile that the first mention of Marchand had not come from Jacques Brunel.

Who now said readily, "Yes, I wish I could have had a talk with him. But I gather he got priority on the trip through an old flying friend, he's probably in Rio de Janeiro by this time, even if he were held up in Lisbon or New York."

"You haven't heard for certain?"

"Not I."

"Extraordinary."

"Not a bit," said Jacques. "Michel's a very sudden fellow. This is just the way he went off to Bucharest, after he recovered from that bad crash four years ago. Air France made a job for him, and off he went, sight unseen—I think he regretted it afterwards."

"So that's what he was doing before he came to London, I didn't know. Do you think he'll regret going to Rio de Janeiro?"

"I don't see why he should—in fact I as good as suggested it to him when Alison brought him to Dykefaulds. Michel's a rich man in Brazil: his uncle made a large settlement on him when he was twenty-one. It was Ferreira money, but Michel's quite independent of the Ferreiras."

"They're in coffee, aren't they?"

"It's a mining fortune, but Mr. Pedro Ferreira was a merchant banker before his retirement. Michel didn't tell you anything of this?"

"No reason why he should. We had a lot of other things to discuss the day he came to see me at the Ministry. In fact we talked so long that he insisted on taking Alison and me to luncheon. Said he owed it to the Comforts Committee, whatever he meant by that."

"It was a lovely lunch too, at the Claridge's 'Causerie.' One of my absolutely favourite places," said Alison.

"One month in London, and she has her favourite places already," said her brother, and Jacques, smiling as he looked from one to the other, marvelled that the same kind of family looks, red hair, white skin, blue eyes, should have turned out so plain and humdrum in the brother, so charming and vivacious in the girl. He was excited by Alison in her black dress, with the bell of bright hair already falling nearly to her shoulders, as he had never been by the kind little visitor to his hospital bed. He recalled himself with an effort to the subject in hand as the waiter brought the coffee and told them the All Clear had sounded.

"Good," said Neil Grant. "That Alert didn't last too long. —Yes, that's how it was," he continued, "we had a long talk and lunch on a Monday, the fifteenth that would be, and on Wednesday he telephoned to say he was off to Eire by the boat train the next morning, just like that."

"He rang me at Dykefaulds the same night," said Jacques. "And before he left he wrote me a long letter about the flat."

"Oh, the flat, yes, that's all right," said Neil. "Alison telephoned the house agents this morning, to make sure you'd have no trouble about the keys."

"That was very sweet of you, Alison."

"I checked, because there was a flap about the keys," said the girl. "The police, or whoever, complained that the front door wasn't securely fastened, and we're all more security-conscious than we used to be. Oh, and the cleaning woman will come in tomorrow, the agents in Curzon Street knew where to locate her."

"You've thought of everything," said Jacques gratefully. Neil had asked for his bill, and while it was being paid he asked Alison in an undertone if he might phone her at the Ministry next morning. She nodded, with sparkling eyes.

"Thank you for the best meal I've had for months," said Captain Brunel to his host. "I know you don't want to be too late getting home, but could I ask you just one question first?"

"Of course."

"Was Michel really in danger of being deported, or interned?"

"I'm not sure how the law stands on deportation in a case like his, but yes, I think he was in some danger of internment after the row at the White City. He told you about that?"

"I know he hit some fellow who insulted him, if that qualified him for internment."

"The fellow being one of de Gaulle's *Deuxième Bureau*—"

"What does de Gaulle need with an Espionage and Counter-Espionage Service?"

"Exactly what your cousin said," Neil sighed.

"You see, what I'm trying to get at, is *why* did it happen? Ordinarily, Michel's the last man to take an interest in politics, apart from damning *all* the politicians who let the Aéropostale down."

"These aren't ordinary times."

"Exactly, and what I do regret is that it was I who asked him to go and see one of my men at the White City. That triggered the whole thing off."

"You're not planning to go out to the White City yourself, by any chance?"

"Don't worry, Mr. Grant, I'm not going to start slapping Gaullist officers around. And Corporal Dupont and his mates are back in France by this time—they were repatriated on the eighteenth."

"Thank goodness they weren't in the *Meknes*," said Alison.

"They were all sailors in the *Meknes*, worse luck."

It had happened less than a week ago, the sinking of the *Meknes*, a French merchantman carrying thirteen hundred of the sailors interned after the seizure of their ships in British harbours. She had been brilliantly lighted, with huge painted Tricolores outlined in electric lights, when a German torpedo sank her off Portland, with the loss of three hundred lives. The German propaganda line that the British had sunk the ship themselves had been swallowed eagerly by most of the French internees.

"I think you have to face it, Captain Brunel," said Neil, "everything that's happened since General de Gaulle arrived in London has worked out in his favour. It's true that no single French personality of any importance has joined him, it's true his recruits are only coming in by twos and threes. But the goings-on at Vichy, yes, and even the tragedy of Mers-el-Kebir . . . and the sinking of the *Meknes* and the French reaction to it, have all worked to make the general look better in British eyes than he really is. If you're going to live in London for a bit, better make up your mind that as far as public opinion is concerned, to be with de Gaulle is to be with the honour and soul of France, and not to be with him is equal to capitulating to Hitler."

"I'll remember what you said," promised Jacques Brunel, and pulled Alison's chair aside as she got up.

It was a quick drive across the darkened city, the moon rising late, from Euston to Mount Street. Jacques declared that he knew the street well, had always liked its Dutch architecture of red brick and crow-stepped gables. "Those two little ruffians I tried to tutor in French ten years ago," he said, "lived just round the corner in Grosvenor Square."

"You'll have to come and see my little ruffians," said Neil Grant as they pulled up outside what had been Mike's front door. "I know my wife wants to meet you soon. How about coming down to us for Sunday lunch?"

"That's very kind of you," said Jacques. "Is Mrs. Grant really receiving guests already?"

"Of course, she's delighted to see people. Alison'll tell you about the trains from Waterloo, and we'll meet you at Watermead Halt. Here, let me give you a hand with your valise."

But Jacques carried it to the door himself, while the Grants waited to make sure that he was admitted. They saw a grey-haired woman open the street door after a few minutes' delay, and then Jacques turned round to wave the keys triumphantly in the left hand that was only slightly distorted, before saluting with the right at his blue Chasseur beret, for what Alison thought with a pang might be the last time.

"That's a thoroughly good chap," said Neil, driving towards Park Lane.

"You do like him, don't you?"

"Very much. And you and he like each other, that's easy to be seen."

"Why not?"

"Why not? Because these are uncertain times, my child, I don't want you to get too involved."

"I'm not 'involved'!"

"But the more you see of Brunel, the more likely—"

"Now listen to who's talking! Who's the one who invited him to come to lunch on Sunday? I thought we weren't going to have any visitors until that starchy nurse went away!"

"Nonsense, it'll do Lucy good . . . He talks well, that chap. Not as excitable as his cousin."

"Poor Mike Marchand," said Alison. "I was sorry for him that day at the 'Causerie'. I don't think he was feeling well at all. I think something had happened to him that he didn't want to talk about."

"Imagination," said her brother briefly, accelerating in deserted Knightsbridge.

"You ought to be telling me how good I was," said Alison. "I didn't interrupt you once when you two were discussing poor old Mike so solemnly. All his reasons for going to Brazil! The wealthy uncle, and the settlement, and the danger of internment if he stayed here—as if those were the only things that mattered to Mike Marchand!"

"What on earth are you talking about?"

"I'm talking about Dina da Costa. *She's* the big reason for going home to Rio de Janeiro!"

"But good heavens, he hardly knows her."

"He took her out to dinner, didn't he? That smashing girl? My guess is that Mike fell for her like a ton of bricks that night. Didn't you notice at the Causerie how he kept beginning to talk about her, and stopping, and then bringing in her name again?"

"That's too subtle for me, I'm afraid."

"*Men!*" said Alison profoundly. She threw her gloves and bag into the back of the car, and stretched luxuriously as she settled down in the passenger's seat.

"Tired?"

"Not a bit." But Alison closed her eyes and said no more until they were well on the way to the Great West Road. Then, with her eyes still shut, she said, "You're up to something, aren't you?"

"What d'you mean?"

"You've figured out some way that Jacques can help in whatever it is you're doing at the Ministry. And I don't mean the oil exports from Spain to Germany."

"Nonsense!" said Neil. "I asked him down on Sunday because I thought a day in the country would do him good. But I admit we could use advice from some steady, sensible Frenchmen at the Ministry these days. We're beginning to have our doubts about General de Gaulle."

*   *   *

Whatever doubts were disturbing back-bencher MPs and junior members of the Ministries which had to deal with him—and these doubts were first engendered by his own hostile and unpleasant attitude to men who had befriended him—de Gaulle developed his plan for personal glory with more confidence every day. Although not even his parade through Westminster on Bastille Day, the 'big occasion' on which Mr. Churchill had insisted, had brought many more volunteers to his tiny force, his staff had so enormously increased that the suite of rooms at St. Stephen's House was far too small to hold them. An entire building was requisitioned to serve as the Free French headquarters. Number 4, Carlton Gardens, was a handsome place, with many historical associations, although the tenants who were moved out to make room for the general were business people, prosaically occupied in selling paint and varnish. Moving on from the bare rooms and lavatory-tiled passages of St. Stephen's House, General de Gaulle, it was felt, would be in suitably dignified surroundings in Carlton Gardens, and only cynics with some recollection of ambitious Frenchmen remarked on the coincidence that from Carlton Gardens Louis Napoleon Bonaparte had gone forth on the adventure which made him, after a *coup d'état*, the Emperor of the French.

The general's mind was at ease about his family, on holiday at the time of his flight from Bordeaux. They had caught the last boat from Brest and were now safely in England, which gave his publicity man a chance to plant some human interest stories in the newspapers, and even some photographs of the general, tall and more awkward looking than ever, looming over Madame de Gaulle as she sat before a piano. It was not in the public interest to reveal that Mr. Churchill, still full of enthusiasm for his protégé, had sent a Sunderland aircraft to find de Gaulle's wife and children while they were still in France, and that the Sunderland and all its crew were lost.

The PR man, who had his work cut out to persuade his difficult client that he was not being 'sold like a new brand of soap', scored one success when he devised a poster which appeared in various pubs and restaurants, catering to the French colony in particular, after the move to Carlton Gardens. Addressed 'To All the French' and signed 'C. de Gaulle' it was less authoritarian than the claim to take All the French under his protection, and proclaimed that 'his aim, his only aim' was to ensure that France took part in the final victory. How this was to be achieved the poster did not explain, but de Gaulle himself had already decided that the seat of the French government (as he called it) which was continuing the struggle should move from England to French soil. Very soon after Bastille Day he had told the inner circle of his officers that they should be prepared to leave London for Africa in four to six weeks. "I have decided to establish the capital of our empire at war at Dakar," he said.

While the general dreamed of Africa, with all the ardour if not the genius of a Hannibal, another drama had been played out in the Far East. As soon as the Germans had forced the French to surrender, the Japanese addressed an ultimatum to General Catroux, the French Governor-General of Indo-China. He was required to close the border with China to all convoys of war *materiél*, and to admit Japanese officials to supervise the border traffic. Catroux made the usual appeals for help. There was no help to be had from France, stunned by defeat and surrender, or from Britain, fighting for survival. The United States was officially 'in no position to provide Indo-China with any support', for the names of Saigon, Hanoi, Cambodia and Laos meant nothing to the vast majority of Americans. But even the government at Vichy, prepared to collaborate with Germany and Italy, declined at that time to collaborate with Japan, and when General Catroux yielded to the Japanese ultimatum he was relieved of his post. He was now on his way to join de Gaulle, the first army officer of high rank to do so, although an elderly admiral named Muselier had 'rallied' soon after de Gaulle's first appeals. It was the absence of any Frenchman of known worth and stature in his entourage which fostered the doubts of de Gaulle that Neil Grant had expressed to Alison.

In Jacques Brunel's mind the doubts were very strong by the end of his first week in London. Although he steered clear of Carlton Gardens, and the offices in Whitehall which now housed what was called the Spears Mission—for as soon as General de Gaulle was 'recognised' by the British government the faithful Spears was accredited to him like an unofficial ambassador, and made responsible for all matters concerning relations with the Free French—he met many members of the French colony. He began by offering his services to the Refugee Committee, and in their rooms near Marble Arch did his best to help the Frenchmen and their wives who had trustingly come to Britain from the north-western ports. As a refreshment he saw Alison Grant nearly every day.

Getting ready to spend the day with her family on the Sunday after he came to London, Jacques thought, as Mike Marchand had thought before him, how quiet the Mount Street rooms were, overlooking the little park, over the hot summer weekend. There was not the faintest sound from the flat next door, for Mrs. Lindsay's nerves had been shaken when she found her neighbour insensible at the foot of the stair, and she and So Long were now with relatives in Wales. The sound of the sirens might have shaken her nerves still further, for the Alerts sounded intermittently in London as the air fighting intensified over the Channel. The enemy was shifting his attack from the east coast, from the Wash to the Thames, to points all along the south of England, and in retaliation Bomber Command was striking at the French ports where his invasion barges were mustering. Jacques had swiftly learned that everyone in London treated the Alerts with contempt.

It was far too warm to close the living room windows and put up the blackout before leaving for a day in the country, but Jacques made sure the bedroom, bathroom and tiny kitchenette were darkened before he left. As he moved from room to room it occurred to him, as on the evening of his arrival from Scotland, that never had any man left so little imprint on a place which had been his only home for nine months as Mike Marchand. The flat, with its chintz-covered furniture, its anonymous beige carpeting and flat water-colour pictures, might have been a hotel suite vacated for the next guest. The only things Mike had left behind were three suits in the wardrobe, which he had asked Jacques to use, and an address book begun by the flat's owner (now serving in the Middle East) with such useful names as a plumber, a dry cleaner, a locksmith and so on. In the same ring-leaf notebook Mike had filled a few pages with the names and addresses of his friends, nearly all French, and a diagonal line had been drawn across these pages with the word in Mike's handwriting 'Rapatriés'. Also in the same sprawling hand, a few lines had been added for Jacques' own benefit:

"*The Grants* you will know about from Alison! *Edmond Leblanc* is a good friend of mine; call him at the *Daily Journal* and ask for Eddie White, his *nom de plume*." At the bottom of the page Mike had scribbled, perhaps in a last minute inspiration, "If and when you go back to the Côte d'Azur, try to meet the *Baron de Valbonne*, formerly the naval attaché here. He was one of the best of them. Villa Rivabella, route de Fréjus, Cannes."

Even the shortest railway journey in wartime England was fraught with mystery for the foreigner since all identifications had been removed from the stations, and after Jacques' train left Waterloo he was carried through a number of places called Waverley Pens or Stephen's Blue-Black Inks. He hoped by keeping an eye on his watch to get off at the right destination, and when he reached what had once been Watermead Halt the best identification of all was there in the shape of Alison. She left the elderly ticket collector, the only other person to be seen, and ran up to the train laughing and waving—Alison in green cotton as bright as the summer day.

"You were going to get out at the right place, you clever Jacques!" she cried. "What d'you think of Watermead? Isn't it like a country station in the movies?"

"In the most English kind of movie," Jacques assured her, and bent his head to avoid the branch of rambler roses which trailed unpruned over the gate by the ticket collector's wooden kiosk. There were cabbage roses and mignonette in the flower-beds round the station, and when the train had gone it was possible to hear the sound of bees.

"They were going to close the Halt if it hadn't been for the war," Alison told him, as they walked away. "Now it's too useful for people like us who live this side of Kingsmead, and have to get up and down to London every day."

"You've stopped using the car, you said?"

"Neil thinks it isn't patriotic, even with his petrol allowance . . . It won't be too far for you to walk along to the cottage, will it? We reckon it isn't quite a mile."

"It's a perfect walk. Look at those water meadows, covered with yellow flowers! What do you call such flowers, in English?"

"Celandine, but they're almost over now." She named the wildflowers in the hedges twisted with eglantine and traveller's joy, and Jacques looked from foxglove and Queen Anne's Lace to Alison's blue eyes until she blushed and slowed her pace, and in the utter peace of summertime and an English lane he put his arms round her and kissed her with passion for the first time.

She realised the difference between that long and slow embrace and the spontaneous, almost brotherly hug he had given her when the train came in from Glasgow, and Alison, without a word spoken, let Jacques Brunel see and feel that love was in her heart. But under the storm of his kisses, the Frenchman's silence frightened her at last, and Alison, moving away a little, told him they were waited for—people knew what time the train came in—they must go on.

"Is your brother watching the clock?" said Jacques teasingly, as she led the way down the lane.

"My brother had just arrived when I left. He's been in his constituency, up on Thursday night, down on Saturday night, and you know what the trains are like."

"And Mrs. Grant and baby Mary, are they well?"

"Very well, and thank heaven Nurse Fielding leaves on Wednesday. She disapproves of us all so terribly—says she's never been in a place where no proper staff was kept. As if anyone had staff these days! I'm afraid Lime Tree Cottage was a dreadful come-down for Nurse Fielding."

A footpath from the Watermead lane led to a wooden gate set in a high wall. Beyond that lay an orchard of neglected apple and pear trees where two little boys in blue jerseys were playing in the uncut grass. They ran away at the sight of a stranger, though Alison called to them to come and shake hands nicely, and disappeared behind the screen of lime trees which gave Neil Grant's house its name.

Lime Tree Cottage was only two storeys high, but solidly built a century earlier of red brick which had faded to a pale rose, only a shade darker than the pink and cream clematis round the french windows. There was a tiled patio outside the front door, and there a gentle dark-haired young woman, sewing in a deck chair, was introduced by Alison as her sister-in-law, while the starched nurse, sitting bolt upright by the new baby in its pram, seemed prepared to resist attack by boys or foreigners.

"She's going to have red hair!" said Jacques, bending over the tiny girl, and Lucy Grant laughed.

"Yes, the boys are dark like me, but we think Mary's going to look exactly like Alison . . . Oh good, here comes Neil with the drinks trolley. He meant to meet you, but he wasn't ready in time."

"Sorry I didn't get to the station, but I only got home in the middle of the morning," said Neil, shaking hands. He had changed into an old blazer and flannel slacks. "Have you met all my family? Boys, come and say how do you do properly."

Colin, who whispered that he was five years old, and Peter, who was four, soon got over their shyness. They leaned against Jacques confidingly while he talked to their mother and Alison, and Neil poured little glasses of lemonade for them, which they tried to share with an elderly bull terrier called Sam. Very soon they were suggesting that the visitor should come and see the lovely air raid shelter Daddy had made down in the wine cellar.

"I expect he'd rather see the wine," said Neil. "We'll take him down and get him to select a bottle for us to drink at lunch, shall we? . . . No, Colin, not just yet! Let Monsieur Brunel finish his drink in peace."

"He's not Moosyoo Brunel, he's Captain Jack!" said Colin, and Alison laughed apologetically. "That's my fault, I'm afraid," she said. "Your hospital nickname's going to stick!"

"That's all right with me, I've got to like it."

"Time my little girl was back in her nice fresh nursery," said Miss Fielding, ostentatiously flapping away the smoke from the men's cigarettes. "Mrs. Grant, will it be convenient for me to have a tray upstairs?"

"Oh, certainly," said Lucy unconvincingly . . . "Alison, do you think Lottie—?"

"I'll look after it myself."

Jacques watched the green cotton dress disappear through the french windows with regret. He had already made up his mind that Alison was the effective member of the household, and when they all sat down to a rather haphazard meal, he noticed that it was she who carved the chicken and helped the panting girl called Lottie to serve fresh peas and new potatoes from the kitchen garden Neil said he had no time to cultivate. Alison made coffee in a glass percolator at the sideboard and served it in the patio; Alison said that while Lucy had her rest she would help Lottie with the dishes—"poor dear, she always hankers for the hectic excitements of Kingsmead on Sunday afternoons!"

"She doesn't live in the house?" said Jacques.

"She cycles from Kingsmead; it's just over two miles away by the main road."

"You'd never guess we're only fifteen miles from London," said Jacques. He stretched luxuriously. The place and the friendly people exactly suited him. The shabby old house, scented with pot pourri and lavender, the garden where the box hedges needed cutting back, the cows standing beneath the elms in the fields which belonged to a neighbouring farm, all added up to a fleeting dream of peace. But Neil, with a quick look to see if his wife had heard—and he thought not, for she was picking up her sewing—said, "Unless you're specially attached to that deck chair, Captain Jack—well, Jacques then—let's take the boys up the orchard and start them on a game of cricket. Otherwise they'll start yelling around here and disturb their mother and the baby."

The cricket match began in some confusion, for Neil was adamant that Captain Jack had been in hospital, and didn't want to bowl to little boys, but when it was settled that each boy was to bowl an over, turn and turn about, the men settled down on a rough log seat between the apple trees and a bare patch of turf which ran up to the farmer's fence.

"I wish we were a damned sight further from London than just fifteen miles," Neil began, as he filled his pipe. "Lucy gets so horribly nervous when there's a daytime Alert. I only wish I could have taken the whole lot of them to Scotland when I went up on Thursday night."

"Would that have been quite impossible?"

"Well—for one thing Lucy's doctor wasn't keen on it. You see, her parents live near Oban, which means changing trains at Glasgow. It's a tiring trip with a new baby and these two, so she's going to wait till the end of the month, when the House rises for a short recess and I can go along with them."

"What about Alison?"

"Alison says she can cope here by herself. I'll only be gone about a week—can't stay away longer from the Ministry, though I'll have to stop off in my constituency on the way south."

"Even though you were there yesterday?"

"Yesterday there was a big War Aims fête in Burns Bay, that's the largest town in Carrick, and I had to make a speech of sorts. They collected a lot of money for war charities, so I hope it was worthwhile."

"That's what I've been doing myself this week—trying to get people to give to charity."

"Through the Refugee Committee? Alison told me you had started work with them. But not on a permanent basis, surely?"

Jacques shrugged. "Is anything permanent?" he said. "It's something to do. It gives me time to look around—and to meet people."

"Forgive a blunt question—are they paying you?"

"Certainly not! They're all voluntary workers at Marble Arch . . . and I don't think they're half as efficient as Alison and her Comforts Committee friends."

"Apart from them, what other people have you met?"

"I've had dinner twice with Michel's friend, Edmond Leblanc. He's a reporter with the *Daily Journal*, under another name. I went to a meeting of the *Français de Grande Bretagne* with him last night, and made an appeal on behalf of the Refugee Committee. I daresay they knew far more about it than I did. One decent old boy, a butcher from Soho I believe, looked quite disgusted. He told me afterwards that an able-bodied young man like me ought to be with de Gaulle."

"I didn't know that crowd was so enthusiastic about de Gaulle."

"Leblanc says a good many of them are for the Marshal, but they daren't say so. They kid themselves that Marshal Pétain is playing a double game, pretending to go along with the Germans, but really backing Charles de Gaulle."

" 'Where ignorance is bliss'," said Neil . . . "Hey, Colin! Don't get in among the nettles!" Most of the cricketers' time seemed to be spent hunting for the ball, of the soft tennis variety, stained dark green.

"Michel was right, you know," said Jacques, when Neil came back from the nettle bed, blowing on his fingers.

"Right about de Gaulle, you mean?"

"Yes. Of course, being Mike Marchand, he had to go at it like a bull at a gate, and he needn't have made quite such a fuss about the enlistment oath—"

"I thought so at the time. 'I John Doe swear by Almighty God that I will be faithful and bear true allegiance to His Majesty King George the Sixth, His Heirs and Successors'—that's what Marchand would have had to swear if they'd let him join the RAF, and he wouldn't have kicked at that, would he?"

"But General de Gaulle isn't a sovereign—yet," said Jacques drily. "What I meant was that Michel needn't have made the personal oath an issue for his conscience. He'd plenty of other facts to go on. De Gaulle *is* creating a network of sympathisers, for *him*, not for his little legion, all round the world. Here he already has the *Français de Grande Bretagne*. In the United States, a group called *France Quand même*. Henri de Kerillis, the editor of *L'Echo de Paris*, has gone to represent him in Canada. He's got committees in Mexico, Havana, Egypt, Turkey, and half a dozen other places. He'd spread his propaganda round the world, if only he'd the money."

Neil Grant was tempted to tell him that within a few days, if his own information was correct, General de Gaulle's financial problems would be solved for the duration of the war. But there was no sense in jumping the gun. He wasn't sure yet of Jacques Brunel. The chap might turn out to be no more stable than his cousin Mike, who had passed on a vital piece of information on which action had been taken, and who had then left England without even attempting to do a follow-up. Neil was aware, also, that like ninety per cent of his colleagues at what was sometimes called 'the Ministry of Ungentlemanly Warfare', he was a rank amateur at the subtle science of espionage. He said,

"What exactly do you mean by 'propaganda'?"

"The line that's being pushed every day and every night on the BBC. Not only by de Gaulle and his official spokesman, but by the Frenchmen already working at Broadcasting House. That the Vichy government is illegitimate, and only *le Grand Charles* embodies the sovereignty of France."

"Do *you* think Pétain and the new French State are 'legitimate', as you call it?"

"At least they were elected by the people's Deputies. Which doesn't mean I approve of what the Deputies did."

"So if you won't accept Pétain *or* de Gaulle, you stand exactly where Mike Marchand stood?"

"Exactly. And I'm sure, sure as the sun is shining, that there are thousands like me all over France, who above all won't accept the German occupation. You don't hear about them yet, it's too soon, but before long—" Jacques broke off, and threw the grass-stained tennis ball, which had rolled to his feet, back to the shouting boys.

"Does that mean you want to go back to France?" said Neil carefully. "If so, it can be arranged. The hospital ships will be sailing right up to the end of September."

"Provided there isn't a repetition of the *Meknes* tragedy. No, I want to stay in London for a while. I've found a useful little job to do, and the Refugee Committee's a good listening post." Jacques had been watching the little cricketers. Now he looked directly at Neil Grant, and the older man for the first time saw that in spite of the black hair and deep brown eyes, the more aquiline features, there was a certain resemblance in Jacques to Mike Marchand.

"Do you realise how much I owe to my cousin Michel?" Jacques went on. "A roof over my head, and the clothes I'm wearing. Yes, and even the money he brought me from his uncle when I was in hospital. Just this breathing space—to see Alison, and be with your family today, and live in England, free to come and go—is due to Michel's generosity . . . I know you think he was wrong to take off for Brazil as if the devil were after him: for all we know the devil was. But I wouldn't worry about Michel if I were you. About now, he's just beginning to realise that he ran out when he should have stayed in the battle. And if I know him, it won't be long before he's back.''

9

JACQUES BRUNEL WAS wrong, but only by a few days, in his estimate of Mike Marchand's reactions after his return to Brazil. On the same day as his cousin tasted the fragrance of an English lane and an English orchard, Mike's thoughts as well as his body were six thousand miles away from the English scene. At a different hour, under a night sky where the Southern Cross was blazing, he was dining with Dina da Costa at the Yacht Club in Rio de Janeiro, looking, from their table in the garden, at the amazing view of the Sugar Loaf mountain and the lights of the city on the other side of Botafogo Bay.

Dina, who had some of Mike's own facility for living in the present, was as unconcerned as he was at that moment with the quarrels of the continent they had left behind. Since his telephone call on the previous Thursday morning she had thought about very little but Mike Marchand.

"Who? Who is speaking?" she said incredulously when the call came through to her office in the city. "Mike? At the airport? I don't believe it!"

"I've just cleared Customs," said the disembodied voice. "Got in half an hour ago."

"But—when did you leave London?"

"Four days after you did."

"Four days . . . but then you've been nearly two weeks on the way!"

"Not my fault. Our friend Jerry O'Hanlon got me out of Foynes, top priority, but there was a hold-up at Lisbon, and then at every whistle stop on the way south from New York. Dina, how are you? When can I see you?"

Dina hardly knew what she was saying. As they talked, she was looking across her desk at her own reflection in a mirror which hung on the office door, glad that the young man who had danced with her at the Hungaria could not see this different and unglamorous Senhorina da Costa of Capricorn Airways, with her black hair screwed into an uncompromising knot on top of her head, and a pencil stuck through the knot instead of a comb. But she was cool enough, when she heard her brother Tony entering his own office—an arrival always announced by cheerful whistling and much banging of desk drawers—to go in and say at once:

"Guess who's here! Mike Marchand just flew in from London!"

"How d'you know?"

"He called me from the airport."

"Quick work," said Tony da Costa. He was less dapper than on his visit to London. On the first of August it was mid-winter in Rio de Janeiro, and their ancient office building was cold enough for Tony to wear a sweater under his jacket, the sleeves protruding underneath his cuffs.

"He's done exactly what I advised him to do," said Dina complacently. "Got out of all that mess and come back here."

"You didn't know this was what he planned?"

"I? Certainly not!" But the little complacent smile was still there, and Tony said teasingly, "Don't take all the credit to yourself, my dear. Knowing the people Marchand was mixed up with in London, the place just *might* have got too hot to hold him—"

"You can ask him about that yourself."

"When am I going to meet him? When are you?"

"He's gone off to his uncle's house at Alto da Boa Vista. He asked me to dine with him tomorrow night."

"Where?"

"At the Copacabana Palace Hotel, where else?"

"Does he know we *live* at the Copa?"

"He does now."

"So you won't be flying me to São Paulo this weekend. Or should I stay in Rio and be your chaperon?"

"Tony, please—"

"All right, sweetie, I'll leave you on your own. Maybe Marchand needs a little time to settle down before I have a talk with him."

"He says he's going to take a week's holiday and then look for a job."

"I've got the ideal job lined up for him, if he wants it."

"I hope he does." And I pray, oh how I pray he does, said Dina's heart, when she was back in her own small office, too restless to sit down to her waybills and manifests, but looking down from her window at the crowded Rua do Ouvidor, where the shoeshine boys and the peddlers carrying their different loads of flowers, fish or candies on their heads jostled through the throng. Although it was a business district the wireless was blaring from half a dozen open windows, samba music challenging popular songs, and two or three mulatto beggar children were dancing where they stood in time to the samba rhythm. The stream of Dina's countrymen went past beneath her windows, of all colours, in Brazil's multiracial society, from white to the blackest black of Africa, *cabras, morenos, chulos,* Japanese. Dina wondered if the procession of human types, seen again for the first time after six years, would seem strange to Mike Marchand's European eyes.

He had been aware of the differences time had wrought as soon as he landed at Santos Dumont airport and walked to the Immigration Building, above which the green flag of the United States of Brazil was flying, with the world in blue on its golden lozenge. The airlines had changed. Panair do Brasil had enlarged its office buildings, Capricorn was new, Trans-Andean had disappeared, of course, swallowed up by Air France, the colossus which had taken over the Aéropostale, after *La Ligne* itself went down in 1933. There was no sign of life round Air France at Santos Dumont, and there probably had been none since the French surrender, but the victor's line was powerfully represented—Lufthansa, which had been trying to oust the French from South America since the earliest days of hydroplanes. It was a reminder to Mike Marchand of all he had been hoping to forget in Rio de Janeiro.

There was a new chauffeur to meet him, an unsmiling fellow who said his name was Emilio, and a new Packard waiting to take him to his uncle's house. That involved taking a new way home, for Senhor Ferreira had retired from banking while Mike was in Europe, and had gone to live at some distance from the city. It was not until the car had traversed Rio, that astonishing composite of hills and mountains, lake and beaches, all protected by the giant figure of Christ the Redeemer, and swung north through the forest, that Mike realised he had subconsciously been expecting to enter the old family home in the Gavea valley, tall and painted dark blue with white shutters, where from his bedroom window he had looked over tropical gardens to the distant ocean. Emilio told him the house and its grounds had been bought by the city, and would be used to enlarge a public park.

It was to be hoped that the protection of El Cristo Redentor was extended to the *favelas,* for the *favelas,* while not new, had spread further along and down the hillsides since Mike was last in Rio. As the city grew, so grew the slums, the wretched shacks which housed those who came from the vast hinterland of Brazil to find work in the city and found poverty and a life of crime instead. At some points the shacks, painted like foul flowers in pinks, yellows, blues, came very close to the streets of dun-coloured stone which formed the bourgeois background to the panorama of the splendid beaches which ringed the city. But where the Packard swung up the Tijuca highway there were no *favelas*. Only the tropical birds and butterflies haunted the forest, and above the birdsong there was no other sound but the ripple of the great Cascade.

Alto da Boa Vista was not a new development. It had been built a hundred years earlier by English settlers in Rio, who hoped by living in the mountain woods to avoid the yellow fever which regularly scourged the city. Senhor Ferreira had bought one of these old houses, which were built round a park, and although small by the standard of his previous home, it was surprisingly modern in its use of patterned woods and varnished bamboo screens dividing the verandas. He was on the veranda outside the front door when the car drew up, ready to greet his nephew with Brazilian embraces and words full of his old warm affection: Mike was concerned to find that his uncle's shoulders felt very thin and frail.

"Come straight to your room, my dear boy," he said. "Emilio, bring Senhor Marchand's bags . . . Are you exhausted, Mike? Do you want a drink first, would you like a bath, are you hungry, was it a terrible trip?"

"No, not too bad, and last night we had a stopover at Belem, so I had a good sleep. Let me clean up a little bit, uncle, and then I'd love to have a drink and hear all about everything."

"Maria will give us something to eat whenever we feel like it."

"Wonderful." The bedroom with its low wide bed looked pretty good too, and the bathroom with a new shower and tub. Mike stripped and looked at his reflection in the door mirror. The heavy bruising from his fall in Mount Street had stopped hurting, but there were still marks, blue and yellowish-green, on the skin above his ribs. He felt glad it was winter in Rio, and not the season for lying half-naked on the Rio beaches. The stitches in his scalp had been taken out in New York, and his thick fair hair was growing quickly where the cut had been.

Emilio had not only brought in the bags, but had laid out

fresh clothing in the bedroom, and Mike put on slacks and a thin turtle-necked sweater with a distinct sense of well-being. His uncle was waiting in a large room which extended to half the breadth of the house, with a dining table at one end and low modern chairs and tables at the other, set round a fireplace filled with a bouquet of pink camellias instead of logs.

"Do you like it, Mike?" Senhor Ferreira asked anxiously. "You don't think it's too—bare?"

"I like it enormously." In fact Mike thought the new furnishings, in their use of light and space as well as colour, a great improvement on the heavy mahogany and huge silver chandeliers of the former home.

"I gave all the family pieces to Heitor and Ruy when I moved up here," Senhor Ferreira explained. "Since both of them set up house in Ouro Preto those dear girls" (this was how he always alluded to his daughters-in-law) "have gone mad over colonial furniture and what the magazines call period reconstruction. So I thought they might as well have their share of my Empire pieces now as later, don't you agree?"

"It was a very kind thought, Uncle Pedro. But when did they move to Ouro Preto? I thought the boys were fixtures at Belo Horizonte."

"The offices are fixtures, but those dear girls thought the city was becoming 'impossibly vulgar' and when one persuaded her husband to move to Ouro Preto, of course the other had to follow suit. They're great competition for one another . . . I ordered *feijoada* for lunch, you'll have a *batida* first, of course?"

"Ouro Preto's seventy-five miles from the offices, they can't drive a round trip every day," said Mike, following his uncle to the drinks table. He wasn't quite sure about the *batida*, that mixture of *maracuja* and *cachaça* might be too sweet for a taste which of recent years had been based on Scotch, but his uncle was at work already with the bottles and a cocktail shaker. He told Mike, as he poured the drinks, that since Capricorn Airways had started a service between the two centres of the Minas Gerais, Heitor and Ruy got through a good deal of work now on the daily flights. "*Seja bemvindo!*" said the old man, lifting his glass to Mike. "I'm glad to have you home again, dear boy."

"I'm very glad to be back." Mike looked appreciatively round the room, at the flowers on the low tables and in the fireplace, at the mantel bare except for a few carved pieces of semi-precious stones on gold stands, and at the painting above the mantel. "Ah!" he said, going towards it, "you didn't give *that* away—I'm glad. It must be worth a fortune now."

He stood looking up, with his uncle silent by his side, at the portrait of his uncle's wife and his own mother, painted in the Paris of the *belle époque*.

In Renoir's glowing canvas of *Les Demoiselles Verbier*, the artist had painted the two sisters on a park bench, with their name flowers massed in the background and foreground, pink roses twined above their heads, and a bed of violets on the other side of the gravel path under their feet. Violette, newly engaged to the wealthy banker from Brazil, was pensively regarding her folded parasol as she traced a pattern in the gravel with its tip; Rose, in a schoolgirl's short white dress with black shoes and stockings, was perching on the arm of the park seat.

"How pretty they were!" said Mike. "1903. *Maman* must have been about fourteen then."

"Yes, for Violette was twenty. Rose was our little chaperone when I used to meet them in the Parc Monceau. Your grandpapa Verbier would never allow us to go for walks alone, even after we were engaged."

"He gave you a hard time, didn't he?" said Mike with a grin.

"Well, can you blame him? A Brazilian, working in a foreign bank, and fifteen years older than his cherished daughter? I commissioned that portrait from Renoir, you know, to console Monsieur and Madame Verbier for taking their girl so far away. I think they took it as solid proof that she wouldn't be going to a pauper's home."

"And then you turned out to be the family benefactor," said Mike, but his uncle was still studying the portrait.

"Lovely girls . . . they didn't make old bones, poor dears . . . You're a little bit like your mother, Mike . . . at least you have her colouring."

"I wish I could remember her looking young," said Mike. "She aged by thirty years after my father fell at Douaumont."

"Yes, Renoir painted them in happier days. And now, what a catastrophe! Poor Paris! Poor France!"

"Is it permitted to serve the gentlemen?" said a woman's submissive voice from the doorway.

"Are you hungry, Mike?"

"Yes thank you, Uncle Pedro."

It was a polite fiction, for after the haphazard meals in indifferent restaurants—in San Juan, Port of Spain, Belem, on his flight from New York—Mike's appetite was not adjusted to Rio time. But the *feijoada* brought it back at once, it had always been one of his favourite dishes, that mixture of black beans with pork and beef, covered with a boiled green leaf of kale and served on cassava flour with slices of orange. It had another taste than the tastes of Europe, and *batida* was the right drink to go before it. He had another.

"Your cook makes a first-rate dish of *feijoada*," he said.

"Maria? Yes, she cooks everything well. She's Emilio's wife, you know. They came to me, when I moved up here two years ago, from the State of São Paulo."

"Italians?"

"Emilio's parents emigrated from Turin, I believe, and Maria's from Verona."

That didn't make them Fascists of course, any more than drinking the excellent beer from one of Brazil's German breweries which accompanied the *feijoada* made Mike Marchand a Nazi. Italian or German immigrants, they were all *brasileiros* now, and prosperous good citizens. As he would be, once he settled down to it.

"I beg your pardon, uncle?"

"I was asking if you think the British really mean to carry on the war with the Axis?"

"Absolutely. Why? Don't people in Rio understand that they won't give in?"

Senhor Ferreira shook his head. "There's a great deal of pro-German propaganda in the city. Enormous bribes have been given to certain sections of the press, the radio and the cinema industry, and of course the smashing victories in June impressed everyone who saw the movie newsreels. Last December, when the *Admiral Graf Spee* was scuttled, it was different. I had Emilio drive me down to the docks to see the aircraft carrier, *Ark Royal*, when she put in to Rio to refuel on her way to the River Plate. People were swarming over the waterfront, cheering the British sailors. At heart, I believe Brazil would welcome a British victory."

The talk went on, from the war to family affairs and back again, until even after the stimulus of several *cafézinhos* the old gentleman grew drowsy, and went off to take a long siesta while Mike explored the beautiful mountain suburb and its flowering park. It was cool enough at that altitude for a wood fire to be lighted when dusk fell, and before the candles were lit Heitor Ferreira telephoned from Ouro Preto to bid Mike welcome home to Brazil, and say how much he and his brother, and their wives, looked forward to seeing him soon. A word to Heitor about the air service between the eighteenth century capital of Minas Gerais and the new was all Mike needed, when the telephone call was over, to introduce the subject of the da Costas.

"Capricorn Airways must be doing well," he said casually. "I met Tony da Costa and his sister when they were in London."

"Did you indeed? Didn't you know Tony when you lived in Rio last?"

"He spent most of his time in São Paulo then. Didn't he marry one of the Chaves girls?"

"Yes, Tereza. Poor dear, she died when their little boy was born. The da Costa parents have him in São Paulo; I suppose he must be six or seven now."

"Tony da Costa didn't marry again?"

"Too busy being a playboy to need another wife."

"He can't be much of a playboy if he's running an airline and selling canned foods to the British government."

Senhor Ferreira grunted. "And conniving with the President's advisors about the building of a new capital, which was the big project in my father's day. I don't believe I'll live to see it realised. At least not by young da Costa and the new *Bandeirantes*."

"The *Bandeirantes*?"

"Have you forgotten your Portuguese history, boy? The Flag-bearers of the Conquest. That's what the popular press calls the da Costa mob—the Flagbearers, brought up to date."

"I can see you don't care for Senhor da Costa," said Mike, and was glad that beyond the firelight his face was in shadow. "His sister's a very attractive girl."

"What's her name?"

"Diviniñha."

"Ah, then it's not the one Ruy's wife was at school with. That would be the older sister, Ester, a girl about your own age. The Saint of the *favelas*, they call her up at São Paulo. A deeply religious girl, and a dedicated social worker. The young one goes around flying in some sort of air circus, I've been told."

"She's got a pilot's 'A' certificate, and she works for Capricorn Airways."

"Indeed!" said Senhor Ferreira. He snapped open a lighter, and before holding it to his cigar studied Mike by the light of the tiny flame. "You seem to have learned a good deal about the young lady in a short time. Did you see much of her in London?"

"No, not much. But I'm taking her out to dinner tomorrow night."

"By previous arrangement, if I may ask?"

"I telephoned her from the airport as soon as I got in. Emilio had to wait ten more minutes, he didn't seem to mind."

"I see." Mike's uncle smoked in silence for a few minutes. "I've never met Senhorina Divinĩha, and I hardly know her parents. But a combination of mixed blood and new money is something I have never liked."

"Everyone has mixed blood in Brazil."

"Mixed European blood—of course, my own sons have that, Portuguese and French. But the da Costas are Euro-Afro-Indio, Mike. That can be a lethal combination."

"There's good French blood in the family, only two generations back. I've heard you talk yourself about the great Bernard Bresson—"

"Peddling fat from door to door? I've nothing against old Bresson, he was a real buccaneer!" And the serious moment was blown away in a gust of laughter, as Emilio came in to light the candles and switch on subdued electric lamps in dark corners before he laid the table for the evening meal.

Euro-Afro-Indio. Mike knew quite well that it was a Brazilian mixture, and one which in all its shades and nuances from ivory to bronze produced some of the most exotic girls in the world. He saw many of them next day, when his uncle took him into the city to lunch with old friends at the Jockey Club. The Leblon district was full of lovely girls, strolling in twos and threes round the lake or heading down the broad avenues to the beach. They were wearing the American styles which their dressmakers copied from *Vogue*, with sweetheart necklines, tiny waists and wedge heels, their beautiful hair—often true blond or copper-coloured—combed into a pompadour and then falling free to their shoulders, and as they went past their black eyes glinted with appreciation of the tall, fair young man whom they took to be an American. Senhor Ferreira murmured in French that they seemed to find Mike *séduisant*. But for Mike none of them had the fierce charm of Dina da Costa, and when he saw her coming to meet him across the lobby of the Copacabana Palace at nine o'clock that evening he thought that no artist would paint her in a setting of roses and violets. The bird-of-paradise flower, which with its stiff petals of flame and purple grew so luxuriantly in Brazil, was the right background for Dina.

Dina herself had given time and thought to her appearance. The suite she shared with her brother in the city's leading hotel was not a large one, and most of her clothes were kept in her parents' house in São Paulo. But she had two dinner dresses in her wardrobe at Rio, one of scarlet chiffon bought in London, and the other which Mike Marchand had already seen her wear. After consideration she decided on the white. By intuition, she believed he would like to see her again exactly as he left her, on the night of 'The Last Time I saw Paris', when he asked her if she believed in love at first sight. So she wore the white dress, the gold belt and the gold sandals, and only changed the gold bag for a white satin purse so that she could pin on to it a bud cut from the bouquet of dark red roses which Mike had sent her in the afternoon. The windows of the little sitting room were closed, because the night was windy, and the scent of the roses completely filled the air.

When the reception clerk announced Mike's arrival by telephone Dina took a deep breath and looked round the room regretfully. That was where they ought to be meeting, alone, with the wintry sound of the South Atlantic rollers just audible beyond the windows, cutting them off from the world. But not even Dina da Costa, whose unconventionality had outraged society more than once, dared risk inviting any man to the suite in her brother's absence, or even—the more straitlaced Brazilian matrons might have said—in his presence too. A 'millionaire playboy', which was how society thought of Antonio da Costa, was not a suitable chaperon for an unmarried girl. So Dina picked up her bag and the same wisp of summer ermine she had worn in London, and went downstairs.

"Maria da Gloria!" he said when they met, with an emphasis on the *Gloria* which made the name an anthem, and all Dina could reply was, "I told you we'd meet again, I didn't know it would be so soon!" It was exactly three weeks since the night they met in London.

She thought, as he settled her at a table in the dining room, that though three weeks was an amazingly short time considering the immense distance they had covered, it might in time have been three minutes, as if the *batidas* the Brazilian waiter brought them were the liqueurs they had been offered at the Hungaria. Mike and Dina were together again, plunged at once into the professional talk so important to them both, and discussing the technicalities of all their flights between London and the City of San Sebastian of January River. But Mike was quite aware that he was not talking to another flight engineer. His eyes were learning Dina again, from her own cool grey eyes under the black silk hair to the creamy curve of breast just visible beneath her dress, and resting, more than she liked, on her square and capable fingers with the unpainted nails.

"Don't look at my hands," she said defensively. "I've had no time to go to the beauty parlour. I've been flying every day this week, except yesterday."

"Lucky you."

"But you just—oh, but of course you were a passenger. Would you like to take up the Puss tomorrow?"

"I only wish I could."

"Probably you'd rather try the Beechcraft. But Tony won't be back until next Friday, I'm afraid. He left his best regards, he's dying to have a talk with you. But he did want to spend the weekend in São Paulo with his little boy."

"I only heard yesterday about the little boy. I didn't know your brother was a widower."

"Yes, poor Tereza died when Tony was only twenty-nine. That's one of the reasons why I work for Capricorn—because he and I have always been very close, and he likes having someone he can talk to about little Tonio, as well as about our work."

"Otherwise you'd cut out all the paper work, and qualify as a test pilot?"

She had a suspicion Mike was laughing at her, but she answered seriously enough, "I don't think Brazilians are ready to accept a woman *test* pilot yet. And anyway I rather enjoy the paper work, as you call it. It's a real job, and when I was at school here in Rio I made up my mind I'd *do* a real job, and not be like the lazy Carioca girls who couldn't talk about anything but who's the best hairdresser, and which is the best beach . . . They're nearly all married now. Most of them have had their second child and their first lover by this time, and they're still talking about the beaches. Only it's about their kids going there, and is the nursemaid teaching them voodoo, and the worship of Ipanema instead of the Holy Virgin—"

"But the beaches are part of the Carioca way of life."

"Not for me, thank you. I'm a Paulista girl, and proud of it."

Mike laughed, and the *vatapá* was served, and the Paulista girl ate it with a zest which showed that she enjoyed Bahian cookery. They drank *vinho verde* from Portugal, and talked about Lisbon, where Mike had a three day stopover on his way to New York, and the *fado* music they both loved, and the time went by so quickly that both Mike and Dina were surprised when a big burst of sound came from the Copa's nightclub on the floor below.

"Shall we go downstairs and dance, Dina?" After the Hungaria, he had to ask it, although he felt too tired for the samba rhythm. But Dina declined: if the saxophones had started it was half past eleven, and high time for a girl to go to bed who had to be on duty at the airport at first light.

"Do the passengers still turn up before dawn no matter where they're going, and stand around drinking *cafézinhos* until the pilots are ready to take off?" said Mike.

"They do indeed, and bring all their families with them to watch the take-off. Would *you* like to come out tomorrow? I'd love to show you the Capricorn set-up."

"I can't tomorrow, but I will come soon. Now, how about tomorrow night? Do they still sing *fados* in that little place on the beach at Leme? If I pick you up here, could we go along there about ten o'clock?"

She said she would love it, and they rose to go. It was not late by Rio standards, but the lobby was very quiet, and Mike drew Dina towards the revolving doors.

"Come round the colonnade with me, darling. It isn't cold, and you've got your fur."

With her senses throbbing, Dina followed him into the stone courtyard which separated the hotel from the Avenida Atlántica and the ocean. The wind had dropped, and the roar of the breakers was very loud. Some of the boutiques under the stone arches round the courtyard were still lighted, and the coloured lamps turned Dina's white dress, as she passed from the shadowed pavement to the light, to the purple and flame of the bird-of-paradise flower.

"Dina!"

They were sheltered, behind the stone pillars, from every

prying eye, and they could see, along the vast curve of the beach, from the spit of land on the right which divided Copacabana from Ipanema to the strangely shaped green hills of Leme to the left, the famous 'diamond necklace' of lights which was the pride of Rio, and the throb of samba rhythm came from the club behind them. With the samba in her blood and the ocean roll in his, Dina knew the first satisfaction of her life in Marchand's arms.

*   *   *

And yet, when she was alone in her bedroom, with the heat of those wild kisses still in her lips, Dina da Costa's first reaction was to wonder what she had done wrong. Once again, as at the Hungaria when the girl sang 'The Last Time I saw Paris', she had sensed Mike's sudden and complete withdrawal of spirit. There had been no such withdrawal in the Copa restaurant; they were on the same wave-length and Dina had kept it that way, not for a fortune would she have alluded to her brother's intervention, before they left London, in the matter of the German pilots masquerading as Gaullist officers. That was a matter for Mike and Tony, not for her, and no shadow fell across their harmony until the very end, when they were walking back dreamily to the door of the hotel. Then she had said—something silly—about blown sand from the beach getting inside her shoes, but *that* wasn't important, surely? And after that, walking so slowly, with his arm round her, she had said from the depth of her content, "No air raid warning tonight!"—was *that* wrong? Mike had said abruptly, "No, we're quite safe here," and that was when she felt the chill.

The chambermaid, who knew her schedule, had laid out the newly-pressed blue skirt and jacket with the Capricorn emblem on the lapel which Dina wore on airport mornings, with the fresh white blouse and black court shoes which completed the uniform. The clothes made her think of that other awkward moment, which Dina had passed over quickly, when she had asked Mike if he would like to take the Puss Moth up, and he had said he wished he could. Why not? What was the reason? Were there to be perplexities, evasions, in what she had felt to be a certain happiness? Dina comforted herself, as she turned on her hot pillow, with the memory of Mike's kisses.

In the succeeding days there was nothing but serenity. Mike called for her on Saturday evening in a Duesenberg which he had bought that day from an American businessman about to return to Florida. It had been through a good many hands before it reached Mike's, but it had the fashionable merits of being powerful, noisy and painted a violent shade of yellow, and in the supercharged roadster, with Dina's black hair blowing in the wind, they went screaming along the beaches to hear the *fado* singers at the little place in Leme. On Sunday night they went to the Yacht Club, on the next nights to mountain resorts near the waterfalls and the tropical forest, and then on Thursday at lunch time Mike announced that he was moving in to town to live.

"You mean you've taken a flat? With servants and all that?"

"No, I can't be bothered with servants. I've got myself fixed up in a new hotel in Flamengo. Central, and handy for Flamengo beach too, you and I can compare notes on which beach we go to, like your friends at school—"

"Mike, please be sensible. I'm thinking about your uncle. Won't he be hurt? Wasn't he expecting you to make your home with him?"

"Darling, I can't go on using his house as a hotel, can I now? And it takes far too long to get up and down to Alto da Boa Vista, even in the Duesenberg. Uncle Pedro never expected me to live there permanently."

"But I thought you did live permanently, if that's the word, in that beautiful house beside the park at Gavea."

"Only for the year after I left school, when I first came out from France. Afterwards I lived in the Trans-Andean crew quarters, here and at Santiago de Chile. It's all right, Dina. Uncle Pedro understands." What the old gentleman had actually said was, "I'm here when you need me, dear boy. Come up often, and remember, when I was your age I liked my freedom too." He was not ill-pleased to return to his solitary routine, catered to by Maria and Emilio, the kitchen maid and the garden boy, with the painting by Renoir his only reminder of the troubled world beyond Guanabara Bay.

"When are you moving to Flamengo?"

"Monday morning. Now, what are we going to eat?"

They were in the 'Cabaça Grande,' a famous fish restaurant in the Rua do Ouvidor. It was only a few steps from the Capricorn Airways office, and Dina herself had suggested it for that very reason; in her brother's absence she was kept close to the office and the telephone. The service was fast at the 'Cabaça Grande', and also noisy: the clatter of plates in the kitchen sinks was as loud as the clatter of china in the dining room, and each table was crammed with talkative businessmen. There were very few women in the restaurant, and by the prompt and respectful service Dina received Mike was able to estimate Senhorina da Costa's high position in the business community of the Rua do Ouvidor.

They decided on grilled salt cod moistened with olive oil. Dina never drank wine at lunch time and asked for a *cafézinho* instead of dessert. Mike drank Brazilian-brewed German beer. It was the first time they had met for luncheon, and then only at Mike's insistence 'because he had news for her'—Dina had not expected the news to be that he meant to start his Rio life all over again, this time in a hotel in Flamengo. He was restless, she had realised that since their first evening at the Copa, and it was a restlessness she had come to know very well among the pilots she met out at Santos Dumont or in São Paulo. Now he apparently had another restless project, which was to take the Duesenberg and visit Petropolis on Sunday, he hadn't been in Petropolis since he was a boy. Dina tried in vain to tell him that Petropolis, the summer capital, would be buried in wet fog at this time of year, that he ought to take his uncle for a drive instead (though it was hard to imagine a staid old gentleman in the Duesenberg) and that her parents insisted she return to São Paulo for the weekend. To all these objections Mike replied with smiles and shakes of the head. It seemed to Dina that he would have brushed her arguments aside with a Brazilian gesture, if such a gesture would not have meant upsetting, in their crowded surroundings, at least one tray piled with plates and glasses.

Or if he had been able to hear what those arguments were.

Dina had thought once or twice before that Mike was hard of hearing. Not that he ever failed to answer her, but he had a concentrated way of listening, or rather of trying hard to listen, which in itself was revealing, and at the wheel of the Duesenberg, in the thick of the Rio traffic, he clearly made no attempt to listen. The uproar of the street outside and the under roar of the 'Cabaça Grande' made the restaurant the noisiest place they had ever visited together. Today it was clear that he couldn't hear her at all, and the key to much that had perplexed Dina was in her hands.

"I must go back to the office, Mike," she said loudly.

"Senhorina Lobos will collapse if she's left in charge much longer. And I've got to leave my desk tidy if I'm flying to São Paulo in the morning."

"Oh, what's all this about going up to São Paulo?" But Mike followed her amiably, a few crowded yards past the newspaper boys and the candy vendors, to the heavy door of the building Capricorn shared with two other firms. "Aren't you going to show me round?" he said as they entered the dingy lobby.

"Tony'll do that tomorrow. Mike! There's something I want to ask you, something very personal, do you mind?"

"What is it, Dina?" He watched her close the door to shut out the noise from the street, and Mike's head dropped, his mouth set mulishly, as if he anticipated what was coming next. "Are you deaf?"

He said with a twisted smile, "That's a pilot's occupational hazard, dear."

She knew about some of the hazards: the open cockpits of the early days, the changes in atmospheric pressure, the thunderheads that hung above the Amazon. But Dina continued bravely,

"But you're deaf because of the crash in Senegal?"

"Yes."

"That's why you don't want to fly the Puss?"

"That's why I'm *not allowed* to fly the Puss, or any other kite. I'm grounded, Dina. I've failed three medical examinations because of vertigo. It can hit me any time—on a staircase, twice this year already. On a roof top once, in Bucharest. And other times as well. Darling, it kills me to talk about it, especially to you. I'm so ashamed—"

"What's there to be ashamed about? I know three—four— flyers who've had the very same thing, and got over it. They were *cured*, Mike, as you could be! . . . What sort of doctors were they, who grounded you? The house surgeons, at Dakar?"

"No, it wasn't at Dakar. That's where they patched me up and started me walking again. The vertigo began later, back in France. The company doctor diagnosed it first, before I started work in Bucharest. Then two military doctors turned me down, for the French Air Force and for the RAF."

"But you never saw a specialist?"

"No."

"And that's what's been destroying you all this time. that you couldn't fly for the RAF?"

"Yes."

She was too proud to ask him the question which might have meant the destruction of her own confidence: "Was that why you left England? That, and not because of me?" But not too proud to embrace him, like any little Brazilian typist kissing her boy friend behind the door, and whisper, "It'll all come right, darling! I'll ask my sister Ester—she'll know the best doctor in Brazil!" so that Miss Lobos, coming indignantly downstairs to her belated lunch, gasped "*A estimada senhorina!*" as she fled past the shamelessly embracing couple into the Rua do Ouvidor.

* * *

Mike Marchand went back to Santos Dumont airport next morning at nine o'clock. The scene of his early triumphs had not changed much in six years, for civil aviation had just begun to expand in the vast country, where barely one hundred civil aircraft were licensed to fly. There was some expansion of the private hangars, and Mike, having asked the direction from a bored policeman who made no sort of security check, walked round the concrete apron to the hangar where the da Costas kept their own planes.

Dina was there, just finishing—as she had told him she would be—the maintenance checks on the Puss Moth, with two mechanics looking on. Mike, who knew the routine so well, saw that she had completed checking the wiring and switches and was examining the air screw for truth; she gave him, across the fuselage, the pilot's half salute. Dina was wearing overalls, with her hair tied up in a red bandanna, and she might have begun wearing rubber gloves, for Mike saw a pair on the ground beside her, but like all good workmen she was carrying on the job with her bare hands, now black with oil and graphite.

"Shan't be long, Mike," she said tersely, and as soon as she had finished her check for torn fabric and cracks she rubbed her hands in the tin of solvent one of the boys brought up, and wiped them on a filthy towel.

"Do you do this every day?" Mike asked.

"When I'm flying I do. Otherwise the boys do it, they're pretty good . . . Thanks, Pedro," she said to the senior mechanic. "I'll take off as soon as Senhor da Costa arrives."

As they walked away towards the terminal building, Mike smiled at the vivid and now dirty face. "You're a proper grease monkey," he said. "Are you working for your 'C' licence as well as your 'B'?"

"Ground engineer? I'll never be good enough for that. But I *am* filthy, Mike; come and talk to our traffic manager while I clean up. Rinaldo's a bit of an old woman, he's always complaining about being overworked, but he gets on well with the station bosses, which pleases Tony. Here he comes."

Senhor Rinaldo was a thin, anxious mulatto, shivering in the grip of one of the minor fevers which still afflicted Rio: he showed Mike the Capricorn ticket counters and freight offices with many references to the races won by Mike Marchand. To Mike it didn't seem as if the manager need be overworked, because Capricorn Airways was a long way from the realisation of Tony's dream of an air bridge with planes flying every hour on the hour between Rio and São Paulo. What they had was two flights a day, early morning and late afternoon, in each direction on the three-leg-route Rio–São Paulo–Santos, using their sixteen-seater Brazilian Deodoros, supplemented by two return flights each day on the 'milk run' between São Paulo and Santos only, using Beechcrafts. Twice a week they flew Deodoros from Rio to Salvador in Bahia via Bela Horizonte, again with the 'milk runs' between Belo Horizonte and Ouro Preto on which the young Ferreiras were regular passengers. Senhor Rinaldo told Mike that the next terminals in the service would be, northwards, to Recife in the State of Pernambuco, and below the Tropic of Capricorn to Porto Alegre in Rio Grande do Sul.

"I'm tremendously impressed," Mike told Dina when she came back. There were not many people in the main concourse of the passenger building. The 'dawn patrol', as the pilots called it, when the early morning planes went out with their loads of nervous passengers accompanied by wailing relatives, was well over, and the incoming flights from Montevideo and Buenos Aires were not expected until the afternoon. There was nobody in Dina da Costa's path as she walked to the corner where the men were waiting, slim and long-legged in her black slacks and thin black sweater, with her flying jacket hitched over her shoulder by the middle finger of one hand and her flying helmet dangling from the other.

"It's a pretty good start, isn't it?" she said, and Senhor Rinaldo, promising to send a girl with two *cafézinhos*, slid quietly away.

146

"*You* look pretty good in that outfit," said Mike. It was the other Dina, the flyer, not the bird-of-paradise flower: he didn't know which of them he loved the most.

"Thank you, darling . . . Ah, here comes the coffee. Bless you, Belinda, how quick you've been!" As soon as the girl had gone (a ticket agent? a stewardess between flights? Mike wondered) Dina took a folded paper from the pocket of her slacks. "I called Ester last night," she said. "This is the doctor's name and address. She says he's the best ear, nose and throat man in Rio."

" 'Dr. Elias Baumeister'," read Mike from the paper. "German?"

"A Jewish refugee from Leipzig. Ester met him through this health service she tries to run in the *favelas*. He was giving his services to the patients, free, while he was getting his licence to practise medicine in Brazil. Mike, you *will* go to see him, won't you? It might just make all the difference—"

"I know it might, darling." And then a few words came through a loudspeaker, so completely indistinguishable to Mike that he knew the Jewish refugee was his last hope, and Dina said, "Here comes Tony now."

They went, with the few people still in the hall, to the big plate glass windows, and in a few minutes saw the Beechcraft coming through the cloud ceiling, low on this wintry day. There was no other traffic in the air or on the ground, and the pilot made a direct approach, landing in a series of bounces which made Mike conclude that Tony da Costa, in flight, was what American pilots called a drugstore cowboy. He taxied gently up to the parking bay where his own mechanic was signalling with a flag.

"I'll go and get another coffee," said Dina. "It's the first thing he wants after he's landed."

Tony, in the passenger hall, made as exuberant an entry as at the Brazilian Embassy in London, with a Hello, Dina; coffee, good! and a Hello, Monsieur Marchand, glad to meet you properly at last, and a word to Senhor Rinaldo, and another to Dina about the cumulo-nimbus front closing in fifty miles south of São Paulo.

"I'd better be off then." the girl said. "Tony, the Recife report's at the office, Senhorina Lobos knows. Mike, *don't forget!*"

"I won't," said Mike. "Happy landings! Will you call me when you get in?"

"Call you where?"

"At the office," said her brother, draining his coffee cup. "At least, I hope Monsieur Marchand's coming back with me?"

"I'd like to." Mike's eyes were on Dina's face. Under the close flying helmet, with her hair hidden, her high cheekbones revealed the Indian heritage in what Mike's uncle had called the Euro-Afro-Indio blood of the da Costas. She smiled goodbye to them both, and the men watched in silence as she walked across the concrete to the Puss Moth, which the mechanics had rolled out of the hangar in readiness. They helped her aboard and pulled away the chocks.

"Off she goes!" said Mike, as Dina, gaining altitude quickly, disappeared through the clouds, and at the note of regret in his voice Tony said jokingly, "Did you think she'd come back and waggle her wings at us?"

"She's too much of a professional for that."

"She is. How about hunting up a taxi?"

"I've got a *chignole* of my own in the parking lot."

*   *   *

Tony da Costa's private room was the largest in the unpretentious offices on the Rua da Ouvidor, and with the window shut against the noise of the street it was also warm and comfortable. There was no attempt at expensive furnishings, but there was a handsome map of Brazil behind Tony's big desk, showing the actual and future network of Capricorn Airways, and a still handsomer map of the Eastern and Western Hemispheres in the form of a mural, which occupied the entire wall opposite the window. Senhorina Lobos, bringing the inevitable *cafézinhos*, was told No visitors, No telephone calls for the next half-hour.

"I've drunk more and better coffee in ten days in Rio," said Mike, accepting a thin black cigar, "than I drank between September and July in London."

"London coffee's pretty foul," said Tony. "We enjoyed our time there, though."

"You did me a good turn, just before you left. Telephoning to Mr. Grant about those two creeps from Condor."

"Oh yes, I remember. You'd had some sort of row with them, hadn't you?"

"You could call it that."

"I called Neil Grant to tell him my sister gave a positive

148

identification on Lachmann, and from her description the other chap sounded to me like Schnaebel. He told you about it?''

''We had a long talk later on. Whether he'll *do* anything about it, I don't know. I left right after that.''

''I hope they're both in the Tower of London. I'd do anything to see that Condor mob in trouble—they moved heaven and earth to keep Capricorn from going in to Salvador.''

''You mean that was why you—''

''Why else? Why should I care if General de Gaulle has two ex-Nazi pilots at his GHQ? De Gaulle's Mr. Churchill's problem child, not mine . . . Anyway you're well out of that mess, Mike. Can I call you that? Mike Marchand—it's still a name to conjure with, in Rio.''

''I haven't seen much sign of that since I came back.''

''You haven't been around for long. What are your future plans? Any possibility of your joining up with the Ferreira brothers?''

''None at all. Heitor's a mining engineer, Ruy's an expert gemologist, and aviation's been *my* line, ever since I first came out to Rio.''

''Then could I interest you in coming in to Capricorn Airways?''

Marchand was not unprepared for the question. He extinguished his cigar before he said, ''In what capacity?''

''We could call your job assistant managing director. Assistant to the president of the company, if you like—that's me. Directing all the Rio operation, to begin with, so that I can spend more time at the factory in São Paulo.''

''I haven't heard about the factory.''

''I'm setting it up to manufacture small two-seater planes, designed like the De Havilland Moths. The kind of aircraft men like your cousins could fly to the mines themselves. There's a big market for the executive aircraft in the State of São Paulo alone—and you know, of course, that it's five times the size of Great Britain.''

Then the New Flagbearer, tilting himself back in his chair, treated his visitor to a glowing account of the future of civil aviation in Brazil and its rôle in opening up the enormous country from a humanitarian as well as an economic point of view. He pictured the twenty-five thousand paying air passengers of the previous year becoming twenty-five million, the ailing Indians of the Amazon jungles being transported to hospital or cared for by a flying doctor service, he described new links forged by air between Brazil and the other republics of South America. Mike nodded at intervals. It was as good a sales pitch as he had ever heard in his Air France days, and he thought a great deal of it made sense. He also thought that when Tony da Costa was roused to enthusiasm—and that was often—the African element in his blood-lines seemed to become more pronounced. The European predominated, the other lines were there.

"You're on to a very big thing, Tony," he said when the enthusiast at last paused for breath. "The factory'll eat up your capital at first, but if you get the new charters north and south you'll soon be in the black. As to what *I* can do for Capricorn, that'll take a bit of thinking over."

"Take all the time you want."

"Just give me one assurance. If I join you, in any capacity, and if I pass my next medical, will you give me a chance to fly?"

"Oh now," said Tony da Costa, "flying? That's something else again—if you mean flying as a pilot?"

"Yes."

"How long is it since you took up a plane?"

"Four years."

"Mike, I've *got* six pilots, as good as any in Brazil, and not one of them a day older than twenty-five."

"You sound like the old chair-borne commodore I met in England, who told me flying was a game for younger men."

"He had an angle there."

"He meant combat flying, of course. I could fly a Beechcraft, or even a Deodoro, tomorrow if I had to."

"But you could do a damn sight more than that without touching the controls of any aircraft. You and I could be in at the start of transatlantic flights out of Brazil, in Brazilian planes. Look what BOAC did this very week. In spite of the war, in spite of the Luftwaffe, they sent their first passenger flight across the North Atlantic from Foynes to Newfoundland. Their first challenge to Pan Am. And in the job you had in London you must have known the British are working on jet propulsion —think what that'll mean to us, after the war! I'm giving you a chance to get in on the ground floor in passenger transportation—"

"Yes, I know. But I've never had anything to do with passengers, except listening to their complaints at Bucharest."

Tony da Costa sighed. "I know your trouble. I used to suffer from it myself, because I'm only a few years older than you are. When we were boys, flying was heroic. Now it's a matter of getting from there to where. We were brought up on Lucky Lindy, and Guillamet crashing in the Andes and walking out on foot, and the fifty-three take-offs of Jean Mermoz. The next great adventure was flying the mail. And then flying by night, when St. Exupéry had only three petrol flares in a triangle to guide him down to the airstrip. Those days are over for good. Lindbergh and Saint-Ex. and Mermoz are yesterday's heroes now."

"Meaning that I'm one of yesterday's heroes too?"

"Yes you are, Mike. I hate to say it, but it's true. You and Bert Hinkler and Amelia Earhart and Jim Mollison—all the second flight of record-breakers—are as out of date as Santos Dumont or the Wright Brothers. You, yourself, were just unlucky in your timing. You were too young for the glamour days of the Aéropostale when Mermoz was the shooting star, and you're too old, let's face it, for the RAF. But last Monday BOAC's *Clare* crossed from Foynes to Newfoundland in sixteen hours. You and I can be in business, bang on time, and barely middle-aged, when passengers cross from London to New York in six."

"Yes, I know," said Mike, almost absently. "The airways are shortening every day. But the route Jean Mermoz opened ten years ago is just the same as it ever was. I've been thinking about it a lot lately." He got up. "Your mural shows it as clear as print. Until Mermoz flew the South Atlantic, from Senegal to Brazil, it took ten days for the mail to cross the ocean. Mermoz carried the first air mail in twenty-one hours. And it's only seventeen hundred miles from Natal in Brazil to Senegal—the nearest point between two hemispheres. The whole of the United States and South America could be threatened by war planes flying to the bulge of Brazil from the bulge of West Africa. From this little place on your map called Dakar.''

10

WHEN MIKE MARCHAND first knew Dakar, during his long stay in hospital there in 1936, it was a port town of less than one hundred thousand inhabitants, and although officially the capital of French West Africa, was notable only for the export of groundnuts. Where groundnuts had once gone out, reserves of gold had now gone in, but Dakar was still the same greasy, sweaty, feverish, tropical town, which in the eyes of two great Powers had, by reason of geography, become a prize. Those seventeen hundred miles of ocean which separated it from the Western hemisphere had narrowed, in some anxious minds, to the breadth of the English Channel.

From the time of the French surrender, President Roosevelt and his advisers had seen the dangers which Dakar presented to the Americas. A Dakar governed from Vichy was to them a Dakar governed from Berlin, and they foresaw a German armada of sea and submarine vessels, supported by long-range bombers, setting out from Dakar to cut off the United States from all commerce with South America and turn the Monroe Doctrine into a scrap of paper. In Germany Marshal Göring was thinking along exactly the same lines. He saw Dakar as an Atlantic Gibraltar, a splendid U-boat base, and in 1940 he tried to persuade the Führer that Gibraltar, Suez and Dakar, in that order, should precede England as his invasion target.

What the British thought, or if they thought at all, about Dakar was not immediately clear, for over the vast Empire where men of all the imperial peoples were under arms they had many bases more important, but General de Gaulle suspected the worst. He believed that since the French collapse one of Britain's war aims had been to rob France of her colonies. Although Britain had West African ports at Bathurst and Freetown which served as coaling stations, and might have been used by submarine packs, the general believed, and warned his entourage, that perfidious Albion had her eyes fixed on Dakar as a submarine base and future possession. Hence his announcement to his staff, shortly after

Bastille Day, that he had decided to establish his capital at Dakar.

Mr. Churchill was not told of de Gaulle's decision until August 3, but he accepted it with enthusiasm. In its original form it had all the charm of the forlorn hope, which particularly appealed to his romantic nature, and yet in that form it might well have given him pause. For the general proposed to land 'a column' at Conakry in French Guinea, south of Dakar, and then 'advance through the bush' to attack the town. This showed a fine disregard for geography, since even along the coast line Conakry was five hundred miles from Dakar, and double the distance 'through the bush'—which incidentally would have meant advancing through Portuguese Guinea and the British colony of Gambia as well. The column would have been in no shape, if it ever got there, for an attack on a town held in strength by a governor-general loyal to the French government at Vichy, and supported, in Dakar harbour, by warships and submarines.

So the first project had to be revised, but the mischief was done, and the impulsive Mr. Churchill was now committed to a Free French attack on a Vichy French possession, which following on the action at Mers-el-Kebir might lead to war with France.

It was nobody's business, at the War Office, to examine General de Gaulle's war record beyond the two abortive actions at Laon and Abbeville. That he had advocated a last-ditch stand by France in the Brittany Redoubt, as it was called, was known at the time when the 52nd (Lowland) Division was committed to a landing near Cherbourg, with every prospect of ending in the prisoner of war camps with the 51st. A last-ditch stand sounded well, except that the ditch contained neither blockhouses nor fortifications, nor tanks in the Vannes depot, nor explosives to mine roads and bridges, and had no labour force except three thousand exhausted Belgians. What sounded equally well, and was equally impractical, was de Gaulle's proposal, in mid-June, that the French Admiralty should ship 900,000 Poles and 100,000 tons of equipment from Bordeaux to Casablanca, with a view to continuing the war in North Africa. Admiral Darlan, not having two hundred merchant ships at his disposal for their transportation, declined to move the Poles across the bombed and congested railroad system to Bordeaux.

This, of course, was in the past, but since coming to Britain General de Gaulle had hatched a new plan, which he divulged to the head of the Spears Mission: it was to send a corps of motor cyclist signallers to 'rush across France from north to south', disrupting the wireless and telegraph systems as they went, and, in Vichy, 'hanging most of the government as they rushed through'. It was a pleasant fantasy for a boys' adventure story; from a man who expected to be taken seriously as a soldier, it was the raving of a lunatic.

Obviously none of this had been taken into consideration by August 7, when the publication of a government White Paper revealed the conclusion of a new Agreement with the Leader of All Free Frenchmen. Of a highly personal nature, it took the form of an Exchange of Letters between Mr. Churchill and General de Gaulle. It provided, among many clauses defining the status of the French volunteer force, that Britain would pay for the whole thing in the first instance, the repayment for what would be a colossal loan to be 'a matter for subsequent arrangement'. It also contained the intriguing proviso that de Gaulle's force would never be required to take up arms against France.

Jacques Brunel bought a copy of the White Paper (price 2d at any bookseller) but found that its clauses were too complicated to be understood and discussed by the simple, anxious French people who were befriended by the Refugee Committee. And he himself was becoming too deeply involved with Alison Grant to spend time discussing Gaullist politics with her brother. On the Saturday after his first visit to Lime Tree Cottage he declined Neil's invitation to go back and spend another day, and persuaded Alison to come up to town for lunch and a matinée.

"I suppose we ought to be out of doors getting the fresh air," said Alison, as they walked from 'Chez Victor' to the Coliseum, "but this is a lot more fun!"

"Mrs. Grant wasn't offended because I didn't go down to the Cottage today? I did want to have you all to myself!"

"No, she didn't mind a bit. Her mother's coming down from Scotland next week, and Lucy's busy getting the guest room in order now Nurse Fielding's gone away. Mrs. Macdonald's a real old battle-axe, everything has got to be just so for her."

"Will she be staying long?"

"Until they all go up to Oban, and then she means to keep the boys in order in the train. She couldn't come any sooner because she's something terribly important in the Women's Voluntary Service."

"You're all so tremendously organised," said Jacques. He never ceased to be impressed by the women of Britain, in all sorts and varieties of uniforms. The Service girls, now—he could imagine the horror of any one of his mother's friends in Menton if her daughter wanted to join the Forces. A little genteel work for the Red Cross was all that could be expected from a well-brought-up French girl, style 1939. He wondered what the French style, 1941, would be.

Alison must have been thinking about the Service girls too, for she turned her head to look at three officers of the Women's Royal Naval Service who had just gone by. "They're awfully smart," she said. "Those three-cornered hats!"

"Would you have liked to be a 'Wren', Alison?"

"I was turned down for the 'Wrens', didn't you know? They have to be awfully clever, and my maths. wasn't nearly good enough. Now I'm only a typist in the Ministry typing pool, but at least I'm here in London, and not stuck in some dreary place like Scapa Flow." And Alison gave a little skip of sheer pleasure as they turned the corner of St. Martin's Lane.

They both enjoyed the show and came blinking out into the late afternoon sunshine with a sense of anti-climax. Alison was adamant about not staying in town for dinner, Lucy would worry too much if she heard an Alert in the distance, but she agreed to walk down to the Charing Cross Hotel for a glass of sherry, and so more than an hour went by. Then Jacques insisted on taking her home by train; the evenings were beginning to draw in now, and he couldn't let her walk up the lane from Watermead Halt alone. They missed a train at Waterloo and had to wait: it really was growing dark when they stepped out under the arch of rambler roses into the silent countryside.

"Now you've come so far, Jack, you must come in and have supper. I told you we were going to have it late."

"Yes, because of the friends coming in for a bridge game. I don't want to interrupt the party."

"It's only the Weldons, Mr. Weldon's in the Home Guard with Neil. I know they'd love to meet you—"

"This was going to be a day just for our two selves, remember?"

Alison smiled and raised her face, half-expecting to be kissed. But Jacques walked on, keeping the breadth of the lane between them; by now he wanted her so much he hardly dared to touch her hand.

"Anyway we had a lovely afternoon," said Alison contentedly.

She began to hum a song from the show, with last year's summer hat in her hand, its flowered ribbons trailing among the real flowers in the hedgerow. They reached the high gate in the orchard wall.

"Are you sure you won't come in?"

"Alison, wait—I want—I must—"

She threw her hat down in the grass beneath the apple trees and moved into his arms. Jacques put his hand on her breast as he kissed her, and felt her heart beating beneath the thin silk of her summer dress.

How long they stood embraced Jacques never knew, but the moon came up and silvered the trees above their heads. It was nearly at the full, what the British people would soon learn to call a bomber's moon.

"I feel as if we were alone in the world," Alison murmured, and Jacques turned his head to look down the long garden to where the cottage stood. At that hour there should have been the glow of lamps everywhere, from the kitchen, from the dining room, and from the big, flower-filled living room where the bridge game was in progress. In the moonlight he could see the heavy blackout curtains masking every window. It looked as if there had been a death in the family. Alison shivered.

"Don't catch cold, _chérie_, the dew's beginning to fall." He let her slip from his embrace, kissed her hands, and watched her run between the trees, across the flower garden and round the cottage to the kitchen door. Then Jacques let himself out of the orchard, and took a short cut across the field to the main road for Kingsmead town. At that hour there were no more Up trains from Watermead Halt.

The train to London was signalled late at Kingsmead station. Jacques had time, leaning against the wall of a packed and stuffy waiting room, to think as calmly as he could about his relationship with Alison. He was in love with her, and he was sure that she loved him. The time was right for the consummation of their love, but everything else was against it. Marriage? He had nothing to offer her. His worldly goods amounted to less than £200 in a safe deposit box, so placed on Mike's advice just before the government froze all French assets in Britain. He had £200, or barely, and the tenancy of a flat paid up to the Michaelmas quarter day, and that was all. Then, an affair without marriage? For a moment the thought of the privacy of the flat on Mount

Street, and the bedroom overlooking the quiet park, rose temptingly before him, only to be dismissed. It was impossible to propose a liaison to a girl like Alison. If she refused him—and he was sure she would—he could never again face the brother who had trusted him with her.

The Kingsmead station-master made his way round the baffle wall into the waiting room, and announced another delay of half an hour on the London train. "Has there been trouble on the coast?" somebody shouted—the man made no reply. "Looks as if there's been a bit of a strafe on," one elderly man remarked to Jacques, who nodded without speaking. There was nothing to say, after nearly a month of enemy action all along the southern shores. A woman with a string bag full of fresh vegetables, with a bunch of dahlias, purple and lemon, on top, began to talk enjoyably about the corpses of German soldiers washed up between Plymouth and Cornwall. "They was practising for the invasion, like," she said.

"Bit off course, weren't they? Too far west, eh?" said the inevitable wag, and another humourist said you had to allow for the drift of the tides. All so jokey, all so patient, this English crowd, the only ones whining and tearful were the very little children. And even they were silent, they had learned already to be silent when a siren sounded, not very close, but unmistakably an air raid warning. It was a few minutes before the conversations started up again.

"That could've bin over Croydon way," said the elderly man to Jacques Brunel. "They're comin' closer."

*   *   *

'They' came much closer in the next few days. The attackers, who had been trying to bring the RAF to battle by bombing the Channel convoys, now moved inland to bomb the airfields and aircraft factories in southern England. The Luftwaffe formations were launched in a series of thrusts intended to soften up the defenders in preparation for Göring's 'Eagle Day'. This the German marshal had named, after a few postponements, as August 15, and on that Thursday England rocked from north to south as a 'balbo' from Norwegian bases fell upon Tyneside, while the twenty-two RAF squadrons in the south were engaged many times against eight hundred German bombers, coming from the French bases in successive waves.

On this tremendous day, when a few young men held the fate of Britain in their hands, the battle was fought out over English villages and English harvest fields, where anti-aircraft guns were manned among the corn stooks. London, which Hitler had intended to enter in triumph on Göring's *Adlertag*, had only one Alert, lasting for ten minutes in the early evening. Jacques Brunel, walking down Fleet Street to join Edmond Leblanc for a drink in El Vino's, found everything normal under the moon sailing serenely above St. Paul's.

"We got eighty-eight of the bandits," said Edmond with satisfaction. "Eighty-eight of theirs to nineteen of ours; very nice work indeed."

"Are the figures right?" asked Jacques.

"They must be right, they were given on the BBC. And they'll be printed in the DJ tomorrow morning."

The re-named Eddie White spoke with authority. He was doing well in his new job, and his background as an aviation writer in the great days of *La Ligne* and the southbound mail had earned him several assignments to RAF stations in the day-to-day reporting of the Battle of Britain. He had spent most of this historic fifteenth of August at Biggin Hill with a group of correspondents from the American media.

"I didn't see much in your paper about de Gaulle's great Agreement, if that's the right word, with Churchill," Jacques said. "Just two lines at the bottom of page three. I thought it was worth more than that."

"Of course it was, but you won't catch us saying it. We don't write puffs for *mon général*, in fact most of the handouts from Carlton Gardens are spiked, but neither do we write the faintest criticism of Mr. C. Our boss is gunning for a viscountcy; we don't do anything to upset the applecart—at least until the next Birthday Honours."

Jacques looked round the crowded bar. It was a quarter to ten, and the drinking time was growing shorter as the noise grew louder. The bar was full of men, many in uniform, many in the tweed jackets and mismatched trousers of the Fleet Street regulars, older men in respectable blue suits. "Eddie," he said, "I know on a day like this all that matters is the RAF, and de Gaulle counts for nothing, except to himself and the boys on his band wagon; but do you think your pals here realise that by the Exchange of Letters Mr. Churchill has committed Britain to paying for everything in de Gaulle's movement, every penny from the food he eats and the shirts on his back down to the upkeep of the youngest kid who signs his enlistment oath? All the weapons, ammo, offices, committees, the GHQ? Even the *Deuxième Bureau*?"

"Of course they don't realise it," said Edmond, "and neither does the British taxpayer. But I'm more concerned with the French taxpayer, who hasn't been consulted any more than the British have. Some day the loan, which is bound to be enormous, will have to be paid back. And you and I and forty million others will have to foot the bill . . .Well, that's in the far future. Myself, I think the most *chic* clause in the Agreement is the one that says de Gaulle's force will never be required to take up arms against France." He lowered his voice. "I hear on the Carlton Gardens grapevine that *mon général* is very anxious to get back on to French soil. How the devil does he expect to do that without fighting his way in?"

Jacques smiled. "Why don't you do a piece about that for the DJ? Is nobody ever going to speak the truth about this man?"

"Ah," said Edmond, "*speak* the truth—you have a point there. The Press can't write it, because the Press is muzzled by the censorship. But an MP could *say* something, ask a question, maybe in the House of Commons. D'you know any reliable MPs?"

Yes, he knew one. He knew Neil Grant, the Member for Carrick, who had shown him, Jacques Brunel, much kindness and hospitality. But whether Neil Grant could be persuaded to make what Jacques thought of as an *interpellation* in the House of Commons, revealing those flaws in the Gaullist movement which were carefully concealed from the British public, was quite another matter. Grant was a lawyer, like Jacques himself: he had been called to the Scottish Bar and practised his profession in Edinburgh before entering Parliament. He would certainly view any criticism of the formally recognised Leader of All Free Frenchmen with due legal caution. He had never, in talking with Jacques, uttered the slightest breath of criticism except for one phrase about events 'making de Gaulle look better than he really was'.

On the other hand he had offered to 'help' Mike Marchand (and Mike, on the telephone, had been insistent that the offer had been made, unprompted, by Neil Grant) and had helped by listening to Mike's story, supported by two Brazilian visitors, of German agents in the uniforms of the Chasseurs Alpins. It was not impossible that Grant was himself a British agent. Mike had explained that the Ministry of Economic Warfare was only as old as the war itself, and was supposed to be concerned with top-level Intelligence as well as the control of shipping and seizure of German cargoes under contraband control. Jacques took the trouble to study the current proceedings in Parliament before going down to Lime Tree Cottage for lunch on the following Saturday.

He had seen very little of Alison during the week. She had made excuses of increasing pressure of work for not meeting him in her lunch hour, and as the German raiders came ever nearer to the capital (Croydon had actually been reached on Tuesday) all office workers were in a hurry to get home at the end of the day. He tried not to think that she was playing him up a little, playing hard to get, back-tracking from those passionate embraces in the moonlit orchard, but when he was at the cottage again Jacques had to admit that she was elusive, finding half a dozen occupations in the kitchen and the dining room instead of sitting down to talk to him.

It was a rainy day, almost the first in that amazing summer, and no sound of Alerts, even in the distance, broke through the peace of the Surrey countryside. To the optimistic, this was due to the RAF bombing raids on Berlin, Essen, Düsseldorf, and other German targets, undertaken in reprisal for Wednesday's *Adlertag*. "They can dish it out, but they can't take it!" said the optimists, as Saturday moved on in peace; even the rain was a blessing as it put an end to the long drought. It was not a blessing to Jacques Brunel, for when he arrived, dripping, from Watermead Halt, Alison was nowhere to be seen, and it appeared that on wet days the little boys could not be kept out of the air raid shelter which their father had constructed in the wine cellar, with a reinforced ceiling and heavy timber beams. She was down in the bowels of the earth with them, 'playing at prisoners and dungeons', explained Lucy as she put away what had been Mike Marchand's raincoat. "Now you must come and meet my mother."

Mrs. Macdonald was a large dogmatic lady, who insisted in addressing Jacques in bad French, and by his professional style of Maître Brunel—it was nearly a year since anybody had called him that! Almost her first statement was "I think your General de Gaulle is just a darling!" and from there she proceeded to an account of the work of the WVS in Oban, an analysis of the campaign in Norway, and an expression of her particular disgust with the French Army. While she talked—and Lucy Grant, sitting between her mother and Jacques, seemed powerless to stem the tide—she knitted "for the Forces, of course", the object being a balaclava helmet which she was fashioning with such ferocious swipes of the steel needles as could only remind a Frenchman of the *tricoteuses* of the Revolution. The sound of the drinks trolley, pushed by Neil across the stone-flagged hall, was very welcome, and more welcome still was Alison's gay voice, as she took her nephews to wash their hands in the downstairs cloakroom.

Neil kept his mother-in-law at bay during luncheon, while Lottie, unnaturally formal in a black dress and creased white apron, stumbled between the sideboard and the table. But in spite of Neil it was a relief to get away from Mrs. Macdonald, when the boys insisted that Captain Jack should join their game in the shelter, although he couldn't understand from their gabbled explanations what the game was about until Alison came to join them. She had been helping Lottie with the dishes.

"I've been telling them about the princes in the Tower," she said. "They want you and me to be the murderers."

"And cover us up with leaves," said Peter.

"That's the Babes in the Wood, you silly," said his elder brother. "That's where the robins come in."

"We could be robin murderers," suggested Jacques, and while the children played their parts with a grave passion he and Alison flapped and trilled round the air raid shelter, from which the wine bins had been cleared out into a dark passage, until they were both hysterical. Lottie, coming downstairs to take the boys to the nursery for their naps, found the murderers collapsed on the pallet beds beside their indignant victims.

"You didn't play properly, Captain Jack," accused Colin as he was led away. "You're not supposed to *laugh*!"

" 'Cheerfulness breaks in'," said Alison, whose face was wet with tears of laughter. "Heavens, I must look a sight!"

"You look lovely," said Jacques, pulling her down on the pallet beside him. "Darling, don't run away again. Stay with me."

"They'll wonder what we're doing."

"Let them wonder." He kissed her roughly, and Alison at once responded, parting her lips to his kisses, letting him put her hair aside and kiss her neck, her throat, the lobes of her ears, in an erotic frenzy through which she heard Jacques whisper,

161

"When are they going to Scotland?"

"On Sunday. Not next Sunday. The first of September."

"Not until then, for God's sake?"

"Lucy won't go till the House rises. And Neil couldn't get train reservations earlier."

He was more in command of himself, winding her red hair round the distorted fingers of his left hand.

"And you'll be all alone here?"

"Lottie's going to sleep in the house. It's only for a week."

"Couldn't you stay in London? Stay with one of your girl friends from the typing pool? Wouldn't it be easier?"

"Wouldn't what be easier?"

"I mean—no travelling. The trains get worse and worse—"

"They think it's dangerous in London now."

Jacques was silent. It was impossible to say, "Then let me come to you here. Tell Lottie to stay at home and let me be with you." He was in the old impasse, the old quandary; he knew that Alison felt it too. He made no effort to prevent her when she slid off the pallet and stood up.

"Let's not make plans too far ahead," she said lightly. "The way to live now is a day at a time. An hour at a time! And at this very moment Granny Macdonald is sulking because Neil's in his study, Lucy's having her rest, and there's no one to listen to the Oban gossip—"

"Doesn't *she* ever have a rest?"

"She's probably finished that helmet and started on a fisherman's stocking by this time. Come on, Jack! We can go for a walk after tea if it clears up."

But it was raining harder than ever after tea, and Neil took Jacques off to what was called his study, although it was more often used by Lucy as a sewing room.

"What on earth were you all doing down in the shelter after lunch?" he said good-naturedly, as he offered Jacques a cigarette box with the arms of Glasgow University on the lid. "We heard you shrieking like mad creatures."

"The kids were acting out the little princes in the Tower, and Alison and I were the heavies."

"The Tower of London?"

"Mixed up with the Babes in the Wood."

"By George!" said Neil, "that's a coincidence. I remember Marchand talking about the Tower of London—"

"*Michel* was talking about the little princes?"

"No," said Neil. "He was talking about General de Gaulle."

Jacques drew a breath of satisfaction: this was the opening he had hoped for. "I wonder what Michel would have to say about the general now," he said. " 'Fed, lodged and laundered', as the French expression goes, and all at the expense of the generous British. When's he going to do any fighting, to pay you back?"

"The recruiting's gone much better since the Agreement was signed, now the men know their rights will be protected. De Gaulle has three battalions now—"

"Less than one per cent of one drop in the bucket, and you know it, Neil."

Neil Grant did know it. He also knew that there was a plan called Operation Menace, to set de Gaulle ashore in French West Africa, which might cost some British lives and much British prestige before it was completed. He listened thoughtfully as the younger man went on, and thought how well the arguments were presented, with what French logic, and how little chance there was that the story of de Gaulle's overbearing authoritarianism would ever be told to a Britain at war. He said so.

"But isn't that what your Parliament is for?" cried Jacques. "*You* could do it! When the Allied Forces Bill comes up for its second reading next week you could tell the Deputies what sort of men are sheltering behind de Gaulle's movement. Like Prince Stahremberg—"

"You needn't worry about Prince Stahremberg. A grand old warhorse called Josiah Wedgwood, the Member for Newcastle-under-Lyme, is going to take care of *him*. Colonel Wedgwood's going to speak about the men in the Foreign Legion who were at Narvik, and chose desertion rather than de Gaulle—"

"But you know more about it than Monsieur Wedgwood does. All Mike told you, all I've told you myself about the people who were bullied and frightened before they came to the Refugee Committee—"

"It isn't quite my line, Jacques. It's not what my constituents elected me for."

"Your constituents have a right to know how their money's being spent. And to be told how a foreign general, called a deserter in his own country, is using Britain as a springboard for his own ambition."

It was exactly the right plea to make to a man whose

profession was the law. Neil Grant knocked out his pipe angrily, but the battle was won, and Jacques knew it. With a sense of triumph he heard the other say, "All right, I'll see what I can do. The Bill comes up on Wednesday afternoon. Come to the House of Commons then and ask for me."

"Thank you." Soon after that Jacques rose and said he must be going back to London; the last Up train from Watermead, he believed, left in three quarters of an hour. Neil did not press him to stay to supper and get a train at Kingsmead; he was plainly concerned and worried about the promise he had given. Jacques thanked him for it, most sincerely, when he said goodbye to his hostess and her mother; Alison, wearing a jersey and holding a big umbrella, said she would let him out at the orchard gate.

"What was it you promised Jacques Brunel?" Lucy Grant asked curiously, when she and her husband were at last alone together. She was already in bed, and Neil was undressing in the dark. They had opened the heavy blackout curtains when they came upstairs, and the bedroom was fresh after the rain, the smell of tobacco flowers and stock rising from the neglected garden.

"Promised?" Neil looked round, he could just distinguish her features against the dark mass of her hair on the white pillow. "Oh—something to do with next week in the House of Commons."

"With the Committee you sit on, from the MEW?"

"With a Committee, but not the one you're thinking of. With the debate on the Allied Forces Bill."

"Are you going to speak, darling? Can I come and hear you?"

"You most certainly can not, and I shan't be on my feet longer than two or three minutes. Just a point I'm going to make, it won't take long."

"Mother was saying you ought to speak oftener. She thinks your constituents would like to see your name in the papers every week."

"They didn't elect me for my oratory, Lucy."

Neil heard the tiny sound of Lucy winding her watch, and thought she had dropped the subject. He opened the window wider and leaned out. There were still raindrops on the sill.

"I don't see what Captain Jack's got to do with your speeches in the House of Commons," said the voice from the bed.

"Most Frenchmen are interested in the Allied Forces Bill."

"Neil, is it going to be something—controversial?"

"It could turn out that way."

"Something the Scottish Whip would rather you didn't say?"

"I'm not a mind-reader, darling. And I'm not sure what I'm going to say, yet."

"Oh dear, you will be careful, won't you?" He knew exactly what was in Lucy's mind. She enjoyed being an MP's wife, and Neil held Carrick by a very narrow margin. If he started being 'controversial' to such an extent that the Whip was withdrawn, he had no hope at all of being returned as an Independent member. It would be back to the Scottish Bar, and goodbye to Lime Tree Cottage and all it stood for, if Lucy's husband forsook the party line.

"What a pack of cowards we are," he said, almost to himself, "if we let that one Frenchman bully us into silence now."

"What Frenchman, Neil? Who are you talking about?"

Neil pulled his shirt over his head. "Not about Jacques Brunel, at any rate. But I've got to do my best for poor old Jacques. Because very soon now, I'm going to ask him to do something I would never have the guts to do myself."

*   *   *

"Are we to keep these people in prison indefinitely," said the Member for Newcastle-under-Lyme, "when their only crime is that they wish to fight with the British Army? I wrote to try to get General de Gaulle to disclaim any authority over these men and to let them go. They fought bravely at Narvik . . ."

That was one word, with all its emotive memories of the campaign in Norway, which Jacques Brunel could catch and hold on to in what was to him the baffling setting of a House of Commons debate. Neil Grant had got him admitted to the Strangers' Gallery, and he had been sitting there since question time, trying to follow the proceedings and identify the famous among the men in the Chamber. It was all so much smaller than he had expected, smaller by far and yet in a way grander than the Chambre des Députés, where Monsieur Herriot's favour had granted admission to the son of Théophile Brunel on two or three occasions in his Paris days. He remembered Herriot himself, seated on his high rostrum as president of the Chambre with the *huissiers* below him, the vast *hémicycle* with the Deputies sitting to the Right, Centre and Left—positions which had given the names of political affiliations to groups all over Europe—and the animation, the eloquence, the violent quarrels which swept the ranks of the Deputies among whom the young Jacques had hoped one day to be numbered. Here the places seemed so few, the Members so quiet, even bored, the Chamber so completely controlled by the Speaker enthroned, in his wig and gown, with the Mace on the table before him. There was only one dramatic figure on the Treasury Bench, and in him all the drama of a nation at bay seemed to be concentrated. Mr. Churchill had made a fine speech on the day before, not one of his great orations, but precise and reassuring about the prospects of victory. The Luftwaffe had resumed its heavy attacks on Sunday.

Now, in the most gentlemanly way possible, the Member for Newcastle-under-Lyme was being ruled out of order. He had a letter from General Spears, he explained, saying that General de Gaulle would not release the men of the Foreign Legion who had been interned for refusing to join the Free French Forces. The Under-Secretary for War and the Attorney-General rose in turn to point out that the question raised was not germane to the Bill before the House. Although Jacques spoke English well, the word 'germane' confused him by its likeness to 'German', and he lost the thread of the argument. But he had been trained to appreciate the atmosphere of the law courts, and he felt instinctively that the two Ministers had lost the attention of their hearers. In the Press Gallery the only men who were writing steadily were the crack reporters of *Hansard*, who noted every comma; some of the others appeared to have lost interest after recording that Mr. Wedgwood was 'sharply called to order'. Nobody cared very much for a few Légionnaires, some imprisoned and some being hidden from the police by Mr. Wedgwood's sympathetic constituents, who were in just the same dilemma as Jacques Brunel, having refused to serve both Pétain and de Gaulle. Mr. Churchill himself seemed restless and impatient. He looked up once at the Ladies, Gallery, where his attractive wife gave him an affectionate smile. Neil Grant glanced up too, and gave Jacques a little nod. He was obviously very nervous, and was twisting his order paper in his hands.

The doughty Member for Newcastle-under-Lyme had returned to the attack, and was now descanting on the presence of undesirables in the Free French Forces.

"I want to know if it is our money which is going to pay

Prince von Stahremberg. We all know him," he said. "He is apparently now a French officer under General de Gaulle—a Jew-baiter, commander of the Heimwehr against the workers of Vienna. He ran away when the fight came, he ran away again when Dollfuss was murdered, and again at the *Anschluss*. He appealed to Hitler to use his services after the *Anschluss* and was indignantly refused. I think we may fairly ask whether Stahremberg is not too much to the right to be fighting for the good old cause in the year 1940."

With a throb of sympathy Jacques saw that Neil Grant had caught the Speaker's eye. He rose to his feet and began to speak in what was at first a low and husky voice.

"My honourable and gallant friend the Member for Newcastle-under-Lyme," he said, "has drawn the attention of the House to some of the abuses existing in the force commanded by General de Gaulle. There are others of which the House should know. There has been consistent intimidation of a group of French trawler skippers and their families who came to Britain in their own boats at the time of the fall of France, and press-gang methods have been employed to enlist their sons in the Free French Forces. The same methods were employed among the men awaiting repatriation at the White City. We have heard today that General de Gaulle believes he has the right to intern, which is another way of saying 'to imprison' French soldiers who have refused to join him, and he has also attempted to seize the French aviators who joined the RAF in June and who now wear British uniform. When the Bill we are now debating becomes law, it is essential that General de Gaulle be made to understand that the rights he claims over his own nationals do not permit him to mete out punishments no longer legal in the British Army. One of his officers, Colonel Maigrin Verneret, had to be restrained from sending two of his men to face a firing squad for creating some sort of disturbance in the streets of Aldershot. The general himself believes in the French Army discipline of fortress arrest, and since we have no fortresses as such in Britain, he has declared his wish to incarcerate offenders at a certain level in the Tower of London."

There was some laughter in the Chamber, not joined in by the scowling Churchill, and a cadaverous Member with long grey-black hair interrupted in a strong Glasgow accent, "Are ye no' feared to hurt General de Gaulle's feelings?"

It was exactly the spur Neil Grant had needed. The colour came up in his face and his voice was louder and sharper as he retorted, "I must remind the honourable Member for Glasgow Tollcross that Number Four, Carlton Gardens, is not a girls' school, and General de Gaulle is not in a position to indulge in hurt feelings. Let him remember that we are paying all his officers and all his men. The whole thing is financed by us. We have a right, as has already been said and well said in this debate, to make sure that the Free French movement is not a traitors' gate through which men like the Austrian Prince Stahremberg can penetrate to ranks which should be closed against them. I have personal knowledge of two German nationals, by name Schnaebel and Lachmann, who were found at de Gaulle's headquarters posing as officers of the Chasseurs Alpins who had escaped from France. One of them, I am happy to say, has paid the penalty exacted for espionage. I hope one result of the Allied Forces Bill (1940) will be a much stricter screening and scrutiny of all those who join any one of the six foreign armies now being formed on British soil."

Neil sat down. There were one or two cries of "Oh!" and some of "Hear! Hear!" which to Jacques Brunel sounded like "Yah!" Mr. Churchill, with a face of storm, left the Treasury Bench and with due formality crossed the Bar of the House and left. Another MP was already on his feet, and embarking on a speech about the need to include the Jews in the Bill. Neil waited for ten minutes, and then with a nod at the Strangers' Gallery he too left the Chamber.

"Congratulations!" said Jacques, when they met in the lobby. "That was very good. Will it be in all the newspapers tomorrow morning?"

"They'll probably slap a D-notice on it," said Neil. "Did you see the Prime Minister's face? He doesn't care for overt criticism of his protégé. But at least he didn't walk out while I was speaking."

"You gave it to them—how do you say—straight from the shoulder."

"Yes, but I can't think on my feet like old Josiah Wedgwood. He really fixed them with the letter from General Spears." He looked at his watch. "I can't stay out too long, it doesn't look well when you've trailed your coat as I did, but we've time for a quick cup of tea. You can go back to the gallery again if you want to."

"Just one question first," said Jacques, catching him by the sleeve. "That about the men who came in through the traitors' gate—the men Michel recognised. Which of them paid the penalty?"

"Schnaebel. And it was Mike who first used that expression: traitors' gate."

"What happened to Lachmann? He didn't call himself Lachmann here, did he?"

"He joined de Gaulle under the name of Corbeau. He slipped through our fingers at the last minute, thanks to the stupidity of a man called Dempster, who had a watch put on the ports too late."

"You mean he's left the country? Gone back to France—or Germany?"

"Not exactly," said Neil, choosing his words with care. "There's some reason to believe he was heading for West Africa."

II

O N GÖRING'S *Adlertag*, when the Royal Air Force threw
back the Luftwaffe in the north as well as in the south,
Mike Marchand went to consult the Jewish refugee doctor
who had found asylum in Brazil. He had put it off until he moved
into the new hotel at Flamengo, partly because he didn't want to
discuss what he thought of as his 'disability' with his uncle, and
partly because he was fatalistic about the attacks of vertigo, and
hardly believed that German medicine might have come up with a
cure. But Dina was expected back from the Capricorn office at São
Paulo, and he wanted to be able to tell her that he had gone to see
Dr. Baumeister—even if there was nothing more to tell.

Senhor Ferreira, who was growing deaf himself, had not
noticed Mike's difficulty in hearing, which seemed to have grown
worse since his return to Rio. It was the noise of the traffic,
beginning to be a serious problem, mixed with the shouts, the
singing and above all the music adored by a lively population of
mixed blood, which seemed to ring crazily in Mike's head after
the quiet streets of London. Even in the mountain peace of Alto
da Boa Vista he had been at a disadvantage when Senhor Ferreira
took his nephew to visit his friends. There had been parties over
the weekend in more than one of the handsome houses round the
lake, the householders being old enough to live in the past, in
their fond memories of the Braganza Empire, and their grand-
children—in their late teens or very early twenties—too young
to attach any significance to the name of Mike Marchand. Young
and old, they had chattered like the Amazon parrots and lory birds
caged at the gates of what had been the Braganza palace and was
now an ethnic charnelhouse of museum skulls and bones, and
the chattering bored through Mike's head in a meaningless
stream. He hated to seem ungrateful to his uncle, but he was glad
to get out of the Ferreira house, away from the living room which
since the day of his arrival had seemed to echo, every time he
looked at the glowing canvas of *Les Demoiselles Verbier*, with the
words, "Poor Paris! Poor France!"

Dr. Elias Baumeister, consulting hours 10–12 noon and 4–8 p.m. daily, lived in one of the drab streets immediately behind the luxury hotels of the Avenida Atlántica. This hinterland was the home of minor government employees, municipal clerks and the better paid among the public transport workers, and also of the midwives, dressmakers and fortune-tellers who catered to their wives. There were cheap shops of all kinds here, and fruit and candy barrows took up a good deal of space on the narrow pavements. Wireless music came from inside the shops, competing with the song of canaries in cages slung to the brackets of the street lamps. It was not a wholesome neighbourhood, and it declined sharply to the northward, for after one or two parallel streets the chain of *morros* began, the hills which ran from the peak of the Sugar Loaf to Gavea, and down those hills the *favelas* were spilled in all their degradation.

A Jewish woman of about sixty, wearing a clean white overall, opened Dr. Baumeister's door to Mike, and said in halting Portuguese:

"Please to come in, sir. The doctor has a patient, will you take a seat in the waiting room?"

Mike thanked her. He was pretty sure that the receptionist was Frau Baumeister herself, and that the waiting room was also the Baumeisters' sitting room, for the flat was obviously small, and smelt of cooking. There was no other patient waiting for the man who had been a specialist in Leipzig.

There was a round table of light polished wood in the exact centre of the room, and on it a few newspapers and magazines, the paper on top carrying a photograph and an article which Mike had seen before. The picture showed the man who had been his chief less than two months before, walking down the gangway of the RMS *Highland Brigade* on her arrival at Rio after a three weeks' voyage from Southampton. "Former French envoy to London to study economic problems of Brazil," the headlines said. "Denies he is representative of General de Gaulle." Mike's lips twitched appreciatively. The former ambassador was about the last man on earth to represent a *général en dissidence*; it amused Mike to think that the post had actually been offered to himself. He took up the paper and studied the photograph more closely. That was the ascetic face he had known so well, the face seamed with tragedy as the fall of France drew nearer; and to Mike there was something tragic in the man's intention to study the economic problems of Brazil. The ambassador doesn't give a damn about their problems, he thought, any more than I do myself. Poor Paris! Poor France!

"Monsieur Marchand?"

"Dr. Baumeister." Mike shook hands with a small grey man in a white coat, wearing pince-nez on a nose which proclaimed its owner's race. The doctor ushered Mike into his consulting room, which was very well equipped—Mike guessed that all the money the Baumeisters had earned or scraped together had gone into it —on the other side of the little hall.

"I'm sorry I don't speak French, Mr. Marchand."

"I don't speak German."

Dr. Baumeister smiled. "I'm a Brazilian citizen now," he said, "I'm ashamed to say I still have difficulty with Portuguese. Shall we speak English?"

"That seems to be the answer, doctor. I just arrived from London—"

"A three weeks' journey—very tedious."

"I came by plane, in fact."

"You came by plane. I'm flattered, Mr. Marchand, that you waited to consult me, when no doubt you had your choice of all the specialists in my field in London. You said on the telephone you were disturbed about your hearing. Is this a new condition?"

"No, but it's got worse recently."

The doctor had asked Mike to sit in a comfortable chair opposite his own desk. He offered his patient cigarettes, and took one himself, watching shrewdly as the small routine of the matches and the ashtray and the first perfect smoke ring seemed to relax a man who, with his fair good looks and well co-ordinated body, his clear eyes and skin, looked the picture of animal health. About the nervous condition of his patient, Dr. Baumeister was not so sure.

"What started the trouble in the first place? Tell me exactly when it began."

Dr. Baumeister was in no hurry to examine the young man. He felt that the important thing was to establish confidence between them, for Marchand was reacting like a scared horse to the clinical equipment of the consulting room, and its faint smell of medicines and antiseptics. He was rewarded by getting the whole story of Mike's flights at very high altitudes for Trans-Andean, and the disastrous crash in the desert near Dakar.

"And it was after that you had attacks of vertigo? Never before?"

"I always passed my physicals before. Not since."

"The attacks being quite frequent, since 1936?"

"I've had three or four a year. Two this year since the end of June."

"Under what circumstances?"

"Each time on a staircase, looking down."

"I see." The doctor sat forward with his elbows on the desk. "Now, Mr. Marchand, you've told me you came to Rio from London by plane. Did you feel no symptoms of vertigo on that long trip? At those altitudes?"

"I kept my eyes shut going up the airplane steps at Foynes," Mike confessed. "In fact I kept my eyes shut most of the way to Lisbon!"

"Yes, but you didn't travel blind all the way to New York, and down to Rio, did you?"

"I did look out when we were over the Atlantic, and when we were coming in to land at the way stations."

"With no ill effects?"

"None."

"None, several thousand feet in the air, but a sensation of imbalance, nausea and actual falling on a simple staircase. Tell me the particular features of the staircase," said the doctor very gently.

"It wasn't the staircase so much as the ground below," said Mike. "The dusty yard in Glasgow. The beige carpet in London. I feel the desert rushing up to meet me . . . and when someone speaks . . . I think it's Francolin, my navigator, calling out when we knew we were going to crash . . . and I think it's happening all over again . . . I'm sorry, doctor." He felt the sweat break out on his brow and fumbled for his handkerchief.

"This other man, the navigator, was he a close friend?"

"I hardly knew him. But I felt responsible for him. We wouldn't have been going all out for the record if it hadn't been for me."

"But like all young men since the start of aviation, you knew you were putting yourselves at risk?"

"Oh, sure we did. We used to have a saying, 'Everyone ends up in the drink!' Like Jean Mermoz, and Guillaumet, and Pranville, and Alcock and Brown, and God knows how many others. Eighty, so far, over the South Atlantic alone."

"And how long had you been a pilot before this accident took place?"

"Seven years. Well, call it six, counting from the start of my military service in France. But I first flew solo here in Rio, out at Santos Dumont, when I was about eighteen."

"How old are you now?"

"Thirty in November."

"I imagine they were flying rather obsolete planes here, when you were a boy."

Mike laughed. "My first instructor took me up in a World War I Salmon biplane, there were a few of these still kicking about in 1928. Jean Mermoz had to fly a Latécoère monoplane when he was carrying the mail from Casablanca to Dakar, and later on a Bréguet: *La Ligne*—the Aéropostale—never could afford the latest in aircraft design."

"And Trans-Andean?"

"Trans-Andean went broke trying to manufacture the Salado, which I used to test. The Salado was the prototype for the Deodoro, a much better aircraft, which Capricorn's using now."

"You'd like to fly a Deodoro?"

"I'd like to fly a Spitfire or a Hurricane."

Dr. Baumeister nodded. "Now let me have a look at your ears," he said, and turned to his instrument cabinet. The examination, while thorough, did not take long, and when it was over Dr. Baumeister sat down at his desk again, and looked very kindly at his patient.

"You are suffering from labyrinthitis in the inner ear," he said, "and it's not attributable to your crash in Senegal. You had been flying for years before that, in obsolete planes with open cockpits, to and fro across the Andes, and at a time when no research had been done on the effects of flying on the human body. Well, we are better informed now, and I can help you, but first of all let me assure you that the vertigo which has naturally alarmed you is—in my opinion—caused only by the loss of equilibrium due to the labyrinthitis which has also affected your hearing. I say in my opinion because I know that some of my colleagues—even in Germany—believe that vertigo can be cured by hypnotism, or by psychiatric medicine: they would be interested in what you have told me about floors which look like desert sand and voices ringing in your ears. My dear Mr. March-and, these are fantasies, and you've indulged yourself in them because you have strong feelings of responsibility and even of guilt, but you must try to put them out of your mind now. I'm going to use the technique we were developing in Leipzig . . . some years ago . . . it's really very simple. This is what we call an insufflator" (he held up an instrument) "I'm going to insert it in your nostrils and blow up your Eustachian tubes."

There was a sharp crack inside Marchand's head, a brief explosion of sensation, hardly to be called pain, and then to his amazement a flood of song.

"Singing?" he said, and his own voice sounded like a shout to him, "am I hearing singing?"

Dr. Baumeister looked at the open window. "It's the canaries," he said. "The cage birds on the lamp posts. You didn't hear them before?"

"Of course I didn't . . . Are you raising your voice when you talk to me?"

"I'm hardly talking above my breath." The doctor laughed, and patted Mike's shoulder. "You can hear properly, that's all, but it may take a bit of getting used to. And remember the vertigo won't come back."

"Just because you blew up my nose with that thing? It was as easy as all that?"

"As easy as all that."

"Then why didn't those Air Force medics who gave me my last two physicals diagnose labyrinthitis? Why didn't they know about the insufflator?"

Dr. Baumeister shrugged, in a perfect Jewish expression of patience and cynicism.

"Would you pass me as fit to fly?" persisted Mike.

"Of course I wouldn't! I haven't given you a complete checkup. I don't know your pulmonary capacity or the nature of your reflexes. All I can guarantee is that you'll no longer suffer from vertigo, but if you do fly again, you'll have to take better care of your ears than you ever did in the past."

"Can I come back and see you again next week, doctor?"

"Why? Do you think this is some piece of quackery, and that you'll wake up tomorrow morning with your head spinning, and your hearing as bad as ever?"

"No, but another visit would give me more confidence in what I mean to do." The doctor nodded. "Next Wednesday, then, at five o'clock," he said.

"I'd like to pay your fee for today now." When Mike sat down to write the cheque—not exorbitant, but at the same time not small—Dr. Baumeister continued to watch him shrewdly.

"You said you'd like to fly Spitfires or Hurricanes," he said. "What you mean is that you want to fly in combat, don't you?"

"Yes."

"I hope you get your wish."

"If I do, it's thanks to you."

"Then that's one item cancelled in a very, very long score."

Mike asked no questions of the refugee. He had known already what the score must be: the loss of motherland, home, family, but not, at least, of profession. He wished Dr. Baumeister good luck in his adopted country, and went out through the vegetable-smelling lobby, down the dark stairs to the canyon of the street.

The street sounds were almost unbearably loud. Mike took the first turning to the right and came out on the Avenida Atlántica near the far end of Copacabana beach, where the Leme district began. The city had started to expand in that direction, and there were some apartment buildings as well as little restaurants like the one where he and Dina went to listen to the *fado* singing, but Leme was still a sandy, lonely place, with an old barracks on the point where the beaches ended, with the Sugar Loaf in the distance high above the Morro de Leme hill.

He sat down in front of a sidewalk café. It was not much better than a shack, selling cups of coffee to the idle boys who spent their days kicking a football along the beach, and sometimes glasses of *cachaça*. Usually the alcohol, made from fermented cane sugar, was spat out on the sidewalk, for it tasted very like airplane fuel: to Mike it was now nectar and ambrosia. He sat smoking and smiling to himself, exulting in the knowledge that the old nightmare of vertigo was laid for ever, until the sound of firing from the rifle range at Leme barracks brought the thought of war uppermost in his mind. Only then, he began to realise the other implication of Dr. Baumeister's verdict. Supposing, in that lost hour of amnesia in London, he had been telling the truth to the police? Supposing, instead of falling in an attack of vertigo, he had been struck from behind on the landing of that silent house? It meant that somewhere in the world his assailant was walking free, and Mike Marchand had run away without even

176

trying for revenge. It was not a welcome thought, and he made an effort to dismiss it. Throwing down a few coins, he left the miserable café.

Mike crossed to the beach side, separated from the avenue by a low stone wall, and stood breathing in the salt air, aware of the first real peace he had known since the day that France surrendered. It was a warm, sunny, winter afternoon, and there were a good many children on the beach. One of them was flying a huge kite, and looking down Mike saw that he was standing near one of the concessions, roughly marked out in the sand, where the big butterfly kites were sold. There were at least a dozen of them, a yard across from wing tip to wing tip, all neatly aligned and pointing in the same direction, like Spitfires or Hurricanes ready to go into action.

Mike watched the airborne butterfly, painted like all the others in an elaborate pattern of orange, green and scarlet. It went higher and higher against the winter blue, flown on a very long string, and as he followed it with his eyes he saw a shadow of steel, flying higher still, come out from behind the Sugar Loaf and make for the south. He knew exactly what it was: a plane from the Argentine flying its first leg on the return trip, ETA 11 p.m. at Montevideo. And Mike Marchand said aloud, as he watched it go, "I'll be able to do that again! I'm going to fly!"

*   ✳   ✳

Mike was in the same exultant mood next morning, when he went to meet Dina at the airfield. Even Santos Dumont field looked different to him: no longer an airport run by an almost new generation, but the place where he had learned everything he knew about flying, where in his early days he had flown his triumphant chandelle round the hangars at the end of a race. Senhor Rinaldo was seeing off a flight to Salvador with a stopover at Bela Horizonte, as Mike left the Duesenberg in the parking lot.

He stood chatting with the traffic manager for a short time. Dina, of course, had plotted her return for one of the long lulls in the airport's morning, and she came in exactly at her ETA, pulling back the Puss Moth's cruising speed until she was about twenty feet above the ground, and then flattening out to touch the ground in a perfect three-point landing. Mike applauded her professionalism even while he was running across the apron to greet her outside the private hangar; he was able to beat the mechanics in helping her out of the plane.

"Oh, Mike!" She knew, as soon as she saw his face, that the news was good. "You saw the doctor? Is it all right?"

"Absolutely. He cleared the whole thing up in five minutes!" He couldn't kiss her there, in front of the grinning mechanics, but Mike hugged Dina to his side as he took her flight bag and log-book from her hands, and hurried her across the apron to the waiting Rinaldo. She had some written reports from São Paulo to give the traffic manager, and Rinaldo looked amazed when the *estimada senhorina,* in her excitement, dropped the whole sheaf on the floor of the lounge, and then spilled half the contents of her open flight bag when she tried to help the men to pick them up. A *cafézinho,* proffered by the eager Belinda, was drunk by Dina da Costa in two gulps. She said confusedly that she was in a hurry to get to the office, Senhor Tony was waiting, and let Mike take her out to the Duesenberg and to his arms.

"Oh darling, I'm so excited and so glad! What did the doctor say? What did he do?" she stammered through his kisses.

"Cleared my tubes with a new thing called an insufflator . . . You smell of lilies and petrol . . . Oh, Dina, it's so wonderful to have you back!"

"But did he say you can fly?"

"Sure. I'm going back to see him next week for a final check. But I feel great, Dina, no more vertigo ever; it was just all the flying in the Andes that messed up my ears. The doctor seemed to make up his mind to that, as soon as I told him I came from London by air, without a touch of dizziness—"

"Well, that's what I thought," said Dina. "I'm not a doctor, but I didn't see how you could fly six thousand miles, even as a passenger, if your vertigo had been real."

"It was real, Dina."

"Yes, oh yes, I don't mean you imagined it," she said quickly. "I mean, now you know what caused it, it makes a difference, doesn't it? Does Tony know? Isn't he pleased?"

"He's not exactly thrilled."

"Not . . . good heavens, is he crazy?"

"Of course he's glad about the doctor, and about your sister Ester knowing the right man, but he didn't encourage me to think about flying for Capricorn."

"Wait till I've talked to him."

178

But Tony da Costa was too clever to embark on a three-sided argument with his sister and Mike. Assuming his rôle of millionaire playboy instead of New Flagbearer, he took them both to lunch at the 'Cabaça Grande,' congratulated Mike on being able to hear every word of their conversation in the maelstrom of that busy restaurant, and promised, when telephoning home that afternoon, to convey Mike's most grateful thanks to the Senhorina Ester. He listened with noncommittal urbanity to a suggestion which Marchand made, and it was not until much later in the day that he spoke his mind to Dina.

She was in her room at the Copacabana, getting ready to have dinner with Mike, her scarlet chiffon dress lying ready across her bed, when Tony called her into the sitting room.

"You'll be having a long talk with our French friend tonight," he said. "I just want to warn you—don't make any rash promises that he can fly one of the Deodoros. I don't want any busted pilot putting my aircraft at risk."

"He's not a busted pilot. He could get a Clearance tomorrow if he wanted to."

"Let him get it then. It'll take more than some Jewish quack with an insufflator to make me believe that a man who's been grounded for years is fit to fly the biggest commercial aircraft in Brazilian skies."

"He hasn't said anything about the Deodoros. He told you today he wanted to work with the ground staff first."

"Which is pure affectation—Mike Marchand staging a come-back as a grease monkey—"

"I think it's very sensible. As Mike said at lunch, if he starts in the traffic office poor little Rinaldo'll be jittering and breathing down his neck all day, scared stiff that he's going to lose his own job."

"There's something in that," conceded Tony. "But I can't get you to see that there's no need for Mike to start anywhere at Santos Dumont. I've offered him a perfectly straightforward job as assistant managing director. The place for him to learn the ropes is here in this office, right next to you and me. Any objections?"

"None. But he feels he's got to start at the beginning again. Tony, why are you so anxious to get Mike into Capricorn?"

"Because he's just the man we need. With a terrific record in aviation, a lot of experience in other ways, and a fine Brazilian background—old Ferreira's name still counts for a good deal. And because you've been carrying a torch for him since you were sixteen."

"How do you know that?"

"I know a lot of things about you, Divininha. Enough for me to keep father and mother off your back, all these years they've been trying to arrange some sort of marriage for you . . . Tereza knew about you too. She used to say to mother, 'Don't worry about Dina. She'll be happy with her airplanes for a few years yet'."

"Did she, the darling?"

"Yes," said Tony, and went to pour himself a drink. "But a lot of things changed after Tereza died. Me, for one."

"Oh Tony . . ."

"Do you want to tell Mike tonight that he can start the way he wants to, along with the mechanics?"

"No, that's just what I *don't* want. He mustn't think I'm meddling, or manipulating him. Give him a ring at that Flamengo place, first thing in the morning, and tell him yourself. And Tony, please don't hustle us. It's all so sudden and so new—"

"And you're so good at getting your own way," said her brother. He surveyed the slim excited girl in her long white satin wrapper. "You look stunning just as you are, my dear, but perhaps you should put your dress on before you go down and knock his eye out."

* * *

They danced that night for the first time since London, to the big band at the Copa nightclub, and between the sambas to some of the London tunes. 'The Last Time I saw Paris' had not as yet crossed the South Atlantic, much to Dina's relief, but 'We'll Meet Again' had arrived, and was sung to the dancers by an importation from Spain. She gave the very English, very romantic song a new dimension of flamenco and castanets which made dancing difficult, and Dina complained that she couldn't understand the words.

"I did in London, I can't here!"

"I don't think What's-Her-Name—Margarita—understands them very well herself. Anyway it ought to be a man singing, not a girl."

"Why?"

"Because it's a man saying goodbye to a girl before he goes to war. Listen." And Mike sang very softly, so that only Dina in his arms heard:

So will you please say hello to the folks that I know,
Tell them I won't be long,
They'll be happy to know that as you saw me go
I was singing this song—

"You could call it the soldier's farewell," he said, and Dina, looking up, was happy to see his face amused and unperturbed. He never talked to her about the war.

Next morning, after Tony's telephone call, Mike Marchand presented himself at the Capricorn hangars out at the airport, with new dungarees under his arm, and started work with the mechanics. His psychology had been accurate, for where the mulatto manager would have fretted and fussed, the two Negro mechanics accepted him with true Carioca good humour. If a boss-man, the Lady Divininha's beau, wanted to service aircraft, they were glad of the extra help, and within an hour, as Mike regained his expertise with tools, the two boys knew that he was a good workman. On the first day they shared their lunch with him; on the next, Mike brought a lunch box and shared with them. They came and went by bus and he in an American sports car, and that was the principal difference between Mike and his workmates. One other, which Pedro and Julio soon noticed, was that the foreigner was particularly interested in servicing the Deodoros, even to the point of watching the Capricorn pilots take off and land the big sixteen-seaters. In dimension they resembled British bombers, and were heavier aircraft than Mike had ever flown.

Immediately after a second and most satisfactory consultation with Dr. Baumeister, he again asked Tony da Costa to give him a chance to fly.

"I'm sorry, Mike, I can't put my pay load at risk," said Tony.

"I wasn't asking to fly passengers, I haven't a valid commercial licence. I was hoping you'd let me take up a Beechcraft."

"Even a Beechcraft costs too much money to end up as scrap," said Tony.

"You can have my Puss Moth any time you like," said Dina.

"Not if I warn the control tower, he can't," said Tony grimly.

"If I take another physical, and it's okay, you can't refuse me —at least on medical grounds," said Mike.

"I grant you that. Shall we see if the doctor who does our pilot checkups will give you a certificate?"

"No, I don't want a civilian certificate. Could you fix it for me to see an Air Force medic?"

"Are you planning to join the Brazilian Air Force, man?"

"Brazil's not in the war."

"Not yet," said Tony da Costa. "But the war's a long way from being over, Mike."

"That's why I want an Air Force medic's line. Come on, Tony, you're the greatest fixer in town: get me a pass to the nearest Air Force hospital."

When the Brazilian colonel, effusive and flattering, had reversed the judgment of his European colleagues, Mike put the certificate in his pocket, drove the Duesenberg to the airport and got his Clearance, and then went in search of Dina.

"The Puss Moth's ready," she said when she rose to face him in Rinaldo's little office. "As soon as I got your phone call I had the boys bring it out. There's a jacket and a helmet for you inside."

"But you're coming too," he said, and took her hands. "I want you to fly me the first time, before I go solo. This is the start of the road back, Dina! You're my wonderful mascot—I need you to bring me luck."

"Very well," she said with stiff lips. "Senhor Rinaldo, will you clear me with traffic control?"

. . . Mike sat in the passenger's seat behind her, adjusting the headphones which were part of the helmet and earpieces, while Dina went through her Before Engine Starting Check, and headed into the wind for her take-off. They were airborne almost before Mike realised it, and Dina began to fly her familiar pattern, westward across the city on the first leg of the flight to São Paulo. Mike looked down: he saw the railway line, and then, in rapidly diminishing size, the old Braganza palace and the Zoo. Dina's voice came through the speaking tube.

"Are you all right?"

"I'm fine."

"No buzzing in your ears?"

"No, they're okay."

"I won't go above 5000."

"Fine with me."

Everything was fine except the nervous feeling, much more acute in a two-seater than in the Pan Am Clipper, of being flown by somebody else, but then the somebody was Dina, competent and secure. She turned south in about ten minutes and flew back over the Tijuca forest, giving him a view of Alto da Boa Vista and the pagoda which marked the Chinese View. She said once or twice, "Keep looking down!"—he guessed she wanted him to test all the angles of vision which had previously caused him distress. But vision and hearing were unimpaired when they returned to the airport, and Dina set her wheels and her tail skid down simultaneously to taxi back to the Capricorn apron.

"You can really do a daisy-bender, darling," Mike said as they got out of the plane. "Better than your friend Amy Johnson, she was a real banger. I've heard it said she didn't land, she just arrived."

"Oh never mind about Amy Johnson," said poor Dina. "Mike, it's you! Are you sure you're really ready to go solo, after so long? Should you put it off until tomorrow?"

"It has to be today, Dina. I've wasted too many years already."

"Happy landings!" she said, and Mike waved once, with his left thumb up, before the Puss Moth headed down the runway. Dina stood clutching her helmet while she watched. This is the road back, he had said, and she was looking on at the beginning; but the road back to—what? To some revenge for what he'd called the wasted years? She saw with a pang of alarm that Mike was flying out to sea.

He made a wide sweep over Guanabara Bay, flying north with his eyes moving between the instrument panel and the once-familiar scene below: the piers at the foot of the Avenida Rio Branco, where the Brazilians had flocked to see HMS *Ark Royal* refuelling before the Battle of the River Plate, then the beautiful Paqueta Island, and the Niteroi ferry, with people looking up from the decks of the paddle steamer. The great bay was studded with islands and spurs of land, some crowned with old fortifications: real sea and real islands, nothing which at all resembled his fantasies of the desert, nothing spoke to him but the familiar sound of the engines. He settled into the pilot's seat. There had never been an easier plane to fly than the Puss Moth, the taxi of the air, and with every minute at the controls Mike Marchand felt himself more completely absorbed into what had been his

183

native element, more at one with the wind and the sky. He left the islands behind him, flying east at 90 m.p.h., thinking of Africa ahead, and—but without the old neurosis—of the sands of Senegal, and then he changed course with an Immelmann turn, and flew back, as he had often dreamed of doing, over Botafogo Bay, with the Sugar Loaf on his starboard wing and the great statue of Christ the Redeemer on the port. Santos Dumont airfield lay ahead.

Mike had been told that nobody chandelled any more, it was a stunt that belonged to yesterday's heroes, and was probably as corny as hell. But he couldn't resist it: flying in from the Andes it had been his custom to chandelle round the hangars to celebrate his arrival, and he did it now. Then he was beginning his approach to the runway, easing back the stick to reduce the angle of glide, and the concrete was rolling up at him, and his wheels and tail skid were down in a three-point landing. He saw Pedro running with the flags to guide him to the parking bay, and as he cut the engine switch Mike Marchand felt intolerably tired.

But Dina was beside him when he clambered stiffly down, and Dina's vivid face was like a song of triumph. She had something in her hand—could it be a notebook and a fountain pen?—and,

"Can I have your autograph, Captain Marchand, please?" she said.

12

"I HAD A CABLE from my cousin Michel," said Jacques Brunel, almost at the pitch of his voice. "He's started flying again!"

"He's started what again?" asked Edmond Leblanc in the same tone. The two men had literally bumped into each other in a crowded public house in Soho.

"Flying!"

"He'll be happy at last," said Edmond, saving the contents of his glass as a burly young man in French uniform pushed his way up to the bar. "But did he send you a cable just to tell you that?"

"No, it was about the flat. He said if I wanted to stay on after Michaelmas he'd fix the rent with the estate agents."

"And do you?"

"I can't live on charity for ever."

"Well," said Edmond, "you know where the money is!"

He jerked his head significantly at a poster on the wall above the bar, one of the posters which de Gaulle's publicity agent had devised and which now appeared in many places of public entertainment. This particular house was 'The York Minster' in Dean Street, more familiarly known from its clientèle as the French Pub, but also patronised by soldiers of the other foreign legions now assembled in Britain. The French, on this August evening, outnumbered the other foreigners by about three to one.

De Gaulle's poster, under crossed Tricolores, began:

To All the French
France has lost a Battle!
She has not lost the War!

"The money's there all right," said Jacques indifferently, "I don't care for the smell of it. And I especially don't care for the sound of that big lie."

"What lie?"

" 'France has lost a battle, she has not lost the war'. De

185

Gaulle obviously believes with Dr. Goebbels that if you're going to tell a lie you'd better tell a good one. Of course we lost the war! Two-thirds of our country, including the capital, are occupied by our conquerors: what d'you call that—the result of a skirmish? Only our Allies will ever get us out of the mess we're in, and if the fellow who signed that poster thinks otherwise, he's living in a megalomaniac's dream."

"For God's sake take it easy, Jacques," said Edmond warningly. They had moved back against the wall and were talking in lowered voices, in English, but the Gaullist NCOs pressed up against them by the crowd might possibly understand the language of their hosts, and to Edmond Leblanc, that accomplished sitter on the fence, there was no point in starting an argument. Rows were only too common in the French Pub, but it was early yet, hardly eight o'clock, and belligerence usually set in about ten. Jacques caught and understood his look, and grinned.

"No, I haven't been drinking," he said, and held up his mug. "Half a pint of draught, and it's my first today." In fact he had already dined off a cup of coffee and a cheese roll at Lyons' 'Old Vienna' café in Coventry Street, and had moved on to 'The York Minster' in the simple need of feeling other human beings near him. The Luftwaffe had got through to London at last. On the previous night there had been a six-hour raid, from half past nine until after half past three in the morning, and Jacques, who like millions of Londoners had no air raid shelter to go to, had sat up in his lonely flat listening to the sounds of combat until the first light appeared in the sky.

"Here come the Americans," said Edmond, not without relief. "I told you, we were at Brize Norton together this afternoon." Jacques nodded. In the last few days, the damage done on the ground had been punishing: the enemy bombers had destroyed forty aircraft on the station at Brize Norton, twenty at Tangmere, with comparable losses all over southern and southeastern England, and his attacks on radar stations and arms factories had been devastating. The moment of truth for England was approaching fast.

The two well-fed individuals who now emerged from the men's room collected whiskies at the bar and made their way to the corner where Leblanc stood with Jacques. "Here's your refill, Ed," said the younger one, sliding one of the two glasses he carried into Edmond's hand. "Found a friend?"

"Jacques Brunel," said Edmond. "Meet Bill Barclay, Eastern Broadcasting Corporation. And Irving Greenbaum, of the Chicago *Clarion*."

"Hi Jack," said Mr. Greenbaum. "You with de Gaulle?"

"No, I'm working for the refugees."

"Do-gooder, eh?"

"Captain Brunel was severely wounded at Namsos," said Edmond quickly.

"Oh, that little side-show," said Greenbaum disparagingly. "*That* didn't amount to much. Now when I was with Georgie Patton in the Argonne in '18—" As he launched into an account of his service as a war correspondent in the Other War, Jacques saw that the *Clarion* man was about Edmond's age, nearer fifty than forty, and plump with years of good living. The other was younger, tougher, with a pleasant smile: he at once offered to get a Scotch for Jacques.

"I'm all right, thanks."

"You don't want to drink that warm slop."

"I like it, thanks all the same."

Bill Barclay nodded amiably. He had summed Jacques up in one sweeping professional glance as a quiet, nondescript guy who had probably done well in Norway when it came to the crunch, but who wouldn't have breath enough for the long haul, unlike those Gaullist daredevils who had swamped the bar and were drinking some toast or other, he couldn't make out what. He was going to ask Eddie White, the DJ man who'd been such a help at Brize Norton, when he heard Greenbaum say something about Caporetto, and the nondescript guy reply equably:

"Caporetto was where the Italians ran away in face of the enemy. They haven't done that so far, because they've had too good a chance to stab their enemies in the back: first the French when we were nearly down and out, and now the British in Somaliland."

"*That* was a lousy little show, if you like," grunted Greenbaum. "How long did the British last in Somaliland? A week? How long are they gonna last when the Eyeties invade Egypt?"

"They'll last all right," said Jacques. "They'll hold the Italians in the Delta; and one day there'll be another Caporetto, somewhere in the desert."

"Fat chance the British have of landing troops in the desert now."

"Perhaps your lot will turn up and give them a hand?" suggested Jacques.

"Not a hope in hell!" exploded the *Clarion* man. "We saved democracy in the '17–'18 War and you couldn't make it stick; why should we send another army of fine boys to do your dirty work again?"

"Steady, Irv," murmured Bill Barclay, but Jacques actually smiled.

"I'm inclined to agree with you," he said. "Why the hell should you? You've got a whole lot out of the war already, without putting one fine boy at risk—"

"Whaddiya mean?"

"I mean those 99-year leases on Britain's air and sea bases in the Caribbean, that Churchill's giving you in exchange for fifty clapped-out destroyers from your mothball fleet," said Jacques.

"It certainly was a very, very impressive offer," interposed Bill Barclay. "The folks back home will surely be convinced now that Britain means to see this thing through to the bitter end . . . Eddie, let me freshen your drink for you. Jack, change your mind and have a Scotch."

"Thanks, I think I will," said Jacques. "Let me help you with the glasses." He needed an excuse to get away from Greenbaum, although Bill Barclay muttered, as they made their slow way to the bar, that he didn't have to take old Irv too seriously. "I know he's a bigmouth, I know he likes to needle people," he went on. "Every sortie we've done together, he's had our Limey conducting officer foaming at the mouth. But I've seen the copy he's sending home, and believe me it's warm, compassionate stuff. He really feels for the British, he thinks they've got a lot of guts. And so has he, of course he's an old hand, but he was the coolest of the lot of us last night, down in the Savoy air raid shelter when the blitz was on . . . I don't mind telling you I was scared stiff when I had to get out and do my broadcast."

"Which was when?"

"One a.m. Greenwich Mean Time."

"Rather you than me." They laughed; the ice was broken, and when they struggled back with drinks for their companions Bill Barclay manœuvred himself into the position of a buffer state between Greenbaum and Jacques Brunel.

"Are you going to broadcast to America about the French Pub?" Jacques asked him.

188

"It could be part of a mood piece, probably. The mood's changing, don't you think?"

"I haven't been in London long enough to tell."

"Where've you been, then?"

"In hospital in Scotland."

But of course he was only putting the American off. Jacques had no intention of being quoted in the mood piece, and the man was quite capable of noting the changing mood of London for himself. It was hardening, not in the determination to see the war through to victory, for that had always been there, but in the stoic acceptance of increasing danger, of the loss of small personal liberties, of the shortages of food and fuel. And with the stoicism there was another hardening, shading more and more into lawlessness and brutality, of theft and violence in the darkened streets. Here in Soho, among the crowd of men in the French Pub—for there were very few women present, the women were in the alleys and lanes outside—and among the foreign inhabitants who had lived so long in London, there was now an impulse to lust and cruelty which had not been felt by the almost idyllic crowds whom Mike Marchand had seen drifting through Piccadilly and Kensington in the balmy evenings of July. The bomber's moon had risen over London, distorting all things with its smoke-stained light.

"What's that toast they all keep drinking?" asked the radio reporter, turning to Edmond Leblanc. The young Free French soldiers, now monopolising the bar, were not so much drinking as chanting their toast.

"They're saying *'Vive le Gouverneur Eboué! Vive le Territoire du Chad!'*"

"Who's Eboué, and where in hell's the Chad?" asked Greenbaum, who had a smattering of French.

"You missed the news when you were out on your 'sortie', as you call it," said Jacques Brunel. "There was an announcement from Carlton Gardens, carried on the BBC. The Chad's a French possession, about a thousand miles east of Timbuktu and just as useless, and Felix Eboué's the Negro Governor-General, who has decided to throw in his lot with General de Gaulle."

"So that's what the kids are cheering about!" said Barclay. "Ed, is this important news? A Negro colony somewhere in the Sahara joins up with a guy in London, without much chance of sending him recruits—"

"Or he of reaching them, unless the British lend him planes," said Edmond. "I don't see de Gaulle hurrying to the Chad, he's aiming at better things, and Fort Lamy isn't Paris; it isn't even a sea-port. But—yes, Chad *is* important. It's the first possession in the French Empire to declare for General de Gaulle, and when one starts, others may follow . . . *allez, les gars, attention!*" He had been jostled, and badly, by the latest arrivals, who were wearing brand-new, French tropical uniforms. They were greeted with a howl of welcome by their comrades at the bar.

"Looks like those guys are hurrying out to Chad, even if their general isn't," said Bill Barclay drily. "It's a warm night, but hardly hot enough for what they're wearing. That's the kind of kit I was issued with last year in Cairo."

The men in Free French uniforms had full glasses in their hands. "*A la France Libre! Au Général de Gaulle!*" The toasts and the laughter grew louder. The barman, French himself, leant over the bar and seemed to be appealing for quiet.

"*Messieurs, attention aux flics—*"

There was a moment of silence at the name of the police. Then one young voice rose clear and high:

"*Merde pour les tauliers anglais! Vive Dakar!*"

And a dozen voices took up the cry, "*A Dakar! A Dakar!*"

A square, middle-aged man in the uniform of a petty officer in the Royal Dutch Navy lunged forward shouting, "Shut your trap, you treacherous young devil! Do you want to get us all killed?"

"*Ta gueule!*" the young French boy screamed back. "What's it to do with you, grandpa? *Vive Dakar, mes braves! Vive Dakar libéré!*"

The Dutchman hit him hard on the point of the jaw. The boy staggered back but remained on his feet; with one quick movement he broke his glass on the bar and flung the heavy end, with its jagged edges, straight at the sailor's eyes. While the blood streamed down his face two of his friends, also in Dutch uniforms, threw themselves on the young Frenchman. Within seconds, the French Pub was a mêlée of men, kicking, gouging, fighting foul, while the girls shrieked, the barman blew a police whistle, and someone threw a pewter pint pot at de Gaulle's poster on the wall.

"Out!" said Irving Greenbaum, and with a turn of speed surprising in an obese man, he shoved Bill Barclay through the blackout curtains into Dean Street. Edmond and Jacques followed: neither of them wanted to join the fray or to be held as a witness when the police arrived, and not only were the Metropolitan Police arriving from the direction of Soho Square, but the military redcaps were coming up from Shaftesbury Avenue. The blackout rules were being violated as beams of light shone on the pavement with each entry and tumultuous exit from 'The York Minster'. The Dutch seaman came out on a stretcher with a bandage over his face.

"Young swine," said Jacques, watching from the far side of the street, "I wish they'd work off steam on the Germans, not their Allies."

"Or on the natives of Dakar," said the American slyly.

"Are you going to put that nonsense in your broadcast?"

"About Dakar? I tried it once already, and the British censor wouldn't pass my script."

"You mean this isn't the first time—?"

"I was eating dinner at the Ecu de France two nights ago, and a few of de Gaulle's officers were drinking 'To Dakar!' at the next table. A bit more classy than a bunch of bums brawling in a saloon, but a security leak just the same."

"That Dutchman wasn't a bum," said Irving Greenbaum. "And *he* yelled out something about 'getting us all killed'. Looks like they've a combined op. in view."

"Whatever may be in view," said Jacques, "let me remind you that Dakar's a French possession. Unless Governor Boisson declares for de Gaulle like that fellow in the Chad, an attack on the town by Frenchmen constitutes an act of civil war."

"Say, that's an interesting point," said Bill Barclay. "Why don't we all go back to the Savoy for dinner, and thrash the whole thing out? I want to give *some* hint of the way things are going in my next broadcast, because a lot of the folks back home are beginning to take an interest in what goes on at Dakar. Come on, Eddie, what do you say?"

Jacques looked expectantly at Edmond. He hated the idea of cadging a meal from the Americans, but the invitation had been freely given, and his stomach had hardly been filled by the cheese roll and coffee of the 'Old Vienna'. Edmond, however, said he must be getting back to the office. The proprietor had taken to dropping in of an evening, and liked to find all his men on the job. "I'll walk to the Underground with you, Jacques," he said determinedly, and a taxi-driver being at that moment seduced by Greenbaum's offer of £1 over and above his fare for taking them to the Savoy Hotel, there was no more to be said to the correspondents than Good night and See you around.

"You didn't mind, did you, Jacques?" said Edmond as they started off to Shaftesbury Avenue. The excitement at the French Pub was over and Dean Street had returned to normal. "That Bill Barclay's a great brain-picker; I didn't want to end up writing half his broadcast for him."

"He seems a nice fellow, I'd like to see him again. But I didn't really want to dine with Mr. Greenbaum, and anyway I ought to get back home." Jacques said it out of pride, though why he called it home and what he had to get back to would have been hard to explain.

"That was quite a punch-up in the pub," said Edmond. "The kind of show your cousin Michel might have enjoyed. Fancy that lucky young devil flying again!"

But Jacques was thinking less about Mike than about Anders Lachmann, alias Corbeau, reported heading for West Africa. "Something's up at Carlton Gardens," he said. "A trip to Dakar, moving on to Chad and elsewhere, would you say?"

"I don't think there's any doubt of it. We have reports of ships assembling at Liverpool—including *Dutch* ships, Jacques, that was a shrewd guess of Greenbaum's—which don't seem to be the usual convoy, and trolleys have been seen taking assault landing craft north on the main roads; it does look as if *mon général*'s getting ready for a *putsch*." He broke off to say "No thank you, darling," to a lady of the town who had addressed him with a "Hello, handsome!"—the girls 'on the Dilly' were doing good business since appetite had been whetted by the knife-edge of fear. "Of course this must have been in the works for some time," he went on. "My guess is that that was why the Press got a D-notice on Neil Grant's speech in the House of Commons. How did he react to it, do you know?"

"The D-notice? He expected it. But I stayed on until the House rose, after nine o'clock, and by that time Neil was feeling more cheerful. There'd been a whole lot more criticism, and the War Office man said at the end that the foreign forces concerned would be informed of the very strong feelings expressed in the House of Commons. It all sounded very cool and offhand to me, but that seems to be the way they carry on their business here."

"It is. And you haven't seen Mr. Grant since then?"

"I'm going down to his place on Saturday, they're giving a farewell party before Mrs. Grant and the children leave for Scotland."

"Best place for them," said Edmond. "The only thing I could think about in that infernal din last night was that my wife and the kids were safely out of it. Oh hell, not again!" he groaned, as the whine of an air raid warning rang out over the dark and crowded Circus.

"That doesn't mean they're any nearer than a hundred miles away."

"Last night it meant they were directly overhead. Come on, Jacques, let's get down to the Underground. I'll have to go the long way round to the office, confound it!"

"I usually take a bus from Piccadilly."

"Don't be a fool, take the Tube to Bond Street or Marble Arch." The newspaperman was clearly nervous, and Jacques let himself be carried along with the crowd now pouring into the Underground for shelter. Last night had completely destroyed the old pride in treating Alerts with contempt: the women dragging children along and lugging bundles of bedding and wraps were taking this one very seriously indeed. Jacques wondered where they all came from—probably from the old tenements of Soho and the streets round Leicester Square; those young mothers and elderly men were quite unlike the usual denizens of Piccadilly. When Edmond had started on his roundabout way to Fleet Street Jacques descended to the lowest level of the Underground station to see the people already settling into nests of blankets on the platforms, usually—if they were British—with a mug of Thermos tea in their hands. He had heard that the authorities were being urged to install bunks in what many people thought were the best natural air raid shelters in London—unless a land mine or some other blockbuster destroyed the escalators and all other means of getting to the surface, and the tunnels caved in. Jacques shuddered. Since his experiences at Namsos he had a horror of being buried in bomb debris. It would take a very much worse night than the previous one to drive him to a Tube shelter, there to huddle with strangers on a dirty platform—and besides the huddling there were also the problems of ventilation and sanitation, not yet resolved. Before a train came in and picked him up, Jacques had enough of the thick unmoving air which hung over the people like a miasma, although he saw they didn't seem to mind it much. At one end of the platform a sing-song was under way, featuring 'Pack Up Your Troubles' and 'Tipperary'. Always the songs of the Other War, the new songs had never caught on properly, though the new slogans had. Jacques heard a concerted yell of "London can take it!" as the train bore him away.

Back at the flat he made some tea and toast, and cheered himself up with the thought that by scrimping on his dinners for four nights he had saved enough to take Alison to lunch next day at her favourite 'Causerie,' and buy some toys to keep her little nephews amused for part of their long train journey to the Highlands. Jacques was beginning to be worried about money. His only perquisite as a voluntary worker at the Refugee Committee's rooms was a good hot lunch whenever he wanted it, and even the Committee's work would not go on for ever. Some of the younger fishermen had joined the embryo Free French naval forces commanded by Admiral Muselier, and others had been allowed to establish a small fishing fleet at Brixham. The older, married skippers from the Côtes du Nord had been transferred with their wives to a boarding-house in Glasgow, for the simple reason that nobody knew what to do with them in London. Jacques was beginning to consider joining the Air Raid Precautions service, which was paid. He would have preferred the Pioneer Corps if he had been strong enough for heavy manual work after his time in hospital. He lay on the sofa, making plans and discarding them until, the night remaining quiet, he went to bed and slept until the All Clear woke him at four a.m. His last waking thought was of Edmond Leblanc's reminder that the money was with de Gaulle.

*　　　　*　　　　*

Since the Agreement of August 7, de Gaulle had indeed had the money, and was now living on an ample scale. He had moved from the modest hotel in Buckingham Palace Road to the Connaught, one of the finest hotels in London, and there, apart from small dinner parties to male guests in his suite, he lived for the whole of each working week in solitary grandeur. His wife and children were well taken care of. He consistently refused to allow publicity photographs to be taken of his son and daughters, because the younger girl was mentally deficient, but he had begun to learn and even to like what was expected of himself. He consented to be photographed by Cecil Beaton and Howard Coster, and the Leader of All Free Frenchmen even found the time to have his portrait painted by a British artist. This was a real bonus for his PR men. The portrait was photographed and reproduced many times. The *Illustrated London News* gave it a full page on August 17, under the title 'Verdun Hero', and if being wounded in one of the Verdun battles, taken prisoner and remaining in captivity for two and a half years was the touchstone of heroism, then a hero the general was. Both film and still cameras were in action on August 25, when the king went to inspect the Free French Forces at Aldershot, and of course the public were not told that George VI had then remarked to a high official of the Foreign Office that he didn't think much of de Gaulle. Basking in the Prime Minister's favour, prepared to be obnoxious to any official who did not recognise in himself the incarnation of France, de Gaulle disdained any suggestions, made in the House of Commons or elsewhere, that his movement was liable to infiltration by men who were actual or potential traitors to himself or the British. He had come to believe, and later wrote, that he was 'a man thrown by fate outside all terms of reference'.

During those weeks, while the ring of steel tightened around Britain, de Gaulle was the archetypal Man on a White Horse, or—as he once announced to his startled dinner guests—the new Joan of Arc. As the month of August ended, the first successes crowned his cause, and these were exploited to the full. On the day after the Chad rallied to de Gaulle, three courageous Frenchmen led by a cavalry officer called Leclerc, who had been taken to Lagos in a British flying boat, claimed the French Cameroons in the name of General de Gaulle. There was not much opposition from the Vichy officials. There might have been more if HMS *Cumberland*, sent in support of the three musketeers, had not been lying off Douala, but by any standard it was a brave effort and a notable success. On the same day Colonel de Larminat, who had made a long journey from the Levant to Durban and had crossed Africa by air, assumed power in de Gaulle's name in French Equatorial Africa and set up the Free French capital at Brazzaville.

It was officially announced in London that all these territories would receive the same financial and economic help as Britain was giving to her own possessions. General de Gaulle's suspicions of

British ambitions inside the French Empire did not extend to refusing money.

That a considerable territory in Central Africa, with an outlet to the Gulf of Guinea at Douala, had passed out of the rule of Vichy naturally seemed the happiest omen of General de Gaulle's enthusiastic welcome at Dakar. Mr. Churchill, whose poetic vision saw the general and his convoy approaching the coast of Senegal under sunny skies, over blue seas, to the sound of cheering from a grateful city, was even inspired to think of further action once Dakar was in de Gaulle's hands. Dakar was to be the base for a full-scale attack on Morocco, scheduled as Operation Threat. In this, Mr. Churchill's attitude to geography was much the same as de Gaulle's when he planned an advance on Dakar through the bush from Conakry, for between Dakar and Morocco lay a thousand miles of the Sahara Desert and the great barrier of the Atlas Mountains. The Chiefs of Staff tactfully urged the great man's attention back from Operation Threat to Operation Menace. There were soldiers in the planning of Operation Menace who thought the code name much too appropriate.

Only a very few Londoners had heard the toast of 'Dakar!' proposed by men who should have known better, but a great many citizens had heard the cry of 'London can take it!' since the night air raids began. They were the most thrilled to know that Berliners were being required to take it too. The retaliation raids on Germany were beginning to take effect. The marshalling yards at Ham had been attacked so often, or reported attacked so often, that the cynical were beginning to say Ham should be renamed Mince, but now Berlin had been bombed, and so had Kiel and Hamburg, and Hitler had been furious enough to vow he would raze every British city to the ground. It was heady, euphoric stuff, and Alison Grant shared in the euphoria as she ran on to the concourse of Waterloo station on Friday afternoon.

Jacques was there, of course, standing by the gate for the Watermead Halt and Kingsmead train, and looking anxious. Her heart leapt at the sight of that tall figure and thin serious face. Captain Jack—her hospital hero not so very long ago, and now the man she loved, wanted to spend her life with, even if other people, friends and strangers, generals and statesmen, would do their best to part them! We're entitled to our happiness, she told herself defiantly, and hurried up to the gate with her season ticket in her hand.

"Darling, I thought you were going to miss the train!" Jacques took her hand and hurried her along the platform. "I don't even know if we'll get a seat now! Where's Neil?"

"There's a flap on at the Ministry, I don't know what about. That's why I'm late myself. Neil told me to wait, and then phoned through at the last moment and said he'd be detained, he'll try to get the next train," Alison explained breathlessly. "Let's get in somewhere—anywhere! The guard's going to blow his whistle in a minute."

There were no vacant seats in any compartment of the carriage they climbed into, but there was space in the corridor, where a long line of commuters buried in their evening papers moved reluctantly up to make room for the newcomers, and in the corridor Jacques was able to slip his arm round her waist, and Alison to tilt her head back against his shoulder. The ticket collector came along and upset their balance as the train gathered speed.

"I love this bit of the railway," said Alison. "I like to see all the funny things people keep in their back gardens."

They were not very far from the great terminal, and the rows of terrace houses, two up and two down, built almost a hundred years earlier of London's own purple-bloomed brick, now grimed by smoke and soot, lay immediately under the railway embankment. Their long, narrow backyards held a variety of things: a couple of rabbit hutches, home-made greenhouses, love-birds in a cage slung on the washing line, a baby in a pram, hens in a wire run beneath a row of sunflowers. "All the little houses, all the little lives," said Alison softly. "How d'you suppose those people get away with keeping hens in town?"

"I don't know. I never noticed them before," Jacques confessed. "I've always been too keen on getting down to Watermead and you. Alison, it was very sweet of your sister-in-law to ask me to dine and sleep tonight—"

"If you don't mind sleeping on the divan in Neil's study."

"Mind! I said I'd gladly sleep in the air raid shelter!"

Alison giggled. "Mrs. Macdonald might beat you to it. She was so brave when she arrived, kept saying she hoped to see a dogfight won by our pilots, but since the Luftwaffe started night bombing she's been terrified, and runs for the shelter every time the Alert goes off. The Oban WVS is going to hear a lot about Mrs. Mac's adventures in the front line."

"When Mrs. Grant phoned she said you'd all been tidying up the garden for the party. Is it going to be out of doors?"

"It'll begin out of doors, with drinks I mean, but the food'll be inside. It's not going to be a big party, you know? Just a sort of goodbye to some of Lucy's best friends—Mrs. Weldon and her husband, and five or six other couples, you'll like them all."

"It sounds like fun. And when do they actually leave for Scotland?"

"Sunday at ten, the night train for Glasgow."

"You won't come all the way in to see them off?"

"Oh no, not on Sunday. It'll be so late."

But on Monday, thought Alison, I don't care how late it is. I'll tell Lottie to go home as usual, because I'm spending the night with a girl from my office—Freda would do, she'll cover up for anybody, and . . . I'll do whatever Jacques wants, whatever he meant when he asked if I couldn't stay in town when Neil and Lucy go away. I'll tell him what I've planned when we're walking up the lane, and he'll ask me to have dinner with him on Monday night, maybe at Mount Street even, and then—oh then . . . It'll be like it was that night in the orchard. Only this time . . . it'll be everything.

But almost as soon as they left Watermead Halt Alison knew it was no time for a confidential talk. The lane of the wild flowers was picturesque but not winding, it ran straight to the footpath beside Lime Tree Cottage, and at the far end they could see the figure of Mrs. Macdonald advancing purposefully with a grandson in each hand.

"Ça alors!" said Jacques, and Alison nearly laughed at his expression. Mrs. Macdonald had been annoying her of late, particularly when she had the impertinence to ask if Alison thought her parents would like her to be so friendly with a Catholic boy —the good lady, like the Grant parents, was a bigoted Presbyterian. It was like her to come along and break up what she would think of as a flirtation in the lane.

She just managed to say, "Be nice to her, Jack, she's worked awfully hard and done all the packing for the trip, Lucy could never have managed without her!" before the little boys came running up to meet them, and they all went amicably enough to the cottage. There Lucy Grant met them, so pretty and animated since her recovery from a difficult confinement, but looking for the moment rather downcast.

"Jack, how nice of you to come," she greeted him warmly. "Neil just telephoned from the Ministry. He won't be back till ten, isn't it a shame? You'll have to be the man of the house at dinner, and do the carving."

"Is there anything *to* carve?" asked Alison.

"Farmer Brown brought me two lovely ducklings."

"Under the counter, eh? Oh, Lucy!"

"No, he said it was a present, because of my going away. And mother picked all the late peas this afternoon."

"We'll have a feast," said Alison, and ran upstairs to change her dark dress for an old blue cotton and tie on an apron with a bib. Lottie went home at six o'clock, after starting the dinner preparations and setting the table, and there was usually plenty to do in the kitchen. Presently she and Jacques were seated one on each side of the table, shelling the big pile of fresh peas, while Mrs. Macdonald put the boys to bed and Lucy moved in and out between the new fridge and the old stove, basting the ducklings. It was a peaceful time, with the sunset light coming through the lime tree screen, and nothing to be heard but the sound of rooks returning to their nests and the ticking of the grandfather clock in the stone-flagged hall. Alison felt calmed and happy. Much more than her innocent ideas of a night of passion, this scene suited her: Jacques and herself working together at a simple domestic task, in a real home, looking up from their green-stained fingers and smiling across the peas in the yellow bowl. Why shouldn't life be always like this for us? she thought, but no longer rebelliously. We're entitled to our happiness—perhaps it will.

It was not quite ten when they heard the sound of a car, and Neil's voice talking to the driver. Lucy went out in the darkness to meet him, calling to the others to mind the blackout when she opened the front door. They could hear Neil, as he came closer, telling his wife that he thought he had bagged the last taxi in the whole of Kingsmead-on-Thames. When he came into the drawing room they could all see that his face was white with fatigue.

"Was there another air raid, darling?" asked his wife fearfully.

"No, not so much as an Alert, but we had the hell of a flap at the office. Well, Jack, it's nice to see you, have they fed you well? Come and talk to me while I have something to eat myself."

"You've had no dinner!"

"Don't worry, Lucy, I'm not hungry. All I want is a glass of beer, and some of that oatcake and cheese I brought back from Carrick, if there's any left."

"Of course there is, I'll get it," said Alison. "Will you have it here or in the dining room?"

"Be a pet and put it in the dining room, it's stifling in here. That damned blackout!" Neil took his jacket off, and loosened his tie.

"You *are* tired, darling," Lucy said. "I did hope you weren't going to work so hard when the House was in recess."

"I'm all right, dear, don't fuss. How's everything here? Boys behaving themselves? Baby sound asleep?"

"Everything is fine." And Alison at the door, quick and deft as always, said the tray was in the dining room. She'd brought a bottle of beer for Jacques too, and there was plenty more in the fridge.

"Is beer all right for you, Jack?" said Neil. "There's Scotch —would you rather have a nightcap?"

"Beer, please."

"A *nightcap*—dear me, that's a broad hint to us women, isn't it?" said Mrs. Macdonald, stabbing her needles through her knitting. "Come along, girls, let's leave the men to talk state secrets. We'll have to be up with the lark tomorrow morning."

"Yes, let's have an early night," said Lucy Grant. "And Neil, don't you sit up too long."

"*A demain, Jacques,*" said Alison, rather wistfully.

"*A demain, chère, bonne nuit.*"

Bonne nuit—and I still haven't had a proper talk with him, Alison thought, as she trailed upstairs behind Lucy. But there's tomorrow, there'll be time tomorrow, in the afternoon, before the party . . . and on Monday, Monday night . . .

The men went into the dining room. It was certainly cooler there, for the french windows had been left open to the darkness, after dinner. Alison had checked the blackout, and Neil switched on a big centre lamp above the table.

"Lucy says this light's too crude, but I'm not in the mood for dickering about with candles," he said. "Pour yourself a glass of beer, Jack."

The lager bottles were misted with the chill of the fridge. The big Dunlop cheese, only half consumed, had a wreath of fresh watercress around it, and the small pat of butter which accompanied the wooden platter of oatcakes was made more impressive by a few sprigs of parsley. Alison had done her best to make the supper tray appetising.

Jacques sipped beer from a tall fluted glass and kept silent until Neil had taken the edge off his hunger. Then his host stretched luxuriously, and smiled.

"I've been looking forward to a talk with you, Jack," he said. "I've been thinking about you a lot lately. But it'll have to wait until tomorrow morning, I'm too whacked to make any kind of sense tonight."

"Something serious has happened?" said Jacques tentatively.

"Pretty serious. The PM called a Cabinet at six. My Minister's not in the War Cabinet, but he has Cabinet rank, so naturally I had to wait till he was free."

"I was afraid it had something to do with your speech in the House last week."

"Eh? Oh, that's a thing of the past. I got a caning from the Scottish Whip for raising matters which should only have come before the House in secret session—by God, that's an idea, we ought to have a secret session immediately after the recess—and then I was told everything would be forgiven if not forgotten. Unfortunately Mr. Churchill has a long memory."

"I heard about the D-notice."

"Yes, well, that didn't apply to *Hansard,* it's all on record there, and also, verbatim, in the Burns Bay *Gazette.* Which is far too insignificant, in official eyes, to be served with a D-notice. The *Gazette,* being Conservative, described my little effort as 'statesmanlike' and compared me to Disraeli. That started a spate of letters to the editor, mostly unflattering. The Provost of Burns Bay, a grand old Liberal, wrote to say I should think shame of myself for wasting the time of the House on a rabble like the Foreign Legion instead of the needs of my constituents . . . He may very well have been right."

Neil Grant refilled his glass. "What happened in London today was something else again. This morning I couldn't have mentioned it to you without infringing the Official Secrets Act. Tonight it's a public scandal, known far and wide, and I don't see why you shouldn't know too . . . Jack, I know you've got a pretty good intelligence service of your own. Have you ever been given a hint that General de Gaulle was planning an attack on Dakar in French West Africa?"

"More than a hint," said Jacques. He described what he had seen at the French Pub and what he had heard of the toasts drunk 'To Dakar!' at the Ecu de France.

"So you were there," said Neil Grant slowly. "We've had reports on all these incidents, of course, both in and outside London, but—you were actually there. You didn't only hear the words, you saw the men. How did the incident really strike you?"

"I thought it was good theatre," said Jacques Brunel. "Good acting, at any rate. Not the Dutchman; he was asking for trouble, and he obviously hadn't been rehearsed. But the—the Free French, we have to call them, were just a bit too melodramatic to be true."

"You're a smart fellow, aren't you?" said Neil. "I think you deserve a sight of what the Cabinet was summoned to discuss. It's not exclusive, don't think that; every porter and sweeper-upper at Liverpool Street Station has had a chance to look at this already."

He took a couple of crumpled leaflets from the pocket of his trousers and passed them across the table. They were printed in French and signed with the name of General de Gaulle. The first began,

> *Soldats Français*
> Your Duty is
> To fight with us
> For France!

and the second,

> We have come to defend Dakar along with you!
> We have come to bring food to Dakar!

and so on, and on, to the dramatic ending:

> *Vive Dakar français!*
> *Vive l'Afrique française!*
> *Vive la France!*

"*Et vive Moi de Gaulle!*" said Jacques. "These papers were found at Liverpool Street *Station*? How?"

"When the Gaullist troops entrained today for the port of embarkation," said Neil, speaking with the precision of fatigue, "a crate full of these proclamations burst open. The intention had been to drop them by aircraft over Dakar. They've been blowing all along Liverpool Street instead."

Jacques drew in his breath. "So the target of the expedition is known before it even sails," he said. "That's what the Cabinet met to discuss?"

"They met to discuss whether to cancel the whole thing at the eleventh hour."

"And the decision?"

"To go on with it."

Neil got up. "I think we'll have that nightcap after all," he said. He went to the sideboard and poured two level drams of Scotch. "Here's to Dakar," he said, "the popular toast of the moment. Here's to another Dunkirk, another Somaliland, another Mers-el-Kebir. Here's to another fiasco. When our armada gets to Dakar—British ships, British planes, three British soldiers for every Gaullist—what do you suppose the guns of the *Richelieu* are going to do to us? Or the Glenn Martin and Curtiss planes at Ouakem? How long will it take for us to be at war with Vichy France?"

Jacques was silent. The news was very bad, but it was no worse than he had been expecting since that strangely artificial scene in the French Pub. And Neil, as if he could read the thoughts of the younger man, broke in on his silence:

"What did you mean when you said those men in the pub were too melodramatic to be true?"

"I was just . . . wondering . . . if all these calculated indiscretions aren't the result of very careful planning. Those toasts in bars and restaurants—they don't sound natural. We never drank 'To Helsinki!' when we expected to go to fight in Finland, nor yet 'To Trondheim!' when we embarked at Brest for Norway. So why 'To Dakar' when the only toast that matters is 'To Berlin'? Unless explicit orders had been given to do it? And now those leaflets—God knows I've learned something about how to make a nonsense of an embarkation, but a crate containing propaganda like this, absolutely top secret, would be fastened with metal bands and clasps, not in some flimsy covering that bursts open at the first handling. Unless that was what was meant to happen! Part of the big coverup of boyish exuberance and plain downright carelessness, hiding the real, deliberate leak of news which must have taken place already—"

"How?" said Neil Grant. "Where?"

"Through what my cousin Michel called the traitors' gate," said Jacques. "To Vichy, possibly. Certainly to Berlin."

13

JACQUES AWOKE NEXT morning with the feeling, so vexatious to a lawyer, of having said a great deal more than he could prove. If he were on trial in the Palais de Justice at Nice now, how could he prove that de Gaulle's headquarters was a nest of traitors out to sabotage the Allied cause? It was true that de Gaulle himself had been throughout his army career, and was now in London, an unpopular figure, but as yet nobody outside of Vichy had accused him of high treason. The worst that was said —but 'everybody' said it—was *'son entourage est lamentable'*; no one, at least in Jacques' hearing, had ever taken the logical step of suggesting that General de Gaulle, and he alone, was responsible for the entourage. Not even Neil Grant, another lawyer, had so much as mentioned that if de Gaulle was not received with open arms at Dakar, but had to fight his way ashore, he would be violating his own Agreement with the British government in its most sensitive clause, that the Free French would never be required to take up arms against other Frenchmen. And if he wins nobody will dream of mentioning it, thought Jacques, as he got out of his divan bed and pulled the window wider to enjoy the freshness of the morning. He could hear the wireless going in the kitchen and Lottie chattering with the little boys. Jacques took the towels folded on a chair in the study and went off to take a cold bath as an antidote to melodrama.

Neil seemed to be of the same mind as himself when they met in the dining room. He had time to mutter to Jacques, " 'Fraid we got a bit over-excited last night, old chap!" before Lucy arrived to pour the tea. She was followed by Alison with a big cup of *café au lait* for Jacques, and they all had a cheerful breakfast. Afterwards everybody had jobs to do. Lottie had stripped the divan bed in the study before breakfast was over, and everything there was back to normal when Neil sat down to the telephone with the door shut and the extension in the hall cut out. Jacques, who had been detailed to carry all the suitcases for Scotland downstairs and put them in the garage, saw him coming out of the study with a very grave face, and knew that his host's thoughts were far away in a northern port where the ships and men so urgently needed by Britain were being despatched in support of a Frenchman's desperate bid for power. He said nothing, however, but a cheerful "*Allez!*" as he began to manhandle a tin trunk containing the boys' toys and clothing towards the back door. Neil, recalled to the needs of Lime Tree Cottage, came up behind him and took the other end.

Then they both set to work in the garden, Neil mowing the small lawn and Jacques sweeping the patio in readiness for the arrival of the pram and its tiny occupant, when he went to bend with Lucy over the baby girl who had Alison's red hair.

"She's growing, isn't she?" he hazarded.

"Of course she's growing, what do you suppose? Mother's big, big girl!" crooned Lucy, and the baby cooed.

"Are you going to take her pram to Scotland, Mrs. Grant?"

"I do wish you'd call me Lucy! No, she's going to travel in her Moses basket, and my brother's wife's going to lend me their old pram while I'm at home." Unconsciously Lucy sighed and straightened up.

"Aren't you looking forward to the Highlands?"

"Very much, for the children's sake. I only wish I knew when we'd be coming back to Lime Tree Cottage." Then, remembering how uncertain his own future was, Lucy said in her sympathetic way, "Jack, it's so nice having you here! Why don't you go and help Alison now? She's going to pick some raspberries for lunch."

It could have been idyllic among the raspberry canes, down at the foot of the tangled kitchen garden out of sight and sound of the cottage, but the little boys were enticed by the twin attractions of Captain Jack and free access to the raspberries, and came squealing at their heels. Colin, as conscientious as his father, was a responsible picker, but Peter had to be restrained from putting the red berries into his own mouth. The two adults kept an eye on him and picked quickly, the yellow bowl which had held the peas was nearly full when Neil appeared at the foot of the garden, with a freshly cut lettuce in his hand.

"Lucy's calling you to elevenses," he said. "Here, Colin, take this lettuce in to mother."

"What are elevenses?" said Jacques.

"A cup of tea and a bite of whatever is handy, and an excuse to sit down for a good gossip in the middle of the morning."

"I couldn't possibly eat and drink after all that breakfast," said Jacques, and Alison laughed. "I never say no to a cup of tea," she said. "I'll carry in the raspberries, and put them out of the reach of little hands."

The two men followed her slim figure in the green cotton dress past the garage to the front of the house, where thanks to Mrs. Macdonald's energy during the week the garden was in good trim for the visitors.

"How do you think it looks?"

"*Magnifique!*"

"Let's stroll up to the orchard, then, and see how the apples are doing."

The apples looked suspiciously worm-eaten to Jacques, but as Neil philosophically said, there was no sugar for apple jelly this year, and Lucy was going away. They moved on to the rough grass and the fence beyond which Farmer Brown's cows were grazing, and there were overtaken by Colin and Peter, carrying their little cricket bats and half-eaten slices of bread and jam.

"Captain Jack, you promise and promise to play cricket with us, and you never do!"

"All right, an over each, then, and that's all."

He bowled underhand and very gently. It was not difficult to get the batsmen out, because as their father crossly told them they stepped out too soon to every ball, and the game was further complicated by the bull terrier, Sam, who did most of the fielding.

"Where's your Aunt Alison? Why doesn't she come and play with us?"

"I don't know," said Peter. It was the stock answer for a child of his age, but Colin said, "She's in the kitchen, Captain Jack, having tea with grandmother and Lottie."

But Alison at that moment was in the big old-fashioned pantry with Lucy, and smiling at Lucy's exaggerated air of woe.

"Alison, I really am a rotten housekeeper! There simply isn't going to be enough bread to get us through to tomorrow night!"

Alison inspected the bread crock. "I don't think there's enough to get us through the party!" she said. "What happened to the brown bread you were going to put the anchovies and things on?"

"What happened to the *white*?" said Lucy. She was looking at the lists pinned to a cork board on the pantry wall. "Can it be possible *mother* forgot to buy bread when she went into Kingsmead on the bus yesterday? Look, there's bread on the list all right! She brought everything else, two huge baskets full—"

"Can we get by with oatcake?" said Alison, opening a tin. "No—only four pieces left. Neil must have *devoured* it last night!"

"We'll need bread for toast, anyway," said Lucy. "How I wish I'd checked everything when mother came home! But she's usually so efficient . . . There's no help for it, I must send Lottie back to Kingsmead on her bike. The baker shuts at one on Saturday—"

"I'll go," said Alison. "I'll take your bike, and *dash*. You know what Lottie's like when she gets a chance to go into Kingsmead, she'll meet some of her pals and stand there gossiping, and there's such a lot for her to do here—"

"All right," said Lucy. "You *are* an angel, Alison. Get a loaf of white and a loaf of brown, that's all you can carry in the basket, and—oh dear! I haven't ridden for months, the tyres'll be flat!"

"I'll get the pump, it's in the garage," Alison said, and pocketing the purse Lucy held out to her, she ran out of the back door. The women in the kitchen heard her whistling as she mounted Lucy's bike at the side gate and set off down the Kingsmead highway. That clear whistling might have been audible as far as the rough grass beyond the orchard, but it was drowned by the sounds of bat and ball, and the barking of an excited dog. And the two men leaning on the farmer's fence were too absorbed in their talk to hear anything.

"I think you've guessed," Neil Grant was saying, "that the Ministry of Economic Warfare isn't solely concerned with such vital matters as the blockade of enemy-occupied territory?"

"Yes, I think I had guessed that," said Jacques quietly. "Our talk last night was enough to convince me."

"This summer we've started one or two new projects. Similar enterprises, you might call them."

"Parallel enterprises," said Jacques. "—Sorry, it's a French expression."

"Parallel; that's exactly what they are. And I can get you a job in two of them."

Jacques shifted his position on the fence. "What sort of job?"

"The first one could be called editorial. No, nothing to do with newspapers or radio broadcasts! Editing, writing leaflets and other propaganda of that sort, British propaganda, for distribution to the occupied countries of Europe. Letting them know what we're doing for ourselves, and how we intend to work for their liberation."

"Who's going to do the distributing?"

"The RAF, we hope."

Jacques smiled. "The RAF wasted a lot of petrol dropping leaflets over Germany at the beginning of the war. I don't think they convinced any German that the war was a criminal mistake."

"I agree; and I admit that after last night's fiasco at the station 'leaflets' could be a dirty word. But we have to wage war by every means, including political warfare, if we expect to win, and this new plan could turn out to be something very useful. You'd have to live in the country, but not too far from London, and you'd draw a salary as well as your living expenses."

Jacques was frowning slightly. "What's the other job?"

"The other job is something very different. There would be payments, but not guaranteed, and certainly not regular; there would be much more responsibility. There could be danger. You could find yourself operating alone, behind the enemy's lines, or even face to face with the enemy."

"Obviously that means working outside England?"

"It would mean going back to France."

Jacques Brunel's expression had not altered while his friend was speaking. Leaning on the wooden paling, chewing a stem of grass, he looked like a meditative countryman. Now Neil saw his lips tighten, and the colour rise in his thin face.

"Can't you give me more details?"

"No," said Neil. "I've no authority to tell you any more. That's for my associates to do, if you decide you want to meet them. Don't decide in a hurry! I'll be back from Scotland next weekend, and you can call me here or at the Ministry. Then you and I can meet, to fix up the editorial job, or you can meet my colleagues and discuss the other. Good luck to you either way."

"I really don't have much choice, have I?"

"If you can think of something better—"

"Neil," said the Frenchman. "I've got to tell you—I think you ought to know—that the reason I'd want to take the job in England, not that I think I'd be much good at it, is that then I could go on seeing Alison. That would mean—everything to me."

Her brother looked away from him. He wanted at all costs to avoid an emotional showdown, and the use of such expressions as 'everything to me' grated on his Scottish ears, but while he was fumbling with words Jacques continued, "If things were different, if we'd met a year ago, if I had anything to offer her—then I would ask Alison to be my wife."

Neil sighed. A proposal of marriage, to his legal mind, meant settlements, wills, the disposition of family heirlooms, the purchase of a house, plate and plenishing, and all the covenants devised by Church and State. And here was the Frenchman, with the extravagance of his race, clinching his intentions with the still more embarrassing words:

"I love her with all my heart."

"Have you told her so?"

"Not in so many words. But I am sure she is—aware of it. Do you—do you think I would have any chance?"

It was a lot to ask of a kind-hearted man. Neil was remembering his own sedate courtship of Lucy Macdonald, teaching Latin in an Edinburgh boarding-school, when he was a rising young man at the Scottish Bar. It was only ten years ago. In the emotional climate of the summer of 1940, it seemed like a chapter from Sir Walter Scott.

"I can't say," he said. "It's obvious she's very fond of you. But man, you've said it yourself, 'if things were different'. They're not different, and we have to make the best of things as they are. Don't be in too great a hurry—"

He was aware of two things: the stubborn look on the troubled handsome face before him, and the way in which his last word was caught up, like the rooks rising from the elm trees in the pasture, the word *hurry hurry hurry*, on the siren note of the Alert.

"Damnation," he said, "we'd better get the kids indoors. Come on, boys, you can play in the shelter."

"Oh, daddy—"

They heard a throb in the distance, and the heart-stopping crump of a bomb.

"My God!" cried Neil. "Lucy! The baby!"

"Run!" said Jacques, "I'll look after the boys!" He seized the frightened children, one in each hand, as the second crash came, much closer. They had got halfway through the orchard—and Neil, running like a madman, was nearly at the house—when he heard the wings of death overhead. Jacques flung the children to the ground and threw himself above them, when the great explosion came in the meadow at their backs and the earth heaved.

While the green apples and the appletree branches hurtled about his head and shoulders, he saw the gun-pocked snows of the mountains above Namsos, and the houses sliding down into the sea. There was a brief silence, and then the zoom of two British fighters in pursuit of the frightened Prussian boy who had lost his bearings, jettisoning his bombs as he went, and then a more terrifying crash than any that had gone before. Then nothing.

Jacques sat up. His back and side were aching, he rose to his feet stiffly and held out his hands to the little boys. Colin's dirty face was stiff with shock, his mouth half open, but he scrambled obediently to his feet. Peter lay on the ground shrieking, with blood oozing from a long scratch on his cheek. Jacques had to stoop painfully and take the child up in his arms.

"Mummy! Mummy!" sobbed Peter, and Jacques, with a glance behind at the meadow where the crater was, where the cows had been, said to Colin, "Don't look! Let's go back to *maman* now!" It seemed as if the boy was rooted to the ground. Jacques pulled him forward gently, and there, thank God, was his father, running again, with the bull terrier at his heels. Then Colin screamed with fear and relief, and was taken, in a strangling hug, to his father's arms.

"Are you all right? Peter, my God, what happened?"

"It's only a scratch," said Jacques. "A sharp stone, or a bit of bark, on the ground—"

"Captain Jack laid down on top of us," said Colin with his thumb in his mouth, and Neil, with his free hand, took Jacques' arm in a hard grip. "Jack, I don't know how to—"

"Never mind that," said Jacques. "The others? No harm done?"

"They were all in the shelter."

"Thank God for that," said Jacques, relaxing. They were nearly at the house now. Blast had shattered the upstairs windows and the glass was scattered all over the patio. The french windows had been wide open and were intact.

"One bit of damage indoors and that's all," said Neil. They found Mrs. Macdonald already lamenting over the grandfather clock, "an heirloom in my own family for two hundred years!" she said indignantly, which was lying face down on the stone flags with its glass in fragments. Lucy, very pale, was in the big hall chair clutching her baby; she handed Mary to the dishevelled Lottie as the little boys were set on their feet and ran sobbing to her arms. In the extremity of relief everybody spoke together and there was even some hysterical laughter.

"But where's Alison?" said Jacques.

"Good Lord, she must be down there still," said Neil.

"She wasn't in the shelter, sir," said Lottie.

"You said they were *all* in the shelter—"

"I took it for granted. The blast caught me before I got down there myself. I just managed to dodge the clock—" said Neil.

"Damn the clock!" said Jacques. "Where's *Alison*?"

"Now, now," said Mrs. Macdonald, who had been the first to lead the rush to the shelter, "there's no need to shout, Mr. Brunel. Alison's not here, she took Lucy's bike and went in to the shops in Kingsmead, half an hour ago; she'll soon be back."

"We were short of bread," said Lucy. "I'm sure she won't be long. Mother, why don't you and Lottie make us a cup of tea, and then we'll start sweeping up the glass? Peter, you need first aid, and both of you can have some barley sugar from mummy's special tin." She pushed them gently in the direction of the downstairs cloakroom, but Colin, very much the elder brother now, hung back on her hand. "Mummy, was baby frightened?" he wanted to know.

"Frightened? Look at her! She never even woke up!"

"But what if the Germans come back again?"

"They're not coming back."

"*Kingsmead!*" said Jacques, when the two men were alone.

"You don't think—"

"I think that first bomb fell over Kingsmead way."

"It may have fallen in the fields. Ours fell in Brown's meadow, didn't it?"

"Bang in the middle of the herd," said Jacques grimly. "The farmer has a lot of paperwork ahead of him . . . Neil, I'm sorry, I can't hang about here. I'm going down the road a bit, to meet Alison."

He walked away quickly, he was too angry to say more. Bread! Why the hell did they have to send her out for bread? He went as far as the milestone which said 'Kingsmead-on-Thames, 2 miles', and stopped. The carnage in the meadow, where he could see people moving around the bomb crater, was hidden from the highway by a belt of trees. Everything was normal again. A breeze blew through the grasses and the birds were singing. But the road was empty, there was no bicycle, no girl with red hair in a pageboy bob and a green cotton dress, waving to him as she came . . . In the exhaustion of nervous shock Jacques stood there —he had no idea for how long. Then the thought that she might have telephoned sent him back to the house, walking faster than his wrenched body could tolerate, and there he found Lottie, the first to recover, sweeping up broken glass from around the fallen clock.

"Has mademoiselle telephoned?"

"No, sir."

"Here," said Jacques, "let's get this thing on its feet again, then the hall won't look so bad." He lifted the clock back to its place. It was heavier than he expected, and he saw that the naked face, painted with emblems of the four seasons, was badly scarred. He went into the drawing room, where half-empty cups stood on the coffee table. The baby still slept in Lucy's arms, and the two boys were huddled on the sofa, sucking sticks of barley sugar. Jacques saw for the first time that Neil's shirt had been torn when the blast carried him off his feet. They all turned towards him hopefully, and then their faces fell.

"No sign of her?"

"None."

Nobody else spoke except Mrs. Macdonald, who appeared to be defending herself on a charge of forgetting to bring bread from Kingsmead. She certainly had not forgotten, it was not the sort of thing she ever did forget, it was Manston's Bakery, always short of everything by the middle of the afternoon, there wasn't any brown bread to be *had* . . . Neither Neil nor Lucy appeared to be listening, and Jacques sat still, hating her.

"There she is now!" cried Lucy, jumping up as the telephone rang in Neil's study. He almost ran out of the room, was gone for only two minutes, and at the sight of his face when he came back only Mrs. Macdonald had the nerve to say, "It wasn't Alison?"

"Wrong number," said Neil. "Jack, come out here for a minute, would you? . . . No, Colin, stay with mummy, you can't go into the patio until the glass is all swept up." He led the way across the hall and into the kitchen passage before he spoke.

"That was Jim Weldon on the phone, speaking from Kingsmead. He saw Alison there earlier on, before the—the incident."

"Then there *was*—"

"Yes. And Jim—Jim's afraid that Alison was hurt. He wants

me to meet him before I check with the hospital. He said not to telephone the hospital, they're all demoralised at the switchboard. Will you stay here and look after Lucy and the kids?"

"Your mother-in-law can get them down to the shelter, can't she?" said Jacques furiously. "I'm coming with you."

"Then let's get the car." Neil snatched an old tweed jacket from a hook beside the back door, and the two men ran together to the garage. Jacques felt a pain start up in his side, a souvenir of Namsos; it grew worse as he started hauling out the tin trunk and the suitcases he had stored earlier in the morning. Neil struggled with the car, it had been out of use and the battery was nearly dead, but at last they were out of the garage and on the Kingsmead road.

"Are we going to Mr. Weldon's house?"

"He said he'd be at 'The Water Bailiff'. It's a pub just outside the town."

'The Water Bailiff' came into view, a pretty Thames-side inn with little tables on a well-kept lawn and a white painted garden seat on each side of the front door. There was nobody to be seen but a small bald man in plus fours, standing beside a Baby Austin car. He took off his deerstalker hat, with fishing flies in the band, to wave Neil to a stop.

"There he is," said Neil, as the man came up at a run. "Jim, how did you find out about Alison? How badly is she hurt?"

"Neil, I couldn't blurt it out over the telephone. Lucy—I don't know how to break the news of a thing like this—a tragedy—"

"Get in the back seat," ordered Neil. "Just talk fast, and tell us what you know."

The man took a gulp of breath and mopped his bald head with a blue bandanna handkerchief. "I was *talking* to her," he said. "I met her in Victoria Square just a few minutes before the Alert. She was laughing, and told me she was going to Manston's to get brown bread for—for the party tonight, and—you know the bomber came over only seconds after the Alert—"

"Yes, I know," said Neil. "Go on!"

"The bomb fell in the Square, they think the bakery was hit —Neil, where are you going?"

"To Victoria Square, of course." The car moved a few yards up the road and stopped when Weldon put a hand on the driver's arm. "They won't let you through," he said urgently. "The whole

Square's cordoned off. The Heavy Rescue squad's working in the rubble now—they're worried about fire from the gas mains."

Jacques in the front seat had spoken not one word. Now he stirred, and looked at his hands, aware for the first time in days of their slight deformity: his fingers were crooked now like claws. Gas, rubble, fire: those were the words he recognised in any language, just as he recognised the odour which came floating over the red brick streets of Kingsmead on the dust-laden breeze as the very odour of destruction. He heard Neil say,

"Where were *you* when it happened?"

"Under the table in my bank manager's office."

"So you don't know Alison actually went *inside* the bakery!" said Neil with a kind of harsh triumph. "She may have changed her mind and gone off to some of the other shops, or she may have been knocked out by blast, or just bruised and someone's looking after her—I'm going to the ARP headquarters now!" Jacques recognised all the symptoms, the utter refusal to believe bad news, the urgent need to be doing something, to accuse somebody . . . Mr. Weldon intervened again.

"I still think you ought to go to the hospital," he said gently. "There's a young constable there, getting first aid, who seems to know some names . . . I spoke to him when they were putting him into the ambulance. His own name's Tibbetts, they'll tell you at the desk."

They had to stop several hundred yards short of the hospital entrance, behind a line of ambulances and some private cars.

"My *God!*" said Neil, stopping almost in the middle of the road.

"They won't let you—"

"It's all right, Neil," said Jacques, speaking for the first time. "You go on in. I'll see to the car." He moved over into the driver's seat and parked the car against the kerb. Then he turned round and looked at the Englishman.

"There's no hope, is there?" he said.

"Terrible," said Mr. Weldon. "Most terrible thing I ever saw in my life. And Neil, poor devil—I just could not bring myself to tell him the whole truth—"

"Sir, I would appreciate it if you would tell me."

Mr. Weldon seemed to become aware of a foreign accent. He said, "You must be the French officer we were going to meet tonight—"

"I'm Jacques Brunel. A friend of Alison—of all of them.'

"God help them," said the Englishman. "I phoned my wife. She'll be with Lucy now. Women are braver at this sort of thing than men. I just could not tell Neil that the policeman saw Alison go into the shop. He'd been showing her where to park her bike, after she left me. And then the Jerry bastard came over—"

"Was it a direct hit?" asked Jacques. He saw nothing but his own crooked fingers. The rest of his body seemed to have turned to the ice of the Arctic seas.

"A five hundred pounder, right on the baker's shop. The place was a shambles. But it was so quick, they can't have suffered . . . Monsieur Brunel, are you all right?" He laid a tentative hand on the young man's shoulder. For the French officer, the veteran of Norway, had slumped forward with his head on his hands, and he was whispering in his own language, which Jim Weldon did not understand:

"Just for bread! Just for a loaf of bread!"

. . . Much later, Jacques Brunel went back to London. It was the end of an afternoon when the Alert and the All Clear had sounded constantly in and around the capital, and the Kingsmead tragedy had been repeated in many quiet streets. The Up train was far from crowded, but Jacques stood alone in the corridor. It was just twenty-four hours since he had travelled to Watermead Halt with Alison, happy and loving, by his side. Now there were piles of rubble and smouldering fires at many points where the old houses had stood beneath the railway embankment. The rabbit hutches were in matchwood, the chicken runs a tangle of wire and feathers, the home-made greenhouses mere shards of glass beneath the uprooted sunflowers. "All the little houses, all the little lives," as Alison had called them, had been destroyed in a moment, like her own.

* * *

Jacques went back to Kingsmead for the funeral. It was not held till Tuesday morning, for the identification of the victims of Victoria Square had taken a considerable time. In the bakery shop alone there had been seven deaths: Mr. and Mrs. Manston, both serving behind the counter, Alison Grant in quest of brown bread, twin sisters aged ten on an errand for their mother, an old age pensioner waiting her turn to be served, and a vagrant who had come in hoping for a handout, and who never was identified at all.

There had been deaths in the houses on either side, which collapsed when Manston's shop was hit, and three on the pavement outside, all strangers passing through the town. In all, the shreds of seventeen bodies had been recovered, and were to be interred in a common grave.

Jacques stood on the fringe of the crowd which had gathered in the churchyard beside the old Norman church, and tried to follow the Service which the white-haired Rector was reading in tremulous tones. His own words, drowning the splendid liturgy, kept ringing in his head. *"Pour du pain! Rien que pour du pain!"*— he was never quit of the thought of the uselessness of her death. And yet there was more comfort than he could now realise in the presence around him of that sturdy, silent crowd. For after all they had not come to pay their respects to the victims of a railway accident, a single and never to be repeated episode. The dead had died by enemy action, an action which might be tragically repeated in that very place before night fell: the living waited with that stoicism which Jacques was certain would win the war for them. There was no panic, no defeatism in the undistinguished town of Kingsmead-on-Thames. On Saturday, as he knew, there had been heroic attempts to rescue the injured from burning houses, after the gas mains burst and the fire broke out. Not far from where he stood, Jacques saw the Weldons, a worried bald man and a fussy, twittering lady who looked as if they would be good for nothing, but who in the horror of Saturday afternoon had risen to the occasion, saying and doing everything that was helpful and kind for Alison's stricken family. It was just this capacity for rising to the occasion which Adolf Hitler underrated, and Charles de Gaulle, paranoically suspicious of the British, would never understand.

They were singing a hymn now, and an elderly woman standing next to Jacques pointed out the words in her hymnary. He couldn't sing and didn't want to sing, but he could read the verse:

> For all the saints who from their labours rest,
> Who Thee by faith before the world confessed,
> Thy name, O Jesus, be for ever blest,
>
> > Hallelujah!

It was obviously a favourite hymn, for everyone was singing, but it filled Jacques with despair. The girl he loved was no saint, and she was too young to need rest from her labours; the words had no relevance to one destroyed in the zenith of her youth.

> O may thy soldiers, faithful, true and bold,
> Fight as the saints who nobly fought of old,
> And win, with them, the victor's crown of gold,
> Hallelujah!

Neither a saint nor a soldier. Just a girl, his girl: he remembered the moonlit orchard, and the young breast beneath his hand, and the living, beating heart. Now she was in one of those seventeen coffins—what was left of her—being lowered into the common grave. Yet it was at the moment of the committal, earth to earth, ashes to ashes, that Jacques Brunel made his choice of the road he was to follow. He bowed his head for the benediction, and gave the red hymnary back to its owner, who was wiping her eyes.

"Thank you, madame."

"It was a beautiful service, wasn't it?"

"Yes, madame."

"They're going to put up a monument later on, with all the names we know, and underneath, 'They lived and died as free citizens'."

Free citizens. It was what the British still were, what the French were not; and how many million others besides the French? He walked slowly through the dispersing crowd. From the beginning of the service he had seen Neil Grant, standing with the close relatives near the row of coffins, and beside him an elderly man, his father, in whom the Grant red hair had turned to pepper-and-salt. Mrs. Macdonald had taken her daughter and the children to Scotland on Sunday night, their train crossing the train which brought Alison's grieving father south from Glasgow.

Jacques watched for his opportunity. Everything that could be said had already passed between himself and Neil, and there was only one thing to be added now. When the senior Mr. Grant began to move slowly down the churchyard, talking in low tones to the Rector, Jacques Brunel confronted Neil. He wore a black suit and a black tie, a Scotsman's mourning; the marks of grief were on his face.

"Jack!" he said, and held out his hand. "It was good of you to come."

"Lucy and the children," said Jacques. "Have you news of them?"

"They didn't have too bad a trip. Lucy phoned last night, after they arrived. She was very tired and miserable, but at least I know they're safe . . . I'll be seeing them tomorrow evening. I'm going back to Scotland on the night train with my father . . . Father!"

"Don't disturb him, please. Just give them my love when you get to Oban. And Neil—"

"Yes?"

"Those friends of yours, colleagues, you talked about last Saturday, do they know where to get in touch with me?"

"They do."

"Tell them I'll be waiting to hear from them."

*   *   *

The summons did not come immediately, for the British did nothing in a hurry, and the prime consideration now was not the recruiting of an agent to a new secret service, but how to repel the Luftwaffe's increasing attack on London's defences. It was Thursday when a polite impersonal voice on the telephone asked Jacques to report at a certain time and place on Saturday. On Friday night the enemy aircraft again attacked London. This time the docks and the working-class area round the docks were the target, for the indiscriminate bombing of civilians was Göring's approach to the date for the invasion of England. Hitler had postponed it twice. Now it was estimated, as events proved correctly, that the time of the full moon in September would be planned for the German invasion.

The daylight hours of Saturday, September 7, were a bad continuation of the noisy Friday night. The East End was again the target, and when Jacques walked across the Green Park just after six o'clock on a very hot afternoon he could smell burning on the east wind, while the aircraft of friend and foe throbbed above his head. He felt safer in the park than in the streets. There were no buildings to crash down about him, and if a direct hit were registered his end would be as quick and painless as he hoped Alison's had been. He remembered Edmond Leblanc's saying, after the first night attack on London, that he'd been glad to think Betty and the kids were out of it. Now he knew that Alison was out of it too, never to return; death, which she had never feared, had set her free.

The Royal Standard was flying as he passed in front of Buckingham Palace. Jacques had an idea that the King and Queen slept at Windsor Castle, but they were tireless in every form of war work, and he imagined some committee meeting, or audience, had brought George VI to London. He looked up at the central balcony. That was the place where Hitler must dream of appearing, as he had appeared in other conquered capitals, while the swastika banners floated overhead and a forest of upraised hands saluted him from the courtyard below. The executions would begin at once on the Horse Guards Parade, a more distinguished death roll by far than last Saturday's victims—the girl, the little twins, the old age pensioner, the nameless vagrant. Unconsciously Jacques squared his shoulders. Hitler would never enter London in triumph as long as there were men ready to avenge the dead.

He had been told to report to a numbered suite in a large and not particularly distinguished hotel in Caxton Street. The St. Ermin's Hotel was not so famous as the nearby Caxton Hall, where stage and society divorcees were photographed after being remarried by the Registrar, and Jacques was surprised to see that it was an enormous building, with a courtyard before its main entrance, and two wings all in red brick: the place was obviously a warren of old-fashioned rooms. Equally obviously, it had been requisitioned by the government, for Jacques was given a pass and told it must be countersigned before he left the building. Then a uniformed guide conducted him in silence to the suite. He had no means of knowing that he was on his way to the headquarters of what had been set up, just six weeks earlier, as the Special Operations Executive.

Three men were waiting for him in a room too impersonal to be called a living room, too bare to be called an office or a library. One was a tall man with drooping features like a hound dog, and the next, Jacques instinctively felt, owned the black homburg hat, called an 'Anthony Eden', on the bentwood hatstand in the tiny hall. The third was a youngish and very dapper general officer, wearing a Sam Browne belt and the medal ribbons of the Other War. None of them were introduced by name, Jacques supposed for security reasons, though it made him feel at a disadvantage, but the All Clear, sounding at half past six, helped to relax the slight tension in the room.

They asked him questions about the campaign in Norway, then about his stay in hospital—how long? and his stay in London—

220

how long? and his volunteer work for the refugees. That, of course, could not be permanent? No, sir, he had never expected it to be permanent. He spoke English very well, did he speak German? He thought, perhaps rather better than he spoke English. Italian? Everybody in Menton had a smattering of Italian. Ah yes, now would you tell us about your home in Menton?

"It's a little way out of Menton," Jacques explained. "The district is called Garavan. It stands rather high, and just a mile from the Italian border, more's the pity."

"Was it damaged when the Italians invaded?"

"Not a great deal, I'm told."

"You've been in touch with your family?"

"We've exchanged letters."

"Have your parents a country cottage, or any kind of second home?"

"I have a two-room apartment at Nice for my own second home. It's in the Old Town, not far from the Palais de Justice."

"Is anyone living there now?"

Jacques shrugged. "My father undertook to pay the rent when I was called up with the reserve."

"Where is this place exactly?" said the man who looked as if he owned the homburg hat.

"It's in the Rue Droite, near the old Palazzo Lascaris."

The two civilians exchanged glances. They knew Nice well. Both pictured the secrecy of the narrow streets in the Old Town, the blind alleys near the market on the Cours Saleya, the tenement rookeries round the ancient churches. For the Special Operations Executive, it was ideal.

"You're prepared to go back to France now?" said the soldier.

"Yes, sir."

"Very good. Now let me explain what our organisation has in mind. Our mandate, in so many words, is to *set Europe ablaze*, that is, to use the skill and courage of thousands like yourself who refuse to accept the German occupation. We also have a special directive to get as much information as possible out of France. The Prime Minister is not satisfied with either the quality or the volume of the information we are getting at present. General de Gaulle refuses to allow any Frenchman under his control to be sent to France unless he's consulted and given full details of the mission. That of course is out of the question. So we'll have to use our own people to keep a continuous movement of agents to and fro."

"What are my orders, sir?"

"The first is very simple: you are to return to France. We can get a berth for you aboard a hospital ship sailing from Southampton on Wednesday, and provide you with a medical certificate for whatever treatment you could have had during your time in London. That's all you need for cover. The ship docks at Marseilles, you'll ask for a railway warrant for the journey to Menton, and after that you simply resume your civilian occupation in the Law Courts at Nice. All you have to do for the present is provide a safe house for the agents who'll be sent out to the South of France via Gibraltar. And assist them in the field in every way you can."

"You'll be a soldier in a secret army, Captain Brunel," said the man with the drooping face, who had been studying Jacques intently while the general talked. He saw the young man brighten at his words.

"Am I to work entirely on my own?"

"You'll be on your own in your sector until the first agents contact you. But in the case of emergency you can get in touch with a man who's on the spot already. His name is the Baron de Valbonne, and he lives at the Villa Rivabella, route de Fréjus, Cannes. Can you remember that?"

Jacques repeated the name and address.

"Good. Now don't write it down! The first lesson is, you mustn't keep any written records, of names, dates, safe houses, enemy dispositions, *anything*. Don't be like that man Passy at Carlton Gardens—he started out with three rooms there, and now he's got two more in an office building in Trafalgar Square, all for his precious records and his files—"

"I don't know Passy, sir."

"You've probably heard of Captain Dewavrin, General de Gaulle's right hand man. He's taken the alias of Passy, a station on the Paris Métro, and others have done the same. It's to protect their families in France from reprisals by Vichy, so they say."

"Captain Brunel looks as if he doesn't approve of aliases," said the homburg hat man.

"I've defended too many of them unsuccessfully, sir."

"You'll have to use one yourself before very long. Not an alias exactly: a code name. Any ideas?"

Jacques remembered Dykefaulds Hospital and his first nickname in the ward, adopted by the pretty red-haired girl who brought gifts from the Comforts Committee. "I used to be called Captain Jack," he said. "Will that do?"

"An English name? Very well indeed. But tell me, have you kept your French uniform? You have? It would be an idea to wear it until you reach Menton."

"But I have my discharge papers already, sir."

"So you have. I was thinking of your railway warrant to Southampton . . . Then there's your medical certificate. You'd better come back here on Monday at three o'clock, and somebody will settle all the housekeeping details with you then. That'll be the time to give you a complete briefing on our operation in the South of France."

"Thank you, sir."

They all shook hands with him then, and wished him luck. The dapper little general countersigned his pass in a totally illegible scrawl which seemed to satisfy the man at the door of that discreet building, the St. Ermin's Hotel, and Jacques, having asked directions, crossed to Victoria Street and made his way past the equally respectable bulk of the Army and Navy Stores. He had an impression that he was being followed, and wondered if the three men he had left wished to make certain of their new recruit's movements. He thought it was quite probable. They all appeared so casual, even bored, and he had learned that this was the British way, but they had their own secret ways of working, and making sure . . . And he would have to get accustomed to the idea of being followed once he got back to France. Once he became responsible for the lives of British agents.

Jacques experienced the slightest flicker of exhilaration. It was the first indication that he was emerging from the deep shock and grief of Alison's death. For the first time in a week he even felt the sensation of hunger, and the need of some companion to share food and drink with him, but although he was still alone there was no need to save his money now. He entered the Grosvenor Hotel, so conveniently placed at the station formerly called 'the Gateway to the Continent'—a gateway for the time being locked and barred. The dining room was almost deserted. He had expected this, for few people were willing to linger in London now, and the grey-haired waiter, when he took his order, advised Jacques to make use of the Underground as an air raid shelter if the Alert went off. Jacques nodded. He had bought an evening paper at the station bookstall, and read it over his first glass of wine while he waited for the food to come.

It was plain English wartime fare, not particularly appetising, but Jacques was suddenly, ferociously hungry, and as he ate, he thought: of his mother, and how glad she would be to have him at home again, and of Captain Dewavrin, alias Passy, whose zeal for espionage and counter-espionage had led him to fill five rooms already with his research files. Had the fellow compiled a dossier on every recruit to the Free French Forces, every French sympathiser in the British Isles? Jacques thought it entirely possible. He knew the French weakness for *la paperasserie*, of doing paper-work for its own sake, which finally defeated its own ends: his father's *étude* in the Avenue Félix Faure at Menton was lined with filing cabinets in which no relevant document could be found without frustrating search. Jacques intended to avoid that mistake in future.

He had paid his bill, and was finishing the wine when the air raid warning sounded, and almost at once a bomb fell so close that the walls and ceilings shook. As plaster began falling Jacques hurried out with the other diners. He had lost his nerve on that terrible Saturday in Kingsmead, and was prepared to face the Tube shelters rather than be buried in débris above ground. Moving with the crowd, he found a place with some Poles in uniform. There was always a lot of the foreign troops hanging around Victoria Station, meeting their friends or picking up the girls who came across the Thames from Lambeth way, looking for a night's fun. Tonight they hadn't long to wait for the fun to start.

It was the worst raid ever to hit London. The Germans attacked over a ten mile front, sending four hundred bombers supported by six hundred fighters across the Channel in successive waves, and the exhausted pilots of the RAF, with their depleted force, fought gamely back. No part of London was spared that night. The bomb which fell in Victoria Street, rocking even the deep shelter to its foundations, quenched all the ritual songs and joking in the Underground, where many told their beads or said their prayers instead. The great Arsenal at Woolwich was in flames, the Surrey Docks and all the docks up river to Millwall were destroyed with all the dwelling-houses near them. In the West End houses were ripped open in Dover Street. The famous shops in Regent Street, Oxford Street, Bond Street were torn apart and lay open to the sky. The men of the Fire Service and the Heavy Rescue squads were scalded, blackened, thirsty, the ambulance drivers and the ARP wardens worked tirelessly through the long night. It was a quarter to five in the morning when the All Clear sounded, and Londoners surveyed the havoc of their city.

Jacques arrived back in Victoria Station after five o'clock, his jacket wrapped round the sleeping child he was carrying in his arms, and the child's mother trudging beside them carrying a suitcase.

"Are you sure you'll be all right in the ladies' waiting room?" he said.

"Oh yes, ever so snug till the trains start running. Seven o'clock, I think ours is. What my mum and dad thought when we didn't turn up last night—! They'll be worried to death, thinking we'd been caught in the street, like. Is Kenny still asleep?"

Jacques showed her the little dirty face. "Sound asleep," he said. "He's as right as rain."

"Still it's hard on the kiddies, isn't it? Don't know what my hubby's going to say about tonight, when he hears about it! Oh! what wouldn't I give for a nice cuppa tea!"

"Here comes a tea trolley now," said Jacques. "Is this your place?"

"It is, and thank you ever so much. Hope you'll soon see *your* folks again!"

Jacques walked out of the station, declining Salvation Army tea. Most of the people from the Underground had surfaced now, helping each other along just as he had tried to do, bound together in some strange comradeship by their experience of the night. Two policemen, in filthy uniforms, were surrounded by people asking for directions.

"Number two bus? Number thirty? Be along in about 'arf an hour, just form a queue at the bus stops, please. Buckin'am Palace Road, miss? That's all right, so's Wilton Road; not Victoria Street, madam, that's cordoned off—" It was on fire, and still blazing. Jacques wondered if the St. Ermin's Hotel had been in the line of fire. He walked off past the Grosvenor, and glanced up at Marshal Foch on his horse under the trees, staring in disbelief at a London such as he never knew.

It was peaceful enough going up Grosvenor Place in the morning sunshine, past the brick wall of the palace gardens, and a policeman encountered at Hyde Park Corner reported no damage done in Mount Street.

"Jerry's given us a fair bit of a dusting, though," the man said. The clouds of smoke and grit were still billowing along Piccadilly, making them both cough. "Still he's right back where he came from, ain't he, and that's what we'd ought to be thankful for."

But the place where 'he' came from was his airfields in France, surrendered and occupied France, and the people who lived there had 'him', Jerry, *les Boches*, in their midst all round the clock. Jacques thought of the inscription to be placed above that grave at Kingsmead. *They lived and died as free citizens*—that was at the heart of the British ethos. That was what, in the end, would give them victory.

At the flat there was ground coffee, and milk in the fridge. Jacques made himself a bowl of *café au lait* and drank it standing. He was too strung up to think of sleeping—he had slept in the shelter, intermittently, when even the Poles were silenced by the hell of noise outside, and children like little Kenny fell asleep from sheer exhaustion. He had to make a list of things to do before he left London—it wasn't too soon to start on plans; and there was one thing he wanted to verify before he took off his dusty clothes and went to bed.

Jacques sat down at the writing desk and took the ring-leaf address book from one of the pigeon-holes. He had added nothing to it since Mike went away except some telephone numbers connected with the Refugee Committee. But in the air raid shelter, at the height of the raid, he had remembered where he had seen the name of his contact in Cannes before.

There it was in Mike's familiar handwriting: 'Try to meet the Baron de Valbonne, formerly the naval attaché here. Villa Rivabella, route de Fréjus, Cannes.'

Was it a hint, or was it merely a coincidence? Had his cousin Michel deliberately left him a message? 'If and when you go back to the Côte d'Azur'—had Mike expected him to go back, and did he intend to return to France himself one day? I wish he would come home, Jacques thought. I believe I'd understand him better now.

In the meantime he would begin as he had been ordered to go on, and destroy these pages—the only personal records of Mike Marchand and himself in the flat they had occupied in London.

There would be no clue left for the next tenant as to what had been the interests and sympathies of two Frenchmen stubborn enough to refuse to accept defeat. It was easy to detach the pages from the ring-leaf book, not only the personal notes made by Mike and himself, but the names and addresses of those Mike had cancelled with the word *Rapatriés*. He read them over. They meant nothing to him. Before he began the work of tearing up he wrote his own name, for a whim, at the foot of the list:

'Jacques Brunel, *rapatrié le 11 septembre 1940.*'

And under the word *rapatrié* he wrote in capitals: RESISTANT.

14

ALL UNKNOWN TO the Londoners in their air raid shelters, and also unknown to Mr. Churchill and the Chiefs of Staff, the code-word 'Cromwell' had been issued by GHQ Home Forces when the night saturation raid on London began. 'Cromwell' meant 'invasion imminent', and on that Saturday evening the forward coastal division went to action stations while the enemy planes were streaming overhead. The church bells were rung to call the Home Guard out in various parts of the country, and rumours of an invasion by parachutists and light coastal craft were spread all over Britain.

It was not possible for the British censors to kill all such stories without a complete blackout of news, and now that the Battle of Britain had become the Battle of London it was thought right to let the neutral correspondents bear witness to London's courage and the successes of the RAF in their epic struggle. Bill Barclay of the Eastern Broadcasting Corporation was only one of several American broadcasters who told the London story to their countrymen; the Swedes and the Swiss too sent accurate reports back to their newspapers. But it was a man from the Chicago *Clarion*, Irving Greenbaum by name, who first broke the story of the expedition to Dakar.

Mr. Greenbaum had been temporarily knocked out by the effects of blast during one of the daytime raids on the first of September, and when he flew back to the United States for rest and recuperation he had one of the Liverpool Street leaflets in his pocket. He made it the basis of the story which he telephoned to his paper as soon as the Pan Am Clipper reached New York, and which described in reasonably accurate detail the departure of General de Gaulle from Liverpool docks on the last day of August, to capture Dakar with the assistance of a considerable British force.

"Your old stamping ground's back in the news today," said Tony da Costa, when Mike and Dina came into his office on the Rua do Ouvidor at the end of their working day. "Dakar. You pal de Gaulle is having a crack at it, in case the naughty Germans have a crack at *us*."

"Dakar, eh?" Mike snatched up the evening paper on Tony's desk. " 'Nazi threat to Natal will be averted. Menace to peace of Western Hemisphere removed.' Well, I'll be damned!"

"Exactly what you were saying not so very long ago."

"They've given it a big play, haven't they? Dakar's always been a topic in Rio, ever since *La Ligne* started flying in the mail."

"But what's General de Gaulle going to do in Dakar?" Dina wanted to know.

"Make the world safe for democracy, we hope," said Tony flippantly.

"Like hell he will! He wants to get another chunk of French territory taken over in his name, and then he'll be all set to get after the gold."

"What gold?"

"The gold we shipped out of Bordeaux just before the *débâcle*. It's under French guard at a place called Fort Croisé now." Mike remembered—not looking at Dina—how a woman called Denise Lambert had betrayed the story of the gold to him, on a sunny afternoon in Mayfair.

"This Fort Croisé—is it anywhere near Dakar town?" asked Tony.

"About fifty miles to the north-east. Look!" Mike glanced at the huge mural, and then bent over Tony's writing pad with a pencil. "Here's Dakar, on a kind of a peninsula sticking out into the Atlantic, with the town guarded by Fort Manuel to the south, and by the batteries of the two harbours. Here's Yoff Bay to the north and Goree Bay to the south; the civilian airfield's at Yoff. That's where I was making for when I crashed in '36. There's a military airport at Ouakem now, it's new since my day. It should be an easy trip to Fort Croisé from Ouakem—if and provided Dakar surrenders as easily as Douala and Brazzaville. But somehow I don't think it will."

"There's nothing you can do about it anyway," said Tony. "Why don't you two have another wash, and I'll take you out and buy you a drink." The weather was growing warmer, it wouldn't be long now until spring, and Tony's office was uncomfortably hot. To his critical eyes, his sister and Mike Marchand always looked, these days, as if they had been decarbonising engines.

Dina, when she came back from the washroom, seemed impatient to be gone.

"Let's make it a very quick drink, Tony," she urged. "I want to get back to the Copa and have a proper bath, and change."

"What's the plan for tonight?"

"Dancing at the Copa."

"You're getting yourself talked about, my dear."

"I thought Rio was tired of talking about Diviniñha da Costa."

"Diviniñha plus a plane, that's old hat. Dina plus a man, that's something new. Changing the subject, did either of you take the Puss up today?"

"We both did. Why?"

"The Controller at Santos Dumont is beginning to fuss about those aerobatics you indulge in, Mike especially."

"We only go up when we're cleared, on the off-schedule hours."

"Yes, but there's too much traffic at the airport nowadays for solo flying. I've got an idea—we can talk about it later on," he concluded, as Mike came back to the office. Nothing more was said about Dakar, or any other reports from the United States about the war, and soon Dina and Tony, in his American sedan, were driving down the long beach avenues to the Copacabana Hotel.

For once he was ready to go out before her. Tony da Costa, in his rôle of millionaire playboy, was in pursuit of a Hollywood starlet who had arrived in Rio to promote her latest film along with the star of the show, a *jeune premier* of some fifty summers, and he wanted to be at her hotel in time to cut her out from that old goat and the rest of the entourage. He was actually looking at his watch, a rare gesture for a Brazilian, when Dina came into the sitting room of their suite. She had been buying clothes extravagantly, and was wearing a dance frock of chiffon striped in a barbaric pattern of orange and vermilion.

"You're looking tired," her brother said abruptly. "How long d'you think you can keep this pace up?"

"What pace?"

"Working all day and dancing half the night, with as much flying and studying as you're fit for, in between."

"You know Mike won't be happy till he gets his 'B' Licence back."

"First, he wouldn't be happy till he was passed fit to fly again. Now it's the 'B' Licence, next it'll be the Beechcraft, and pretty soon the Deodoro."

"He says he's *got* to be able to handle a heavy plane. Oh, Tony!"

Tony stroked the back of her neck, where the chiffon dress was cut in a deep slit to her waist. "What are you afraid of, baby? You think he wants to get back in the war, don't you?"

"Yes, I do."

"A guy who travelled six thousand miles to get away from it isn't going to be in all that big a hurry to get back. Now here's what you do. You take one of the Beechcrafts, with Mike aboard, and fly him down to Parana, to the ranch. He can use our airstrip there to practice his take-offs and landings without anybody being a penny the worse, at least I hope not, and you could both stay out of the Rio rat-race for a week."

"The ranch!"

It was a completely new idea to Dina. The da Costa ranch in the State of Parana, close to the border of the great State of São Paulo, extended over almost the most northerly acres of the great pampas grasslands of the Gaucho country, and the cattle which her family raised there ended as the processed meat which had made the fortune of her grandfather, the immigrant from France. At the ranch house no one mentioned the canning factory. It was all romance: moonlight and Gaucho songs and barbecues, even horse-back riding across the pampas, though that had given place in the last few years to the airstrip and the Beechcrafts.

It was so completely romantic that a younger Dina had often thought of it as the place for the consummation of a happy love, and even now the idea of the country music and the barbaric woods and fabrics of the ranch house made her grey eyes glow. Then she shook her head in a sad but decided No.

"Then I really would get myself talked about, going off to Parana with a man."

"Stop off at São Paulo and get Ester to go along with you as chaperone."

"Not on your life!"

"I didn't know you thought of *Ester* as competition."

"Competition? Are you crazy?" She threw her head up arrogantly. "I wasn't thinking about that at all. Ester's worth more than you and me put together, we know that, but she *is* my sister, and to invite Mike to one of our own homes, with my sister there as well, seems like taking him into the family."

"Well, what's the matter with that? Father and mother really want to meet him soon."

"I told you before, please don't *hustle* us." Dina took up her gold evening bag and looked at her reflection in the glass.

"Divininha, I know Mike Marchand loves you. Hasn't he told you so?"

"He says he believes in love at first sight—our first sight."

"Well then, what are you waiting for?"

"*He's* waiting for something," said Dina, and almost ran out of the room.

Tony da Costa whistled. I give up on those two, he thought. He took one of Mike's red carnations from a vase, threaded it through the button-hole of his dinner jacket, and went to find his car.

It was well after dinner-time when he saw 'those two' again in the Copacabana night club, where he had taken his starlet to drink champagne. She was very blonde and very silly, and Tony thought she would be sillier still if he plied her with too much wine. Intending to bring the evening to a satisfactory conclusion, he ordered a light supper to mop up the champagne, slowed down the whole Latin-lover tempo, and while the starlet prattled on, looked round the room in search of Mike and his sister.

They were entirely absorbed in one another. There was a champagne bottle in an ice bucket beside their table too, but Mike had pushed the glasses aside, and was using his coffee spoon to trace out some sort of diagram, hidden from Tony's view. He looked serious enough to be explaining the formulae of aerodynamics, or the outer defences of Dakar, but from time to time he touched Dina's wrist possessively, and her answering smile showed how quick was her response. They were deeply in love, but not yet lovers—of that Tony was certain; and they were not quite lost to the world, because when the samba music stopped and the second of the two big bands came out, Mike Marchand gave something to the waiter and obviously asked for a special number. The conductor bowed in their direction, and the girl singer, a Brazilian this week, smiled as if she knew already what they wanted.

> We'll meet again, don't know where,
> Don't know when,
> But I know we'll meet again some sunny day.
> Keep smiling through, just like you always do,
> Till the blue skies drive the dark clouds far away

Listen, they're playing *our* song—it was a Hollywood cliché, and Tony's attention was recalled to the starlet, who was beginning to pout. But he saw Mike and Dina when they got up to dance, cheek against cheek, one so fair and the other so dark, and thought they were good-looking enough to be in pictures themselves. And the only thing that worried him (snapping his fingers at the waiter and nodding at the champagne) was that *their* song, those two so close together in the present, should be a melody of parting and farewell.

*   *   *

Tony da Costa said to himself, as the days went by, that this was the damnedest courtship he had ever known. At one time you saw them lunching at an open-air café on Flamengo beach with a crowd of bright young people; at another, racing off to Gavea or the Freitas lagoon like any wild young Carioca couple. But then there were the long hours when they were shut up together in the Capricorn offices out at the airport, studying, for Mike was determined to be reinstated in his 'B' licence, and for that new requirements in navigation had to be satisfied. Dina's navigation had always been sketchy. Like most light plane pilots of the day she flew cross-country by landmarks instead of following a compass course, and working with Mike was an education to her. Privately Tony thought that no Brazilian examiner would dream of failing a pilot with over two thousand flying hours on his log, and he was rather surprised when yet another physical was required at the time of the examination, and successfully passed by Mike. After that, when Mike was licensed to pilot a plane 'for hire or reward', Tony felt in honour bound to let him take the controls of a Beechcraft with himself as passenger to Bela Horizonte. It was a good opportunity for a reunion with Mike's cousins Heitor and Ruy, and the sight of their impressive offices in the capital city of Minas Gerais made Tony more anxious than ever to add the Ferreira connection to Capricorn Airways. A few days later he asked Roberto Sanchez, the senior Captain of the Line, to take Mike on his crew as second pilot on the next early morning Deodoro flight to São Paulo and Santos.

Mike got on famously with all the pilots. Capricorn was still too small to have crew quarters at any airport except São Paulo, but they used the offices for briefing, met. reports, airlines gossip and the drinking of innumerable *cafézinhos*, and everyone was willing, when the senior Captain approved, to give a once-famous pilot a chance to brush up on his instrument flying.

One evening when he had not been flying, but had put in a full day with the mechanics, Mike with his dungarees rolled into a ball behind the driver's seat overtook Senhor Rinaldo as he trudged off to his bus stop, and offered him a lift into town in the Duesenberg. The traffic manager accepted gratefully.

"I promised to take my wife to the cinema tonight," he said. "We were disappointed in the Sunday show, so this is an extra week-night treat to make up."

"What did you see?" asked Mike. He had never been a regular movie-goer in Rio de Janeiro, for the Brazilian cinema industry hardly existed as yet, and in his younger days the star attractions had been Laurel and Hardy.

"The play was called 'Fire over England', and we were expecting to see pictures of the blitz on London. So exciting! So dramatic, no? Instead we see a costume affair about the English Queen Isabel. My wife says costumes are for Carnival, and all the queens and emperors should be dead . . . Her father was a Russian, you see."

"Russian, was he?" said Mike abstractedly. ". . . What made you think you'd see pictures of the war in London?"

"It was so announced in the newspaper, sir. And there *were* news pictures, some, not many. Not enough for the sake of sitting through the story of Queen Isabel."

"I guess not," said Mike. "What cinema was all this at?" Rinaldo told him, and while his bath was running in the Flamengo hotel Mike telephoned to the address given, and then to Dina.

"About dinner at Botafogo beach tonight—is it all right if we go to a movie first, for half an hour?"

"A movie—what movie?"

"Just a newsreel about the goings-on in Europe. It only runs for twenty minutes. Can I pick you up at eight o'clock?"

"That doesn't give me much time—but yes, of course, whatever you like, darling." She was always very willing and agreeable about a change of plan.

Because of that they reached the downtown end of the Avenida Rio Branco with time to spare, even after the Duesenberg had been parked in a garage near the Fine Arts Museum.

"I don't suppose you want to see the tail-end of a movie set in the days of Henri de Navarre?" said Mike.

"I certainly don't, let's stroll." Dina put her hand confidingly through Mike's arm, and they began walking towards the Ciné Capri. There were several ramshackle cinemas in that neighbourhood, a magnet for all the strolling youth of the *cidade maravilhosa*, marvellous indeed in its blend of land and sea and lake water, its mountains and its necklaces of light. Dina had dressed for the occasion in a short-sleeved black frock with a white lace wrap embroidered with red flowers, and wore her hair knotted on her neck. It was a variant of what every second girl was wearing on the Avenida Rio Branco, clinging to her escort's arm as they stopped to gaze at the jewellers' windows, rich with the spoils of the Minas Gerais, and the flowershops, and the entrances to the huge beer halls where the jukeboxes were playing at their loudest.

There was a stampede of people from the Ciné Capri when 'Fire over England' ended, and Dina stepped aside to examine the stills in the lobby while Mike bought the tickets.

"She's lovely, isn't she, Vivien Leigh?"

"Very attractive."

"I saw the show when Tony and I were in London."

"Oh! you did!"

"Yes, you confused me, talking about Henri de Navarre!"

"Same period." Mike knew his answers were too abrupt. He took care that Dina was settled comfortably in her seat, but something in his throat was tightening, and chat in the lighted theatre, with ice cream and soft drinks being noisily sold during the intermission, became impossible. He was remembering the last time he had gone to the cinema, alone, in a place as small and uninviting as this, in Coventry Street, to see the newsreels of the retreat from Dunkirk, and the German armour raging over France.

The lights went down, the shabby curtains parted, and there it was on the screen, the very fire over England of the featured film. But now the fire was real, and London stood on the brink of the inferno; as Mike watched horrified he saw the familiar landmarks crumbling before his eyes. No faith was spared. The great Wren churches of the City went down with Our Lady of Victories in Kensington and the Scots kirk in Pont Street. Mike saw Bruton Street in flames, so near the street where he had lived, the shops he knew in Savile Row and the Burlington Arcade ripped open like Cavendish Square and Lambeth Walk. He saw the miles of desolation in the East End, and the king, the queen and Mr. Churchill picking their way among the ruins.

There was hardly a sound in the Ciné Capri but the voice of the commentator, dubbed into Portuguese. The audience, for all their Carioca liveliness, were shocked into silence. But applause began, in ripples at first and then in a storm, as the film cameras picked up the RAF planes going out to battle over the Narrow Seas which had helped them to save Britain from invasion. Mike sat tense-lipped, identifying the Spitfires, Hurricanes, Blenheims of the one side, the Dorniers, Heinkels, Messerschmidts of the other. And he sat safely in a neutral city! The cameras panned to an aerodrome. Young Englishmen ran out to their waiting aircraft, took off into the summer sky. The aerodrome was bombed and vast craters appeared where the aircraft should come back to land. Then there were still pictures of faces suddenly become famous: Paddy Finucane, Skipper Malan, Cobber Kain. Today's heroes, victors of the Battle of Britain, leaving Yesterday's heroes a long, long way behind.

Mike wanted the thing to be over. He had seen enough, and too much, but Dina's strong fingers were intertwined with his, and Dina, when he gave her a sidelong look, had tears in her grey eyes. When he turned back to the screen he knew why. For without a linking word the scene had changed, he saw the last and worst of it, heard that music, once revered and now dreaded. He saw French civilians glancing nervously over their shoulders at German soldiers patrolling the Rue de Rivoli and the Place de la Concorde, he saw the German ranks marching up the Champs Elysées to the Etoile. And the sound track was playing the *Marseillaise*.

15

ON SUNDAY, SEPTEMBER 15, the news from Britain was very grave. The great raid on London eight days previously had been followed by eight consecutive nights of heavy bombing, in which many people had been killed and wounded. On this Sunday, the Luftwaffe mounted a daytime attack, repelled by Fighter Command during the daylight hours, and avenged by Bomber Command's attack on all the invasion ports by night. There was an alarming list of sinkings in the Atlantic. The Italian army had crossed the Egyptian frontier, and was driving on to Sidi Barrani, while the troop transports coming round the Cape of Good Hope had hardly steamed as far as the Gulf of Aden. It was a tale of suffering and endeavour very far from the restaurant in Tijuca forest, where Mike Marchand and Dina da Costa went to have luncheon on that fine September day.

The place had been part of the slave cabins of some colonial landowner in the days of the Braganza Empire, and Mike and Dina drank their *batidas* in an old flagged patio, where sunlight filtered through the palm fronds and tree ferns of the tropical forest. Indoors, the restaurant was not crowded. Most of the guests came from the mountain suburbs of Muda and Alto da Boa Vista, and some of them were known to both Mike and Dina. There were greetings, and covert glances at Senhor Ferreira's French nephew and that wild da Costa girl, but Sunday was a family day at Floresta da Tijuca, and most of the young women were preoccupied with their beribboned babies. Mike and Dina, at a corner table, were soon dismissed as just another courting couple.

Mike was sitting with his back to the room, and only Dina saw his downcast face. She was trying in vain to amuse him, for Mike, so exuberant since he had begun to fly again, had been serious and depressed since they saw the war newsreels at the Ciné Capri. As soon as lunch was over he seemed impatient to be gone. "Let's drive around a bit," he said. "Let's get away from all those squalling kids." He then drove the Duesenberg, too fast, down the Floresta road to the Emperor's Table, once a favourite picnic spot of the deposed Braganza emperor and his family. The table was still there, hewn out of stone, but instead of the imperial court there were happy Carioca groups with picnic baskets and bottles and of course guitars, the young ones dancing while older people had their siesta in the shelter of the trees. The view remained the same, of Rio among its hills and lakes stretching to the blue ocean, with Christ the Redeemer spreading His protective arms above.

"It's wonderful, isn't it, Mike?"

"Unique in the whole world," he said slowly. "But noisy up here, don't you think? Let's see if we can find a quieter spot."

"All right."

"Want to drive?"

"Oh, Mike, may I?"

"Of course." She handled the yellow sports car nearly as well as he did, and knew the winding mountain tracks even better. "Let's go to the big waterfall," he said.

On the way there, close to another group of handsome houses, set back from the road in their large gardens, they passed the beautiful Mayrink chapel, a small colonial jewel gleaming white among the trees.

"Both my Ferreira cousins were married there," said Mike.

"Did the brides live up here?"

"No, they both lived in the city. But you know as well as I do that Mayrink is *the* place for what's called a society wedding."

"I remember hearing that when I was at school," Dina said primly, but her lips curved in a smile. Every teen-age girl in her boarding-school had dreamed of being married in the Mayrink chapel, wearing white satin and gardenias, with no expense spared on lilies and wax candles. The bridegroom was a shadowy figure, usually an American movie star. Dina's smile grew wider as she remembered what her own fantasy had been.

"First to the right," said Mike.

"Sorry!"

They passed the Cascatinha, where a few people were picnicking, and Dina drove carefully along a woodland trail for about two miles. "I don't think we should take the car any farther," she said, "and it's lovely here."

They were parked on a plateau of bright green grass at the entrance to a little dell, where a miniature waterfall splashed into

238

a pool near a rough timber bench. The clearing had been made among giant cacti, ferns and pink camellia trees, and was carpeted with the red and yellow blossoms of impatience. Snake plants grew beneath the trees, and there were clumps of the bird-of-paradise flower which Mike always associated with Dina. Tiny lory birds, brightly coloured, twittered at them from the boughs, and a cloud of blue butterflies danced just above the spray from the waterfall.

"It's perfect," said Mike. "Dina, sit here."

He made her perch on the timber bench, turned sideways, with her hands folded in the lap of her white dress. Around her the dell glowed green, amber, purple, rose, like the gemstones of the Minas Gerais.

"Wonderful!" said Mike, "but Renoir couldn't paint you. No Frenchman could, unless perhaps Gauguin. It ought to be a Brazilian artist—"

"What *are* you talking about?"

"A painting of my mother in the Parc Monceau, when she was fourteen. Renoir painted her with her elder sister, who married my Uncle Pedro. All roses and violets and pink cheeks and white lace parasols—"

"It doesn't sound a bit like me! And I'm twenty-four, darling, not fourteen."

Mike sat down beside her and took her in his arms. "Yes," he said, "you're a woman, Dina, the woman I love. Tell me that you love me too."

"*Amigo do coração!*"

The marvellous body was yielding in his arms, the vivid face suddenly blurred with tears. A hank of the black silk hair fell across Mike's mouth as he kissed her eyes, her lips, her cheeks, and then as he buried his face in her neck Dina felt rather than heard him sigh.

"You're worried about something," she said softly.

"No I'm not. At least, not about anything that concerns you and me."

"I think I know what it is."

"What, then?"

"I saw how excited you were on Friday when you and I had coffee with the pilots from Panair do Brasil, and they hinted about a big hush-hush operation Pan American's getting ready to mount at Natal."

"I didn't get much out of *them*."

"No, and that's why you were so depressed afterwards. But you got enough, and so did I, to make you believe Pan Am's going to sponsor a flight from Natal to Dakar."

"I had the failure of my life at Dakar, Dina. I'd dearly like to see de Gaulle getting *his* comeuppance there. But that wasn't what was bothering me last week. I'm sorry if I was a bore—"

"You weren't."

"Sweetheart, I didn't want to talk about it then. But the thing is, when I went back to the hotel at seven I found a cable from my cousin. It must have been delayed in London."

"Yes?"

"It was to tell me he was on his way back to France."

"*When?*"

"Last Wednesday. He may have reached Marseille by this time."

"But the German submarines—"

"He was sailing in a hospital ship." Mike sighed again. "And that wasn't all of it, Dina. He had to tell me that Alison Grant, the girl he met in Scotland, had been killed in an air raid."

"That pretty red-haired girl? Mr. Grant's sister?"

"You remember her at the Brazilian Embassy?"

"Of course I do. Oh Mike, how terrible! Your poor cousin! Was he very fond of her?"

Mike shrugged. "I don't know. We never had a chance to talk about it. But I've a hunch her death's the reason why he's going back to France. Otherwise there's no explanation. It was the one thing he said he wouldn't do. Either he's going home because he's ill, or just knocked endways by that poor kid's death, or else—"

"Or else what?"

"Or else he's found some way of carrying on the battle."

"Is that possible—inside France?"

"Perhaps not yet. But if there ever is a real resistance, inside France, it'll be led by men like Jacques Brunel."

"You're very close to your cousin, aren't you?"

"No, not really," said Mike. "We haven't seen very much of each other since we grew up. But we were a pretty good team at school, and maybe we could be good again, if we ever got together for long enough . . . I'm sorry I didn't wait to talk to him in London when he got out of hospital."

"Are you sorry you came back to Brazil?"

"Oh, Dina!" He turned to the girl and took her in his arms

again. "How could I ever be sorry, when Brazil has given me you? And you are mine, aren't you, my darling? You've said you love me. Say you'll be my wife!"

She clasped him then in so close an embrace that Mike believed his victory was won, and Dina felt that she held all her past and all her future in her arms. It was with great self-command that she answered only with the words, "Some day."

"Some day? What does that mean?"

"It means 'don't know where, don't know when', as the song says."

"But why should we wait, Dina? We love each other, we're free, there's no reason on earth why we should wait at all—"

"Except that the times we live in aren't geared to happy endings."

"Oh, damn the times we live in! That's no reason for putting me off with 'some day'! Darling, what's the matter? What have I done wrong?"

"Nothing," she said. "Nothing at all. Except that you haven't got over your mistress yet."

"My *mistress!*" The word, so totally unexpected, came like a physical blow. How in the world could Dina have heard about Denise Lambert, or any of her predecessors? He said angrily, "Who the hell are you talking about?"

"I don't mean *who*. I don't mean another woman." Dina laid her hand tenderly against Mike's cheek. "I mean France."

"That's absurd," he said. "I'm not sentimental about France."

"No, not sentimental. But you can't get over it—you can *not* get over what has happened to your country. I knew it that first night in London, when they played 'The Last Time I saw Paris'. I knew it for certain at the movies, when the soundtrack played the *Marseillaise*. Your face—"

"I never could bear to hear the *Marseillaise* played after our defeat, or in honour of Charles de Gaulle, who seems to think it was written just for him—"

"You see? Your heart is mine; your thoughts are all with France. You'll never be happy till you've been back there. Try Pan American; they *may* plan a flight to Dakar, though I can hardly believe it. Talk to Tony, it's the kind of thing Tony knows all about. And then go to France, or Dakar, if you must. And some day, when they let you fight for France, I'll marry you."

*   *   *

"I don't know if I should congratulate you or condole with you," said Tony da Costa. "I came back from a happy Sunday with little Tonio to find your future bride in floods of tears, and now you arrive with a face of doom—" He turned away from Mike and handed the menu to the Copacabana waiter. "We'll have this, and this, and make sure the wine is properly chilled. But don't bring anything for half an hour. Drink, Mike?"

"No, thanks."

"On the wagon too, eh?" Tony poured himself a small white vermouth. ". . . I thought we'd have more privacy in the suite than anywhere downtown. You haven't been in our sitting room before?"

"Never."

"You've been keeping it filled with beautiful flowers. Pink camellias today, I see. Of course they grow all over the place at the Cascatinha."

"Oh, cut it out, Tony."

"Too bad they're wasted on me. You know my versatile sister took the stewardess's place on Deodoro II to Salvador this morning?"

"The girl reported sick, Rinaldo said."

"Belinda's the swing stewardess, but never mind that. We have a chance to talk without interruption for the next half hour. I'll begin by telling you that you and Diviniñha are a couple of fools."

"You're her brother. I'm going to give you a chance to say your say."

"Be glad you aren't listening to my father. I don't know what he'll say, or Senhor Ferreira either, to two young people with everything going for them, who're obviously madly in love, and who want to risk their whole future for some quixotic idea which one of them, at least, doesn't even understand."

"Meaning me or Dina?"

"Dina, of course. What the devil does she care about France? Now she says she won't marry you till France is free. What does she know, or any of us know, about the kind of France we'll find after the war? In any case that's years from now." He clipped the end off one of his small black cigars. "Dina seems to think I can pull strings to have you set down in France tomorrow. I don't know what sort of reception you imagine you'd get there."

"Better than I would in England, probably."

"You've blotted your copybook there all right. The British wouldn't even consider you for a re-entry permit. So what are you going to do?"

"Have a word with Pan Am about their mystery flight from Natal to Africa."

Tony pounced on the word. "To Africa? Not to Dakar?"

"I don't know enough about the operation to pin-point the landfall yet."

"Dina said both you and she got the impression that the mystery flight was to Dakar. Did you also get any impression of why it was being undertaken at all?"

"No."

"Perhaps I can fill you in on that. Last night I had a long-standing engagement to dine at the presidential palace, and I took the matter up with Senhor Vargas after dinner. He's extremely worried about the Dakar situation. If the Vichy French declare war against Britain for trying to ram de Gaulle down their throats in Africa, then the Germans *will* move into Dakar, and the whole Western hemisphere will be at risk."

"That's the United States view, I know."

"Ours too. Now, President Vargas is very anxious to implement the agreements we made with the United States in '39 —even to the extent of allowing American military aircraft to be flown to the British in West Africa from a base on Brazilian soil."

"Which has to be Natal."

"It could be Belem, with a stopover at Ascension Island. The two routes will both be tested before the final decision is made."

"Will the American public stand for that? It sounds like a big step nearer getting the US into the war."

"Exactly. And this is an election year up north. Roosevelt can only sanction one proving flight, and that under wraps, until he's safely re-elected President."

"And this is the flight we've been hearing rumours about?"

"Yes, but it isn't going in to Dakar, it's going in to Freetown, British Sierra Leone."

"That's the devil of a long way from Dakar, but naturally the Yanks don't want to get mixed up in the de Gaulle operation."

"It's also a long way from Takoradi, if you know where that is?"

"Sure I know Takoradi, I once landed there, in 1935 it must

243

have been. It's a miserable dump in the British Gold Coast colony, about two hundred and fifty kilometres east of Accra."

"Good man! I never heard of the place until last night. That's the new British base for ferrying their own fighters and bombers to the Middle East. Eventually American supplies will go to Takoradi too."

"My God, it'll take a year to turn Takoradi into an operational base. Why not Lagos? BOAC have had a service between Lagos and Khartoum for quite a few years, and obviously Khartoum'll be one of the refuelling stops between West Africa and Cairo."

"Sorry, I wouldn't know why not Lagos."

Mike ruminated, and Tony da Costa studied the ash forming on his cigar.

"It's really a very clever bit of politics," Mike said at last. "President Roosevelt sets up the machinery for sending more military aid to Britain without alarming the voters in an election year. President Vargas is doing the Good Neighbour a favour, and he'll get his reward for it. Perhaps a state visit from Roosevelt, and some public declaration of solidarity with Brazil. How does that sound?"

"Very good indeed."

"The British get planes to fly to Egypt, and a big air base in the Gold Coast will help them to keep the French territories calm, if de Gaulle takes too many of them under his famous authority."

"Right again."

"And Pan American Airways gets a bridgehead in West Africa, and can start a new civil air service there after the war. Nice work all round, except for Mike Marchand."

"What's the matter with him?"

"He's twelve hundred miles from Natal as the crow flies, and seventeen hundred miles east of that to Dakar."

"You're obsessed with Dakar, Mike. I told you, the destination's Freetown. And if you especially want to visit Natal, you can fly up there tomorrow by commercial airline."

"And then?"

Tony da Costa drew out his wallet and extracted a letter in a stiff white envelope. "Are you really serious about all this?" he said. "Do you really want to get to Takoradi, God knows how, and try to join the RAF as a ferry pilot?"

"I tried to get taken on as a ferry pilot in the Auxiliary, before

I left England. I've learned my lesson, Tony. Yesterday's heroes aren't good enough to pilot Spits and Hurricanes. If you can get me on the proving flight, I'll be eternally grateful."

"It's as good as done," said Tony, handing him the envelope with the heavy crest on the back. "A letter from the President."

Mike opened the letter disbelievingly. It was true: President Getulio Vargas begged that the courtesy of Pan American Airways might be extended to the bearer, Senhor Miguel Marchand, his special observer—

"Now tell me I'm a good brother-in-law."

"*Mon vieux* Tony, you are the very best." Tony jumped up, and they fell into a Brazilian embrace, pummelling each other's shoulders and shaking hands, to the amusement of the waiters rolling a dining table into the sitting room.

"When's the take-off?" Mike asked in English, as the men began to set out the food and wine.

"Friday, I believe."

"*This* Friday! Wonderful."

"Listen to the happy lover," Tony said drily. "Mike, you're running true to form, and so I suppose is Dina. The thing I don't understand is how you can bear to leave her now."

"She insisted, Tony."

"Yes, when she was with you, and then she cried on my shoulder all Sunday evening. You've sold her on the Dakar idea, and I couldn't get it through her head that the flight's going nowhere near Dakar, it's going to Freetown. What are you grinning at?"

"Tony, you're a genius. You've only missed out on one little bit of homework. You didn't listen to the twelve o'clock news. De Gaulle's not at Dakar. He's gone to Freetown instead."

*　　　*　　　*

"My dear boy, isn't this a very sudden decision?" said Senhor Pedro Ferreira. He was sitting with Mike on the veranda of his home at Alto da Boa Vista, looking at the yellow Duesenberg parked beneath them, close beside the steps.

"Everything's sudden in the airline business, uncle. I hope it won't be a nuisance to garage the car till I come back?"

"We've space for three little sports models like yours, of course. Leave it now, if you like, and Emilio shall drive you back to the city."

"That'll be a great help, because I'm leaving Rio on an early flight. But I've a feeling Emilio doesn't think my car a fit companion for your Packard."

"He's a terrible car snob. When d'you think you'll be back to pick up that little animal—a Duesenberg, d'you call it?"

"I don't know, honestly. It depends on how things go at Natal."

"And does this trip mean you've definitely thrown in your lot with Senhor da Costa?"

"Yes, I suppose it does. If he can get a charter to go in to Recife and Natal, which is one of the things I'm supposed to study in the north-east, he should soon be doing very well indeed."

"He has steep competition in the north-east, from Condor."

"A Nazi-controlled airline may lose *its* charter in Brazil before too long."

"They say Antonio da Costa has dropped a packet of money on Capricorn already. Luckily his father can afford it."

"He expected to operate at a loss in the beginning."

Maria, discreet in her black dress, appeared from the interior of the house. "Will Senhor Marchand be staying for dinner, sir?" she asked.

"Mike?"

"I'd like to, uncle, if I may. And if there could be some of that wonderful *feijoada*, Maria?"

The Italian smile flashed in Maria's dark face. "Of course, *o senhor*," she said. "Emilio will mix you some *batidas*."

"Maria's flattered, and so am I," said the old man, "I thought you would be dancing attendance on the fascinating Senhorina Dina on your last night in Rio."

"No, I'm not seeing her tonight, she's got to do some packing. She's flying up to Natal with me tomorrow," said Mike casually.

"She's *what*?"

"Flying to Natal on business for Capricorn."

"Considering that you'll arrive on Saturday afternoon, and any office she might want to visit will be closed until Monday, I don't think the young lady has chosen a very businesslike time to travel. And really, Mike, I'm not strait-laced, but—is it wise?"

"Uncle, this is 1940. Surely a man and a girl can take a business trip together without the worst being suspected?"

"Not in Brazil." The wrinkled old face wore a look of distress. "You know I hate gossip, even good-natured gossip, but

246

I can't help hearing, whenever I go out to a little party, that you're seen everywhere with this girl, and I can't help wondering . . . You're not going to do anything rash like elope with her, are you?"

"Good God, uncle, of course not! Dina only means to stay in Natal till the beginning of the week. She's flying back to Rio on Tuesday night."

"And you're staying on alone?"

"I'm not coming back with Dina."

"That doesn't answer my question. Mike, you're up to something! Don't attempt to deny it—you never were the slightest good at dissembling. Now they've let you fly again, you're going out after some crack-brained record—"

"Nothing is further from my thoughts, Uncle Pedro."

"I'm very glad to hear that"—relaxing. "Because in spite of what Dr. Baumeister says, you oughtn't to take more risks with your hearing—no more mountain flying, no more taking chances in the desert—"

"Sometimes you have to take chances, to get anywhere."

Abruptly: "Mike, do you remember your father?"

"Hardly at all. I remember him coming on leave once, it must have been 1915, not long before he was killed. He brought a little Christmas tree, and presents—"

"Just now you look exactly like him. Oh yes, you have your mother's colouring, so fair, my Violette had it too. But your features are your father's and your height . . . the Verbiers were short and small-boned. Poor Jules! He was an impulsive fellow, just like you. Taking chances, taking risks, especially at the wheel of his car. Do you know that he won the first motor race from Paris to Bruxelles?"

"Yes, I do," said Mike Marchand. "And I also know that he gave his life for France."

*   *   *

The pilot began his descent on Natal, and Mike swallowed and pinched his nostrils as his ears began to crackle. On the port side of the plane he could see the coastline, so enticing from that altitude, with the blue sea breaking in white-capped waves against long yellow beaches, so deceptive an invitation to the ugly tropical town where they were going. Dina was sitting in the single seat in front of him. She too was studying the capital of Rio

Grande del Norte as they came in to land over the ocean, and she turned to smile at Mike reassuringly. He had been worried about her for no reason, since she had stood up to the long gruelling trip splendidly; perhaps he had been stampeded by Tony's violent opposition to their plan.

"No, you will *not* fly as far as Salvador by Capricorn! Mike as second pilot and Dina as stewardess, that's a little too much! If Dina insists on going to Natal to see you off, you must both travel the whole way by Panair do Brasil, and at least give the impression of respecting the conventions! I tell you one thing, I'm keeping out of São Paulo until Dina's safely back in Rio, and then mother needn't know about your damnfool trip too soon!"

It was only Tony's bluster, of course. He always did what they wanted in the end, and in this case it was his own words to Mike, "How can you bear to leave her now?" which had inspired Mike to beg her, when she was in his arms again, to come just that much further along the road to Africa with him. She agreed at once, his proud Dina, with such a touching eagerness to please him that he was almost ready to give up the whole far-fetched scheme of enlisting as a ferry pilot half way round the world. But one short flight as pilot in the Deodoro, one more radio bulletin that de Gaulle had sailed again from Freetown for Dakar, and Mike was more eager than ever to satisfy his need to fly and to return to what he chose to think of as the forefront of the battle.

The tropical heat of Natal surged up to meet them as soon as the doors were opened and the landing steps wheeled into place, and "Goodness!" said Dina, "this is a lot worse than Salvador!" But she had no real objection to the sweltering heat. In a sense it was in her blood, and when they entered the dingy transit hall, Dina in her dark blue skirt and jacket, worn without the Capricorn emblem, was the neatest person in the sweating, shuffling, miscellaneous crowd which always gathered to see the plane come in from Rio.

"I've sent a boy to get a taxi, and I want you to go right into town, don't wait for me," said Mike, returning from the baggage claim counter. "I may be quite some time at the Pan Am office. There doesn't seem to be any senior person around."

"Probably out drinking coffee. Okay, I'll check in at the hotel and send the taxi back for you. Taxis seem to be in short supply in this flea-pit, and you don't want to ride the airport bus, do you?"

"Talk about fleas . . . !"

Fortunately they had reservations, for there was only one moderately respectable hotel in the whole crowded city. Dina's taxi, with torn fabric covers over the cracked upholstery which inspired her to sit far forward with her skirt well tucked beneath her knees, took a long time to travel the eight miles from the airport along a road congested with motors and donkey carts, and nearer the city centre, with ramshackle buses and streetcars. Natal was a town which lived by the salt industry, producing nearly all the supplies needed by a country larger than the European continent, and there was something salty and gritty about Dina's hotel room, where the water ran rust-coloured into the washbasin, and outsize cockroaches scuttled across the zinc pan which stood beneath the shower. But the bed, which she gingerly inspected, was clean beneath a grimy mosquito netting, and Dina herself was perfectly groomed by the time Mike came in sweating from the airport, to find her drinking gin and lime in the hotel lobby and talking to a Pan Am pilot.

She waved eagerly. "Mike, look, Captain Bennett's here!"

The American pilot uncoiled his long legs as Mike came up, and held out his hand. "Mike Marchand?" he said, "glad to meet you. We had a signal about you yesterday from Washington."

"Did you though," said Mike. "Your airport staff have been hunting for that signal for the past half hour."

"My fault. I brought it in to the town office in my pocket, and had them file it with the signal about our other VIPs. What'll you have to drink?"

Mike inspected the sticky glasses of gin and lime. "Can I have a beer?"

"Captain Bennett says the take-off's postponed till Monday morning," Dina interposed.

"So they told me at the airport . . . Have you two met before, or what?"

Captain Bennett laughed. "Dina was one of my crew when I was flying for Panair," he said. "As good a little stewardess as ever worked for us. And now she's the boss-lady of an airline 'way down south—"

"Miss da Costa and I are going to be married," Mike told him crisply. "Didn't she happen to mention it?"

"There wasn't time," said Dina, enjoying herself.

"Well, say, that's great news," said the pilot. "She's darn right there wasn't time. I just came in to fix up rooms for two more VIPs, two guys from the CAA, and Dina and I got talking about the ride you're hitching on our hush-hush trip—"

"Oh, you're not staying in the hotel?"

"No, I'm at the Panair crew quarters, out beyond the airport. Not much to choose between that and this place when it comes to spiders and fleas. Say, I hope we get you out on Monday, Mike. Twenty-four hours of Natal's about as much as anyone can take."

"Why, do you think there might be another holdover?"

"If we get a bad met. report there could be. Why don't you come down to the lagoon about nine tomorrow morning and let me show you over the *City of Brotherly Love*? She's under guard right now, but I could give you a pass." He produced a notebook and a pen.

"Thanks, I'd like that."

"Me too?" said Dina pertly. "*I'd* like to compare a fifty-passenger flying boat with my own Puss Moth!"

"Just so you don't try to take her up, Dina baby . . . Say, I've got a great idea. I don't know what Mike and you plan on doing, but why don't you come on the round trip with us? My ETA back here is Friday of next week at the very latest—"

"Don, what crazy thing will you think of next? The CAA men would never stand for it."

"They'd have to if I put you on the manifest, wouldn't they? Only thing is, you'd probably need some extra shots, like for yellow fever; they know about all that at our town office. It's right here on the main drag, just past the Gloria church." Don Bennett once again levered his long length out of his chair. "Well, see you tomorrow, Mike, great to have met you. I used to read about you when I was a boy." He slapped Mike painfully on the shoulder. "Didn't you barnstorm in the mid-West in one of the early Jennies?"

"No, that was Lindbergh," said Mike Marchand. "Before my time."

"I guess it was. Well, good night, Dina baby, see you." He retrieved a cap with a broken visor from beneath his chair, and turned back to say,

"If you folks want to see fascinating Natal, better not put it off too late. The rain comes down like Niagara every night around nine."

"Fresh kid!" said Mike, when the swing door creaked behind the pilot. "Dina baby, what are you laughing at?"

"At your face when he asked if you flew Jennies. He didn't mean to be fresh, Mike, it's just his way. And he *is* a good pilot, one of Pan Am's best. I'm glad he'll be flying you tomorrow, Monday I mean. I wonder what the Civil Aviation Authority men are coming for?"

"To raise a pack of difficulties, they always do. What do you bet the whole flight gets re-routed via Belem and Ascension? Especially if Bennett gets a bad met. report. God! I nearly laughed in his face when he said that. I felt like telling him about the fifty-three take-offs of Jean Mermoz—only I was afraid he'd ask me who Mermoz was."

"Don was right about one thing," said Dina, rising. "If we're going out, we'd better go now, for it'll very soon be dark."

"Do you really want to go out? Not too tired?"

"Tired of sitting still all day. Besides, I want to see the Bomfim lagoon."

"Oh, Dina!"

She knew him so well, and he knew her so well, that there was no need for explanations. The Bomfim lagoon was a sacred place to both of them, the scene of the first flight of Jean Mermoz back across the South Atlantic after carrying the mail from Senegal by flying boat; the scene of the fifty-three take-offs, doggedly persisted in even after the orders to abandon the attempt and return by boat. The scene of a man's triumph.

Nothing could have made Mike happier than to go there with Dina, through the sweltering evening streets of Natal, where Negroes in limp clothing were jostled by Brazilian soldiers in their green uniforms, and hawkers danced in front of Mike and Dina, brandishing chewing-gum and tinsel dolls. She had not the heart to remind him that even Natal must have changed since that great flight of 1930, when the only man to welcome Mermoz was an old French convict, escaped from Cayenne, who was down on the shore of the Rio Potengi with a home-made Tricolore and a gramophone playing a cracked record of the *Marseillaise*. There were more houses now and many more people as they approached the Bomfim lagoon, and the fifty passenger Clipper flying boat was floating on the water which had cradled the Laté 28. But the eternal south-east wind was ruffling the water, and the beam from the lighthouse of the Magi was beginning to twinkle through the dusk. In Mike Marchand's imagination the scene had never changed.

"I wonder how far it is from Cape St. Roques to the Pot au Noir?" he said. "Captain Bennett will make nothing of it, I'm sure."

"The Pot au Noir? They've been overflying it for years."

It was true, but as they turned to walk back to the hotel through the lowering darkness, in which a few drops of rain began to fall, all the jungle inheritance in Dina's blood made her shiver with ancient superstitition. The Pot au Noir had almost been the death of Mermoz on his first flight. That density of black cloud down to the surface of the sea stretched, according to some old pilots, for nearly three hundred miles along the air route to Natal. A man had to find a tunnel or risk a long detour. Jean Mermoz had found the tunnel, and lived until the South Atlantic claimed him six years later, when his luck ran out.

They were both very quiet over the tasteless dishes served up as dinner by the comfortless hotel. The heavy rain began as punctually as Don Bennett had foretold. The windows had to be closed, the atmosphere was stifling. Even so, the place filled up with men, the waiters slopped the drinks from one table to another, and a full orchestra broke into samba music in the combined dance and beer hall next to the hotel. Dina, at last, put her hands to her ears.

"Darling, I know you're tired, but there's something I must say to you," said Mike in desperation. "Should we try sitting in the lobby?"

"There's more of a racket there even than in here. Let's see if there's a parlour, or even a little lobby with two chairs, on the next floor."

"I don't think this place will rise to anything so fancy."

"We'll have to sit in my bedroom then."

"Do you care?"

"No, I don't care." But Dina cared, her heart was beating furiously when in the shabby room Mike put his arms around her, and they kissed for the first time since the long hard flight to Rio Grande del Norte began. His body was burning hot against her own, but yet there was a coolness in the room, and listening to the creak above her head Dina realised that a maid had started the ceiling fan. She looked over her shoulder, and saw the bed made down, the mosquito curtains draped around it like a bridal veil, the grime in the netting obscured by the half dark. Looking up, she saw Mike's blunt features and blue eyes now dark, now light in the flickering of the electric sign above the cinema across the street. The words came one at a time, illuminating his face, her hands clasped behind his neck, his white shirt, her carved ivory bracelet, each in turn. Ciné . . . Paris . . . Ciné . . . Paris. Paris.

"Mike, what is it you have to tell me?"

"Darling, I want you to decide."

"Decide what?"

"Whether I should go or stay."

"Isn't it a bit too late to think of that?"

"It won't be too late until the *City of Brotherly Love* takes off on Monday morning."

"But I don't understand, Mike! I thought this was what you wanted more than anything else in the world—"

"The thing I want more than anything in the world is you."

"When did you realise that? When you saw me with another man tonight?"

Mike groaned. "I was jealous, I admit it—"

"You don't have to be jealous of Don Bennett. Or anybody else."

"But what if we're parted longer than we think?"

"Then remember it was your choice, not mine." She had dropped her hands from his neck, but they still stood enlaced, with Ciné . . . Paris writing its legend of light and dark.

"Mike! I don't want you to leave me. I dread the danger, I hate the war. But I can't decide for you. If you turn back now, nobody will blame you. You've tried so many take-offs, not as many as Mermoz at Bomfim, but more than anybody knows but you. Perhaps this one wasn't meant to succeed. There must be some other way—"

"*No!*" he said, from a dry throat, "there isn't any other way Forgive me, darling. You mustn't think that I'm a coward. It was only—now, at the last moment, I can't bear to be parted from you."

She embraced him then, whispering that she understood, that her heart was breaking, that she loved him beyond parting, beyond life, until Mike, gathering her up in his arms, kicked aside the mosquito netting and sat down, still holding her, on the side of the low bed. He held her like a child, rocking her, for Dina was weeping.

"Darling, don't cry, listen to me. Do you think Bennett was serious when he asked you to fly on to Freetown?"

She was quiet at once, a little less relaxed in his embrace, listening.

"If you do, would you consider—would you for one moment consider—doing just that? Going on the proving flight, so we'd be together just a few more days? Dina? Darling?"

"I couldn't," she said faintly. "Oh, Mike, don't ask me! I can't leave Brazil. My father—"

"I know," he said at once. "My love, forgive me. It was too much to ask, for so few tomorrows—"

At that she cried out, and moved so strongly in his arms that Mike, as he laid her down on the cheap sheet and the thin pillow, whispered, "There's still tonight!" And Dina understood that this night there would be no parting: that her innocent romantic dreams of the Mayrink wedding, the Gaucho honeymoon, the lilies and guitars, the unknown bridegroom, were to be consummated with the body of this man, whom she loved, in the staleness and the grime of a room rotten with paid lust and made clean only by her own body's honour. In the pain and joy of that first consummation Dina for a time lost all awareness of her surroundings. It was only after Mike's grateful kisses had lulled her to sleep, after sleep blurred into a drowsy awakening, that she heard the rain and the south-east wind, blowing over the Lago do Bomfim, and saw the electric lights across the street still spelling out the message: Ciné . . . Paris . . . Ciné . . .

Paris.

16

THE FLYING BOAT *City of Brotherly Love* took off from Natal in Brazil in the very early hours of Monday, September 23, and after passing over Noronha Island set her course for the British Crown Colony of Sierra Leone. At approximately the same time, Skuas and Swordfish of the Fleet Air arm were assembled on the flight deck of HMS *Ark Royal*, ready for the fly-off which was to open Operation Menace and prepare the triumphal entry of General de Gaulle to Dakar.

Operation Menace had taken a long time to get under way. Two months had passed since the general told his staff that he intended to establish himself on French soil at Dakar, and in those two months the planning had veered from an exclusively French operation to a predominantly British expedition, which it was hoped would be a friendly one. Not all the planners believed this was possible. The Foreign Secretary complained that information had been leaked to Vichy; the Chiefs of Staff thought that if Dakar resisted it would lead to war between Vichy France and Britain. General Irwin, commanding the British troops in Operation Menace, took the precaution of embodying his doubts in an official memorandum before the operation started.

In de Gaulle's headquarters there was unqualified optimism. Dakar, and with it all the states of French West Africa, would yield to the general's magic touch as other African territories had done already. He had, by what means was not revealed, received many messages of sympathy from the inhabitants of Dakar. One zealous school inspector, by name Maurice Kaouza, had been distributing leaflets in Dakar since the end of August. "Frenchmen of Dakar! Martyred France must rise again!"—they were not very different in tone from the leaflets allowed to flutter over Liverpool Street station before the Gaullist force embarked in the Mersey.

Messages from secret agents, leaflets and radio broadcasts were highly esteemed as weapons of war at 4, Carlton Gardens, and de Gaulle's publicity had been so well handled since the eighteenth of June that when the Dakar expedition put out to sea none of the reporters assigned to accompany it had eyes for anyone but the leading man in the melodrama. They did not harass the actual commanders, Admiral Cunningham and General Irwin, by requesting interviews and photographs. General de Gaulle was the one sought after, but he believed in scarcity value. Remote and unapproachable by the common herd, he remained in the company of the indefatigable Spears aboard the Dutch ship *Westernland*.

"Couldn't you have fixed up His Nibs aboard a French ship, Eddie?" enquired the correspondent of Empirex, an Australian news agency, who had joined the expedition when HMS *Ark Royal* rendezvoused with her sister ships in the middle of September. "Looks bad, him being aboard a Dutchman. There *are* French ships in the convoy, aren't there? Seems to me I've caught sight of a French flag from time to time, dead slow astern."

"Three sloops and four armed trawlers—hardly good enough for *mon général*," said Edmond Leblanc placidly. He hardly believed in himself as Leblanc any longer. He was Eddie White of the DJ, good old Eddie, the one Frenchman you couldn't get a rise out of, as his colleagues said in the Fleet Street taverns. All the others got fighting mad at the mere names of Pétain or de Gaulle.

"*Free* French sloops and *Free* French armed trawlers," emphasised Fred Clapperton spitefully. "In other words, part of our bag in Portsmouth harbour last July. Part of Operation Catapult, remember?"

"Are you two suffering from cabin fever?" asked the man from Empirex. Edmond and Clapperton had been in one of the old British battleships from the day the convoy sailed until the rendezvous with the aircraft-carrier, sharing a cabin for nearly two boring weeks. The battleships, having to take their time from the steaming rate of the slowest vessels in the convoy, waddled south and west with some of the majestic clumsiness of the Invincible Armada.

"We're suffering from a rough trip in the cutter," Edmond said. "I never cared for small boat sailing." There was loud laughter, for the Atlantic was at its calmest, with flying fish leaping and playing in seas of summer blue.

"Well, they've got us all in one floating press camp now," said the Australian. "And my word, you couldn't be in a better berth than the old *Ark Royal.*" Nobody contradicted him, for the air-craft-carrier, launched less than three years earlier, was the pride of the Navy. Her crew of fifteen hundred men was almost as big as the entire force General de Gaulle had been able to muster for Operation Menace. She was battle-scarred, for she had been at Rio de Janeiro, refuelling before the Battle of the River Plate; she had shared in the disaster of Namsos; her Captain had tried, by negotiation with the French, to avert the tragedy of Mers-el-Kebir. Now she was on her way to Dakar, carrying one squadron of Skua fighter-bombers and four of torpedo-spotter-reconnaissance Swordfish.

There was only one objection to being a war correspondent, or a neutral observer according to status, in HMS *Ark Royal*, and it applied to every other ship in Operation Menace—the constant feeling of being isolated aboard one ship, and cut off from whatever newsworthy incidents might occur in any of the others. The man from the *New York Times-Herald*, who completed their four-some, said he was suffering from this sense of isolation to such an extent that he preferred remaining in the cabin he shared with Dashwood, the Australian, to going on deck and trying to make news items out of nothing. "Let me know when things start happening, gentlemen," he said, "and I'll be there!"

The arrival of Eddie White and Clapperton from the *Resolution* had been happening enough to tear Mr. Prentiss from his type-writer (he was said to be writing his memoirs) for the ritual drink of welcome in their cabin, and when the newcomers grew tired of the artificial light and the whisper of air through the ventilators all four men went on deck to watch the return of the afternoon reconnaissance. It was an invigorating sight to see the Skuas and TSR Swordfish take formation round their leader while the arrestor wires fixed athwartships on the long flight deck were raised on their stanchions and the Deck Landing Control Officer began the complicated drill of guiding the aircraft in. It was no less invigorating to see the destroyer screen beyond the two old battleships, *Barham* and *Resolution*, the cruisers and the supply ships which had sailed nearly a month earlier from Scapa Flow. It was even possible, on this late afternoon in the apparently peaceful tropics, to forget for an hour that each day the news from home was worse than the day before.

No one, not even the Chiefs of Staff in London, could as yet say with confidence that the danger of invasion was over. It was not even possible to assess fully the importance of that great Sunday, September 15, when the Luftwaffe was decisively beaten in the skies of Britain. But within a few days it was clear that Hitler had temporarily abandoned his plans to invade by sea and land. The brilliant fatal summer was over, the Channel waves were rising, the equinoctial gales would soon begin to blow. The RAF had saved the island fortress, and Adolf Hitler would never see the swastika banners lifted as he drove in triumph up Pall Mall.

But many terrible nights of bombing were in store for London, the great seaports, Coventry and other cities, and there was hardly one Englishman in the Dakar expedition who was not racked by anxiety for someone, some family, some home in the beleaguered island far away.

Afterwards the correspondents remembered the day when White and Clapperton were transferred to the *Ark Royal* as the last optimistic day of Operation Menace. White had always been the least optimistic of the four; he had had too many hints of trouble since the night in the French Pub, but even he had been lulled by the uneventful two weeks' voyage south. Besides, he was pleased with his assignment. He had got the job because of his background as an aviation writer, but it was a sign of status to be on a job as big as Operation Menace with men like Prentiss of the *Times-Herald*, who was pooling his stories with the whole American press corps in London, and Dashwood, who was doing the same for the Dominion correspondents. Eddie White knew he was not in the same class as Clapperton, who was the chief cameraman at the Crowborough Film Studios, and had brought movie journalism to a new level; he also knew that his boss's determination to saturate every theatre of war with his reporters had caused the men themselves to be known as the DJ Ragtime Army. But that was not the sort of gibe which ever worried the former Edmond Leblanc. He had only one unspoken fear: that of seeing the bloody beginning of a French civil war.

It was not long after he went to his new quarters in *Ark Royal* that the threat of civil war came a handsbreadth nearer. The greatest danger of resistance at Dakar lay in the mighty *Richelieu*, which the British had partly disabled during Operation Catapult. Her 15-inch guns were still capable of doing great damage to an attacking fleet. Now, to the dismay of the Menace commanders, it was announced that a very strong French naval force had passed the Straits of Gibraltar and was heading south.

Allotting the blame for this misfortune was to be a subject of recrimination for many days to come. There had been nothing furtive about the French action; it would not, in fact, have been possible to conceal the movement out of the Mediterranean of three French cruisers and three destroyers, all of a modern class. The French Admiralty had even informed the British naval attaché at Madrid that the passage of the Straits was intended, and both the attaché and the consul-general at Tangier had telegraphed to the Admiralty accordingly. There was a fatal delay in the passing on of these telegrams to the highest authorities. Officers were reprimanded, excuses of blitz conditions were made, orders to pursue the French ships were given, but nothing could conceal the fact that there had been a major blunder at the Admiralty. On the other hand, the departure of the flotilla from the Mediterranean in the direction of Dakar seemed to be proof that, as had been so often asserted, there was a leakage of information from de Gaulle's headquarters to what could only be called the Axis satellites at Vichy.

"Why the hell doesn't de Gaulle give a press conference?" fumed Dashwood. "Why can't he level with us, and make a statement to clear this whole thing up? Say what his opinion is on carrying on with this caper now the Vichy French have beaten him to it?"

"They don't give press conferences in France, Dick," said Mr. Prentiss. "Not conferences like you and I know them. Personally I'd settle for a broadcast. We're hooked up for it, and even if the crewmen couldn't understand it all, they'd hear the man's voice . . . Maybe he could even say a few sentences in English?"

"He hasn't got his PR men to advise him now," grunted Fred Clapperton. "Eddie, if this squadron from France attacks us, what'll de Gaulle do then?"

"He'll have to fight back, or else turn tail and run."

"That's the way I see it."

But that was not how the British Chiefs of Staff saw it. Between blabbermouths at Carlton Gardens and bumblers at the Admiralty, they were driven to make a stern decision: Operation Menace must be broken off.

By this time the British flotilla had passed west of Dakar and was steaming for the Crown Colony of Sierra Leone. It was impossible to make for Dakar until the dispositions of the Vichy reinforcements were clearly known, and also—one more delay in the intolerably prolonged operation—*Ark Royal* had developed faults in her valves which had to be repaired. The nearest British territory to Dakar was Gambia, but there were not adequate facilities for refuelling at Bathurst, and to Freetown the expedition accordingly went. This was de Gaulle's first arrival at Freetown, which had been reported before Mike Marchand and Dina left Rio de Janeiro for Natal.

The correspondents in *Ark Royal* had not been kept entirely in the dark about the government's wish to abandon Operation Menace—or Operation Muddle, as it was now being called. Too many signals flashed from ship to ship, too many visits were exchanged between the Admiral's flagship, HMS *Barham*, and the *Westernland* in which General de Gaulle was travelling, only a few decks above a refractory body of Free French soldiers, most of them North Africans, whom the Dutch captain ruled, as he ruled his own stokers, with a rod of iron. It was not possible to conceal that something was up, and rumour was rife in the *Ark Royal*, where nerves were already frayed by the BBC reports of the heavy bombing of England.

It was a relief to enter the harbour of Freetown and see people bathing off Lumley Beach, a touch of civilian pleasure on the shores of the vast bay where vessels of every kind were forming in convoys, the merchant vessels daring the run home to England, the ships of war making ready for the voyage round the Cape to the Middle East. The ratings hoped for shore leave, but were disappointed; the correspondents, after the usual bluster about press priority, were sent ashore in one of the *Ark*'s cutters to transmit copy.

"Here comes His Nibs at last," said Dick Dashwood, who had his binoculars at his eyes as the cutter threaded its way through the press of shipping. "The admiral must have sent his own launch out to fetch him."

"The one and only launch in Freetown."

Edmond focused his own binoculars while Clapperton was busy with his movie camera. There was no mistaking the tall figure of de Gaulle, with two British officers beside him, and then the launch was hidden behind a string of native boats bringing fresh fruit and vegetables to the ships from England.

"Going to be a big day for him," said Mr. Prentiss.

"What do you bet he backs down, and calls the whole thing off?"

"No takers. He's got too much at stake."

In truth General de Gaulle had come to another cross-roads in his life. The British government, his paymasters, had signalled that the arrival of the Vichy fleet at Dakar had altered the whole picture of Operation Menace, which should now be abandoned. But at the time when he persuaded General Spears to carry him to England, de Gaulle had registered a vow 'to climb to the heights and never again to come down'. After such a vow, no matter who died in its fulfilment, it was impossible for him to slink back to England with his tail between his legs. During the conferences of those days at Freetown, he persuaded the British commanders that all his information showed Dakar ready to open its gates to him, and that his plan to land his troops was a purely French affair in which no British interference would be necessary.

With extraordinary naïveté, no one enquired what the plan involved. The inhibited British officers, typical of their class and time, 'were afraid of seeming to be inquisitive', as one of them put it, and vehement representations were made to London that the operation should go on. In due course the reply came from the Cabinet, leaving the decision to the men on the spot, and giving them full authority to go ahead.

Edmond Leblanc, in the name of Eddie White, sent a long cable from Freetown to the *Daily Journal*. It wasn't much more than a recap of what he had transmitted by wireless, and was sent by way of insurance against a mutilated text. It also wasn't much of a *Journal* story, being short on human interest of the sort to appeal to a busdriver's wife in Sheffield, the figure whom Mac, the editor, had fixed on as the norm of DJ readers. The mythical lady, Edmond thought, was at the moment more interested in what the Luftwaffe was doing to Sheffield than in what General de Gaulle wanted to do to Dakar, but he tried his best with the cable, and afterwards sent a much shorter one, at his paper's expense, to Betty and his boy and girl in Bath. While he wrote, standing at a desk by the window of the cable office, he had a view of the building where the leaders of Operation Menace were in conference. There was no chance of getting in, he had tried that, and had been warned off by Negro soldiers of the Crown Colony, very smart and very ready with their bayonets fixed. But he knew who had gone in; what interested Edmond at that moment was the identity of the strangers who might come out.

He had seen one or two Free French officers chatting by the

261

door, not as smart as the Negro sentries but very businesslike with the inevitable folders in their hands (containing *dossiers*, no doubt, on all the leading citizens of Freetown) but no one he recognised until an officer of about his own age, equally grizzled, and wearing an old tropical uniform, came out and walked towards the entrance gate where the sentries were, without looking to left or right. Edmond cut across the street and intercepted him.

"It's Georges Lasserre, isn't it?" he said, holding out his hand. "Edmond Leblanc."

"*Mon vieux* Leblanc!" exclaimed the other, wringing Edmond's hand warmly. "How many years has it been? What in heaven's name are you doing here?"

"I might ask you the same thing, Jojo. Last time I saw you was at Toulouse, in the great days of *Courrier Sud*—"

"When it took thirteen hours to fly the mail from Casablanca to Dakar—"

"And you had a revolver on your belt, just as you have today. You've joined de Gaulle then, you old fire-eater?"

"It's a long story. *Allez, mon vieux, il faut arroser ça!* I've found a tavern where they sell adulterated spirits and good wine—"

The tavern was a mere shanty, and the good wine could only have got there by a miracle, but it gave as good a view as the cable office did of the building where General de Gaulle was in conference, and of the gate through which as many men in civilian suits as in uniforms were going. Some of them were very smart indeed, in tropical whites; others, like Georges Lasserre, in faded khaki.

"You're looking at my uniform," he said to Edmond. "It was all I could unearth out of my old tin trunk when Colonel Leclerc liberated the Cameroons. Yes, I'd been there for years, ever since I grew too old to fly, trying to make groundnuts pay, and failing. Angèle died five years ago—you remember Angèle?"

"*Sacré bleu*, I was at your wedding, man, back in 1920."

They had been pilots together in the Other War, but Lasserre had gone on flying for *La Ligne* while Edmond had taken to writing about aviation instead. They exchanged the news of many years briefly: Edmond's marriage to an English girl, his life in London and his jobs; Lasserre's near-bankruptcy when the Free French arrived with a new chance for men like him.

"It wasn't just the offer of good pay and perquisites," he insisted, "though I admit that had a lot to do with it. It was the cool way Colonel Leclerc bluffed himself into Douala that took my fancy. We knew nothing at all about de Gaulle before Leclerc turned up. There had been some propaganda about *la gloire* and *la patrie est en danger*, but at our age, Edmond, that doesn't cut much ice. We heard it all before, in the Other War. But that chap Leclerc, with nothing at his back except one British cruiser, took over the Cameroons in twenty-four hours, and I thought, well, what have I got to lose? I signed some sort of oath and here I am."

"So you met General de Gaulle in person today?"

"I had five minutes with him. Very impressive! Very sure of himself! I've been appointed one of the Free French Mission here."

"Here in Freetown?"

"It's the Mission to the Colony of Sierra Leone."

"What's the British Governor going to say to that?"

"What can he say? The British are pledged by their Agreement to help General de Gaulle in every way. And it's best there should be a French presence in Freetown, in case the British get the idea that *they* should move into the Cameroons."

The man had been well indoctrinated, Leblanc could see. He asked who the head of the Free French Mission was to be.

"Captain Hettier's our titular chief, but he has a roving assignment for the present. He was with Leclerc de Hauteville in the Cameroons."

"Yes, I know. I've met Captain Hettier in London. I keep in touch with some of de Gaulle's *Service de Presse*."

"Hettier's a splendid fellow. De Gaulle has great plans for him, I think . . . Here he comes with some of the British now. Do you want to talk to him? I could get you an interview—"

"Don't worry, Georges, the man's busy." He didn't think his boss, who was penurious about cable charges, would thank him for a thousand-word profile of Captain Hettier de Boislambert, although the news of the Free French Mission was worth perhaps a couple of lines. The Governor's reaction was the one Mac would be interested in, and Ed White's next bit of leg-work should take him to Government House. He chatted for a little while longer to Lasserre, watching Hettier out of the corner of his eye. The man seemed in no hurry to go through the gate where the sentries stood waiting to present arms. The Englishmen went about their business, the Frenchman stood talking earnestly to another French officer, short and square with a ruddy complexion, called, said Lasserre, Captain Corbeau, who had been at Douala too. He reminded Edmond of somebody seen long ago, and he searched his memory for old pilots of *La Ligne*, even old mechanics from the days at Montaudon, but the name of Corbeau had no association with anyone he knew. He was in his berth in the cabin he shared with Fred Clapperton, and the ports were open to the stifling night, before a memory trained to observe detail warned Edmond that he had seen a picture, not a man. He had seen a photograph in his own *Paris-Lendemain* of the officer talking to Captain Hettier. He was wearing a flyer's helmet in the full page illustration. He had won an international race from Frankfurt to Strasbourg, flying a Junkers aircraft, and his name in the caption was Anders Lachmann.

*   *   *

Mr. Churchill had predicted blue seas and cloudless skies when the liberators approached Dakar, and nobody had given much study to such weather reports as had ever been collected from that region of Senegal. Any of the ratings in *Ark Royal* who had already been in those waters could have told the planners in London that dense fog was as likely to prevail as sunshine in the last week of September. When the battle for Dakar opened in the early hours of September 23, there was a heavy fog over the oily grey surface of the shark-infested waters. It was even thicker over the town, hiding the palm-shaded avenues of the new quarter and the dark alleys and black basalt of the old. It obscured even the Tricolore fluttering from the bastion of Fort Manoel.

The Tricolore, with a new addition to its white stripe, was flying beside the Dutch flag in the *Westernland*, where General de Gaulle was on deck long before the tropical dawn broke above the fog. He had still not divulged his landing plan, although he had over two thousand of his own men at his command, but that he meant to land at some point, some time, and in person was clear —he had had one of his typical arguments (and lost it) with General Irwin about his right to command *all* the troops in the expedition as soon as he set foot on what he called French soil.

Everything else was cut and dried. At Freetown the *Ark Royal* had taken aboard two little French Fireflies which were to be given the honour of landing on Ouakem airstrip and occupying it in the name of General de Gaulle. Two Free French sloops were to enter the harbour under flags of truce and present letters from de Gaulle to the Governor General, the commanding general of the garrison, and the admiral. The Swordfish from *Ark Royal* were to drop such of de Gaulle's manifestoes as had not been scattered over a London railway station, including leaflets which gave the terms of his Agreement with Mr. Churchill.

The general himself was going to do the broadcasts.

The Swordfish and the Fireflies took off at 5 a.m., into a murky fog which the dawn had hardly reddened, and were soon lost to view. Most of the British ships were hidden from each other as far as twenty miles off the coast: a food ship blundered in where a destroyer ought to be, and reinforcements in the shape of the cruisers *Cumberland* and *Dragon* were keeping station with the destroyer screen. The correspondents who had been allowed to watch the fly-off from *Ark Royal* shivered in the wet fog, and strained their ears to hear a sound of cheering from the land.

There were seven thousand white inhabitants of Dakar, and seventy thousand coloured, mostly native Senegalese. What the latter, largely illiterate, made of the leaflets and the news that General de Gaulle had come to deliver them from famine and German infiltration was never to be known. The white reaction was definite and spontaneous. Unaware that the British planes were carrying nothing more lethal than a few samples of de Gaulle's turgid prose, the gunners of the *Richelieu* and the forts on Gorée Island opened fire.

The firing was heard aboard the *Ark Royal*, the first indication that Operation Menace had gone wrong. "Fire party stand by for crash landing!" was the order, and the correspondents saw the firemen emerge: grim figures armed with foam sprays and dressed in asbestos suits with square enveloping helmets. But none of the Swordfish had been hit on that strike, and on the command "Stand by to receive aircraft!" the planes, flying in line astern, peeled off to touch down on the deck and hook on to the arrestor wires. The handling parties took over, and the British planes were moved to the lifts at a few seconds' interval.

They were more fortunate than the Free French Fireflies.

Edmond Leblanc was waiting anxiously for news of them. He hadn't thought much of the tiny aircraft taken aboard at Freetown. They were dirty and badly maintained, and he hadn't thought much of their crews, who were only following their Leader in being thoroughly unpleasant to their attentive hosts.

They complained of the food, of their berths, of everything, during the voyage to Dakar. But when all was said and done they were Edmond's countrymen, and he wanted to see them win. It took a lot of nerve to fly two midget planes to take over a military airstrip, heavily manned. It would only work if de Gaulle had been correctly informed that the Air Force at Dakar was eager to welcome him.

Unfortunately the general had adapted himself too well to the Goebbels technique of the big lie ('France has lost a battle, she has not lost the war') and now believed that a lie becomes truthful by force of repetition. The Vichy airmen at Ouakem were not eager to welcome the man or his emissaries. They seized the Fireflies and arrested the crews. It was then found that one of the Free Frenchmen, with that passion for paperwork which was a Gaullist weakness, was carrying a complete list of all the Gaullist sympathisers in Dakar.

After that, Operation Menace became all too easy for the defenders of Dakar. The first arrests were made before nine o'clock, and the energetic school inspector, Monsieur Kaouza, accompanied the mayor and others to the city prison. The leaflets had failed, the Fireflies had failed; the last hope of a peaceful investment of Dakar now lay with the sloops carrying de Gaulle's letters and the flag of truce.

It was half past seven in the morning. In not much more than two hours tempers had risen so high in Dakar that the Admiral refused to respect the flag of truce. The envoys, one a former monk, were threatened with arrest, and under the threat they turned tail and ran. Neither by air nor by sea had it been possible to join forces with Hettier, who had been ordered on from Freetown to cut the telegraph wires to the interior. In every single instance the plan for the annexation of Dakar had failed.

"His Nibs is going to broadcast again," announced Dick Dashwood, who had been talking to one of the *Ark*'s wireless officers. "That's all we need!"

There was a subdued groan. De Gaulle had been broadcasting from the *Westernland* since the action off Dakar began, his tone becoming more threatening with each request that the Free French forces be allowed to land. Facing a microphone aboard a ship in a dense fog, shaken by the cannonading from the *Richelieu*, de Gaulle was in a different situation from his appearances on the BBC. At Broadcasting House he had received the VIP treatment.

He sat down to read from a carefully prepared and marked script, fearing no interruption, laying aside his white gloves and his cigarette while his official spokesman bent above him to breath the introductory words, *"Honneur et Patrie, voici le Général de Gaulle!"* Here there was no spokesman, no team of engineers to balance his voice defects, no sense of an audience of millions hushed to receive the Word. Nothing but the guns of Dakar, booming their defiance through the fog.

Before noon the British flotilla and the defences of Dakar had come to an open battle, and the exchange of fire between ships and shore was made totally incoherent by the fog and the breakdown in communications between the units of the steadily less menacing Menace. The Governor of Dakar had proclaimed a general alert. He was a sturdy old soldier, who did not claim to be a Verdun hero but had left one leg on a Verdun battlefield, and he was not shaken by the 'ultimatum' or the threat of reprisals by 'enormous Allied forces' which de Gaulle broadcast hour after hour. If the British wanted a fight he would let them have it, if only in revenge for Mers-el-Kebir. To their final ultimatum, threatening the total destruction of Dakar unless the Free French were allowed to land, Governor Boisson sent the laconic reply:

"France has entrusted me with Dakar. I will defend Dakar to the death."

"He's got to go in now," growled the cameraman from Crowborough, for whom the poor visibility had been one long frustration. It was four o'clock, one of the Vichy destroyers had capsized with great loss of life under the British fire, and still *le général Micro* was brandishing his favourite weapon. "If he had the guts to *lead* his men ashore, who knows, it might just turn the trick, even now—"

"Better ask Eddie about that," advised Dick Dashwood. "Ed, if His Nibs does go in, how about the understanding that his French would never take up arms against France? Is it all shot to hell, or what?"

"Probably not," said Edmond Leblanc listlessly. He thought he had caught cold in that early morning vigil in the fog. "You can't take up arms against yourself, can you? De Gaulle believes he *is* France; he's said so. Also he's Jesuit-bred, he may put a different interpretation on what France means than you would, Dick. Oh hell, what does it matter now? Operation Menace is a total loss."

"He's going in!" said Mr. Prentiss, who had been on deck. There was a concerted rush into the open air.

From the huge flight deck of the *Ark Royal*, where her squadrons were ranged in order, it was impossible to see the *Westernland*. De Gaulle himself remained invisible, and there was no sign of any disembarkation of the Free French troops aboard. The ships crawled on in the fog, hoping for the best in the hit or miss conditions; presently a message was flashed that the Free French Marines had landed.

Landed without a leader, without leadership, a pathetic token force trying to get ashore at Rufisque Bay, ten miles east of the town. So disorganised, so ineffective, that they were promptly chased off again by a few Senegalese soldiers under a white subaltern. Thankful to escape with their lives, the little detachment of Marines crept back to the shelter of the British ships. Then the fog lifted, and the *Westernland* was seen at last. She was full of Free French troops whom it had been impossible to set on shore. A direct hit on the *Westernland* might have meant the end of de Gaulle and hundreds of his followers. The correspondents on the deck of HMS *Ark Royal* held their breaths as they saw two armed Vichy cruisers coming out of harbour to attack. Then the Dutch ship turned away, making for the open sea, avoiding the hopeless battle, as the Leader turned tail and fled. The aircraft carrier waited, the whole flotilla waited until the flagship gave the agreed signal breaking off the action at Rufisque:

"Cancel Charles! Cancel Charles!"

" 'Cancel Charles!' " growled Dick Dashwood. "I wish to God we could!"

17

IN THE SMALL hours of next morning the Pan American flying boat from Natal landed in the great estuary of Freetown, after an uneventful proving flight. The only motor launch available, lent by the admiral, came out to meet it, and the passengers were disembarked. A girl whose name had been added to the manifest was helped down first, then the VIPs from Washington, and then Captain Bennett and his crew, among whom came Mike Marchand. The launch made its way up the swept channel in a darkness broken only by the lamps along the docks and the riding lights of the great concourse of ships awaiting convoy north or south. Dina looked up at them in awe. Much more clearly than when she was in London, she saw the face of an empire engaged in total war.

There were RAF officers on the dock to meet them. The Clipper's proving flight had been conducted with far better security than the expedition to Dakar, and there was nobody but the police patrol on duty to see the arrival of its passengers. There were two civilians in the background, and when all the passengers had been landed from the launch one of them, a youngish man in a white tropical suit, came forward and introduced himself as Thomas Prewitt, the American vice-consul at Freetown.

"Welcome and congratulations, gentlemen," he said, shaking hands with Captain Bennett and the two men from the Civil Aviation Authority. "I hope you'd a successful flight?"

They said "Fine!" and "Great!" in chorus, and one of the men from Washington asked immediately:

"Has General de Gaulle taken over Dakar?"

"Oh, you know about that?"

"We heard a news flash on the radio before we left Natal."

"We've only had news flashes here, but they've been pretty regular. So far it doesn't seem as if the general made it. There's been heavy fighting between the British ships and the Dakar defences, and it looks as if they meant to renew the action in the morning." He looked nervously round the ring of faces. "Well, it's nearly morning now, and you'll be wanting to go to your quarters. The RAF's looking after the transportation, and my wife and I brought our car along for the young lady from Brazil."

"For *me*?" Dina came forward from her place beside Mike as a small woman in a girlish seersucker dress was motioned onward by the vice-consul.

"This is my wife Peg, Miss da Costa—"

"How are you, dear?" said the small woman, and then, in a general appeal to the Americans, "Can she speak any English?"

"Yes, I speak English," said Dina with alarming clarity, and Mrs. Prewitt beamed. "Well, isn't that just lovely?" she said. "You must be just *exhausted*, honey. Tom and I are going to take you right home to our own house and see you get a bath and a good night's rest—"

"How very kind of you," said Dina. She looked down with calm curiosity on the little woman, whose greying hair was unsuitably tied with a striped ribbon. "I shouldn't dream of disturbing you and Mr. Prewitt in your home. I have a reservation at the Victoria Hotel."

"We all have," said one of the CAA men. "Captain Bennett fixed it up before we started."

"Oh, but dearie, we've been specially asked to look after you!" said Mrs. Prewitt. "We can't let you go off alone to the Victoria—" Her husband murmured his assent.

"Tony," said Mike Marchand under his breath, and Dina nodded. "Tony, of course," she whispered back, and then, aloud, "I do appreciate your kindness, but I can assure you I'm in no need of care and protection, Mrs. Prewitt. My fiancé is here to look after me. May I present Mr. Marchand?"

"Well, isn't this *nice*!" said Mrs. Prewitt helplessly. There was a flurry of introductions, broken by the voice of Captain Bennett, suggesting that they ought to get the show on the road. The baggage was all on the dock now, and the RAF trucks moving up: Mike was able to whisper to Dina, under cover of the movement, "I'll bunk in with the crew. Call you at ten tomorrow morning!" His lips brushed her cheek, and then Dina was taken into custody by the Prewitts and led away to the big American car where a Freetown Negro in a khaki uniform was holding the rear door open.

"Mr. Marchand isn't coming with us?" said the vice-consul, looking round. "Is he a member of the crew?"

"He *is* a pilot, but not with Pan Am. He's a special observer for President Vargas on this flight."

"Is that right?" Mr. Prewitt was out of his depth now. His relief was evident when they drew up at the lighted doorway of the Victoria Hotel.

"Miss da Costa, are you sure you'll be all right?" Mrs. Prewitt's wizened little face, like the face of an old child, was poked anxiously from the car window as Dina got out.

"Perfectly, thank you."

"We'll meet at the party, but if there's anything you need don't hesitate—"

"Never mind the party now, Peg," said her husband. "I just want to have one word with Miss da Costa, and then we'll let her get some sleep. No, you stay in the car with Amos, I won't be long. Boy! Take the lady's bag in—"

The two men from Washington were already in the modest lobby of the Victoria, giving their names to a sleepy desk clerk, when Dina was ushered in. "Anything I can do to help you, Miss da Costa?" one of them called out.

"No, thank you, I'm in good hands."

The vice-consul led Dina into a small, badly-lit room just off the lobby, where a waiter in a soiled white jacket was sitting half asleep behind a long table with bottles on it, apparently used as a bar during waking hours. He started up when Dina and the man walked in.

"Could I order anything for you to eat or drink, Miss da Costa? Would you like to have something sent up to your room?"

"No, thank you, we've been eating odds and ends of food at weird hours all day. What I really need now is a good long sleep—"

"I know, and I won't detain you." He cleared his throat. "I have to ask you for your passport, I'm afraid."

"Why? Are you afraid I'll leave the country? I'm going back with the Clipper next Friday night."

"Yes, I know," said Mr. Prewitt. "I'll see you get it back in good time. But first it must be stamped for entry before the British will give you an exit permit, and you have no Brazilian consul to represent you in Sierra Leone."

"Oh, I see." Dina opened her flight bag, hanging on a strap from her shoulder, and took out the Brazilian passport. "I'm really grateful for your help, Mr. Prewitt. Just tell me one thing. How did you know I was on the proving flight?"

"I had a cable from our ambassador at Rio de Janeiro, asking me to be of whatever service I could . . . I'm sorry I didn't understand about Mr. Marchand. Is he an American citizen, by the way?"

"No, he's French. Is there a French consul at Freetown?"

"Er—not now," said Mr. Prewitt. "He was replaced by a French Military Mission, representing General de Gaulle. The acting head of it is Capitaine Corbeau, you'll meet him at a little reception I'm giving at the consulate on Wednesday. But probably Mr. Marchand will be in touch with him before that."

Dina smiled. It was a smile which remained with Mr. Prewitt, uneasily, all through the drive on which he motioned his wife to silence, from the Victoria Hotel up to the colony of red-roofed bungalows on the hill above Freetown. They were inside their own bungalow, in the flower-filled room where photographs of President Roosevelt, King George VI and Queen Elizabeth were prominently displayed, before Mrs. Prewitt dared to utter an eloquent "Well!"

"Isn't she something, though?"

"Tom, I just don't understand. The way that message from Rio was worded, she might have been a fugitive from justice. Or in some awful kind of trouble—"

"I don't think she's in any trouble. Not with that boyfriend of hers around, he looks tough enough to handle anything."

"Could they be eloping?"

"Funny kind of elopement, with a whole Pan Am crew along. No, I don't think there's any real trouble. Somebody got excited, and pulled strings with our ambassador in Rio. And if there *is* trouble, I'd rather not tangle with Miss Dina da Costa, I'll tell you that."

"She's a stunning-looking girl, but Tom, do you really think she's well, you know, *white*?"

"I wouldn't swear she's one hundred per cent White, Anglo-Saxon, Protestant, would you? But Mr. Marchand's French, she told me. He came on the flight as a special observer for the President of Brazil. That's probably what got our ambassador's guts in an uproar."

Mrs. Prewitt sighed. "Why does this have to happen when the Robsons aren't here? Why is it always you and I who have to carry the can? It was bad enough having de Gaulle here last week, when you had to write all those reports to Washington, but why should you have to get mixed up with something in *Brazil*? I just hate it when they spring something like this on you, Tom. I never know what it's going to do to your career. And that girl's bad news—I'm sure of it!"

Mrs. Prewitt, worrying and fretting until the false dawn, which had broken while they talked, gave way to the true morning, slept less well than Dina, who in a bedroom which was cramped but clean lay motionless until the sounds of traffic woke her about nine o'clock. Then she felt so rested, her vitality so completely unimpaired by the long flight from one hemisphere to another, that she rang at once for tea and fruit, and sat up in bed, hugging her knees in the exhilaration of the thought that Mike and she were still together.

It was a new day, and in its heat and sunshine the exasperation of the night before was all but forgotten. She was even inclined to smile at the evidence of Tony's far-reaching power; she had known of course that he would be furious when she failed to return from Natal, and it was Mike, in fact, who had sent a telegram to say she had been invited to take part in the Clipper's proving flight. All that long Sunday in the grimy hotel near the Lago do Bomfim the determination had grown in her to go with her lover to Africa, to bind herself more closely to him, to prolong their joy for a few days more. All that Sunday, and on Monday crossing the South Atlantic, she had forgotten everything but her love for Mike and the satisfaction of their desire. She was prepared to leave parents, brother, work, everything in the lurch to spend those last days with her lover. They would be worth all the anger and rejection she might meet with when she had to leave him, and go home.

As soon as the Negro chambermaid brought her tea, Dina gave her a little money, and told her to make up the room while she took her bath. The girl, with a brilliant smile, took away two dresses to be pressed, and Dina looked after her with curiosity. Although she knew all the mixtures of Negro blood which Brazil could offer, and was well enough aware of the faint trace of African in her own heritage, it was the first time she had talked to a Negro girl in Africa, or wondered about the tribal, primitive life which this girl's ancestors and her own had shared. Everything that was primitive in herself was alive at that moment, but there was no crack in the veneer of civilisation when, instead of his telephone call, Mike Marchand himself was announced in the ordered room, to the immaculate girl, at ten o'clock.

"Darling!"

"Oh, Mike, my darling!"

There was nothing coherent about their greeting. Only kisses, and lovers' words, and long hungry embraces which seemed unending until Mike began to ask Dina, "Are you all right? I mean, after you left us at the dock, was everything all right?"

"Perfectly. I was in bed and sound asleep within half an hour."

He drew a breath of relief. "I hated to see you going off alone with those people, but it did seem the best way. I mean, why add to the commotion, in the middle of the night? But I brought my bag over from the airfield, and I checked at the desk downstairs. They've got a room for me all right. We're together again!"

She pressed herself against him as she thought how short their time together had to be, and tried to smile and speak lightly. "Mr. Prewitt took away my passport," she told Mike.

"He did *what*? An American vice-consul? He had no right—"

"He had his instructions from the American ambassador in Rio. Prompted of course by my dear brother Tony. I think Tony pictured me setting out for the Gold Coast, or even Egypt, instead of flying home like a good little girl."

"Oh Dina," said Mike remorsefully, "I shouldn't have begged you to come. I hate to think of you going back to face the music alone."

"I don't care," she said. "There won't be too much music to face. Mother'll cry, and Ester will pray for my soul—if she hasn't given it up as a lost cause—and father will storm, and then Tony'll soothe them all, and send me across to Bela Horizonte or Santos until it all blows over. That's one thing about working for an arline; we do see life."

"Don't we though!" said Mike feelingly.

"After all, Freetown's only another way station, for both of us . . . Mike! Have you made any plans yet, about flying—on—from Freetown?"

"Yes, well, I want to tell you about that."

"Come out on the balcony, then. It's hot enough out there, but it's stifling in the room . . . Who can that be?"

274

A tap at the door announced the maid, who came in with her wide smile, carrying a letter and a bouquet of flowers.

"These must be from your admirer, Mr. Prewitt," said Mike.

"I'd rather have my passport back. It's too big to be in this envelope, though."

She opened the letter while the maid fetched a vase and water. "No, they're from *Mrs.* Prewitt," Dina said, unfolding the sheet of paper round a formal invitation card. "'Just a breath of welcome from a real American garden'," she read aloud. "Mike, how can people write such things? 'Hoping so much to see you and Mr. Marchand at our cocktail party Wednesday. Just an informal get-together to drink the health of all of you who crossed in the Clipper yesterday'—I remember now, she was talking about a party in the car."

"Well, that's all right," said Mike. "They mean to be kind, I think."

"Yes, but I hope she won't call me 'dear' all the time, I hate that kind of slop."

"You don't mind when I call you 'darling'?"

"Don't call me darling now," she whispered, "or I'll never be able to listen to your plans. You've talked to people already?"

Leaning beside Dina on the balcony rail, looking across the estuary to the other shore, where kites were wheeling above the lush green, Mike told her that it hadn't been a bad idea, his going to the RAF station with the Clipper crew. He had seen the station commander after an early breakfast, and told the Englishman he wanted to enlist as a ferry pilot.

"And they'll accept you?"

"He thinks they will. He's going to send a signal to Takoradi, recommending me. They're certainly building up Takoradi as the ferry base, and the first operating party went in a month ago. In fact they've assembled a few Blenheims sent by sea from England, and despatched them to Egypt already. They've got several hundred Negroes building workshops at Takoradi now."

"And how are you going to get there from here?"

"Back at the old problem. Well, the thing is, they've got a twelve passenger Lockheed Hudson due to fly down there on Friday around noon. It handles much the same as the Deodoro."

"Do you mean they're going to let you *fly* it, Mike?"

"They can't do that, officially, until I'm sworn in to the RAF. But I think they might bend the rules a bit more out here, where they're desperately short of pilots. Anyway I can hitch a ride, as Don Bennett would say."

Dina looked over the river at the circling birds. She was trying to visualise the map of Africa. "What route are they flying to Egypt?" she asked.

"From Takoradi to Kano in Nigeria, then Kano to Khartoum, where another team of pilots takes the crates on to Cairo. They're trying to lay out the route in five hundred mile hops for refuelling."

Dina nodded. Her own flight experience in a country larger than the continent of Europe had taught her not to be afraid of distances as such, and she could make (which Mike knew, and loved her for) a professional calculation of the RAF's bomber life-line to the Middle East. But this was not a professional matter. This was Mike, her lover, committing himself to some of the hardest flights on earth, under the worst conditions . . . She thought of the desert, which had haunted him. She thought of what Dr. Baumeister had said about flying altitudes, and she bit her lips against protest.

"Friday noon," she said. "You'll be going out before me. I think I'm glad of that."

"Why, darling?"

"Because I would have hated to leave you on the ground, not knowing what was going to happen to you. I do know now."

"Destination Takoradi."

"Destination Rio de Janeiro," she said, and managed to smile. "Some day, destination Paris."

"Dina, will you ever know how much I love you?"

"Just keep telling me . . . Oh, Mike! Is there any news from de Gaulle's destination—Dakar?"

"There was one flash this morning, before I left the station. Governor Boisson won't surrender, and why the hell should he, he's got them cold. He announced eighty civilian casualties in the town already, and said he was evacuating civilians to the interior." Mike thought fleetingly of Madame Denise Lambert, and wondered how that exquisite Parisienne liked being evacuated to the interior in an army lorry, with a crowd of weeping women and children. "I hope Governor Boisson has reinforced the guard on the gold at Fort Croise," he said. "De Gaulle would love to get his hands on that."

"Do you think he will?"

"It doesn't look very like it. As for the British, they're in a proper mess. Next thing you know, the Vichy French'll attack Gibraltar."

      *   *   *

A thousand miles north of Dakar, French aircraft were indeed preparing to attack Gibraltar as the second day's attack on Governor Boisson's capital began. The fog still lay on the water, and visibility was poor when the Skuas from *Ark Royal* renewed their assault on the *Richelieu* and on Fort Manoel, defended by the much faster and better armed French fighters from Ouakem. No attempt was made, on this second day, to land any troops after the fiasco at Rufisque, although a British force twice as large as de Gaulle's was waiting in the transports to take part in what had been planned as an amphibious landing. It was as if the heart had gone out of the attackers since General de Gaulle ordered the Rufisque action broken off. His turn-away in the *Westernland* was not so momentous as Jellicoe's famous turn-away at the Battle of Jutland, but it had its effect on the morale of the whole expedition undertaken at his insistence and in his interests: the second day's fighting was sporadic and inconclusive. Eight British aircraft had been lost. On the third morning, while the British fire was hampered by a smoke screen laid by the Vichy destroyers as soon as the fog began to lift, one of the Dakar submarines torpedoed HMS *Resolution* and effectively put her out of action. The fire from the crippled *Richelieu* was devastating, and her gunners might well have thought Operation Catapult and the tragedy of Mers-el-Kebir were now avenged. The French fighters attacked the Swordfish and the bombers also attacked the British ships. At about half past one in the afternoon Mr. Churchill sent a telegram to the British commanders, ordering them to "abandon the enterprise against Dakar".

That the Navy of Trafalgar, of the Falkland Islands, of the River Plate, of Jutland, had suffered a humiliating defeat off a small French colonial town, was known in Sierra Leone shortly before the guests began to assemble for the informal party given by Mr. and Mrs. Prewitt at the consulate. The American flag was flying, and the two US Marines on duty at the door were spruce and soldierly when Mike and Dina arrived—at Mr. Prewitt's request a little early. He looked appreciatively at the tall, black-haired girl in the white dress, with a spray of the flowers from his garden pinned to her shoulder, as he greeted them beneath President Roosevelt's portrait in the entrance hall.

"Miss da Costa, Freetown suits you," he began. "You're looking swell. Mr. Marchand, good of you to be so prompt."

"I already thanked Mrs. Prewitt for the flowers," said Dina, touching the spray.

"I hope you'll have time to drive up and see our garden before you leave. Friday evening at seven, isn't it?"

"I believe so."

Mr. Prewitt glanced into a large room where a long table was spread with a white cloth and glasses, and a Negro waiter was putting out bottles and plates of canapés. Women's voices could be heard in the background, and the vice-consul remarked that his wife and his assistant, Miss Ballantine, were setting up the show. "Will you come into my office for a minute?" he said. "I've something important to give to Miss da Costa."

Fans were whirring from all the ceilings in the consulate, but Mr. Prewitt's little room was close and sultry, and almost entirely occupied by a too-large desk, from which he took a square manila envelope. "This is your passport," he said. "It's properly stamped, and the exit permit is enclosed. It's valid for a week in case there should be some unforeseen delay."

"Thank you very much."

"I just want you to know that I sent your brother a cable this morning, to let him know your ETA Natal. I understand he's planning to have you met."

"I'm sure of it," said Dina, who had raised her eyebrows at his first words. "My brother Tony's nothing if not thorough. Did *he* ask you to send him a cable?"

"Not personally, no; it was in the signal from our ambassador at Rio."

"I look forward to meeting His Excellency when I get back. I'm grateful for his interest in my affairs."

"Oh now, Miss da Costa," said the American wretchedly, "I hope you don't think I'm interfering in your private life. I'm only carrying out instructions—"

"Yes, I know."

"I don't want to say any more, except I wish I could have been of more service to you. And now I hear people arriving, perhaps we ought to join the party. Wing Commander Oakley is very anxious to meet a lady who's a qualified pilot in her own right."

"And a very good one," said Mike. "Mr. Prewitt, could I ask one question first? Have you any news of what's happened at Dakar, I mean since the action was broken off?"

"Not a great deal. General de Gaulle is reported to have announced that the failure was due to German infiltration, but I don't think he can make that stick, because our own consul says there wasn't a single German anywhere in the area. I think both de Gaulle and the British will have to admit the expedition was a write-off; just a plain military defeat."

"What's de Gaulle doing now?"

"At last reports he had asked to be set ashore at Bathurst in British Gambia."

"That's probably as near to Dakar as he'll ever get," said Mike. "He can look across the estuary at the guns of Fort Manoel, and lick his wounds."

"You know Dakar, Mr. Marchand?"

"Very well indeed."

"That's interesting. By the way, I've invited two of General de Gaulle's mission to come here this evening. I wish Captain Hettier were here—a very good man—but he was seconded to special duty when de Gaulle arrived. Captain Corbeau and Captain Lasserre are coming; perhaps you've met them already?"

"Not me," said Mike, and Dina gave him a warning look.

"It's all right, dear," said Mike. He walked behind Dina and Prewitt into the reception room. And stood face to face with Anders Lachmann.

"Well," he said without hesitation, "Lachmann! I was wondering where you would show up again. How's Schnaebel? How's the traitors' gate?"

"Mr. Marchand, really!" said the astounded consul. "This is Captain Corbeau of the Free French Mission. Captain, I do apologise—"

"*Je regrette, monsieur*," said Mike. "This is Anders Lachmann, a German national, formerly a pilot with the Nazi Condor Syndicate in Brazil. He wormed his way into de Gaulle's headquarters in London, stirred up as much trouble as he could among the French, and hit me a dirty crack on the back of the head at our last meeting. He's probably given the defences of Freetown to the Germans by this time, as he gave the plan of de Gaulle's fool trip to Dakar to the Vichy satellites. Somebody had better call for the military police."

"This man is raving," said the man who called himself Corbeau. "I knew him in London. He made a habit of denouncing innocent men, loyal and patriotic Frenchmen like myself . . ."

"You weren't a Frenchman when I saw you in Recife," Dina said. "You competed against me at an air meeting there in '37. You were the chief pilot of Condor then, and I can prove it."

Lachmann looked at her for the first time, and no words came. Her simple statement of fact was more convincing to the American consul than Mike's indignant accusation. He said, "I think we'll have to look into this," and turned towards his office and the telephone.

"Look out!" screamed Miss Ballantine. "He's got a gun!"

He had a gun, but the bullet went harmlessly into the cornice as the RAF Wing Commander took Lachmann's wrist in a hammer-lock. The gun fell, the man struck at the airman's neck with his free hand, was free himself, knocked the women aside and got as far as the street. Then Mike and the two US Marines were upon him, rolling down the steps of the consulate on to the pavement, while the other Free Frenchman yelled *"Au secours! Police!"* and two MPs came up at a run, their truncheons drawn. Lachmann's face was covered in blood when they hauled him to his feet. "I appeal to General de Gaulle!" he shouted, while the Negro passers-by stood amazed at such a scene outside the American consulate, and the police whistles shrilled. Mike, sucking his bruised knuckles, replied with satisfaction, "I don't think appealing to *him* will do you much good now."

*   *   *

By Thursday evening Mike Marchand and Dina da Costa—their full names spelled out, and misspelled, on dozens of evidence sheets—had been helping the police with their enquiries for nearly twenty-four hours. There were niceties of legal argument to be defined before the case of Anders or André Lachmann could be heard in court and *in camera*. The man claimed to have been born in Strasbourg of a father who had opted for French citizenship, and was therefore French. Even if he had flown for a Nazi-controlled airline he was not necessarily a Nazi. He had assumed an alias on joining the Gaullist movement, but in that he was only doing the same as a score of others, whose names he could give, in the early days at St. Stephen's House. And so on, while the sworn statements and the affidavits mounted up, and the American vice-consul washed his neutral hands of the whole affair, while Mrs. Prewitt was more convinced than ever that the arrival of Dina da Costa at Freetown spelled ruin to her husband's career.

"It was very fortunate he lost his head, and drew a gun," said one of the law officers of the colony, in his last interview with Mike and Dina. "Now we've got him in custody on charges of intent to cause grievous bodily harm, and resisting arrest, and that'll keep him in cold storage until Special Branch can fly a man out from London with all the evidence they collected at the time when some trusting soul put him on a plane for West Africa. And as a flight from London to Freetown, even with top priority, takes three days at present, it may be a week before we can begin to assemble the charge of espionage."

"But you had that cable from Neil Grant," said Mike.

"Yes, telling us about Lachmann's association with Schnaebel, who was executed by a firing squad inside the Tower of London. Guilt by association is foreign to British justice, Mr. Marchand, and at the same time, this wretched man claims to be outside British jurisdiction. He's cooled off now, you know. He's trying every trick the law allows, and he has Churchill's Agreement with de Gaulle, and the Allied Forces Act, off by heart. I hope the London evidence is strong; I must admit the legal interpretation may be very tricky. I foresee one more complication when General de Gaulle arrives."

"He really is coming back to Freetown? They didn't set him ashore at Bathurst after all?"

"Mr. Churchill felt we couldn't guarantee his safety at Bathurst, and he obviously can't show his face in London for the present. A retreat to one of what he calls his own cities, Douala or Brazzaville, seems to be indicated." The lawyer began to gather up his papers. "The fleet is due at Freetown early to-morrow morning; some of our ships are badly in need of repairs. Gibraltar was attacked again while they were on their way south, and I should say we're within an inch of war with Vichy France. However, that doesn't concern you, Mr. Marchand. Wing Commander Oakley says you're off to join the RAF."

"If there's nothing more I can do here."

"We have your affidavits, and you've both done splendidly.

No, it's over to Special Branch now, and you are free to go. Good luck to you!"

*   *   *

"I believe Lachmann will get off," said Dina suddenly. They were in bed together, sated with love, in her room at the Victoria Hotel. They had been silent, smoking; the red tip of Mike's second cigarette was still glowing when he stubbed it out in the ashtray on the bedside table.

"What put Lachmann in your head, my darling? He's safely behind bars," said Mike lazily.

"I don't know," she confessed. "I don't believe I was thinking about him in particular. I was watching the lights on the ceiling. The headlights and the bicycle lamps, they make a funny kind of shifting pattern. Like the toy little Tonio used to have. You shook it, and all the coloured particles inside made new patterns —what's the name for it, Mike?"

"A kaleidoscope?"

"That's it. I was thinking Lachmann's a particle, I saw him once at Recife, and you saw him in London, and now he may be going to die because of us. And because of Neil Grant—shall we see him again? And your cousin Jacques, whom you like so much? Will they all get shaken up in a new pattern, that perhaps we'll never see?"

"Hush, darling, don't get excited." Mike looked at the luminous hands of his wrist watch as he pulled her closer to his bare breast. Ten minutes to midnight, just over twelve hours to his take-off. This time tomorrow night she would be five hours out across the dark Atlantic, putting the width of the ocean between herself and him.

"We're sure of our pattern, Dina, you and I. It's going to renew itself again and again for the rest of our lives. Look, it began eight years ago, when you were only a schoolgirl, and the kaleidoscope shook and shook until we were both shaken together for always." He didn't quite know what he was saying, but anything to stop her crying. "And now the pattern's set, we belong to each other. It'll begin repeating again . . . when I come back from the war."

There was no singing of the *Marseillaise* as Charles de Gaulle came back from the war at eight o'clock next morning, when the British flotilla brought him defeated to the port of Freetown, which he had left in high hopes only a week before. There was a big crowd at the docks, but it was silent and disapproving, angry and grieved by turns, as the launch brought de Gaulle and his officers ashore, and the British ships sailed in. There was HMS *Cumberland*, which had helped Leclerc to claim the Cameroons, limping from the fire of the *Richelieu*, there were *Inglefield* and *Foresight*, also damaged, there was HMS *Resolution*, battered and listing badly, towed along by the flagship *Barham*. And there, in the *Westernland*, was the man whose self-assurance was reponsible for it all.

"What's that they're flying on the Tricolore?" said Mike Marchand as the Free French sloops came nearer. He could see without binoculars that a new design had been imposed on the white stripe of the French flag.

"Haven't you seen it?" said one of the Englishmen who was going with him to the airfield. "That's the Cross of Lorraine. The Gaullists have adopted it for their emblem—it's something to do with Joan of Arc. Here, if you take my glasses, you'll see it better."

"Thanks, I can see it now." The two-armed cross came into view, and Mike laughed. "The double cross, how very appropriate. Hitler has his swastika; why shouldn't Charles de Gauleiter have the double cross?"

"Here comes the man himself," said Dina.

De Gaulle had disembarked. He came down the gangway to the pier near which Mike stood, ignoring the silent crowd. His face was very pale as the crowd made way for him, and he walked with long strides, looking straight ahead. He already knew in part, and was soon to know in full, of the damage done to his name by the fiasco at Dakar. The British Dominions and the United States were particularly incensed by the failure to carry the city, and Mr. Churchill, bearing the brunt of the criticism, might well feel that his protégé had double-crossed him in the account he had been given of the welcome awaiting de Gaulle at Dakar. Back in London the general's propaganda machine, and in particular the newspaper *France*, was busily concocting reasons for his failure: the massive infiltration by Germans, the general's humanitarian desire to avoid useless slaughter—all the mendacity which Bill Barclay of EBC summed up in a broadcast to the United States in the simple phrase *We wuz robbed*. But de Gaulle himself was there in Freetown, and the petulant mouth was set in a thin line as he trod the path of his humiliation. Mike Marchand drew a breath of satisfaction as for the third time in his life he saw the Adventurer, defeated in the first conflict of his search for power.

"You really hate him, don't you?" Dina said.

"I hate him for what he's doing, and may still do, to France."

"But won't they shoot him now?"

Mike laughed.

"A general like that would be shot in Chile," she persisted.

"Only in Chile? Not in Brazil?"

"We're civilised people in Brazil."

Mike was staring after the retreating figure. A car had been brought up to the end of the pier, and de Gaulle was driven away. "We like to think we're civilised in France," he said. "We forgive our debtors as we hope to be forgiven our debts. That's why I'm afraid—I am very much afraid—that we haven't heard the last of Charles de Gaulle."

It was only a few hours after that early morning scene that the parting came for Mike and Dina. Mike went to the RAF airfield in an army lorry, identical with the one which had taken him to Dykefaulds to see his cousin, on the day when the kaleidoscope of war began to shake him into a new pattern. Dina was driven out by Don Bennett in a borrowed car. It was the first time she had seen the American since the Clipper landed at Freetown. All the crew, and most of the officers at the air station, had left them in peace. There was a conspiracy of silence and privacy around the two whose private hours were well known to be severely numbered. They were all living now on borrowed time.

The Lockheed Hudson was waiting on the concrete, and the cargo and baggage were being put aboard. The station commander came out to speak to Dina in front of the crew room where a cracked gramophone was playing as the men for Takoradi drank a last cup of compo tea. There were three passengers, including Mike, besides the crew.

"You've had a rough time in Freetown, Miss da Costa," said the commander. "Extraordinary thing, this Lachmann affair! Makes you wonder, doesn't it, how some paths seem to be meant to cross?"

"Yes, it does."

"I bet you'll be glad to get back to Rio de Janeiro. Leaving tonight, aren't you?"

"At seven o'clock."

"Well, then—" He glanced in Mike's direction, turned away. The airmen were coming out of the crew room, pulling on their flying jackets.

"Goodbye, Mike. Happy landings."

He held her in a last embrace. "*Mon amour*," he said, "*mon oiseau de paradis. Mon lis tigré.*" He went a few steps towards the plane, and stopped. "I'll be back!" he cried, and ran across the concrete, away from love, back to the war.

Dina went forward to the rough barrier as the props began to spin. Mike paused in the door of the Lockheed to give her the pilot's salute. In the crew room behind her she heard the song they had danced to so many times.

> We'll meet again, don't know where,
> Don't know when

Dina saw the mechanics pull the chocks away and move backwards. The pilot turned the bomber into the wind.

> So will you please say hello to the folks that I know,
> Tell them I won't be long,
> They'll be happy to know that as you saw me go
> I was singing this song

The bomber took off in a rush of sound, the pilot set his course for Takoradi. Dina could watch no longer. She turned back to the waiting men with her head high, fighting the tears, willing herself to belief and hope. I know, I know we'll meet again—

Some sunny day.

THE SNOW MOUNTAIN

CATHERINE GAVIN

The Grand Duchess Olga
impulsive and lovely, saw the cracks beneath the surface
of the last Czar's court

Captain Simon Hendrikov
risked his life in a vain attempt to save Olga from her
Siberian prison

Mara Trenova
straight from school, threw in her lot with the Bolsheviks
and lived to regret it

Joe Calvert
from Baltimore, watched the Russian struggle with com-
passion and waited for the United States to enter World
War I

They all meet in the pages of this great new novel from
CATHERINE GAVIN

'Her writing cuts across life and death, love and war,
debauchery and devotion, with the boldness and not a
little of the grasp of a Tolstoy'
Los Angeles Mirror-News

'A powerful and dramatic novel, beautifully written'
Woman's Journal

CORONET BOOKS

CATHERINE GAVIN

THE DEVIL IN HARBOUR

How can a rough young trawlerman from Aberdeen adapt to life as a naval officer at the time of the Battle of Jutland?

How does a minister's eighteen-year-old daughter at Scapa Flow react to the knowledge that there is a traitor in her family?

Why should a famous Russian dancer, devoted to the Allied cause, become the mistress and tool of a German secret agent?

CATHERINE GAVIN
explores these human questions in her much acclaimed novel of World War I

'*The Devil In Harbour* shows again Catherine Gavin's superb sense of history, her capacity for dramatising the character and thrust of an age with the clear and moving images of the personal conflict. She takes us from the restaurants and theatres of Petrograd to the high seas off Jutland, always with unshakeable confidence and skill'
Los Angeles Times

CORONET BOOKS

Also Available from Coronet Books